The Duke at Hazard

KJ Charles is a British author of mostly historical romance, mostly queer, sometimes with fantasy or horror in there. She lives in London with her husband, two kids, an out-of-control garden, and a cat with murder management issues.

KJ mostly hangs out at KJ Charles Chat on Facebook, where you can find excellent book conversation, sneak peeks, and exclusive treats.

For all the KJC news and occasional freebies, get the (infrequent) newsletter at kjcharleswriter.com/newsletter

Find KJ on Twitter @kj_charles or Bluesky @kjcharles.bsky.social.

Read the blog or pick up free reads at kjcharleswriter.com

The Duke at Hazard

(Gentlemen of Uncertain Fortune #2)

KJ CHARLES

First published in Great Britain in 2024 by Orion Fiction,
an imprint of The Orion Publishing Group Ltd.,
Carmelite House, 50 Victoria Embankment
London EC4Y 0DZ

An Hachette UK Company

The authorised representative in the EEA is Hachette Ireland,
8 Castlecourt Centre, Dublin 15, D15 XTP3, Ireland (email: info@hbgi.ie)

3 5 7 9 10 8 6 4 2

A CIP catalogue record for this book is
available from the British Library.

ISBN (Paperback) 978 1 3987 1578 3
ISBN (eBook) 978 1 3987 1579 0

Typeset at The Spartan Press Ltd,
Lymington, Hants

Printed and bound in Great Britain by Clays Ltd,
Elcograf S.p.A.

www.orionbooks.co.uk

'One can live well, even in a palace.'

Marcus Aurelius, *Meditations* book V chapter 16

Reader Advisory

This book contains depictions of gambling; references to the death of a parent; accident and injury; references to past acts of violence and sexual assault; references to homophobia.

'Daizell' is pronounced to rhyme with 'hazel'.
'Cassian' is stressed on the first syllable.
'Severn' is said like the number seven.

Chapter One

Vernon Fortescue Cassian George de Vere Crosse, the fourth Duke of Severn, the Earl of Harmsford, Baron Crosse of Wotton, and Baron Vere walked into an inn. They were all the same man.

He did not announce himself by all of his titles, or any of them. Nobody did it for him, either. Nobody slipped in front of him to open the doors, or bowed to greet him. In fact, nobody paid him any attention at all. A couple of heads turned at his entry, but their gazes slipped over him without interest and away: he was water off a flock of ducks.

That might have been rather lowering if he'd believed that the usual stir and attention his arrival created was due to his good looks and imposing presence, rather than his slew of titles. However, the Duke was all too aware of his moderate height, nondescript features, quiet ways, and general sad lack of ducal authority. He was nothing without his titles, and he knew it. Nobody would pick him from a crowd; nobody would look twice at him without the trappings he'd been born to.

Well. One man had.

The Duke took a deep breath of the smoky air in the inn's parlour, ripely fragranced by spilled beer, insufficiently washed bodies, and the ghost of a pork joint that had spent too long at the fire. It smelled like freedom.

He probably ought to have a drink, he thought. He had

plenty of money, but he wasn't sure how to apply it. Should he expect to be shown to a table, or seat himself and wait to be attended? There were men standing at an elbow-high bar receiving ale: did one purchase it oneself? Was one meant to join in with the friendly banter they exchanged with the buxom woman at the bar, or would that be a solecism? If one did join in, what did one say?

The Duke of Severn knew to a nicety how to judge a bow to people on every rung of the aristocracy including his equals (all twenty-five of them) and superiors (the Royal Family). He knew how to behave at a rout, a soirée, Almack's or White's. He might be personally negligible but he had never put a foot wrong socially, in large part because he kept to the limited, elevated circles considered appropriate to his station. In the public bar of the Bird in Hand, he was suddenly and terrifyingly uncertain.

'Mr Wotton,' said a voice at his ear. It took the Duke a second to remember that was himself. He turned to see the man he'd come to meet.

'Good evening,' he said, and forgot all about public house etiquette in the rush of relief.

The Duke had been on an informal visit to a school friend in Gloucester, accompanied only by his valet, two footmen, groom, and outrider. He'd shed the lot of them to take the air in a park one evening, and there seen a man in a mulberry coat: a dark-haired fellow with a roguish sort of look. Eyes had met. There had been a little casual conversation, the brush of a hand, a tempting smile.

Very tempting indeed, and the Duke had duly fallen. Not under his own name, or names, of course: he'd called himself George Wotton, enjoyed a brief but very satisfying fumble in the darkness, and agreed to meet a few days later at the Bird in Hand inn. That had meant ridding himself of his retinue by underhand means that involved letting them believe he was meeting a woman, and the sense of release was exhilarating. Just for tonight, he would be an ordinary man, without the weight of rank, his behaviour scrutinised by nobody except his partner. Just for tonight, he would be with a man who was attracted by his person, who didn't need to be paid to be there, who wanted the man, not the duke.

He couldn't wait.

John Martin, his companion, had secured a private parlour to dine, saying it was his treat. The Duke had never had a man spend money on him before. That was his role in the few encounters he'd had, and he didn't resent it: he knew very well he was paying for the company. Now he found himself stunned by the little kindness, which seemed like more than was necessary, more than an assignation. It felt like courting, and it made him warm all over. And John Martin was a witty, amusing man with a lively manner, and the Duke found himself wondering, if things went well, whether he might dare to propose a third meeting.

That was dreaming. He was here for a night's illicit pleasure; he really couldn't have more. But all the same he tingled with anticipation, and ate the stringy boiled fowl with more enjoyment than he took in his own French cook's roasted quail.

They moved upstairs, to a small bedroom. John pulled him over, and kissed him.

And it was ... good. Not perfect, because his head was a little clouded by two mugs of strong ale, followed by a glass of gin which he'd tossed back with unwise abandon, seeking Dutch courage or perhaps just wanting to be roguish and reckless for once. He was unquestionably rather drunk, and also John had very decided views on what he wanted which weren't precisely in step with the Duke's own preferences.

That didn't matter. If he wanted his desires fulfilled to the letter, there was always that discreet London house where he could have whatever he wanted supplied with a smile. He was here incognito precisely because he *didn't* want to be pandered to; he wanted to discover what it was like when the goal was mutual pleasure, not his alone. Which meant that when John said, uncompromisingly, that he wanted to be buggered, the Duke obliged him.

It was good enough. John certainly seemed to enjoy it, though the Duke was starting to feel more than a little dizzy by the end. John suggested another drink before the second bout, and the Duke accepted another glass of gin because he'd already had too much to be sensible, and he didn't remember anything more.

He woke up with a headache like knives and a nasty taste in his mouth.

He blinked his throbbing eyes open and sat up carefully. He was alone in the bed, which was good – discreet, sensible – but also regrettable. How had he fallen asleep so early and foolishly? He hoped John wasn't offended. Maybe he was downstairs; maybe he'd waited.

The Duke cast a glance around the room to see if John had left his things. It was bare of the clothes they'd strewn around, and of the Duke's travelling bag which he'd carried himself. Had Waters, his valet, come in and tidied up? The Duke had a pulse of alarm at that before remembering that Waters wasn't here.

He sat up again, too sharply for his head, and got out of bed, realising he was naked. His clothes were nowhere to be seen. He turned to the single chest, wondering if John had put them away, and saw a sheet of paper on top of it, with a couple of lines of scrawled writing.

You really ought to be more careful. Don't put temptation in people's way.
I won't trouble you further if you don't trouble me.

The Duke stared at that. Then he checked the chest, which was of course empty, looked under the bed in one last desperate hope, and sat down on it, hard.

He'd been robbed. John Martin had stolen his clothes, his money, his silver hairbrushes, everything. And that second line – was that a threat? If he made a fuss, if Martin was tracked down and the Duke prosecuted him, would the villain make counter-accusations? The Duke imagined himself the subject of a prosecution for sodomy, the newspaper reports, his family's reaction. Surely it could not come to anything: he was the Duke of Severn. But the shame alone was a prospect to make his whole soul cringe.

He felt sick to his stomach with bad gin and mortification and crashing disappointment. It wasn't that he'd cared for John Martin, but he'd briefly imagined a world in which he might one day come to care for him, just as he'd imagined that Martin had seen something appealing in his own nondescript person, picked him from a crowd and liked what he'd seen.

Clearly his imagination was overactive. Because he'd also imagined that he could manage one single evening without a regiment of people taking charge of his life.

He put his face in his hands as if that could hide him from the humiliation, and felt something wrong in the touch of his skin. Something missing. It took him a second to realise what, and then it hit him with the force of a slap.

His ring. The Severn ring, wrought of Welsh gold from the Crosse family's mine, a gnarled dragon worn by every duke since the first, taken from his father's still-warm corpse and put, frighteningly loose, on his own six-year-old finger. He'd worn it every day of his life since, with various artful attachments to keep it safe until his hands had reached their adult growth and it had been sized for him. He'd left behind his retinue and his embroidered linen to come to this assignation, but he hadn't even considered taking off the Severn ring. It proved him the Duke of Severn when nothing else did.

And it was gone.

The rest of the day was a bad dream. He had to poke his head out of the door with a blanket wrapped around him, so as not to outrage any serving-maid, and summon the landlord, and beg him to send a message for his valet, on the promise of lavish reward once his money arrived. At this point, he learned that John Martin had left him to pay the shot for last night's meal as well as the cost of the room. He sat on the bed in his blanket for hours, since he had no clothes and the landlord was too suspicious to lend him any, and enlivened the time by alternately kicking himself for his stupid self-delusion, and searching frantically for his ring, as if it could have somehow fallen off his finger.

At last his valet Waters arrived in a flurry of competence for which the Duke could only feel grateful, bearing clothes and money and terrifying authority borrowed from the dukes he'd served for fifty years. He restored the Duke to decency, gave the landlord a dressing-down that left the man in a state of grovelling apology, and swept the Duke into the comfort of his well-sprung carriage.

Waters did not ask what had happened. The Duke told him anyway, a version whereby he had indulged in an evening of manly pleasures of the acceptable kind (drink, gambling, a hint of women), and been robbed. There was no way to avoid that admission: he'd just have to endure the embarrassment and hope the tale stayed within the family. He tried to make a story of it, a comical misadventure, the kind of thing that could happen to a seasoned man of the world, more to practise that version than out of any hope his valet might take it lightly.

As indeed, he did not. 'Your Grace must not jest!' he said, real distress in his voice. 'Anything might have happened. You could have been killed! These brutes have no mercy.'

The Duke put out a reassuring hand. 'Since I wasn't in the slightest harmed—'

Waters wasn't listening. His eyes bulged. 'Your Grace! The ring! Did – did they steal the Severn ring?'

The Duke opened his mouth to make the dreadful admission, and heard himself say, 'No.'

'No? But—'

'A very lucky chance,' said the Duke's voice, which seemed to have overpowered his mind. 'I caught my finger in a door earlier, so I took the ring off in case it swelled. I have it safe.'

Waters pantomimed relief with a hand on his heart. 'Thank heavens. To have lost the Severn ring—'

'Yes,' the Duke said, strangled. 'That would be unthinkable.'

'Unforgivable. Your grandfather was so gracious as to inform me it was his most precious possession, valued over all else. He called it the Honour of the House.'

The Duke knew that. He'd been told over and over that

he was the ring's custodian, that it represented everything he ought to be, that it should always be worn and could never be lost. He felt giddy with horror, sick with shame; he wanted to curl up and cry.

He'd have to admit the truth at some point. Why had he not just done it now and got it over with?

Well, that was easy enough. It was because he'd have no way to explain why he wasn't sending to Bow Street for their best men to track down the thief.

Even so, all he'd achieved by lying was to delay the inevitable. It was pure cowardice, running away from trouble like the child Waters still thought him. His valet would be so disappointed by the truth. His uncle would be furious.

The journey back to Staplow, the ducal seat, seemed to take both forever and not nearly long enough. The Duke spent several minutes greeting the staff who lined up to welcome him back after his brief absence, knowing too well that while he chatted, Waters would be rushing to tell Lord Hugo about the whole sorry affair. The two old men had been allies in guarding and protecting the orphaned child-duke for too long to lose the habit in his manhood. His only hope was to present the whole affair as an absurdity, and hope his uncle could be brought to regard it in the same casual manner as he did his own sons' mishaps.

His uncle did not.

'Are you quite mad, Severn, making light of this?' Lord Hugo demanded. 'And you don't propose to summon the Bow Street Runners? The Duke of Severn made drunk, robbed, his person outraged—'

'My person was not outraged in the least,' the Duke interrupted. That, he was quite sure, was true: his larcenous lover had even tucked a blanket over him to keep the chill off. 'And I can't claim to have been made drunk: that was my own fault.'

'I don't know why you young men are so easily disguised. In my day, anything less than a three-bottle man – but that is not to the point. Of course you will summon the Runners.'

'And have the story get about within days? I really should prefer not to make myself a public laughing-stock. I have been taught a lesson, and will learn it with all the grace I can muster.'

'I damned well hope you do. To go off on your own in such a careless manner – what were you thinking of, boy?'

'I am a grown man,' the Duke pointed out. 'Leo and Matthew go off on their own, as you put it, all the time.'

'Pah! *They* don't matter,' Lord Hugo said of his beloved sons. 'You are Severn, and I will not permit this recklessness.'

'Ah – "permit", Uncle?' The Duke loved his uncle, and owed him a great deal. But his long minority had ended at the age of twenty-five, and he had steeled himself to challenge those many habits of speech when his cousins had informed him that if he didn't, he would spend the rest of his life a schoolboy. It didn't come naturally.

Lord Hugo lifted a hand in irritable acknowledgement. 'Yes, yes, I misspoke. But this is an outrage and you must take it seriously.'

'Believe me, I do,' the Duke assured him. 'Notwithstanding, I have learned a lesson at the cost of fifty pounds, a coat that I was not quite pleased with, a pair of hairbrushes, and a bad head. There are worse fates.'

'I will say for you, you don't make a fuss. Not but what you ought to be a deal higher in the instep,' Lord Hugo added, in one of the instant contradictions that made him such a trying conversational partner. 'That spirit of uncomplaint is a very admirable thing in any man, but you are not any man. You are Severn.'

'So I should rant and rage for my offended dignity?' the Duke asked with a quizzical look. 'Dear sir, why, when you do it so ably on my behalf?'

That got a reluctant laugh from his uncle. 'Insolent dog,' he said, once again forgetting that his nephew outranked him. 'Well, you will decide, I suppose, but no more of this gallivanting around on your own without your proper attendance. You must know your position better.'

He returned to the subject at dinner. It was an informal family meal: just the Duke, his two resident aunts, widowed Amelia and spinster Hilda, their brother Lord Hugo, and his sons, Cousin Matthew, who was twenty and ought to have been at Oxford but for an incident on a racecourse, and Cousin Leo, who was twenty-eight and ought to have been in London but for an incident in a gaming hell. Both aunts had fluttered, worried, and mourned what their poor mother would have said about the boys' wildness. Lord Hugo had accepted both sons' rustication with a deal less dismay than he did any transgression on the Duke's part.

Inevitably, Lord Hugo went over the whole sorry business as soon as they sat down to dine. Leo and Matthew found it hilarious, which the Duke attempted to take in good part, aided by the free-flowing wines, of which he partook more than usual in an effort to numb his still-aching head. In other circumstances, he could perhaps have laughed sincerely – not at the personal betrayal, which he flinched from considering, but certainly at the spectacle of the Duke of Severn huddled in a blanket and hiding from a suspicious landlord. He *wanted* to remember it as ludicrous. He would far rather be the butt of a ridiculous affair than the victim of hurt and unkindness and crushed hope.

He could have laughed, if it wasn't for the ring. As it was, he thanked the Lord for his family's habitual obliviousness, which meant nobody had noticed his bare finger and spared him repeating the lie, and wondered what the devil he was going to do.

He had to get it back, that was all. A discreet – exceedingly discreet – private agent to investigate, perhaps? There would surely be someone who would pursue the matter on his behalf, and who would know how to track down a thief who doubtless wasn't called John Martin at all and of whom the Duke could say little more than the colour of his hair and coat. He wondered how he might seek out a discreet private agent without word getting back to his uncle.

'You are not attending to me, Severn!' Lord Hugo remarked, jolting him from his thoughts. 'I suppose rag-manners are the fashion these days.'

'You've read him the same lesson several times, sir,' Leo observed to his parent with pardonable exasperation. 'Yes, he was reckless to go abroad without attendance. The point is made.'

'Well, and do you dispute it?'

'Of course I don't. The way you have wrapped him in lamb's-wool all his life, it is no surprise that any effort to look after himself should end in disaster.'

'I have done no such thing!' Lord Hugo objected inaccurately. 'Naturally Severn's safety has been my paramount concern—'

'Such that he now can't go on a spree without losing his shirt. Literally. Even Matthew can hold his drink better, and the Lord knows he's a featherweight.'

'I say!' Matthew put in, and was ignored by all.

'You're harsh, Leo,' the Duke said, keeping his voice mild though he felt decidedly stung. 'I grant you, I did not show to advantage last night, and I know I lack worldly experience—'

'Lack experience? That is to understate the case. Could you even survive without the constant ministrations of the faithful Waters, and your groom, and your footmen? Good Lord, Sev, you're held up by a scaffolding of service. No wonder you collapse without it.'

'I say,' Matthew repeated, this time in a more worried tone. There was something unusually aggressive in Leo's voice, more than the usual family give and take, and the Duke's bruised feelings found relief in responsive anger.

'That is unjust,' he said. 'I am not a fool, or a weakling. I have been robbed once—'

'You've been *out* once!'

'At least I have not returned to be robbed again and again at a single spot,' the Duke retorted. '*I'm* not that easily shorn.'

Leo had lost a great deal of money to the same men at the same hell over three evenings, a proceeding on which his father had commented in unflattering terms. He reddened. 'Easy to say from your noble heights. You have no more knowledge of the world than a baby, and no more force of character either, and it is no surprise that you cannot manage without a retinue. If you attempted to take the public stage—'

'I would learn to do it, just as you did. Purchasing a seat in a coach can hardly be a conundrum requiring membership of the Royal Society to solve.'

'And carry your own bags? Command rooms and meals?

Make your own way without the glory of the Duke of Severn opening all doors for you? Admit it: you'd be helpless.'

'Of course I could do all that!' the Duke snapped, and in that moment his great idea rushed upon him, carried on a wave of wine and anger. 'I could,' he repeated, 'and since you suggest it, I shall. Do you care to make a wager of it?'

Leo sat up straight. 'Wager?'

Aunt Amelia squeaked. Aunt Hilda barked a laugh. Lord Hugo said, 'Eh?'

'I would do very well by myself, and I shall prove it,' the Duke insisted. 'I shall fend for myself without all the advantages of Severn for, let's say a month.'

'You will do no such thing!'

Leo ignored his father. 'Without servants, and without use of your title or your social connections for assistance or influence? A month without privilege?'

'Without using any of it. Entirely anonymous.'

'But what are you going to do for a month like that?' Matthew asked.

'Travel,' the Duke said recklessly. 'Explore the country. Gain the experience Leo wishes for me.'

'You'll find it dashed uncomfortable. Dashed dull, too. You must have rats in your attic, Sev. If I were a duke, I shouldn't set foot on the stage for the rest of my life. Who cares if you don't do things for yourself? Why would you bother, when you're Severn? Dash it, what if you're pretending to be nobody and you meet someone you know?'

'I'll just have to avoid fashionable haunts.'

'Nobody will recognise you without your pomp and circumstance,' Leo said, all the more brutally because it was a statement of fact. 'You've a damned forgettable face. If you weren't dressed up, you wouldn't look like anyone at all.'

'I have often observed, my brother didn't consider the breeding stock when he married,' Aunt Hilda said. 'Joan was a delightful woman, but sadly unremarkable. Typical of a Malsham, all their girls were plain as—'

'Hilda, *really*,' Aunt Amelia said.

'This is not to the purpose.' Lord Hugo glowered at his sisters to no effect, then turned on the younger generation. 'And you will both stop this nonsense.'

'It is a wager,' the Duke said. 'I shall fend for myself for a month without using my title or influence or advantages, and when I have done so, you, Leo, will make an apology to me for doubting my capacity.'

'If you do it,' Leo returned. 'Using the public stage and inns as any common fellow might: no hiring a carriage or any such. If you survive a month of ordinary life without disaster, and without resorting to your title or station, I shall admit I was wrong as publicly as you like. And the stakes if you don't succeed...' He paused, thinking. The Duke braced himself. 'Your match greys.'

'What? No!'

'You can't wager money,' Leo pointed out. 'It doesn't mean anything to you, and Father would have an apoplexy.'

'Yes, I would!' Lord Hugo had never permitted betting or borrowing: the ducal estate was the Duke's alone, and he had rigidly avoided any action that might be interpreted as profiting from his nephew. 'You know very well—'

'Yes, sir, we do,' his son said impatiently. 'Stake the greys, Sev, if you're so sure it's easy.'

The Duke adored his greys. He had bought them as foals, trained them himself, and driven them for two years now, turning down extravagant offers. They were his sole point of personal glory. People who would not recognise him in a crowd knew the Duke of Severn's greys: fast, sweet steppers, perfectly matched, high-spirited but never misbehaving. He didn't want to lose them.

'Or if you don't care to risk it…' Leo added.

The Duke set his teeth. He needed this time, this free month in which he would go out into the world and get his ring back by hook or crook. Not to mention, he was cursed if he'd back down now. He would just have to make sure he won his bet.

'Very well,' he said. 'The greys.'

Chapter Two

Waters came in the next morning bearing a tea tray in his hands and the world on his shoulders. 'Your Grace,' he said. 'I am informed of the most distressing news. It cannot be correct.'

'My wager with Leo?' The Duke had been awake for some time, wondering if his great idea was in fact quite as great as it had seemed last night under the influence of several glasses of wine and the flush of insult. The concept was impeccable: a month in which he could track down the scoundrel John Martin and retrieve his ring. It was the execution – specifically, the fact that he had no idea how to go about executing it – that worried him.

'But Your Grace cannot seriously intend this.' Waters looked distraught. 'To travel alone? Without your carriage, or James, or a single outrider, or a wardrobe? Without *me*?'

'It is only for a month,' the Duke said soothingly.

'A month! Your Grace jests. Who will brush your coats and see to your linen? What about your boots?'

'I expect inns have people who do that.'

'Hardly to the standards Your Grace expects.'

'Indeed not. It will teach me to appreciate you.'

'Your Grace,' Waters said strongly. 'You must not. Surely Lord Hugo objects.'

'I dare say he does, but I don't require his permission.' *Or yours*, the Duke did not say, because, exasperating though it was to be nannied, Waters had cared for him all his life. The tightening of the valet's lips suggested he had taken the inference anyway, and was offended. The Duke sighed internally. 'Will you help me select the most ordinary clothes from my wardrobe?'

Waters stiffened even more. 'Your Grace does not possess any *ordinary* clothes.'

This was true. The Duke's coats were made by Hawkes or Weston, and it showed, even if he did not display them to any great advantage. In the end he resorted to borrowing a couple of Matthew's older coats, noting with satisfaction that they were a touch large for him and rather worn. He looked wonderfully ordinary. Waters wrung his hands in the background as the Duke admired his nondescript appearance in a full-length glass, and left in a huff when he expressed his intent of wearing his Wellington boots, which were informal and comfortable and had always grated on his valet's soul. All his linen was of the first quality but hopefully that would not be as obvious as coats were: he took just a few changes, intending to buy more and plainer items, along with toiletries and so on, because everything he had was embroidered or embossed with the Severn crest. He also appropriated a *Paterson's British Itinerary* and a copy of *The Traveller's Oracle* that belonged to Matthew, on the grounds that his need was greater.

As he put his luggage together, realising there was an art to packing and wondering whether Waters was too offended to help, his uncle came in.

'You cannot be going ahead with this, Severn.'

'It is a wager.'

This ought to be a clincher to a man of Lord Hugo's

generation, but he shook his head. 'It is a nonsensical wager. I shall tell Leo to retract.'

'I beg you will do no such thing. I shall come to no harm, and it will be an interesting experience. And it is my choice. I am above the age of majority after all.'

He said it with a smile, but he'd had to make similar reminders too many times over the last year. If he was of Lord Hugo or Leo's temperament he might have said *How many times must I tell you?* or *Will you remember my place and yours!* He could not imagine saying such a thing to his uncle, and so the comments never stopped.

Lord Hugo snorted. 'You are your own master, but you are also Severn, and I wish you would consider your position. This is cursed rash behaviour. You will find it extraordinarily uncomfortable, hobnobbing with the scaff and raff, and sleeping in damp bedsheets. I have no doubt you will catch a chill. And the vile sustenance available at ordinaries will not agree with you. It is very well for the common sort, but I repeat, you are Severn.'

'It doesn't *sound* very well for the common sort,' the Duke remarked. 'Should I not know the hardships my fellow men undergo, that I may strive to alleviate them?'

His uncle eyed him menacingly. 'Don't give me that Quakerish clap-trap. I see you are determined to be defiant.'

'You mean, to carry out my intention?'

'That's what I said. Oh, curse it, boy, you have not the knowledge of the world of a child, and I am not easy in my mind. If anything happened to you, my brother's son ... He entrusted you to my care.'

'Nobody could have fulfilled his request with more attention,' the Duke said sincerely. He would, in fact, have been very happy with rather less attention. 'But it is time I learned to care for myself. I do not wish to be, as Leo said, held up by a scaffolding of service all my life.'

'Nonsense,' Lord Hugo said. 'You are not anything of the kind.'

'You don't think Leo was right, sir?' the Duke said hopefully.

'Of course he was right; naturally you will not manage for yourself. I meant to say, you are quite wrong in your understanding of your position. The service, the attendance, all that – it is not a scaffolding. It *is* Severn; that is the point. You cannot be Severn and live in a cottage on pease pudding. Your position must be filled.'

'My position is filled, whether I like it or not.'

'I should hope you like it, since you are the most fortunate man in England. I dare say it is hard that you had so little time to be Harmsford,' Lord Hugo added, sounding slightly less brusque. 'My brother died too early, and ermine is a heavy weight on young shoulders. You could have got all this independence out of the way if you had succeeded later on. But here we are, and you have your duty.'

'I do have my duty,' the Duke agreed. 'And I am truly not going to live in a cottage on pease pudding. But I also have my wager, which I intend to win, so if there is nothing else, sir—'

Lord Hugo scowled. 'And suppose you fail and people say Leo set you on to this recklessness? I did not coddle you for twenty years in order to have my son blamed when harm comes to you! Good Lord, it was bad enough when that young oaf persuaded you to climb the Great Oak. You might have been killed when you fell, and the world would have called it his fault!'

'I landed on him,' the Duke pointed out. 'I have always

counted it an act of great loyalty that he broke my fall, especially since I broke his arm.'

It had no effect, nor had he expected any. Lord Hugo had always taken his responsibility for his orphaned nephew stiflingly seriously. The Duke sighed. 'Uncle, I proposed the wager and Leo can hardly be blamed for taking me up on it. I am looking forward to my adventure and I shall come to no harm. This is a civilised country under the rule of law. Pray do not fret.'

'I do not *fret,*' Lord Hugo said indignantly. 'If I am concerned, it is because I have more regard for your rank and station and safety than you seem to.'

The Duke let that pass. 'I will – no, I can't write to you here, in case anyone should observe the superscription. But I shall think of you, and send at once upon my re-emergence into Polite Society.'

'You are a feckless young fool,' Lord Hugo told him, surrendering without grace. 'And you will take a goodly sum with you – a hundred pounds at least – and the address of your bank, and your card-case ...'

He finally departed, still muttering, and the Duke had about five minutes' peace to go over his immediate plans before Leo came in.

'If you're on a mission from Uncle Hugo, go away,' the Duke told him. 'I shall not withdraw from my wager, or let you do so.'

'He did tell me to,' Leo admitted cheerfully. 'I told him I thought this lark would do you the world of good. I shan't enquire as to *why* you so badly want a month unsupervised, dear coz, but merely extend my good wishes in your endeavours.'

The Duke's eyes flew to his face. Leo grinned, a little

sheepishly. 'It occurred to me this morning that you might have taken the opportunity of my foul temper to carve yourself a little freedom, and I don't blame you: in your shoes I'd have run mad years ago. Just come back safely, or my father will never forgive me. Sev?'

'Mmm?'

'I apologise for my words last night. I was cursed rude to you, mostly because I was in a shocking rage at myself. Matthew dressed me down for jealousy of your circumstances, which I hope isn't true, although even if it is the little whelp should still respect his elder. Notwithstanding, I took out my frustration on you and I beg your pardon.'

'Oh, nonsense, Leo.' The Duke put out his hand.

His cousin grasped it. 'You're too tolerant. And this doesn't affect the bet. I still want your greys.'

'Are you setting up as a whip? Because horses won't do it alone: you'll need to be a deal less cow-handed first.'

Leo grinned at that accurate hit. 'I have no aspiration to drive your greys: I wouldn't presume. But Vier covets them, so—'

'Vier?'

'Sir James Vier. You know the man.'

'Yes, I do. And since I do, I have refused to sell him my greys several times. Why would you do such a thing?'

'Because he's the man I lost the money to,' Leo said. 'Did Father not mention that, or were you not listening? He's the very devil at whist, him and that smooth swine he partners with, but I'm quite sure he'd take the greys in settlement, so—'

'You are not giving Vier my horses,' the Duke said, not mincing words. 'The man is a brute. He thrashes his cattle like the worst sort of carter. For God's sake, Leo, you cannot!'

'I have limited options,' Leo said, the humour dropping from his eyes. 'I lost heavily. More than I can afford, in truth. Villainous, I know.'

'We all make fools of ourselves now and then; look at my performance. But for heaven's sake, let me give you the money. Or lend it, if you must be particular,' the Duke added, seeing a familiar mulish expression on his cousin's face.

Leo had always made a point of never taking so much as a shilling from his vastly wealthy cousin, supporting his father's position of honest stewardship. As ways of handling the gulf between their positions, it was as good as any and better than many, and the Duke respected that Leo did not expect to be hauled out of the River Tick whenever he fell in. But what was the point of wealth if one could not spend it on people one loved? 'I know you'd never ask or expect it, but just this once? Please? I'd far rather spend the money than see my greys in Vier's hands.'

'I'm not biting your shins. You know how my father feels.'

'He has never treated my money as his to use, and nor have you. It is mine to spend as I choose. I choose to spend it on you.'

'No. I can't ask that, or take it either. Sev, it's three thousand pounds.'

'Good God. What were you thinking?'

'I was drinking, not thinking.' Leo waved an airy hand, which did not fool the Duke in the slightest. 'It was my foolishness and I will bear the consequences.'

'But what will you do? Other than give Vier my greys, which, I must tell you, you should not bank on.'

'I dare say the old man will oblige when he calms down. Or I shall sell out of the Funds, if I need to. Your father was generous with his bequests.'

'Leo, that's your income! For goodness' sake, don't waste your capital on Vier. Let me loan you the money, and you may repay me at a sensible pace. I'll charge you interest.'

'I do not and will not depend on you to solve my troubles,' Leo said. 'Though I shall be delighted if you lose our wager. Otherwise, dear coz, I wish you well on your adventure.' His tone made it clear the subject was closed.

The Duke negotiated starting his travels in Gloucester. The Bird in Hand inn where he'd been robbed was on the outskirts of the town, and he'd ascertained from the landlord that John Martin had departed in a northerly direction. He'd hoped to pick up the fellow's tracks without too much difficulty.

He'd been optimistic. It turned out that ostlers were very busy men who didn't have time to answer the questions of undistinguished greenhorns, whether about who they'd seen or where the coaches were going. In fact, most people were completely uninterested in helping him. One pleasant individual did come up to engage him in conversation; the Duke, having completed a tour on the Continent and not being quite such a Johnny Raw as all that, had declined the invitation to take a drink or pass the time with a game of chance. He congratulated himself on that much, and was feeling quite satisfied by his performance once he managed to take a place on the stage to Cheltenham.

That was a guess, but it was a spa town where one might find idling gentlemen: it seemed plausible John Martin might attempt to repeat his performance there. The Duke therefore boarded the stagecoach in a spirit of hopefulness that was rapidly knocked out of him.

The interior of the coach reeked, of the potations of at

least two of his fellow passengers, a small boy who'd recently been sick, and another passenger's hot meat pie, which somehow left a film of grease on the Duke's lips from two feet away. He was squashed between a rubicund farmer and a buxom lady, both of whom expressed their pleasure that he was such a small man. The coach was unsprung, the seats unpadded, the roads of a vileness, the journey longer than he could have imagined. He staggered out at the other end, cursing John Martin and Leo and himself, and discovered that at some point someone had picked his pocket and stolen twenty pounds.

At least it wasn't more. He'd split his money up and secreted it about his person and in his luggage. But it had gone from an inner pocket, which was rather frightening, and he had no idea when, which was worse, and it was a sizeable part of his entire worldly wealth for the duration of a month. It was a bad blow on his first day.

He'd decided to retire early and ask questions tomorrow, thinking to ensure a good night's rest. That also was denied him, since his person did not command instant obsequious attention, or comfortable rooms, or the choicest viands. He dined on the ordinary, which was extremely ordinary – a slurry of oversalted, overcooked vegetables and a few pieces of gristly meat – and found himself allocated a dismally dark, smoky space under the eaves with decidedly damp sheets and rough blankets. Worst of all, the noise from outside was unceasing: rattling wheels, shouting, an endless hubbub that made him pull the miserable covers over his head and wish himself back in the luxurious quiet of Staplow.

Burned coffee and an inadequate breakfast for a sum he suspected was extortionate did not help his mood in the morning. He was unwashed and had made a poor fist of dressing, and it took a strong effort to command his feelings. If he was uncomfortable, he reminded himself, it was because of John Martin, and he would use his irritation to fuel his enthusiasm for the pursuit.

He set himself doggedly to the task. He asked ostler after ostler if they had seen one not-particularly-notable man out of hundreds, discovering that a shilling was the best coin to win attention but not too much attention. He made his wearisome way around the edges of Cheltenham, and then ventured into the centre with his senses on alert for acquaintances. It would not be in breach of terms for him to be recognised, but he'd have to refuse any invitations, and explain what he was doing in an ill-fitting coat, and word would doubtless get about, and the whole thing would be cursed awkward.

It didn't arise because he saw nobody he knew, and in particular, he did not see John Martin.

He hadn't expected immediate success, of course, but it was still a disheartening and exhausting day that made him aware he was seeking not just a needle in a haystack, but one with the power of movement. He wanted nothing more than a hot, deep bath to rest his aching feet, and if he were going home to Staplow, Waters would have one waiting ready for him. He put that thought out of his mind and made his way to probably the eighth and definitely the last inn of the day, the White Hart on the Birmingham Road.

It was busy. He would have to wait for a quiet moment to speak to the ostlers; in the meantime he went inside and attempted to command a room.

The landlord cast an unimpressed glance over him. 'I might have a bed. Sit you down with a mug of ale and I'll see. Saloon bar's over there.'

The Duke didn't want to sit down with a mug of ale: he wanted to be conducted to a comfortable room without delay. He murmured thanks anyway, wondering if he was being polite or merely weak, and went through to the saloon bar.

It was occupied by a man, who sat opposite a woman wearing a quite remarkable bonnet. He was staring intently at her, and had a sheet of paper with a black patch at its centre in his hands. She was turned sideways to him, clearly posing. The Duke said, 'I beg your pardon.'

'Don't mind me,' the man said without looking at him. 'Have a seat. Mine hostess will be free to attend to you in just a few moments.'

'I am having my likeness taken,' the lady added, casting the Duke a glance and a smile. Clearly she was the landlady; she wore an ordinary day-dress with what looked like her Sunday-best hat. The man was cutting her profile, the Duke realised. He had never seen one done before, only the results. He hesitated, interested but unwilling to intrude.

'You are welcome to observe,' the shade-cutter said, still without looking.

The Duke moved closer, and watched with fascination. The shade-cutter had a pair of tiny scissors which he seemed to be holding very still as he snipped, instead moving the paper into the jaws of the blades in a slow but almost continuous turning motion. The scissors cut smooth, confident curves, paring the blackened paper so that the extra material fell away and the landlady's outline emerged, including the hat. It was a surprisingly quick process. The artist cut the remains of the paper surround free, and made a few additional snips. He took a rectangular card from a leather satchel, pasted the back of the profile from a little pot, placed it neatly on the card, and presented it to the landlady with a bow.

'Well!' she said, delighted. 'Well, good heavens, look at me. See, sir!'

The Duke examined it, looking back and forth between paper and woman. It was a striking likeness, considering it was simply an outline without depth or detail. The artist had been kind to her jawline, and somehow managed to convey a curve to her mouth that radiated the woman's obvious good humour.

'That is quite delightful,' the Duke said. 'You have remarkable skill, sir.'

The cutter glanced up at him with a glowing flash of a smile. 'Why, thank you. And thank *you*, Mrs Sturridge. Will your good man be having a likeness too?'

'I can see all I want of him any day.' She examined her profile again, beaming. 'That's worth a night's lodging to me, and a meal too. And you, sir,' she added to the Duke, 'what may I bring you? Ale?'

He agreed reluctantly. A glass of wine would be preferable but he had already learned the unwisdom of ordering any such thing in an inn outside London. He took a seat, while the other man put away his paste-bottle and card.

The shade-cutter was a good-looking fellow with a cheerful sort of face, the kind that looked wrong without a smile. He had a fine pair of brown eyes, and his wavy hair combined bronze, copper and gold like a handful of coins: no silver there yet. His coat gave the impression he'd worn it for rather too long, and that impression was carried through into the rest of his dress, which was well used to the point of shabby. He looked like a pleasant gentleman, but down on his luck.

He also seemed vaguely familiar, especially the bright glinting hair. The Duke had a panicked moment wondering if he was an acquaintance, perhaps someone met in London – but no, not with that sadly worn coat, and in any case this was a professional profile-cutter and he'd never sat for a profile, even to an amateur. No, he couldn't place the fellow, but all the same, exasperatingly, he was sure he knew him.

The man glanced up, catching the Duke in the act of scrutiny. 'Unlike the dancing bear, you may observe me at no charge. Or may I serve you? Would you care to have your profile taken?'

'Thank you, no. No, I was merely … I beg your pardon, but are we acquainted?' the Duke said recklessly. 'You look very familiar.'

'Do I? I can't say the same, I'm afraid.'

That was unsurprising: the Duke knew himself to be entirely forgettable. That was currently a good thing, just as it was good that the shade-cutter wasn't trying to pin down where they might have met, even if it seemed a rather unfriendly response from a man with a friendly face.

'Perhaps I was mistaken,' the Duke said. 'I beg your pardon. My name is—' He bit *Severn* back, reminding himself that he'd settled on his favourite of his many names, one he never got to use. 'Cassian.'

'Good day to you, Mr Cassian. Charnage.'

'Charnage?' the Duke said. '*Daisy* Charnage?'

He saw Charnage's smile die, his lips staying curved but without any happiness behind the expression. 'Daizell, if you please, and yes, the same. I dare say you have had a long, tiring day if you are travelling, so I won't disturb you.' He reached into his satchel and took out a book.

The landlady returned at that point with two tankards of ale. The Duke took his with a word of thanks, mind racing.

Daizell Charnage, the bizarre first name pronounced to rhyme with 'hazel', usually shortened to Daisy at school. The Duke had been two years behind him at Eton, a fact he was quite sure Charnage wouldn't remember since he had been just another small boy and a particularly unimpressive one at that. Titled, yes, but many of their peers were peers: Charnage himself was a connexion of the Marquess of Sellingstowe, albeit no longer acknowledged as such. There was no reason he would recognise the Duke.

There were a number of reasons the Duke should have recognised him, and refrained from conversation accordingly.

His name had not been mud during most of the Duke's school career. In fact, Daizell Charnage had been a highly popular boy. He'd been expelled, granted, but only for running a gambling ring, which was doubtless very bad, but from a schoolboy's perspective had felt trivial compared to the unpunished cruelty of many of the older boys. The Duke remembered him as that schoolboy might: a glowing, laughing young trickster, to be hopelessly admired from a safe distance.

Not any more. His father's appalling actions had ruined his son's name and left him penniless and disgraced, whether entirely by proxy or because he'd been somehow involved, the Duke wasn't sure. He'd been abroad at the time. Then there was the scandal that Charnage had had on his own account a year or so ago. The Duke couldn't recall the details if he'd ever known them – an elopement, he vaguely thought – but Leo had shaken his head. Either way, Charnage had disappeared from good society and now moved in decidedly less elevated circles, attending the sorts of parties that the

Duke of Severn would never grace with his presence even if anyone had invited him.

And, it seemed, he cut profiles in public houses to pay for his lodgings. That was horribly sordid for a gentleman, or at least a man born a gentleman, and Charnage had doubtless decided to end the conversation before he could be snubbed. He probably received plenty of snubs, and indeed the Duke would probably have snubbed him. Severn could not risk letting an encroaching mushroom grow on the fringes of his ermine robes.

He wasn't currently the Duke of Severn. He was the unknown, unrecognised Mr Cassian who could talk to anybody he pleased, and he was lonely, and he remembered Daizell Charnage so well as that bright young god at Eton.

'So what are you doing?' he asked.

Charnage glanced up from his book. 'I beg your pardon?'

'At the moment. I mean to say, are you, uh, travelling somewhere?'

Charnage didn't make the obvious point that they were in a coaching inn. 'Not urgently. Dawdling on my way to an engagement. And yourself?'

'I'm currently struggling with rather a challenging task, which is what brings me here.'

Charnage's eyelids drooped. 'A challenging task. Really. Does that involve the placing of horses before a race?'

The Duke didn't understand for a moment, and then he laughed with surprise. 'Not at all, no, and I am not going to suggest a game of chance or skill, either.'

'I'm relieved to hear it.'

He didn't enquire further. The Duke was used to people showing rather more interest in his doings. He pressed on. 'The fact is, I was recently robbed.'

'Sorry to hear it,' Charnage said, with no effort to sound sincere. 'Unfortunately, I will not be able to tide you over with a small loan.'

This was entirely unfamiliar ground. As one of the richer men in England, the Duke had never had to fend off accusations of breaking shins, nor had he ever had to work to make people speak to him or feign interest, his family excepted. 'I don't require one,' he said. 'Actually, I was robbed of a certain item of sentimental value and I'm trying to discover where the thief went.'

'Good God.' Charnage gave him an examining look. 'Are you a Bow Street Runner?'

'Me? No.'

'Thief-taker?'

'Again, no. I have no experience in this at all.'

Charnage's brows tilted. 'I suppose there's a reason you are doing this yourself rather than calling in someone competent?'

The Duke's cheeks heated. 'Yes, but – the thing is – well, it's rather a delicate matter. For reasons I prefer not to disclose,' he added, feeling the weakness of it.

'Naturally. Naturally.' Charnage waved that away. 'And you are in this caravanserai to lay hands on the thief?'

'I wish I were. I have been trudging across Cheltenham trying to pick up his trail without success. I don't know he's anywhere near here, to be honest.' He was blurting out more than Charnage wanted to hear, probably, but it had been a very solitary and disheartening few days. 'The robbery happened in Gloucester and the only clue is that the fellow took a stage going north rather than south.'

'Does your thief have an eyepatch? A dramatic scar?'

'Nothing. He looks quite the gentleman, but without any

very distinguishing features. A perfectly pleasant ordinary sort of man.'

'You can't just ask at every inn if they've seen an ordinary sort of man recently,' Charnage said. 'Or rather, you could, but not to any effect.'

'I realise that. I do have his name, but it's probably false. John Martin,' he added in response to a questioning look.

'Oh, certainly false.' Charnage put down his book and pulled his chair round to face the Duke more squarely, as though he'd decided the conversation was worth his interest. The Duke found himself absurdly flattered. 'It's a strangely common habit among the false-name-giving fraternity to resort to Christian names as an alias for a surname. A man who calls himself Mr Martin or Mr Peter or Mr George is never to be trusted.'

The Duke would have liked to query such a sweeping statement, and might have done so if he hadn't currently been using a Christian name as an alias for a surname. Thank goodness Cassian was such an obscure name as to be unfamiliar to most Englishmen. That could have been embarrassing.

'In any case, I can't rely on him using the same name,' he said. 'I need to ... To be honest, I don't know what I need to do. I hoped I would cross his tracks.'

Charnage made a face. 'If I were you – did you say this item was of actual value, or merely sentimental?'

'Both.'

'Then I'd go back to Gloucester and try the pawn shops. If he stole valuables, his first thought will have been to get them off his hands. I'd say try the fences, but that would require the help of someone familiar with that profession. A discreet thief-taker would be best.'

'I've no idea how to go about that. I dare say I seem rather a greenhorn.'

'A little out of your depth, perhaps.'

'Very much so. I'm not familiar with the area, and I'm not used to travelling from home like this' – it was technically true depending on your interpretation of those words – 'and in all honesty, I suspect I have bitten off more than I can chew.'

'Poor fellow,' Charnage said, with a touch more sympathy than before. 'Really, are you quite sure you can't put this in the hands of the authorities? Although …'

'Although?'

'Well, an item both sentimental and valuable – does that make it easily identifiable? Because that isn't an attractive quality to a receiver of stolen goods. A necklace might be more valuable as a collection of matched jewels on a string, but more safely saleable as individual stones. A golden item might be better melted down for the value of its metal, even if that destroys the value of its artistry.'

The Duke's mouth had fallen open in shock. He closed it. 'You think— No. They could not melt it down. *No*.'

'I hope not, for your sake. But you might want to get on and retrieve the thing quickly.'

'Yes. I need to.' The Duke had the distinct sense of another brilliant idea dawning. He wasn't sure whether he ought to trust that sense, since his previous brilliant idea was not going marvellously. Then again, the clock was ticking and he had not done well by himself, and Charnage, for all his reputation – perhaps *because* of his reputation – clearly had ideas.

'I need to,' he said again, and took the plunge. 'Would you help me?'

Chapter Three

Daizell wasn't sure what was going on.

He'd been recognised, but this Cassian fellow hadn't told him where from. That might only mean that he'd been pointed out at some juncture with the usual litany: George Charnage's son; expelled from Eton; the man who failed to elope with Eliza Beaumont; dubious character; scarcely more than a Merry Andrew with his cut-out flummery; bad ton. Then he'd assumed Cassian was attempting to break his shins, in which case the joke was on him, since Daizell had approximately six pounds to his name. Still, he'd started paying attention to the slightly odd young gentleman, who wore a coat that had been made for somebody else two years ago, but whose very fine linen looked to have been fresh on in the last day or so. He was an unassuming sort physically, and modest in manner, yet he'd taken it for granted that Daizell would listen to what he had to say, and he'd been genuinely amused when Daizell had suggested he might be a tout. One could laugh at that sort of thing only if one didn't fear the mud might stick.

Cassian. The name didn't ring a bell, but then it was a long time since Daizell had been in good society. He might be a provincial gentleman who kept himself to himself. Either way, he was pleasant, and he didn't seem to be a humbugger, and this was the longest conversation Daizell had had in a while, so he might as well see where it went.

'Help,' he repeated. 'What sort of help?'

'I need someone who knows how to negotiate this business.'

'Negotiate what, precisely? Because if you mean with fences and thief-takers, I regret that is not my area of expertise.'

'Oh, I didn't mean that!' Cassian said hastily. 'Not at all. I meant – well, someone who knows about this sort of thing in general, or more than I do. Pawn shops, as you said, and people who give false names, and so on.'

'Someone familiar with the more disreputable side of life, not the world of gentlemen.'

'Exactly!' Cassian said, and then his face changed ludicrously. 'Oh. Uh. I didn't intend any insult.'

That was the worst part: he clearly hadn't. He'd stated it as a fact because Daizell Charnage was so very obviously a man one would ask about pawn-shops.

Daizell should probably take offence, stand on his dignity, and consign Mr Cassian to the devil. Any self-respecting gentleman would. But Daizell was rather short on self-respect and indeed gentlemanliness these days, and was there really much point in taking offence at what was, after all, the truth?

Cassian looked exquisitely awkward, but he pressed on. 'I apologise for my clumsiness, but to be honest, I find myself out of my depth. I only have a month, you see, and I've wasted two days of it already.'

'What happens after the month is up?'

'I have to go home.'

Daizell considered him. He looked to be in his mid-twenties. Mid-brown hair, middling sort of build, on the shorter end of mid-sized. Nothing noteworthy about him. If he was asking about a man who looked like everybody else, people might enquire whether he'd tried a mirror.

Except for the mouth. He had a nice mouth, well-shaped in an unobtrusive way, with a gentle, almost wistful upward turn to it as though it was his habit both to smile and to hope. Daizell liked people who smiled and hoped because he did so himself. Sometimes those were the only things he could do.

But, returning to the initial point of the examination, Cassian looked mid-twenties, and he *felt* well off, so why would he 'have' to go home? A wife waiting? Responsibilities?

'And you want a partner in your search?' Daizell asked.

'Yes. Someone who knows his way around, a man of the world, which I freely admit I am not.'

'And you think I am?'

'You have that reputation. Uh—'

'I know my reputation,' Daizell said. 'I might even deserve some of it.'

'I understand you live by your wits,' Cassian said. 'That's precisely what I need, because my own wits – I shan't say they're blunt, but they need to be sharpened by experience that I don't have time to acquire. Naturally it would be entirely at my expense, and—' His eyes flickered over Daizell. 'If it would not offend you, I'd be most glad to recompense you for your time.'

Of course it was offensive to suggest hiring a gentleman. Any man of good birth and self-respect would dismiss him at once. 'What recompense have you in mind?'

'Er.' Cassian looked blank. 'Fifty pounds?'

Daizell did not spit out his mouthful of ale, though it was a close thing. Fifty pounds! That would keep him afloat for a full year if he handled it wisely. He wouldn't, of course: it would be gone in a month, but the concept was irresistible.

'A month assisting you?' he clarified.

'Yes, if you aren't busy. But you said you had an engagement?'

Daizell waved that away. 'No matter. It isn't important.'

He mostly lived on the charity of people who owned large houses and liked to fill them with company. To make that work one had to avoid overstaying one's welcome, and these days he had a limited number of people willing to host him. A month fending for himself at Cassian's expense, then maybe two months living off his fifty pounds if he was sensible... yes, he'd make himself that bit scarcer now and with luck people would be pleased to see him come the winter. This could keep the wolf from the door for a while.

'So,' he said. 'What is this item you're seeking?'

'It's a ring.'

Of course it was. A full-length portrait would have been too easy. 'I'm not a Bow Street Runner either. What if we don't find it?'

'I realise that's quite possible. Likely, even. But I need to try, to know I've done my best,' Cassian said, and his expressive mouth twitched, just for a second, into a look of deep distress.

'Very understandable, but I meant, if we don't find it...?' He let that hang. Cassian looked blank. Daizell sighed internally: people with money never thought about these things. He hadn't, when he'd had money. 'I still get paid?'

'Oh. Yes, of course. Your time and effort will still have been spent.'

What a very pleasant man. 'And you want... what, a companion, assistant, generator of ideas about what to do next?'

'All of that, especially the last.'

'And you said fifty pounds?' Daizell checked, in case he'd misheard and it was fifteen. 'Well, I am happy to do my best, for what it's worth.' Which was, apparently, fifty quid. He'd never been so highly valued in his life.

'You will?' Cassian's eyes lit. 'Thank you. Thank you very much.'

'The pleasure is all mine. I think our first step should be to command a dinner, awaiting which you shall tell me everything, and then we'll make a plan.'

'Of course. Yes.' Cassian looked remarkably pleased with himself, as if he'd achieved something greater than paying an aimless not-quite-gentleman for help. Odd fish, Daizell thought. 'Perhaps we could order a meal, and I must ensure I have a bed. I slept dreadfully last night. So noisy.'

After years in coaching inns, Daizell could sleep through cries of 'Fire!' and indeed had. Mr Cassian was clearly more delicate in his tastes. 'Intolerable,' he agreed. 'Shall I . . . ?'

He didn't particularly want to be a dragoman, arranging Mr Cassian's travels and smoothing his way, but it seemed only right to offer. Cassian gave an automatic-looking nod, then said, 'No! That is, I should prefer to do it.'

'Of course,' Daizell said, since he didn't care, and rang the bell. 'Let's see what the rogue in charge here has to offer.'

The answer to that was mixed. The inn was very busy, the innkeeper Sturridge said dismissively; the gentleman would have to wait, and something to eat would be along in due course. As for a room, he dared say they could accommodate Mr Cassian on the top floor. Daizell listened to Cassian give politely ineffectual objections to the first, thus guaranteeing he'd eventually be served whatever was deemed unworthy of more determined guests, and reluctantly accede to the second, at which point he realised that 'greenhorn' wildly overstated the man's experience of staging inns.

'Enough of that, you wretched villain,' he informed Sturridge. 'I'm eating with him, and we'll have beef collops, sweetbreads, and green peas, plus a bottle of whatever drinkable wine you may have, and *not* watered if you value your life.' If Cassian was paying – and he'd need to be, because Daizell couldn't – then Daizell would be taking full advantage. 'And you'll put him somewhere decent, fool, not the attics or over the stables. Can you not recognise a gentleman when you see one?'

'I might see *one* here, yes,' retorted Sturridge, turning his gaze on Daizell in a meaningful fashion. 'And who's paying for this, I'd like to know? Paying with more than cut paper, I mean.'

'I am,' Cassian said, sounding rather faint.

Sturridge gave a grudging nod. 'Well. As for a room – if you'll share, there's the front room. Best I can do.'

'Then I suppose it will suffice,' Daizell said. 'If the sheets are damp, I shall personally wrap your head in them till you resemble the turnip you are.'

'Sweetbreads and collops,' Sturridge snarled, making it sound like a particularly filthy oath, and departed.

Daizell caught Cassian's astonished expression. 'Old friend,' he explained. 'Acquaintance, anyway. Well, he's a shocking fellow but his good lady is an excellent cook. Now, tell me about this thief of yours.'

Cassian actually blushed, as if Daizell had said something embarrassing. 'Er. Well.' He launched into a tale of a chance meeting, an invitation to dine and gamble, excessive drink. It was all very plausible, except that he told it with a certain amount of care, and the rather charming red stain over his cheekbones persisted. Probably whores had been involved, and the inexperienced Mr Cassian didn't want to admit it, as if Daizell gave a curse.

He wrung out a description of the thief John Martin – medium height, dark hair, hazel eyes, mulberry coat. It wasn't much to go on, although Daizell liked the sound of mulberry. Perhaps he should spend some of his fifty pounds on a new coat. Once he lost the remnants of a gentlemanly appearance, he'd be in deep trouble.

They discussed strategies for finding the thief's destination over dinner. Daizell thought they might as well throw darts at a map of England but the discussion seemed to make Cassian happy and they had a very pleasant meal, since Mrs Sturridge was indeed a fine cook, and had liked her profile. Wider conversation was a little stilted at first, since Cassian wasn't very forthcoming. He lived somewhere in the country to the west of Gloucester but not actually Wales, and that was about as much as he wanted to say of himself.

Daizell didn't press. He wouldn't have wanted to rehearse his own circumstances and recent history, and probably Cassian was aware of that, since he didn't ask. So instead they talked about the news, politics, and anything that didn't address awkward questions such as *Who are you? What's your life like?*

They were to share a room that night. That didn't trouble Daizell, who frequently found himself sharing sleeping quarters or even beds with strangers. A room with two people and two beds, paid for by somebody else and shared with someone who didn't look louse-ridden and wouldn't rifle through his pockets in the night, was luxury. Cassian might even be too refined to snore.

The room was quite adequate, considering. He checked under the beds all the same.

'Er, what are you doing?' Cassian asked.

'I once found a fellow lurking under the bed. No idea if he wanted a free night's sleep or to cut my throat and rob me, but it stays with you.'

'I should think so!' Cassian looked alarmed. 'Is that usual? Ought one always check?'

'It rather depends the sort of inn you frequent.' Daizell had many stories of inns he'd frequented, ranging from absurd to alarming, and he deployed a couple of them now. He wanted to make friends, since he liked to be friends and the next month would be more pleasant that way, but he also had an urge to make Cassian laugh again, because he had a delightful laugh. It was a sort of surprised gurgle, as though he was startled and even a touch embarrassed by his own amusement, and Daizell thought it was charming. So was the smile that lingered after his laugh, keeping those expressive lips in a curve that took a moment or so to fade. One wouldn't call him handsome, exactly, but it was an endearing smile.

Not to mention that he was rather amusing too, offering an account of hostelries in France and Switzerland which had Daizell in stitches, even as he filed away that Cassian had made a Grand Tour.

They chatted very pleasantly as they both got ready for the night. Cassian did so with an odd combination of carefulness and carelessness, including dropping a perfectly good shirt on the floor, as if he expected someone to pick it up for him and to have a clean one waiting tomorrow. Daizell also couldn't help noticing that Cassian's bare torso in the candlelight was perhaps a little more impressive than expected. He was slender, but he had a rider's or a fencer's body, with gentle lines of muscle showing as he moved. Trim, Daizell thought appreciatively, and stopped looking on that thought. He had fifty pounds to earn. Now was not the time to do something rash.

The next morning they got down to business bright and early over a slapping breakfast. Daizell felt he could get used to someone else paying: the knowledge he wouldn't have to argue about the bill added savour to his sausages.

'If we go back to Gloucester and try the pawn shops, we may find the ring,' he said. 'But we have no guarantee it was pawned rather than fenced, or indeed if Martin has disposed of it at all. It will take a couple of days to go through them all, and if that fails, we will doubtless find it more difficult to pick up the fellow's trail. I suppose we could split up,' he added, with a little reluctance. He'd woken with pleasant anticipation of companionship for the day.

Cassian looked torn. 'I suppose perhaps we could, but then, how would you find me again if you did locate the ring?'

'You could give me your address?'

'Oh. Yes.' He didn't leap on the idea, which was fair. He naturally wouldn't want Daizell Charnage turning up at his home claiming acquaintance and a bed for a week. 'It's very hard to know what to do for the best. As you said, I can't simply ask at every coaching inn for an ordinary man in a mulberry-coloured coat.'

'No, although …' Daizell stopped. 'Just a moment. Is that what you've been asking?'

'Yes, of course.'

'In those words?'

'Yes.' Cassian looked a little alarmed.

'What colour is mulberry?'

'Darkish purple with a touch of pink.'

Daizell snapped his fingers at Sturridge, who was walking by. 'Rogue. What colour are mulberries?'

Sturridge gave him a look. 'Black, what d'you think?'

'Anything else?'

'Red if they ain't ripe.' He pondered. 'Green if they really ain't ripe.'

'What sort of red?'

'What d'you mean, sort of red? Red.' Sturridge rolled his eyes and walked off.

Daizell turned back to Cassian, who said, 'I feel exceedingly foolish.'

'Some people will have understood you. Sturridge is more than usually uninterested in the world around him. Nevertheless …'

'Nevertheless, I have wasted two days by asking the wrong question. I should have realised it was the wrong question. I didn't *think*. And now I have lost time and doubtless the trail by making that assumption. Nobody ever said, *what do you mean by mulberry?*'

No, they'd just taken his money, and Daizell didn't blame them. Ask a silly question, get a useless answer. Still, he looked genuinely upset and Daizell felt a stab of sympathy. 'Do you know what? I think we should start again. Let's go back to Gloucester, to the Bird in Hand. I might be able to get more out of the landlord than you did, since you were in an awkward position at the time.'

Cassian's shoulders sagged. 'You probably could. I asked him about Martin, where he'd gone, but he was shouting about his bill, and I was only wearing a blanket, and I could hardly assert myself – or, I should have, I know that, but to start making a fuss in such humiliating circumstances—'

'Hey,' Daizell said. 'You had a cursed nasty time of it. You were robbed by someone you considered a friend, or at least a pleasant acquaintance. That's a distressing thing to happen even without the embarrassment of being caught in a state of nature. You needn't blame yourself for not being at your best.'

Cassian just looked at him for a few seconds. Daizell said, 'No?'

'No. I mean, yes. I mean … Do you realise, you haven't said a word of blame or ridicule to me about the whole affair?'

Daizell blinked. 'Why would I?'

'Everyone else has.'

If Daizell went around telling people when they'd been fools, it would be very like Cassian searching for ordinary men: they should both look in the mirror first. 'I dare say everyone else must have led a very sensible, secure, consistently well-judged, and exceedingly fortunate sort of life where they have never made a mistake,' he said. 'I envy you your acquaintance. That or they're a pack of hypocrites.'

'They are not!' Cassian said strongly, with a flash of colour into his cheeks, which was overtaken by a lurking grin. 'Perhaps a touch inclined to pass remarks. But it was foolish of me, so they have every right.'

'Mmm,' Daizell said. 'Let's find the Gloucester coach.'

They went to the yard. Cassian strode ahead with a determined stance, as if signalling his intention to take the lead. Daizell followed happily along.

Cassian found out about the Gloucester coaches without difficulty, paused, then asked the ostler, 'I wonder if you can help me. I'm looking for a man, who would have come through here perhaps three days ago, or more recently. A little taller than me, dark brown hair.' He gave the rest of the nondescript description. 'And he may have been wearing a coat in a dark purple-pink colour, like an over-ripe raspberry on the turn.'

'Oh, him?' the ostler said. 'Two days ago, that was.'

'You *saw* him?'

'Saw him?' The man snorted. 'You might say. Passed me a dud shilling, he did! Me, done like a right Johnny Raw!'

'I will be very pleased to replace it for you, with another for your trouble, if you can tell me where he went,' Cassian assured him.

The ostler put out his hand, and made a point of biting the coins he was given. 'He took a seat to Worcester.'

Cassian turned to Daizell with a grin of triumph. 'Then we shall need two seats on the Worcester coach.'

Daizell couldn't help a moment of optimism as he smiled back. Perhaps they could track down this Martin fellow; perhaps his aid might make the difference. It would be very pleasant to have a success chalked up to his name.

It was harder to maintain that optimistic frame of mind when they joined the stage. Stagecoaches were punitive things at best and this, a six-seater, was particularly bad. The interior was a little over three feet wide, so to wedge three adults onto each seat was difficult even when they were of slender build.

They were relatively fortunate to grab a centre and corner seat, less to have their backs to the direction of travel, significantly less so to be sharing the coach with several well-built and well-fed men. Daizell pushed Cassian into the corner, and wedged himself next to him, taking the middle seat with the fifty pounds firmly in mind.

He was quickly glad he'd done it. Cassian's knuckles were white on the strap as the coach bounded its bone-jolting way along the road, and Daizell, pressed up tight against his slim frame but not in an enjoyable way, could feel his tension.

'Don't travel much?' he asked quietly. He hardly needed to shout despite the rattling of the coach: packed as they were, a turn of his head brought his mouth all too close to Cassian's ear.

'Not on the public coach.' Cassian spoke with a grimness that made Daizell hope he wasn't going to be sick. 'This conveyance appears to be entirely unsprung, and why are the seats not padded?'

'You *don't* travel much,' Daizell agreed.

'Could be worse, friend,' one of the men opposite said, jovially, and went on to make that a self-fulfilling prophecy by launching into a rambling anecdote. Daizell inferred from the expressions of the other passengers that he was a stagecoach bore, and would probably tell his stories from the start every time a new passenger joined them. He adopted the blank expression of a man who couldn't hear a thing in the faint hope it would discourage the talker, which was quashed by Cassian's polite, 'Very good, sir. Excellent,' at the long-awaited end of the story.

'Ah, if you think that's funny…!' the bore exclaimed. One of the men opposite shut his eyes in despair. Daizell trod on Cassian's foot, for all the good it would do. At least it relieved his feelings.

It was two stages to the Blue Boar at Worcester, through which the dull man talked without pause, mercy, or, as far as Daizell could see, breathing. Daizell clambered out of the coach in the usual exhausted, battered, rumpled state, but with a powerful sense of relief at escaping. He couldn't help noticing Cassian didn't seem to feel even that: he looked wretched.

'Are you all right?' Daizell asked.

'No. That was dreadful.'

'You aren't mistaken. Lord, what a bore.'

'I don't mean him. Well, I do, but – the stage, that appalling conveyance, the smell. The discomfort was beyond anything. I'd rather *walk*. How can anyone bear it?' He sounded strangled. 'What the blazes – for a month? It's intolerable!'

'If you can't stand it, why not hire a private carriage? It would be a deal more comfortable, not to say faster, and not that much dearer with two of us travelling.'

Cassian was already shaking his head. 'No. I can't do that.'

Couldn't drive? Couldn't afford it? A carriage could be hired for five pounds a month. If he couldn't afford to drive himself, that put the promised fifty pounds in a different and significantly less certain light. Daizell wondered if he should ask for money up front, and decided against it as long as Cassian was paying his shot. Nevertheless, he felt a twinge of irritation at the unnecessary hardship that came out in his voice. 'In that case, accustom yourself to the coach, or walk. But we've covered twenty-four miles or so in three hours, and I wouldn't want to do it on foot even for the sake of peace and quiet.'

'Yes, I know I encouraged him,' Cassian said wearily. 'And I should have ignored him, and a misplaced urge to be courteous merely exposes one to encroaching mushrooms. I *know*.'

He looked small and rather defeated. Daizell repressed

a sudden urge to pat him on the shoulder and assure him it would be all right. 'You should have ignored him, but it probably wouldn't have made a difference. That sort of man is like champagne.'

Cassian's brows came together. 'In what possible way?'

'Constantly giving off gas, and if too much builds up without an outlet, it explodes.'

Cassian gave a shout of laughter, again with that startled note to it. His eyes were bright with amusement. Daizell hadn't really noticed his eyes before: last night's inn had been too dark and he hadn't paid particular attention this morning. In fairness, they weren't attention-grabbing eyes, being fundamentally grey. Except, if you looked, the grey had an unusual yellow tint to it, giving it the luminous colour of a rainy day turning to sun. They might be a very striking feature in a more striking face.

Cassian had stopped laughing and was looking at him with puzzlement. 'Is there something on my face?'

Dammit. 'Not at all,' Daizell said. 'I am merely faint with hunger. I suggest we obtain luncheon here – if it is not too late to call it that – and start asking questions.'

Food was indeed restorative. Even more so was an intelligent ostler who had seen the man in the mulberry (very overripe raspberry) coat, and informed them he'd taken the stage in the direction of Stratford-upon-Avon.

'We're on the track,' Cassian said. 'We are on his track and it's entirely thanks to you.'

Daizell didn't deny it. He sat back and enjoyed his ale, a bite of luncheon, being able to move and breathe before they got back on the stage, and, mostly, the pleasant and unfamiliar sensation of being the object of gratitude. He could definitely get used to this.

When the stage arrived, it was at a slapping pace, and pulled up very stylishly. It seemed the driver was encouraged by the applause of his companion on the box, a young sprig of fashion with exceedingly high collar points and many capes to his coat. They both got down, followed by the glares of at least ten outside passengers who looked like their ride had been bumpy, and the young man pressed the driver to a mug of heavy-wet as the horses were changed. Daizell cast them both a jaundiced look and prepared for a journey that would probably be both faster and less comfortable than usual.

Cassian looked a little uncertain. 'I say,' he murmured to Daizell. 'That fellow, the driver, is he quite sober?'

'I highly doubt it.'

'But—'

'If you're waiting for a driver who's quite sober, we'll be here a while,' Daizell observed, which was a gross slur against at least a fifth of the drivers he'd encountered. 'Not to mention that young oaf will probably want to tool the coach.'

Fashionable young men very frequently asked to take the reins of the stage. It was against the regulations, but they would beg, bribe or bully the drivers until they had their way. Daizell might have done it himself in his reckless, feckless days, if the idea had ever occurred to him. He couldn't see the point now, and it meant an uncomfortable journey for everyone else, but there was no point objecting since the driver was already the worse for wear. 'Come on, get in. We don't both want to be stuck in the middle.'

It was another six-seater. Daizell heard Cassian's little despairing noise, but he didn't complain out loud. Daizell took the middle seat next to him once more, vaguely feeling that the fifty pounds made it his duty. That meant he had Cassian's slim frame squashed into one side, and on the other a woman who was buxom to the point of overflowing. Daizell appreciated a trim man, and indeed a generous bosom, but he preferred it when people actually wanted to be pressed up against him. The lady was very reasonable about it, merely remarking how dreadfully cramped these coaches were, and concentrating on her baby, which stared at him with huge eyes.

'A very handsome child,' he remarked to be friendly, and won a beam of pleasure. He just hoped it wouldn't cry throughout the journey.

The coach rattled off at great speed, lurching and bounding. 'Someone's in a hurry,' Daizell said.

'At least they keep to time,' one of the opposite passengers remarked.

The baby mewed. The buxom woman jiggled it soothingly. 'Nasty rattling things, aren't they, my poppet?'

'Very tolerant young person you have there,' Daizell observed.

'Oh, she's a good girl, aren't you? Say hello to the gentleman. Hello, sir,' the woman added in a high-pitched voice, presumably on her child's behalf, and flapped its pudgy wrist. A little starfish hand reached out towards Daizell.

He extended a finger out of curiosity and found it caught in a hot, sticky fist. Enormously round blue eyes stared at him with a look of uncomprehending examination, as though the baby was trying to establish what manner of man he was. Daizell wished it luck, and attempted to extricate his finger, only to realise that babies had rather stronger grips than he'd expected. He tugged discreetly; the baby held on like grim death with chubby cheeks. A choke at his shoulder indicated that Cassian found his predicament amusing.

His smile faded soon enough as the coach continued on its reckless way. If anything, it was speeding up, and Daizell felt the drag as they took a corner too fast. Cassian gripped his knees with white knuckles. 'My God,' he muttered.

There was noise from above now, a few cries of encouragement, more of protest. The mother clutched the baby to her with a little scream as the coach hit a rock or some such and a wheel left the ground. 'Lord!'

The baby wailed, but didn't release Daizell's finger. The coach bounded on.

'This is too fast,' Cassian said. 'Can we make him stop?'

'How?'

Cassian's hands flexed, making fists as though he held reins. 'It's too *fast*. If we take a corner at this speed with the coach top-heavy from all the people up there—'

'Bless you, young fellow, this is nothing,' a man opposite said. 'I've seen eighteen crammed atop a coach before now, and never—' They hit a bump in the road that jolted Daizell right off the seat despite the close-packed interior. Someone swore, in a mumble that suggested a bitten tongue. The coach lurched sideways, and down on one side.

'The axle's going,' Cassian said sharply. 'The axle— Hey! Fellow!' He shoved his head out of the window, yelling for the driver. 'Stop! *Stop!*'

Daizell hauled him back in by main force. 'Stick your head out when we roll and the window will chop it off quicker than a Frenchman,' he snapped. 'Grab the strap. *Everyone* grab a strap. When that wheel comes off, we're going over.'

'My baby,' the woman said on a terrified breath.

Daizell looked at her, at arms that kneaded and scrubbed longer than he ever could but shoulders that weren't used to taking weight, and at the tiny hand that held on to his finger as though he were someone to be trusted. 'Give her to me. I'll hold her safe. Use the straps and brace with your feet when we go.'

'There's no need to fuss,' said one of the men opposite, but his voice suggested he knew that was wishful thinking.

'No, he's right. Hold on!' Cassian said.

The mother gave a sob of fear. 'Please,' Daizell said. 'Look to yourself and I'll hold her.'

She held the child out. Daizell pulled the heavy little bundle into his arms, grappled her to him, wrapped the strap round his other wrist, and readied himself for the moment he knew was coming.

And it came, with a crunch he felt more than heard. The axle gave; the wheel was off. The speeding coach lurched and rocked from side to side, so for a terrifying moment it might have gone either way. Daizell poured every ounce of concentration into locking the baby-holding arm immovably against his chest – why in God's name was he doing this, he'd probably break his neck – and then the coach tipped and fell sideways.

It was one of those moments that seemed incredibly slow. Daizell, who'd been braced and waiting for it, pushed himself up and off the seat with both feet, feeling the strap dig round his wrist, timing the motion to the inevitable crash as the coach hit, and skidded along the surface of the road on its side, and the screams rose.

Chapter Four

The toppled coach dragged along for a few terrifying seconds that felt like forever. They'd gone down on the left side, so Daizell thumped on top of the buxom woman, and Cassian landed on top of them both, with extra feet and legs flailing from the other passengers. It was a maelstrom, a dizzying chaos of movement and bodies and pain and screaming.

They rocked to a stop, in what might have been a deathly silence except for a loud, enraged noise close to his ear.

The baby. He'd still got the baby, and it was howling with infant fury. He felt a moment of bone-melting relief that it wasn't forever silent, and then started wishing it would stop.

He was squashed in a heap of bodies with bones, heels, and elbows sticking into everything of him that was soft and vulnerable. 'Cassian?' he managed, shouting over the squalling. 'Cassian!'

'Urgh.'

He wasn't the only one groaning. There was a low sobbing, and a male voice cursing in a low tone. 'Is everyone all right? Cassian, are you hurt?'

'No. Or – no, I don't think anything's broken—'

'Then get the devil off me. Come on, move. Get out!'

'Where?' Cassian demanded with a note of panic. 'How?'

'Out the window, you fool, above you. Move your arse, I've got a baby down here.'

'My baby,' wailed the woman from under Daizell. 'Connie. Oh God, God help us!'

'She's all right!' Daizell said as if the baby's outraged shrieks didn't tell their own story. 'Cassian, shift yourself before this deafens me.'

He shoved to make the point. Cassian pulled himself together and clambered awkwardly out of the coach window. This involved him treading fairly heavily on Daizell, who expressed his feelings with as much moderation as he could. 'Take the blasted baby!' he shouted once the man was out. 'Come on, get her!'

Cassian reached reluctantly down. Daizell jammed the struggling, crying, distressingly damp bundle into his hands, and then hoisted himself out of the window, attempting to use the coach itself rather than his fellow passengers for leverage.

He found his feet despite shaky legs, and stood on the top, or side, of the coach to survey the scene for a moment. Cassian was kneeling awkwardly by him, holding the baby with dismay. His nose was bleeding. On the road, people were scattered around in little weeping knots, or sprawled and unmoving. At least one had blood spreading around his head in a puddle. Daizell looked away, down at the horses, and swore like a trooper.

'What is it?' Cassian demanded.

'Nobody's cut the traces!'

Daizell clapped his hand to his pocket, and was relieved to find his clasp-knife. He skidded down the sidewise roof of the coach with reckless speed and ran to the horses' heads. Two had already struggled to their feet and if the panicked creatures started to run again, dragging the overturned coach behind them, Christ knew what would happen to the four people still in there. 'Someone help me!' he called to the world in general, and ran to start sawing at the leather straps.

A third horse rose as he started cutting. The fourth was still down but kicking. He couldn't see the driver; the young sprig in the caped coat was watching with a fatuous grin. 'Help me!' Daizell said again, to nobody.

There was a thump and a scrabble behind him, and Cassian was there, babyless. 'Cut the traces!' Daizell shouted. 'Quick!'

'No knife,' Cassian said, with a calm serenity that begged for punching, and moved to the lead horse's head. He was dishevelled and his face was bloodstained, but his stance radiated peace. 'There, boy. There.'

'Get away before it kicks you!' Daizell snarled.

'He won't. Here, now.' He had an uncommonly sweet tone to his voice as he soothed the frantic horse. 'Come, beauty, be a good boy for me. Such a good boy, aren't you? Such a lovely, willing, *very* good boy ...'

His tone was honey and velvet, and somehow Daizell's knife had slowed in its work at the murmured endearments. He gave himself a mental kick, and severed another trace, but he could see and feel the horses calming under Cassian's influence. He cut the remaining traces anyway, in case, and clambered out of the way.

Cassian gave the horse a final pat and stepped back. They looked at one another, and Cassian said, 'What now?' for all the world as if Daizell was the expert on disasters.

'Where's the baby?'

'Oh!' Cassian looked round and hurried to the grass verge, where he picked up the howling infant, keeping it at arm's length. 'Oh. Ugh. It smells really very bad now. And it's... squashy.'

'I doubt she's the only one to have soiled herself,' Daizell remarked. 'Where's the mother? Has anyone got the rest of them out?'

Cassian looked blank. Daizell cursed internally, and clambered up onto the coach again.

The next little while was an aching, relentless slog. Two of the male inside passengers had made it out on their own. One was nursing a broken nose; the other was unharmed, and much bigger than Cassian, so he and Daizell set to getting the last two free. The woman was battered and looked sick as a dog, but she thanked Daizell vocally and went to reclaim her child from Cassian with tears.

The final man was curled in the bottom of the coach, sobbing with pain.

'We need to get you out,' Daizell said. 'They won't be able to get the coach upright with you in. Where does it hurt? Can you sit up?'

'My arm. My arm!'

Daizell offered a cautious, supportive hand. He only wanted to take the fellow's weight, but as the man shifted, his arm moved in a terrible way and he screamed. 'Jesus! Don't touch me!'

'Christ,' Daizell muttered. 'Hey, someone up there! Help us!'

He and the other man managed the job eventually. It took heaving, and shoving, and the victim screamed a lot and then passed out, which was a mercy all round. His arm was bent in bad ways. The other man cut off his coat sleeve, muttering about swelling, and they all saw the bloody, jagged bone sticking out of the skin.

That was it. Daizell sprinted for the ditch and cast up his

accounts, on his hands and knees on the dusty verge, puking with tears in his eyes.

'Charnage!' It was Cassian, crouching beside him. 'Are you all right?'

'No,' Daizell said comprehensively. 'Christ. Did you see—'

'I didn't look.'

'He'll lose the arm if he even lives. He screamed, I hurt him – and the *blood*...' The smell of it, and the look of terror in a man's eyes as he felt his death approach, and his own utter failure to do any good. 'Christ. Useless. I'm useless!'

'Shh.' Cassian reached out. Daizell grabbed his hand, all need and instinct, clutching it hard. Dusty, sweaty, warm, alive. Cassian held on tight, giving him a moment of silence he badly needed, then asked again, 'Are you all right?'

'No. Yes. Of course I am.'

'You've done everything you could. More than anyone else did. Come on.' Cassian spoke in the calm voice, the one he'd used on the horse. 'Come on now, Charnage, I've got you. Good man. Up you get, now.'

Daizell held on to his hand for a second longer, for both the physical comfort and that soothing voice, then let go and hauled himself to his feet. Cassian put a hand on his arm. He didn't say anything stupid about it being all right, or a nasty shock. He just stood by Daizell, and touched him so he wasn't alone.

He got about a minute of that peace, and then people started shouting.

The outside passengers who'd been thrown off had now gathered themselves, those capable of it. Several were demanding what was to be done. It seemed the driver was unconscious; the man on the ground in a pool of blood wouldn't be getting up soon either, they were all stranded on a coach-road to Stratford, and the woman with the baby had assured them all that the very kind, capable gentleman – bafflingly, she meant Daizell – would know what to do.

'I want to know how we get to Stratford!' a thin man said. 'I have urgent business!'

'I want compensation,' someone else added. 'That driver handing over the reins like that—'

'Do I look like the coach company?' Daizell retorted. 'I've no idea what we do except wait for another stage and get help. Or walk to find a house where they can send a cart, I suppose.'

'We need a doctor,' someone said. 'There's three men in a bad way.'

'Someone has already gone back to the last house for help,' said the thin man angrily. 'We could have driven on if you hadn't cut the traces!'

Daizell stared at him. Cassian stepped in, quite literally, moving in front of him. 'You must not realise, sir, the horses were like to bolt with people still inside the coach – one with a dreadfully broken arm, and one a lady. It was a necessary action in a difficult situation. I'm sure you understand.'

He sounded like someone who spent a lot of time pouring oil on troubled waters. The thin man didn't appear mollified. 'So you say, but the urgency of my business—'

'*I* was in that coach,' the mother announced, looking daggers at him. 'I would have been dragged along and killed if it wasn't for this gentleman who saved my baby, and if you think your nasty business should come before my little girl's very life, you miserable old stockfish—'

Cassian and Daizell eased back out of the way in silent synchrony to let her pulverise the fellow unimpeded, and everything might have simmered down if the fashionable young man hadn't spoken up, in a voice that sounded decidedly slurred. ''F we're in a hurry, let's get the tits back on the road, what? Coach back on its wheels, it'll take two minutes, and off we go!'

'The traces have been cut, the axle broke, and we lost a wheel,' Cassian said. 'It will not be a swift repair.'

'Oh, hush, Mother Shipton,' the young man said with a dismissive flap of the hand. 'We've strong fellows enough. We'll be back on our way in no time. Yoicks!'

Cassian stiffened. 'There are three seriously injured men here. What do you propose to do, leave them on the side of the road?'

The young man shrugged. Daizell held up a finger. 'Sir, you were on the box when we set off. Am I correct in thinking you took the reins?'

'That's right!' The young man beamed. 'What a ride, eh?'

'And you didn't feel the axle go? Or think of slowing down?'

'You do realise you overturned us, and people are seriously hurt?' Cassian did not sound soothing any more. His voice rose. 'People might die because you crashed us!'

'Oh, rubbish. Everyone spills now and again, what? Accidents happen. Part of the fun! Lot of fuss.'

Daizell considered that. He nodded slowly. Then he punched the young man with everything he had, and was delighted to feel his nose break.

The youth staggered back, clutching his face. He seemed more shocked than hurt, which Daizell regretted. 'You – what – how dare you?' he said thickly. 'Do you know who I am? I'm Tom Acaster! My father is Sir Benjamin Acaster!'

'You're a slobbering ape, and your father is an imbecile for not drowning you at birth,' Daizell snarled. His throat still stung with the taste of vomit. 'You stupid little turd, you've probably killed that man!'

'You wait till my father finds you! I'll have your name and direction, sir!' The youth's voice was nasal, choked with blood.

'My name is Daizell Charnage. *Charnage*, like carnage with an H, got that? And as for your father—' He grabbed the youth's shoulder, threw him down to the ground with the aid of a foot between his ankles, and assisted him into the ditch by means of a few forceful kicks to the posterior. The howls and the muddy splash relieved his feelings a little.

He turned away, brushing his hands, and realised everyone was staring at him.

'I'm not saying you were wrong to do it,' the baby's mother remarked thoughtfully. 'Not *wrong*. But Sir Benjamin lives just at Upton Snodsbury, not half a mile up the road, and he's powerful careful of his lad. *And* he's the magistrate hereabouts.'

'That young fool overturned us!' Cassian said. 'Surely nobody will defend that!'

Everyone turned to look at him. Daizell contemplated the fact that they were an indeterminate way into the countryside, with a rich man's wrath a short distance off, and any replacement coach some hours away. 'Cassian? I think we'll walk.'

At least Cassian didn't have a trunk. They trudged along the road together, each with his travelling bag, under the April sun. Cassian had wiped most of the blood off his face, and seemed to be breathing without issue.

'Your nose isn't broken?' Daizell asked.

'No. I'm prone to nosebleeds.'

'Good. Not the nosebleeds. That it's not broken.'

They crunched along some more. Daizell had led them off the main road at the first fork, and sincerely hoped they were going somewhere useful: he'd mostly been propelled by the urge not to have an outraged magistrate catch up with him. Cassian was wearing Wellington boots, which seemed not to be uncomfortable, but he looked much as a man might after being overturned in a chaise and forced to walk along a warm road without a drink because his idiot companion had punched a powerful man's heir in the face.

'Sorry,' Daizell said abruptly.

'For what?'

'Hitting that fool.'

'Why?'

'Because now we're probably in a deal of trouble.'

'Nonsense,' Cassian said. 'I'm sure he'll be taken up by the authorities and held to account.'

'Weren't you listening? His father *is* the authorities!'

'There's plenty of magistrates. I don't see anything to worry about. And in any case, you did quite right, since he didn't seem to feel the slightest remorse. *Accidents happen*, indeed. Outrageous. I'm not at all surprised you lost your temper.'

'It was a stupid thing to do. If we get in trouble—'

'I'm not worried about that,' Cassian said, with the serenity of the extremely naive. He would change his tune fast enough when he was faced with a rampaging baronet throwing around his wealth and authority. 'And I had meant to say, too, thank you for what you did back there.'

'I did nothing.'

'You did everything. You saved that child.'

Daizell felt himself flush, as if his face wasn't warm enough. 'I dare say the mother could have held her if need be.'

'At the bottom of that heap? No. It was a good thing to do, and a kind one,' Cassian said. 'But really, I meant thank you for instructing me. I realise I was no great help to you, and I'm sorry for it.'

'You were astonishing with those horses.'

'When I realised I needed to be, which is to say, when you pointed out the problem. I couldn't seem to think.' He sounded as though it was eating at him. 'I simply panicked, which is contemptible. I don't know why; I've had spills before.'

'Being a passenger in a stage is quite different from driving your own team. You can't see what's going to happen, you aren't in charge.' Cassian nodded, confirming that indeed he did drive his own horses. Why wasn't he now? 'Whereas that was my third tumble in a stagecoach, so I'm used to it. Not that sort of tumble,' he added as Cassian choked.

'I should hope not. There would hardly be space.'

'And all the passengers looking on. Puts a man off his stroke.'

Cassian snorted. 'Someone would tell you they'd been on a stage where *four* passengers—'

Daizell's bruised shoulders hurt with the shaking as he laughed. It felt good, though, lifting the cloud. 'What I was trying to say was, I've had that unlovely experience twice before. The first time, I was no use to man or beast: I sat there stunned, and I wasn't even injured. I couldn't seem to take in what had happened. Just useless.'

'Yes,' Cassian said in a low voice. 'That's how I felt.'

'But you weren't. You did what you were told,' Daizell said. 'That's better than the people who stand around and cry, and even they're better than the ones who get in the way. You did as well as anyone could expect, and next time you can deal with the horses and the swine who thinks he's a whip, *and* the one who wants to drive the coach over the bodies to get to his important engagement.'

'I'll look forward to it,' Cassian said. 'You – uh, you think people do get used to these things? To dealing with emergencies?'

'If you have enough of them.'

'Yes, but what if you don't? Or haven't? I mean, if one is used to being held up by a – a scaffolding of other people, and has never encountered emergencies, might one not discover one is helpless without that support?'

Daizell wasn't entirely sure what he was actually being asked, but it sounded painful. 'Everyone relies on other people. And eventually most people let you down, one way or another, so I dare say it's a good thing to practise dealing with difficulties on your own. But I don't see there's any great moral virtue in it.'

'Do you not think independence is a virtue?'

'Overrated,' Daizell said. 'One should be able to do things for oneself, but the world would surely be a better place if we did more for one another.'

'Yes,' Cassian said. 'Yes, that is true. And we can't all expect to do everything.'

'Certainly not right, and definitely not the first time we try.'

'No. Although, even so, nobody wants to be helpless.'

'No.' Daizell knew exactly how it felt to be helpless. 'No, that is an unpleasant sensation.'

'One feels so pointless,' Cassian said. 'Filling a place, rather than being useful.'

That was not how Daizell would have described the sensation of having his entire life torn from his control, ripped up, and thrown away, but doubtless they had different experiences of helplessness. 'Well, you weren't that. You did perfectly well, and better than many would have, and if those horses had bolted, things would have been a deal worse. You've nothing to rebuke yourself for.'

'Then we can both flatter ourselves we made the best of a bad situation.'

'If we weren't trudging along on an apparently endless road with no place of refreshment in sight and an enraged magistrate likely on our tail, I might agree with you.'

Cassian gave his startled laugh. 'Well, there is that, but I'm sure we'll find somewhere. I suppose everyone from the coach is all right?'

'No idea,' Daizell said. 'I imagine someone will have come along by now and we'd reached the limits of what I was able to offer in the way of help.' That met with a silence. He glanced over and saw Cassian looking rather struck. 'No?'

'I was just thinking that I could have done more. Oh, curse it, I know I should.'

'I don't see how, unless you're a bonesetter.' He remembered again the splintered end of bone, the torn skin and obscenely bared flesh, and shuddered the memory off.

Cassian glanced over. 'Are you all right?'

Daizell didn't want to talk about it. 'Is that a farmhouse there?'

It was a farmhouse, and a friendly one. The mistress of the house tutted and sympathised at their shocking escape from danger, as narrated by Daizell with a bit of flair, agreed that coaches were nasty rattling things that went too fast, brought them tankards of excellent home-brewed, and let them sluice off the blood and dirt and dust in the yard with a bucket, while she went to consult someone called Jed Browning as to how they could best carry on their journey.

Daizell thought of nothing but being briefly cool and clean as he stripped to the waist and dumped water over his head. He scrubbed his face, dunked his head in the bucket, and shook it like a dog to get the contamination of the day out of his curls, poured handfuls of water over his torso, and opened his eyes to see Cassian watching. His mouth was slightly slack, his sun-and-rain eyes fascinated, and they weren't locked on Daizell's face, either.

Well.

Daizell had no objection to being looked at, especially not in the hungry way Cassian was looking. He did have a strong objection born of experience to people looking and being caught looking and regretting it, and it somehow becoming his fault that they'd given themselves away. So he shut his eyes again before Cassian could realise they were open, made perhaps a slightly excessive performance of rubbing and stretching, and scrubbed at his face before saying, 'Do you want the bucket?'

'Please.' Cassian sounded a little stifled, but he took it and sluiced himself down in turn, and Daizell took the chance to watch while he could. Turnabout was fair play.

Cassian definitely stripped to advantage: the candlelight hadn't lied. Slim, but not willowy; not tall, not too much sinew and muscle. He was an elegant package, Daizell thought, a picture that repaid attention, with the water running rivulets down his skin in droplets that begged to be caught with a finger. A finger that Daizell might pop into his mouth, or even between Cassian's parted, expressive lips…

Bad Daizell. Bad. *Fifty pounds*, he reminded himself, and reached for the rough cloth to dry off.

Jed Browning, it transpired, had a cart, and was going past a hamlet whose name Daizell instantly forgot, where there was an inn that would give them a meal and a bed. It was now close on five o'clock, still warm and light, but night had a way of springing itself on you when you were on foot in the countryside. They thanked their benefactress, Cassian rewarded her for her kindness – lavishly, Daizell guessed by her expression – and they climbed into the back of Jed Browning's cart, resting on hay-bales.

That was the sort of thing that looked charmingly pastoral in paintings, but was surprisingly prickly in practice. It also tended to insects. But Cassian didn't object, lying back to look at the sky, and if he was happy, Daizell wouldn't be complaining. The hay cushioned the jolting as the cart rumbled over the rough stony path, and it was a while since Daizell had lain back companionably with someone he liked and enjoyed the moment.

'You were dashed good with the horses,' he remarked. 'Do you have your own?'

'A pair I trained myself, of whom I'm very proud. Horses are wonderful creatures. So much life, and feeling, and they hardly ever judge one.'

'Hardly ever?'

'Oh, I've been judged by horses,' Cassian said with a laugh. 'When I've been egregiously foolish or careless. But mostly they're very accepting.'

'But you're not driving yourself now?'

'No.' It sounded a little awkward. 'I had reasons to go by the public coach.'

'I'm sure,' Daizell said. 'Well, it's such a safe and comfortable way to travel.'

'Highly convenient, too, never taking one out of one's way—'

'And so reasonably priced,' Daizell finished. He could see Cassian's grin, and his own lips were curving. 'I expect you'll sell your own pair and become an aficionado.'

'I won't do that,' Cassian said, and though he was smiling still, Daizell felt he meant it.

They were peacefully silent a little longer, then Cassian said, 'Charnage?'

'Daizell.'

'Sorry?'

'If you don't object. Most people call me by my first name, that's all. Daizell, or Daize for short. Unless you'd rather not, of course.' He cringed internally as he spoke, kicking himself for the unguarded offer. Of course Cassian wouldn't want to be on first-name terms with him: this was a temporary association, not a friendship, and Daizell would do well to remember that. 'It doesn't matter. Charnage does very well.'

'No,' Cassian said. 'No, I would like to. Thank you. Daizell.' The name sounded magical in his soft voice. 'That's an awfully unusual name.'

'I should think it's unique.'

'Where is it from?'

Daizell had of necessity told this story a great deal. The familiarity helped him recover himself from the surge of embarrassment and then of pleasure, and the sound of his name in Cassian's voice. 'Are you familiar with the name Dalziel?' He pronounced it in the Scots way and saw Cassian frown.

'Dee Ell? You mean, the letters DL?'

'Pronounced Dee Ell, spelled D-a-l-z-i-e-l. It's a Scottish surname. My mother's uncle Ralph Dalziel took great pride in his roots, and when I was born my parents hoped to curry favour. He was rich. I was to be Dalziel Charnage in his honour, and he was to hand over the readies in his will, you see. Except my father's ability to spell was commensurate with his other talents, so he had me christened Daizell, with the I and L in the wrong places, and wrote as much to Uncle Ralph, who pointed out the mistake. Some people would have corrected themselves and smoothed matters over, but my father did not like to have his mistakes pointed out. He insisted my name was indeed Daizell, pronounced as spelled. Uncle Ralph took the hump, and there went my chance at a rich godfather and an inheritance. But at least I have an interesting name out of it.'

'Good heavens,' Cassian said. 'That's uh, remarkable.'

'Very typical of my father. And myself, I suppose.'

Cassian twisted round to look at him with a little frown. 'Well, it suits you, I think. Daizell, then. Oh. Er. I would return the compliment, but—'

He didn't want Daizell Charnage to call him by his first name. Naturally not. Daizell kept his features pleasant despite the familiar, hateful way his stomach clenched at the rejection, and waved an airy hand. 'As you prefer.'

'I didn't mean I wouldn't want – Um. The thing is, I loathe my name.'

Daizell blinked. 'You—?'

'My name, my first name. I hate it. It doesn't suit me at all, and I think it's hideous, actually.'

'Ah. Right.' He controlled himself for about three seconds, then gave up. 'No, sorry, I have to ask.'

'Vernon.'

Daizell sat up a little, the better to contemplate him. 'Vernon. Ver-non. *Vernon?* Good God, no. What were your parents thinking?'

'It's as though they barely knew me at the time,' Cassian agreed with a lurking grin. 'I suppose it wouldn't be so bad if I were a six-foot Corinthian with huge shoulders.'

'It sounds more to me like a dastard who attempts to seduce the heroine, but is undone by seducing the house-maid.'

'Not me, either way. Whereas Cassian is—'

'Oh, delightful. It has a certain, what shall I say. A fairytale quality.'

'You're thinking of Ossian. The Scottish bard.'

'I probably am, but it still suits you. Charming the birds out of the trees, or rather the horses out of their panic, by the sound of your voice. Of course you're a bard.'

Cassian actually blushed at that, a delightful dusky pink, accompanied by a smile of startled pleasure. 'I can't play the harp,' he protested. 'Or the bagpipes.'

'Thank God for small mercies.' Daizell would have liked to expound more on Cassian's voice, see how much darker he might blush. He restrained himself. 'So your friends call you Cassian?'

'It – uh, it's what I'd prefer to be called. I'd be very glad if you would.'

'Then that's what I'll call you. Is it ever abbreviated, or always used in full?'

'Well, um, I'd be happy with Cass.' He sounded quite shy. It was absurdly endearing.

'Cass. Very well. And at least your name didn't open

you up to the wrath of uncles, unless of course you have a rampaging Uncle Vernon who's offended you don't use it.'

'Oh, it *is* an uncle name, isn't it? A terribly strict one who has control of the heroine's money and intends to marry her to his wayward son.'

'I see you are a connoisseur of elevating literature,' Daizell said. 'Have you read the latest Mrs Swann?'

Cassian had not, but he had a deal to say about the Waverley author, whose work Daizell also enjoyed, and they talked and argued and laughed as the cart jogged along in the evening sunshine.

Chapter Five

Daizell.

The Duke didn't intend to read too much into the move to first names. He'd learned his lesson with attractive men; he would do well to solve the problem his wayward desires had already caused him before following them into more trouble – and Daizell Charnage was trouble. Very pleasant trouble, trouble with shining hair, but trouble nonetheless. His name alone said that, and his erratic history, and now the Duke had seen it for himself.

Not that he blamed Daizell for punching that drunken fool. The Duke would have rather liked to do the same, if only he had been either built or bred to punch people in the face. It was more that Daizell clearly had reason to think it was a bad idea. The Duke didn't share his alarm at possible retribution from a local magistrate, but since Daizell did, he should have thought twice. The Duke tried hard to think twice, since one of his uncle's oft-repeated lessons was that a man in a position such as his own should never act on impulse. A duke must assess his behaviour, consider his course, ponder its rightness, because the consequences of his errors would be large.

His uncle wasn't wrong. The Duke hadn't thought through all the possibilities and implications when he agreed to a night with John Martin, and look where he was now: in the middle of nowhere, jogging in a haycart on the friendliest terms with George Charnage's son. Lord Hugo would have an apoplexy.

Lord Hugo was excessively careful, the Duke decided. Daizell might be erratic, but he was immensely likeable, he'd behaved with notable courage and decency, and anyway, the terms of the bet obliged the Duke to take a holiday from ducal behaviour. There was nothing more to it, and he would call his companion Daizell without further thought.

Or even Daize. 'Daizell' was a magical sort of name that matched his dazzling head of metallic hair, all copper and gilt like coins spilled on a counter, but 'Daize' felt like a friend intimate enough to be casual with, a man with whom one shared a bottle, perhaps slept on his settle after a long night's play. He'd like to have a friend he called Daize. He'd like to have a friend who called him Cass. He'd never asked anyone to do so before now, because nobody in the world was on first-name terms with him.

The Duke had been Harmsford since his birth. He had become Severn at the age of six and that was his name now, when he wasn't Your Grace. A very few people called him Sev, and while he'd be perfectly happy if more did, one couldn't demand that people called one by an intimate nickname. For that, they had to feel intimacy, and neither his position nor his reserved character invited that.

But Daizell had asked if his name was abbreviated, and the Duke's heart had thumped with a sensation he couldn't name as he'd said – lied – that it was, and all but invited him to it. *Call me Cass.*

He knew this wasn't quite fair. He'd tried not to tell more outright lies than he could help, but everything he said to Daizell was at least a lie of omission. Surely it did no harm, though. This way they could be on friendly terms, chatting easily, exchanging jokes. The Duke didn't have that with many people, and for an obviously gregarious, outgoing man, Daizell didn't seem to have much of it either. He looked genuinely happy to have company, and the Duke would take that away from him if he told the truth.

And, he had to admit, he'd also have to behave differently himself and certainly not do things like stare at Daizell's bare torso, the skin wet, gleaming with copper-gold curls. Thank goodness Daizell hadn't noticed his momentary fascination.

'Cass.'

It didn't even register for a second. Daizell prodded him in the side. 'Cass!'

He sat up. Cass: that was his name on this journey. 'What is it?'

'We're here. Were you asleep?'

'Half.' The Duke – Cassian, he reminded himself – looked around. The light was fading, and they were approaching a neat sort of inn. 'Where are we?'

'The Bear and Staff, I understand. Some miles outside Stratford, and that's all I can tell you.'

They clambered down with their bags. Cassian both resented the weight of his, and wished he'd brought a lot more clothes. He would have to ask about laundry. Habit told him to stand back while all was made ready for him; humility reminded him that Daizell knew far better than he did how to command an innkeeper's attention. There was nothing wrong with accepting help as long as one gave it too, and it was very tempting to let someone else arrange matters for him as he always had. But Daizell glanced at him and gave a little wave to usher him forward, so he plucked up his courage and went in.

It turned out that commanding was not required. The

Bear and Staff was no busy coaching inn, and its landlord was obsequious in his delight at their custom. Of course they could have rooms for the night, and he would have the sheets warmed right away. Dinner? Why, the best they could serve; he regretted to his very soul that he had no fine wines to offer, only elderflower wine of his wife's making, unless perhaps the gentlemen would prefer ale?

Cassian chose the ale, having noted Daizell's eyes widen in alarm at the mention of elderflower wine, and they were ushered to a tiny but very pleasant parlour where they both collapsed into chairs.

'Your health,' Daizell said, raising his tankard. 'Good God, what a day.'

'It has been long. And eventful.'

'And, I regret to say, with all the delay, we might have lost the trail.'

'I know. It can't be helped. We'll get on our way to Stratford tomorrow. It's all we can do. And if we can't track him from there, we can…' He wasn't quite sure what they could do. He looked hopefully at Daizell.

'We'll work something out,' his companion said, with cheerful confidence. 'There's always the Gloucester pawnshops.'

'Yes. Exactly. We've only lost a day, really.'

'And we can't do anything at all about that now, so we might as well enjoy the evening.' Daizell held out his tankard, and Cassian clinked it with his.

They did enjoy it. The landlord served them a very satisfactory meal – plain cooking, but good, and the seasoning of hunger and physical exertion made it delicious. Cassian ate with relish, and enjoyed watching Daizell wolf his meal, and half way down his second mug of ale, he felt as comfortable as he'd been in his life.

That was when they heard the noise outside the parlour.

'I understand that, miss, but I've only one parlour and it is commanded already by two gentlemen.' The landlord, pleading.

'Gentlemen will understand that a lady's needs come first.' A young man's voice, trying for firmness.

'But the gentlemen have commanded—'

'Then they must be disappointed. I have a lady here.'

'A lady? Not a wife?' That was a female voice, tone ominous. Daizell, who was eavesdropping as shamelessly as Cassian, gave him a gleeful look and mouthed, *Landlady*, while tapping the fourth finger of his left hand. Cassian blinked, then understood a second later as the young man said, 'No – that is—'

'Not your wife? Your sister, then?'

'Uh, no. I mean, yes,' the young man added, and then, 'Er, well, no.'

'No. And no attendant with you, *miss*?' The landlady's voice was rising. 'This is a respectable house. I won't stand for any nonsense.'

'We came by a misfortune on the journey,' the young man said, sounding somewhat harassed. 'And I am asking you to provide a private room, and two bedchambers, *and* an attendant for the lady tonight.'

'Our girl could—' the landlord began.

'Our girl won't be assisting at an elopement!' his wife said over him. 'And I won't have any such thing here. This is a respectable house!'

Daizell pulled a face that economically conveyed that

he was glad not to be in the young man's shoes. Cassian murmured, 'We could surely …? For a lady?'

'If you don't mind the public bar. Very gracious of you,' Daizell said, with a wink that quivered pleasantly in Cassian's nerves. He went to the door, pulled it open, and went into the hallway. 'I beg your pardon, but we couldn't help overhearing. My companion and I – oh my God!'

'You!' said a young lady's voice, in accents of throbbing accusation.

'What's this?' the landlady demanded.

Daizell retreated rapidly backwards, into the parlour. A young lady came after him, with a sturdy young man on her heels. She was well built herself for a woman, about Cassian's size, and wore a fierce expression; he looked as though incomprehension was his natural state. 'You!' she said again. 'What are you doing here? Have you followed me?'

'Followed?' Daizell said. 'I've been here for hours! And why would I want to see you anyway?'

'He has been here with me,' Cassian added, with no idea what was going on but feeling he should offer support. 'We've had dinner here, as this good woman can—'

The young lady waved at him to be silent with an impatient gesture. Cassian reminded himself, after a stunned moment of outrage, that he was not currently the Duke of Severn. 'Well, what are you doing here if you are not following me?' she asked Daizell insistently.

'Pursuing my own affairs,' Daizell said. 'Yours, as you made quite clear, are not my concern.'

'Eliza?' the youth said. 'Who is this man?'

'Do be quiet, Tony.'

The landlord and landlady had both crowded in. The extremely small parlour was now feeling decidedly cramped.

Daizell had retreated behind a chair, whether to make space or to have something between him and the young lady's militant stance.

'If you are not following me—' she began.

'I am not!'

'If you aren't, then what do you want?'

'I was going to offer you the parlour,' Daizell said. 'I regret the impulse.'

'You were?' The young lady's face underwent an instant transformation, from hostility to bright spring day. She wasn't pretty, Cassian thought, being rather ordinary in features, much as he was himself, with mousy brown hair and a pair of grey eyes, but she moved and spoke with such animation that one might easily be convinced she was very pretty indeed. 'Oh, Mr Charnage, how very kind! Well, that is wonderful and resolves all.'

'It does nothing of the sort, miss, because if this is an elopement—' the landlady began.

The young man came in over her. 'Charnage? This is Charnage? What's *he* doing here?'

'We've been over this,' Daizell said. 'Why don't my friend and I leave you the parlour, and you can finish your conversation with mine hosts. Get your drink, Cass.'

'Wait a minute, sir!' The young man skirted around to block the door, with a threatening look. He was quite sturdy. 'I have a few words for you on your conduct.'

'Don't be absurd, Tony,' the young lady said.

'This wretched fellow had no compunction in attempting a young lady in the most disgraceful manner—'

'What did you call me?'

'Tony, stop it! I *explained* this!'

'You did not know what you were doing,' the young man told her sternly. 'And you, sir, took advantage of her!'

'I *eloped* with her, you idiot,' Daizell said. 'And by the looks of things, so have you, so—'

The young man lunged. Daizell leapt back out of the way. The young lady squawked; the landlady said, 'I knew it!', and Cassian said, 'Stop!' Daizell kicked a chair into the path of the oncoming young man, snapping, 'For God's sake, you oaf!'

Duke of Severn, Cassian reminded himself. 'I said, stop this at once!' He gave the words the full authority and command of his noble house and lineage.

Nobody even looked at him. The young man grabbed the chair and hoisted it, whether to throw it out of the way or at Daizell, and Cassian, giving up on lineage and remembering illicit brawls with Leo, kicked him hard on the ankle.

'Ow!' He dropped the chair and turned on Cassian, and the landlady interposed herself with a bellow of, 'That will do!' that was equally ignored. Daizell leapt at the young man, crashing onto him from behind, and the young lady let out a scream.

It was not a scream of fear. It was pure ear-splitting noise, like a kettle come to the boil, and it was so long and loud and piercing that Cassian, reeling away, briefly wondered if the windows would survive. Daizell had his hands clapped over his ears; the angry young man ducked and cringed.

'*Thank* you,' the young lady said into the stunned silence, giving herself a little shake. 'Really, what great stupids men are. Be *quiet*, Tony, you are being nonsensical and jealous, and it is very tiresome. Hostess, please bring me something hot to drink, and I expect Tony will like ale.'

'Young lady,' the landlady said, swelling. 'I will have no

brawling in this house, nor elopements either. I don't hold with such things.'

'*I'm* not eloping with anyone,' Daizell remarked to nobody in particular. The young man shot him an evil look.

Cassian said, 'Ma'am, I quite understand your position, but it's late. Is there anywhere close by for these travellers to go?'

'Not till Snitterfield,' the landlord said. 'And that's a fair way.'

'Then, while your principles do you credit, you must see it would be quite wrong to turn away a young lady in the dark. I trust you will find yourself able to admit these guests.' Daizell was giving him an odd look, possibly because he didn't want to share an inn with the young lady, but that couldn't be helped. 'My companion and I will happily relinquish this parlour for the lady's comfort. And, as the mother of a daughter, you'll doubtless agree it would be a kindness to give the lady some attendance tonight.'

The landlady's hands were on her hips, but Cassian thought she might have softened a little at that. 'I'll have no fighting and no immorality under my roof.'

The young lady blushed a fierce scarlet. 'I am *not* immoral,' she said heatedly. 'And it is very unkind of you to say so.'

'I think everyone would be better off for a drink,' Daizell said. 'I certainly would, if you'd be so kind, landlord. Cass, shall we retire to the other room?'

The landlady's jaw tightened. 'I can't have an unmarried lady and gentleman left alone. This isn't that sort of house. And my girl is busy making up beds.'

'Then we'll stay in here with them,' Cassian said. 'Nobody could object to that. We will have that ale, please, and tea for the lady.'

The host and hostess departed, he dragging out his irate

wife. Sounds of marital discord rose from the hallway. The four in the parlour stood in stiff silent discomfort while ale was produced, and the table cleared, and a meal ordered. Finally the landlady put down a pot of tea and marched out of the room.

The young lady shut the door behind her. 'Goodness, what a tiresome woman. Good evening.' She smiled at Cassian. 'Thank you for your kindness, that was most gentlemanly of you. My name is—'

'Eliza,' the man said warningly.

She glared at him. 'What?'

'You might not want to—' He nodded meaningfully.

'"Don't give your name, Eliza"?' Daizell mimicked, with some incredulity. 'Good Lord. Also, the lady and I have met, in case you forgot. Miss Beaumont, Mr Cassian.'

'And this is Tony Marston,' Miss Beaumont said. 'Mr Marston, Mr Cassian, and Mr Charnage, so now we can all sit down before I scream.'

'Don't do that,' Daizell said. 'My nerves couldn't take another of those. So, Miss Beaumont, eloping again?'

'Daize!' Cassian said.

Daizell took a healthy swig of his drink. 'In fairness to myself, I should point out—'

'You need not do any such thing,' Miss Beaumont said hurriedly. 'No hard feelings. I have quite forgot the matter.'

Daizell mouthed *forgot*. Mr Marston bristled. Miss Beaumont said, 'Stop it, Tony. You needn't be a dog in the manger: Mr Charnage didn't elope with me or I him because we *liked* one another.'

'Ouch,' Daizell said. 'Although not inaccurate. So *are* you eloping again?'

'Well, yes, actually,' Miss Beaumont said in a confiding tone. 'You can't blame me, can you?'

Cassian couldn't help a surreptitious glance at Mr Marston. Daizell gave the man an openly examining look, then shrugged. 'No accounting for taste.'

'Daizell!' Cassian said, louder, but Miss Beaumont gurgled. 'You are dreadful. And I am sorry for saying you had followed me. I was so startled, and to be honest, I've been jumping at shadows all day. The fact is – oh, don't be stupid, Tony, he already knows most of it, and I dare say we can trust his friend, and if we can't, it's too late anyway. You are a gentleman, sir, you would not betray a confidence?'

'No indeed,' Cassian said warily.

'You see? The fact is that, as Mr Charnage well knows, I am fleeing intolerable persecution. My only means of escape was to elope with Tony. That's why I eloped with Mr Charnage.'

Cassian nodded sympathetically and then said, 'What?'

'Tell you later,' Daizell said.

'And I have finally managed to get out again, so we are on our way to be married—'

'At Gretna?'

She put up her small chin. 'At Gretna. I am terribly afraid that Sir James will have us followed and when I saw Mr Charnage, I panicked. But you will help us, won't you?'

'No,' Daizell said. 'That is, I'm not going to stand in your way, but as for helping, we've an urgent concern of our own.'

'I'm hardly asking much,' Miss Beaumont said, her expressive face flicking to a mask of big-eyed pleading. 'Only that you don't let anyone know that you saw us, or where we have gone.'

'If you want to pass unnoticed, you should make your

arrivals less dramatic,' Daizell pointed out. 'Everyone in this inn will be talking about you for weeks. And why don't you have a story to explain your situation?' He waved a hand at the obviously unmarried lady travelling alone with a man.

'Not a story. An attendant,' Cassian said. 'Clearly, you need—'

'Don't be ridiculous,' Miss Beaumont said over him. 'An attendant, on an elopement? What for, to lend me countenance? I *am* going to get married, and if I can't, I should rather be ruined than go back!'

This was not something Cassian could approve, even incognito, given the possible consequences. He was morally obliged to intervene. His heart sank at the thought.

The landlord came in at that moment with food for the new arrivals. Cassian seized the opportunity. 'I shall get some fresh air while you eat. Daizell, would you accompany me?' The landlord could stay with the couple if he cared about appearances.

Daizell swung himself upright with clear reluctance, and followed him outside. They stood together a little way from the inn, in the quiet of the country night. An owl hooted above them. It was cold compared to the rather stuffy parlour, and the clear air made Cassian's head swim slightly, unless that was the strong ale.

'You probably want an explanation,' Daizell said. 'The thing is—'

'No, wait.' Cassian did want an explanation, because he was consumed by curiosity, but that wasn't the most important thing. 'Miss Beaumont. How can we get her back to her home?'

'What? Why would we do that?'

'Because she's eloping!'

'Isn't that her business?'

'No,' the Duke said. 'It's any decent person's duty to intervene to prevent someone making a terrible mistake. It would be bad enough if she marries foolishly, but if she doesn't bring it off and this escapade becomes known, what then? She's clearly gently bred. This could ruin her.'

'She knows that. It's her risk.'

'She's too young to decide that!'

'Twenty,' Daizell said. 'And surely it's her mistake to make. Do people tell you what mistakes you can and can't make?'

'All the time, yes!' Cassian was beginning to feel quite heated.

'And you listen?'

'I didn't listen when I went off to – to gamble with John Martin, and he robbed me. If someone had intervened to save me from that experience, I should have been very grateful.'

'No, you wouldn't,' Daizell said. 'Because you didn't know he was going to rob you, therefore someone intervening beforehand would, so far as you knew, have merely prevented you from a pleasant evening's play with a friend. I doubt you'd have been happy about that, any more than Miss Beaumont would be about you taking it on yourself to predict her doom.'

'If someone who knew he was a thief had told me so—'

'You'd have taken their word for it? Do you always let other people pick your friends?' Daizell demanded, sounding rather heated himself. 'Surely you should be able to judge for yourself, rather than giving a dog a bad name and hanging him.'

'John Martin deserved hanging! Metaphorically,' Cassian added in fairness, since he was not an admirer of the laws.

'That doesn't mean everyone else is a villain. You made a mistake, and you'll learn from it.'

'My mistake lost me my ring. And Miss Beaumont has a great deal more to lose than that.'

'Yes, she does. But I'm not a better judge than her of whom she should marry, or how, and I don't see why you are.'

'I don't claim to be! I'm saying that she is committing an indiscreet action she will probably regret, which could easily lead her into shame and distress and hardship, and if there is the opportunity to prevent that, I must surely take it. I can't just let a bad thing happen. You said yourself, we should help each other.'

Daizell was looking at him; Cassian could feel it, although his features were barely visible in the faint light coming from the inn's windows. 'But it is *not your affair.* You aren't her friend; you owe her nothing. You've only just met her.'

'And I wish I hadn't,' Cassian said with feeling. 'But now I know about this, how can I ignore it?'

Daizell scrunched his hand into his curls. 'Easily. We go back inside, finish our drinks, go to bed, and let the woman decide her own life instead of getting embroiled in her ridiculous goings-on which, I may say, she is going to pursue whatever you or anyone may think of them.'

It was overwhelmingly tempting. Cassian had absolutely no desire to drag a headstrong woman back to her family home against her will, or embroil himself in what would doubtless be a ghastly mess. The Duke, on the other hand, could only imagine how the news would be received that he had allowed an elopement to proceed under his aegis. *You are Severn*, Lord Hugo would say; *you have a duty*.

'Surely her family will allow the marriage to take place in

the proper manner if it proves a lasting attachment,' he said. 'Or if not, I dare say there is some good reason they don't wish her to marry Marston.'

'There is certainly a reason, and it's not even his beef-wittedness, or his deplorable propensity for jealousy,' Daizell said. 'Although I did attempt to run away with his intended bride so one can't entirely blame him for being testy with me. She's a substantial heiress. Her father was old Giles Beaumont, Golden Giles. Why on earth do you think I agreed to elope with her?'

Cassian would have liked to interrogate that last, but he had other concerns. 'Giles Beaumont? The manufacturer? But isn't his daughter Sir James Vier's ward?'

'Vier got his hands on her when Beaumont died, and controls her income while she remains unwed. Her fortune only becomes hers on her marriage. It's why he hasn't let her make her come-out or any such. She'd be snapped up within a season, and that would incommode Vier very seriously. He intends to claim her hand and thus her fortune for himself, and as her guardian, he is in an excellent position to do so.'

Cassian spluttered. 'A girl of her age? In his power? And he's fifty if he's a day!'

'Quite. Do you blame her for escaping?'

'Good God, no. But for heaven's sake, she's playing right into his hands. If she elopes without even a female attendant, and he has to retrieve her – again,' he added, because the previous failed elopement had been widely talked about, 'she will make herself utterly unmarriageable.'

'Not with her money.'

'Unmarriageable to a decent man. And anyway, it would seem far less of a villainy for Vier to marry his own ward if she so clearly needs to be controlled. People will say she needs a firm hand, an older man to steady her, that she clearly isn't fit to decide for herself. Not to mention that people care far less about a wrong done to a woman who is already soiled goods.'

Daizell made a face. 'True.'

'Would you put it past Vier to haul her back home, let the world know she spent all this time with a man, and present himself as saving her reputation by marriage?'

'I wouldn't put much past him,' Daizell said. 'You're right that she has got herself in a bad position. But do you really think we should return her to that swine's house?'

'Of course not. We should help them get to Gretna.'

Daizell paused for a second. 'Not what I expected you to say, but carry on.'

'Clearly she should marry Marston, if the alternative is Vier. Can we help them on their way?'

'How?'

'I thought you'd know. You must have some ideas, surely? You've done it before.'

Daizell gave him a look. 'I don't elope with heiresses as often as you might think. Just the once, actually, and it wasn't a success. You seem to have changed your stance on the aiding and abetting of elopement rather rapidly?'

'I loathe Sir James,' Cassian said, with immense feeling. 'He's a cruel, grasping, malicious brute who abuses his horses, and I would enjoy nothing more than to put a spoke in his wheel. And I should not like to see a young lady in his power, especially if she had crossed him.' If Miss Beaumont was forced back to Sir James, the Duke would unquestionably have to act, now he knew of her plight. That opened all kinds of ghastly vistas, since people would want to know the reason for the Duke of Severn's interest in a pretty, eligible, unmarried lady. Whereas if she eloped successfully and gained control of her fortune, he could forget about her without guilt.

Not to mention that if he could help now, that would show he could act as himself and not just through his inherited power. He rather liked that idea.

'We must aid her,' he said firmly. 'Surely you can think of something.'

Daizell sighed. 'Let's talk to Romeo and Juliet.'

They returned to the parlour, where the young lovers were in the middle of a very pretty row. Mr Marston sounded aggrieved. Miss Beaumont looked tired, her bravado clearly ebbing.

'I beg your pardon,' Daizell said, taking a chair. 'You said you wanted help. I should mention that I have let Cassian know your situation, among friends.'

'Good,' Miss Beaumont said. 'Oh, do please stop, Tony! We've had shocking luck – one of our horses cast a shoe, and we got lost – and Sir James will be on our track, and you're quite right that we should have had a better story, and now that horrid landlady will be talking and talking and of course he will track us down, and I cannot—' She broke off, jaw firming. 'I shan't marry Sir James. I *will* not. I want to live my life and not be kept in that horrible house with that horrible man and have my fortune in his control forever.'

Legally speaking, once she married, her money would be controlled by her husband. Cassian didn't trouble to mention that: she doubtless knew.

'Sir James won't want to let you slip through his fingers,' Daizell said. 'He made that exceedingly clear on your previous excursion, when I narrowly escaped a horsewhipping, by the way. I mention that merely for context.'

'I'm terribly sorry,' Miss Beaumont said politely.

'Think nothing of it. Did either of you tell people where you were going or who with?'

'No, of course not,' Miss Beaumont said, offended by this slight on her deceptive powers. 'In fact – oh!'

'Oh?' Cassian asked, with a slight sinking feeling.

'Well, you see – and I do beg you won't be annoyed – but one never knows who's watching in Sir James's house and I didn't want him to suspect Tony. I needed to lay a false trail before I escaped. So I wrote various letters to you, Mr Charnage.' She gave Daizell a hopeful look. 'I thought you wouldn't mind.'

Daizell opened and closed his mouth. 'You thought—'

'Well, you had already tried to elope with me, so that made it credible. And you wouldn't have got the letters, since I just sent them to an inn, and they will doubtless still be there. The slightest investigation would show you had nothing to do with the matter. It will be quite easy for you to explain.'

'When Sir James arrives with a horsewhip, you mean?'

'Oh, you're far younger than him,' Miss Beaumont said bracingly. 'I'm sure he couldn't just attack you.'

'On his own, perhaps not. Unfortunately, he tends to bring large men with him.'

'That awful groom? Oh, yes. Oh dear. But the point is, it does seem to me that if he thinks I've run away with you, and he's coming after me, and now you're here with me—'

'I quite see how that could be made to suit you,' Daizell said. 'It doesn't suit me at all.'

'Well, now, wait,' Cassian said. 'Could it not be a good idea? We didn't give the landlord our names. If – how would this work—'

'If we say Tony is Mr Charnage,' Miss Beaumont said. 'And he and I leave together, and you go elsewhere—'

'No use, because Sir James will still be pursuing you,' Daizell said. 'Which, in my opinion, is preferable to him being after me.'

'But I can bear witness you haven't eloped with Miss Beaumont,' Cassian said. It would be cursed awkward if Vier appeared in person, but at least he could ensure Daizell's safety: Vier wouldn't dare touch a man under his protection. At least, probably not. He had never actually put anyone under his protection, and wasn't quite sure how one went about it. 'We can have the law on him if he threatens you. Really, there does surely seem to be an opportunity here if we could think how to use it?'

He looked around hopefully. So did Miss Beaumont. So did Mr Marston. They all ended up looking at Daizell.

That gentleman sighed the sigh of a badly put-upon man. 'For goodness' sake. All *right*. Suppose we leave together tomorrow, the four of us, for Stratford-upon-Avon. Before that, Mr Marston will identify himself as Daizell Charnage here, and inform the landlady that you are to marry in Stratford as soon as the banns are called. Name the church. Does anyone know a church in Stratford?'

'Holy Trinity,' Cassian said. 'I believe it was Shakespeare's parish church.'

'Marvellous. You two can chatter happily about your forthcoming literary wedding. Once we get to Stratford – have you money, Miss Beaumont?'

'Enough. I have been hoarding my pin-money for some time.'

'In Stratford, then, you and I will take a trip to purchase a common licence, consult the vicar of Holy Trinity church as to how soon banns can be published, and make ourselves memorable doing it. With luck the pursuit will be diverted in that direction, and Sir James will attempt to track you down in Stratford, and become embroiled in finding me instead. With even more luck, he won't have his big brute with a horsewhip in attendance. Meanwhile, Mr Marston will organise your journey north. You could go through Birmingham to confuse the trail, though I have always wondered whether one might simply sail up the coast, and arrive in Scotland that way. Anyway, *you* will depart, and *we* will carry on with our own business, while dropping my name in a casual sort of way to anyone who might be asked, and confusing the trail for long enough that you can disappear. There. Happy now?'

'I'd also suggest Miss Beaumont hire a chaperone,' Cassian said, and recoiled at the look she gave him. 'Well, surely Sir James will be asking about a couple, not three people?'

'Might work,' Daizell said. 'Alternatively, Miss Beaumont could dress as a boy.'

'You see?' Miss Beaumont interjected, with a significant look at her fiancé. 'I *told* you I should.'

'No wife of mine—'

'Save it for the honeymoon,' Daizell said. 'Dress up, pretend to be siblings, buy a ring and behave like you're married. Anything but a repeat of tonight's arrival.'

Cassian felt obliged to reiterate his point. 'Nevertheless, a chaperone—'

'Yes, thank you,' Miss Beaumont said, unceremoniously dismissing him once again, and turned her glowing face to Daizell. 'Thank you, Mr Charnage, you are quite wonderful. That is so clever and so very kind, and I do hope not to cause you too much trouble. And I am terribly sorry about last time, really. We're both dreadfully grateful.'

Marston didn't look grateful, and Daizell didn't look gratified. Cassian glanced between them, and said, 'I'm glad he could help. I think I'm going to bed.'

Chapter Six

There was only one bed.

Cassian hadn't thought of that. Doubtless, if they had a room with two beds, Miss Beaumont would be given it so she didn't have to share with the hosts' daughter. Or possibly vice versa.

It was quite normal to share as a travelling expediency, he knew, if one wasn't a duke entitled to always have the best room entirely to himself. He was not currently a duke, so he was going to share a bed with Daizell. To be asleep next to him.

That might have presented more of a problem if he wasn't so tired he could die from it. The long day, the accident, the long walk, and the ale were all catching up with him now, and he found himself swaying as he washed. The lamplight was dim, and he couldn't tell if he'd need to shave in the morning or it was just the speckled mirror.

'You look dog-tired,' Daizell remarked, sitting on the bed. 'Are you always this chivalrous?'

'Chivalrous?'

'Give up the room, save the lady from herself, save the lady from the villain ...'

'I don't think any of that's chivalry. It's just responsibility.'

'You don't have a responsibility to her.'

Cassian sat on the other side of the bed to wrestle his boots off. He had his back to Daizell, but he could feel the heat of his body a couple of feet away, or imagined he could. 'You didn't have a responsibility to anyone in that coach.'

'That was an emergency. Most people help in a dramatic situation, if only to be part of the drama. People aren't so ready to do the same for day-to-day situations – a child with holes in his boots, a man in need of dinner.'

He wasn't speaking with his usual cheer. Cassian pulled his shirt over his head, feeling rather snubbed. 'I dare say you're right. Though I don't really want to be part of Miss Beaumont's drama at all. I suppose I got carried away when Vier came into it. I saw him thrashing his horses once and we had the most appalling row.'

'Good for you,' Daizell said. 'Though risky: I heard the Duke of Severn once squabbled with him on the subject and Vier chased him off with his tail between his legs. But I didn't mean to imply that you were inserting yourself into Miss Beaumont's affairs for entertainment: you were clearly trying to do a good thing. I still don't think Miss Beaumont's affairs are any of your business or mine, and I bet we, or at least I, come to regret interfering. But Vier is an utter swine, and I suppose if we can help a little, we might as well. And I also think you're a very generous man.'

That brought more blood to his cheeks, but this time pleasantly. 'Oh, well, I wouldn't say that.'

The bed creaked as Daizell twisted and he felt a warm hand on his bare arm. 'I would.'

Cassian wanted to turn round, desperately. He searched for some response. '*Do* you think we'll come to regret it? That this runaway marriage is a bad idea?'

'I dare say Marston will be an adequate husband to Miss Beaumont.' Daizell's hand was still resting on Cassian's arm, so casual a touch. 'In her shoes I'd spend my money on an excellent lawyer, but here we are. I was more reflecting that we, specifically I, will regret it very sharply when Sir James Vier and his hulking groom arrive brandishing horsewhips.'

'I won't let that happen.'

'Will you not?' Daizell said. 'Well, that's nice. There's also the small matter of another elopement being ascribed to me, a story which will doubtless do the rounds.'

Cassian's stomach plunged. He turned without thought of anything else. 'Oh Lord. I didn't think – but of course you will be blamed. Your reputation – Oh, no. We can't allow this.'

Daizell blinked at him. 'My dear fellow, I was only grumbling. I don't *have* a reputation. You must know that.'

'Yes, but this charge isn't true!' Cassian said, and then, 'Uh – I meant—'

'You meant exactly what you said.' Daizell shifted back, turning away to pull off his own shirt. 'Correctly. I am, regrettably, my father's son, and beyond his very considerable contribution, I'm the author of my own misfortunes. I did attempt to elope with Miss Beaumont once, so really, what does it matter in the grand scheme of things if people think I did it again? And anyway, it was my idea.'

'But it's my fault,' Cassian said. 'I asked you to think of something.'

That was exactly what he'd done, of course. Asked. Not done it himself, not taken charge or responsibility, just waved a hand and given the order and not considered what it might mean, or cost. A wave of guilt drenched him. 'We can't go through with it. This isn't fair to you. I will explain—'

'Oh, don't worry about it,' Daizell said. 'You look fit to drop. Let's discuss it in the morning.'

Cassian didn't have the mental acuity to argue. He

managed to get his breeches off, and piled his clothes on a chair, since he'd learned that leaving them on the floor meant picking them up off it again. He blew out the lamp, and groped his way to the bed.

It wasn't uncomfortable, really, and the sheets were not damp, but on the other hand, Daizell's body was a foot from his, if that, weighting the mattress. Cassian could feel his solid warmth without touching. He tried to balance as far over as possible, because he knew an accidental touch would be bad even if he found it hard to think why.

And he wished he wasn't so sleepy, because here in the dark with Daizell next to him, he didn't want to fall asleep. He felt they could talk long into the night, if only he could stay awake. But consciousness was passing from his control, and his eyes fluttered shut to the sound of Daizell's quiet breath.

He woke with an arm across him.

The awareness was slow and confusing – a weight, a warmth – and then his mind sprang to life, and it was all he could do not to react. Daizell's arm, around his waist. The thought thudded through him, pulsing in his groin. Was he … could he …

He didn't move, careful to keep his breathing level and regular. A second later, he realised that Daizell's breathing was as regular as his own. It was deep, and a little resonant. Actually, he was snoring.

He was asleep. Of course he was.

Cassian breathed out, slow and careful. Daizell was asleep. They'd shared a bed in a perfectly respectable sort of way – which, he reminded himself, was the only possible outcome of their association. Daizell liked laughing young ladies, or at least he was happy to elope with them, and even if he should happen to like gentlemen as well, he was Daizell Charnage, a gentleman of uncertain fortune and dubious reputation. The Duke had already made a mistake with a man like that. One should learn from experience.

Then again, the nominal purpose of this month as Mr Cassian was to have experiences from which he could learn.

He allowed himself to dwell on that traitorous thought for a self-indulgent moment, then turned his mind firmly away. He should consider the day's duties. They'd lost a full day thanks to the accident; they had to get to Stratford—

Oh Lord. He'd promised to help the eloping couple and tangled both himself and Daizell in what, under daylight and a clear mind, now seemed a quite ludicrous course of action. He had a feeling he might have run briefly mad, through tiredness and strong ale, and a powerful dislike of Sir James Vier.

And, also, a clear injustice. It was not right that a vicious rake should have guardianship over a young woman, and Miss Beaumont's position was intolerable. His information was admittedly from the lady herself, who might be unreliable, and Daizell, who was certainly erratic, but on the other hand, he'd met Vier.

And come off worse, as Daizell had reminded him. That casual gossip about the Duke of Severn's humiliation had stung viciously, not just because it was proof the story had done the rounds, but also because Daizell knew it and, Cassian discovered, he didn't care to have Daizell regard him as a weakling or a figure of fun.

'Umph.' A grunt from beside him. 'Urgh. Eh? Who did I – Cass?'

Cassian made a display of yawning, and gave Daizell's arm

a shrug. He withdrew it, leaving Cassian bereft of warmth. 'I beg your pardon. I'm all limbs at night, or so people tell me.'

'Not at all,' Cassian said meaninglessly. 'Good morning.'

'Morning. Oh God, that woman. Did we really agree to—'

'Yes.'

'Curse it. The ale here creeps up on a fellow.'

'I had the same thought,' Cassian said. 'You said something last night about your reputation. Not wanting to be accused of eloping with another lady.'

'More precisely, the same one twice.'

'Even so. I think we should find an alternative plan, one that doesn't involve your name.'

'Like what?'

Cassian hadn't got that far. 'Um, I'll try to think of one—'

Daizell yawned jaw-breakingly. 'Ah, don't worry about it. It makes no odds: I'm not going to be admitted to White's anyway, so I might as well help a damsel in distress. And if she actually marries Marston that will deal with any scandal attaching to me. I'm more concerned about Sir James. The horsewhipping, obviously, but are there legal consequences for aiding an elopement?'

Cassian hadn't thought of that. 'If she'd agreed to marry him, he might have a case for breach of promise against her, if he wanted to be a laughing-stock. But against people who helped her? I suppose he could mount a civil suit for damages, but I don't think it's likely.' He would engage lawyers if he had to. 'I don't think you should worry about it.'

'I'm glad to hear it.' Daizell stretched. His foot brushed Cassian's leg, just the lightest careless touch, and Cassian couldn't help a twitch. 'Sorry. Actually, this might even be entertaining, and I'm always ready to put a spoke in Vier's wheel. But it strikes me we risk losing our trail while we muddy Miss Beaumont's.'

'That can't be helped,' Cassian said. 'Perhaps I can start asking questions while you go and ... buy a marriage licence under false pretences, and deceive a parson ... oh God.' He couldn't help it; he started laughing, and felt Daizell join him a second later, shaking so hard he could feel the mattress shift under them. 'Oh no. What's happened to me?'

'Well, it's not me,' Daizell said. 'I wanted to be sensible. You're the one who asked me to lie to vicars.'

'That was your idea!'

'It was your idea to have the idea.'

Daizell Charnage was calling him the reckless one. Cassian felt quite dizzy, and stupidly happy, and he didn't want to move. He wanted to stay here in the warm bed next to Daizell's warm body, talking and laughing and just accidentally touching.

'We should get up,' he told himself aloud, and swung his legs out of bed before he changed his mind.

They made a hearty breakfast. Their temporary travelling companions seemed rather more nervy. Mr Marston made rather a point of giving his name as Charnage to their hosts, and talking about their forthcoming marriage and the pleasures of Stratford-upon-Avon. Cassian had never been there, but, based on their companion's speech, he felt confident that Mr Marston hadn't either.

It turned out the eloping couple had a hired chaise. That saved Cassian's own purse, he reflected smugly, without infringing the terms of the wager. The four of them set off very promptly. Mr Marston took the reins, which left his intended, Daizell, and Cassian sitting inside.

Miss Beaumont evidently felt obliged to make conversation. 'So what business are you about in Stratford, Mr Charnage?'

Daizell glanced at Cassian, who said, 'Pursuing some interests of mine. Uh, business interests.'

'Oh. That sounds… interesting. Are you doing that too, Mr Charnage? I didn't know you were a man of affairs.'

'I'm not.'

'Oh.'

'Miss Beaumont, would you care to speak about your situation?' Cassian didn't think he could bear any more small talk. 'Of course, I wish you success in your, uh, mission, but it strikes me, since Sir James has the right to force you to return to his house, you may need to consider what to do if he should catch you. Is there anyone you can appeal to? Trustees, relatives?'

Her jaw set. 'Do you think I haven't tried? My father appointed him my guardian because he had nobody else, and my trustee is only concerned with my fortune, not my wishes. And scarcely even that, the idle lump.'

Cassian considered. 'How long might it take you to reach Scotland?'

'Don't answer that,' Daizell said. 'We don't want to know which way you're going: that way we can't let it slip.'

'Why do you ask?' Miss Beaumont added.

'I was wondering how we might find out if Sir James catches you,' Cassian said. There were surely people he could write to. Leo, perhaps: he'd doubtless be aware of Vier's movements and state of mind. Then again, Leo was unlikely to want to cross a man to whom he owed a lot of money, and also, while Cassian could write to him, he had no idea where he'd be over the next few weeks to receive any reply.

Miss Beaumont was looking oddly at him. 'Why?'

'So we can help. If Sir James finds you, you'll need someone to get you out of his grasp. I'll be travelling for the next three weeks, but after that – hmm. Perhaps you could write to me care of a friend.'

'Help me? How would you propose to do that?'

'I don't know yet,' Cassian said honestly. 'But it is wrong that your guardian should press you to marry him, and I am quite sure something should be done, if only bringing his behaviour to the world's attention.'

'He would inevitably bring Miss Beaumont's behaviour to the world's attention,' Daizell pointed out. 'He enjoys exposing people's sins.'

'Oh, he *does*,' Miss Beaumont agreed resentfully. 'It hides his own. It wouldn't matter if I could just get away. Once I have my fortune, I dare say people will stop caring about anything else. And if they don't, then I shall do very well without their good opinion. I want to have my own life, and live it, and if other people disapprove of how I go about that, they can disapprove till their ears turn blue, because I don't think a good reputation is any sort of consolation for a life of misery. So if Sir James does catch up, Mr, uh—'

'Cassian.'

'If he does, and if you do have any means of finding out and making a fuss on my behalf, whatever the consequences, I would be immensely grateful. I don't know why you're both being so dreadfully kind,' she added, and her mouth twitched then, pulling down at the corners as though she might cry.

'He's chivalrous, and I'm easily led,' Daizell said, his cheerful tone pulling her expression back to a smile. 'You don't have much luggage. Very wise, or will you be shopping on the way?'

Miss Beaumont responded to that opening with a brightness that didn't entirely convince, but she and Daizell kept up a light and meaningless chatter for long enough that the mood lifted. Cassian found it admirable on both their parts. He didn't feel quite able to join in. The coach was travelling at a very good speed indeed, and the road was appalling, bumpy and rutted and badly sloped. He would have liked to take the reins himself, or to join Mr Marston on the box and see his handling of the horses. He didn't want to be stuck in this dark box, jolting, rocking, going too damned fast because any moment there would be a crack and a lurch and they would crash—

Daizell put a hand on his knee.

Cassian looked down at the touch, startled. Daizell's hand, resting on his leg, casual and warm, and as Cassian looked up again, Daizell gave it a squeeze, and flashed him a reassuring smile. 'Mr Marston's a good whip?' he said aloud, with just a touch of a question.

'Oh, yes, excellent,' Miss Beaumont said. 'Are you a nervous traveller, Mr Cassian?'

'I'm very well.' Cassian didn't want to talk about the crash, and hoped Daizell wouldn't. He looked out of the window instead at the landscape jolting by, and took comfort from Daizell's hand resting gently on his knee.

They didn't crash. Mr Marston's furious but competent driving got them to Stratford-upon-Avon in good time. It was a small town, rather low, with a mix of some fine new houses, and some marvellous older ones, black-beamed in the Tudor style.

It shouldn't take long for them to learn if Mr John Martin had travelled through, but first they had a promise to fulfil.

Accordingly, he and Daizell took a room at the White Swan on Rother Street, and then Daizell and Miss Beaumont trotted off to carry out the motions of a wedding. Mr Marston set out to find a way up north that might evade pursuit, and Cassian was left to his own devices.

It felt rather flat, and he realised he would rather have been an actor in the drama. It was of course best that he should stay out of the business. The Duke of Severn could not involve himself in what was, frankly, troublemaking, and Daizell was better suited and placed for the work. And yet—

Maybe, next time he faced a challenge, he would think how to address it himself, before he asked for help.

He filled the time as best he could. He wandered around the town between the various coaching inns, enquiring about John Martin without success, and commanded luncheon at an ordinary with an ease that amazed himself once he was addressing his food. It had only been a few days, but he was becoming used to doing these things already. Or possibly he had so much on his mind that he didn't have room to worry about trivialities.

He certainly had plenty to think about. The crash. Miss Beaumont's problems, which were in no way his, but in which he was nevertheless tangled. His quest to track down his missing ring, which was starting to seem very unlikely indeed, and the question of why that didn't seem to matter as much as once it had. Daizell.

Daizell. He could still feel a phantom hand on his knee, offering silent support for his unreasoned fear, and a phantom arm over his shoulder, close and comfortable in sleep. He wanted those touches to be real.

This was foolish. Daizell was a wastrel who came of bad stock, and attempted to elope with heiresses, and was currently making a mockery of the sacrament of marriage. He needed to remember that those were bad things.

He trudged on around the alehouses in the centre of the little town till late afternoon, then returned to their inn, where he sat in the snug with a book, recuperating his energies after a frustrating day. As the many churches reached a loose consensus on six o'clock, Daizell reappeared.

'Cass.' He looked bright-eyed, hair chaotic, buzzing with energy, and Cassian's moral resolutions were swamped like a sandcastle in the tide. 'Good evening. What a day. Have you a drink? New book?'

'There's a bookseller here. I couldn't find the new novel by Mrs Swann that you mentioned but I picked up *Nightmare Abbey*, which I had not read.'

'How is it?'

'Terrible.'

'Excellent, excellent. Let me just command a drink, I'm parched.' Daizell waved at a barmaid. 'What have you been up to?'

'Nothing as exciting as you, by the look of things.'

Daizell grinned. 'I have been enjoying myself, I will admit. Miss Beaumont has a remarkable turn for skulduggery, and an alarming ruthlessness. It was most entertaining. We purchased a common licence, and had a conversation with the vicar which I am quite sure he will remember. Miss Beaumont discussed our intention to marry and her flight from a wicked guardian with astonishing invention, and confided in his housekeeper that she intended to evade pursuit by dressing as a man. I understand the vicar has no power to forbid the banns from being read, or to refuse to marry us on grounds of disapproval alone, but good Lord, he looked like he wanted to.'

'I imagine he did.' Hoaxing vicars was not a respectable way to go on, and Daizell seemed to have enjoyed it a great deal. Cassian was torn between very natural disapproval, the fear that he would not be able to hoax a vicar with any sort of aplomb, and a lurking regret he hadn't tried. 'Do you think it will help?'

'If Vier manages to follow her tracks here, it's quite possible this will throw him off. And if it does, and they can get ahead, they may be able to lose the pursuit altogether.'

'Worthwhile, then. I hope it doesn't become common knowledge that she proposed to go about in breeches.'

'I don't think she'll care, as long as she gets away with it. And, as she remarked, once she has her money, nobody will worry about how she got it. I hope she succeeds,' Daizell added thoughtfully. 'I'm glad I met her. I rather resented our last encounter, but she made me a very frank apology today and I feel better about it now.'

'What happened?' Cassian asked. 'The elopement, I mean. You didn't seem to be very, uh ... That is, were you awfully fond of one another?'

'Do you want to know? It's not terribly edifying.'

'I should like to. If you don't mind.'

'Ah, it's the truth, so you might as well. It was not a Romeo and Juliet affair,' Daizell said, with a smile that wasn't quite as sparky as before. 'There was a very tedious party, in a house where I was staying. Vier was there, and Miss Beaumont with him. She accosted me and proposed an elopement.'

Cassian blinked. 'Just like that?'

'More or less. We spoke briefly and she said she intended to get out from under Vier's thumb by any means necessary. That was, apparently, me. I was in rather a bad situation myself so a rich bride falling into my lap seemed a stroke of luck. As it turned out, she was using me to get out of the house, and intended to send me off separately by some ruse, with pursuit following in my direction while she fled with her swain – I assume Marston, since he clearly lacks the brains to arrange his own elopement. All's fair in love and war, I suppose. But Vier caught up with us very quickly. He retrieved her, and I had to leg it over a wall to get away.'

Cassian blinked at that. 'You left her behind?'

'Vier is her legal guardian, and he had four men with him including one carrying the much-mentioned horsewhip. Of course I left her behind: what else could I do?'

Daizell sounded a touch strained, as well he might. It wasn't, indeed, an edifying story, but the Duke had known he was Daizell Charnage when he hired him. He could scarcely complain when the details were filled in.

And for all that, he'd seen Daizell act in the coach spill. The Duke of Severn was obliged to take an uncompromising line on what constituted acceptable behaviour, without making allowances; perhaps Mr Cassian might be more understanding.

'Well, I think you're extremely kind,' he said.

Daizell hesitated. 'What do you mean?' He sounded rather wary. 'I know it wasn't a very admirable way to go on—'

'I'd say she treated you exceedingly poorly if she intended you to suffer for her elopement and gain nothing by it. I'm astonished you were ready to help her now.'

'Oh, well, I owe Vier a bad turn,' Daizell said. 'And it wasn't so bad of Miss Beaumont really. I will admit to being extremely annoyed at the time, but she was only eighteen, and desperate for a way out, and I was a tool at hand. She did what she had to do. Don't we all?'

Cassian sipped ale, thinking about people who did what they had to. He'd had to do a lot himself. Had to take up the mantle of his father aged six, had to carry the burden of rank and wealth and lands, had to live under scrutiny because of his position, and always be conscious that he was Severn. The weight he lived under was crushing. He'd wanted to flee his position so much that he had become bosom friends with a notorious rascal under a false name.

He had no idea at all what it was *not* to have money, or people, or prospects. He'd never been aimless or hopeless, or desperate.

He'd been lonely. He'd very often been lonely because he was a quiet man who didn't make friends easily or in great numbers, and his position had got in the way of friendships he could have made. If he'd been merely Harmsford at school, not Severn, the other boys wouldn't have been instructed how to behave to him, and might have been readier to include him. Then again, if he enjoyed parties, or if he was minded to matrimony, or if he let it be known he wanted a crowd of companions to gamble with, he could have made all the friends he liked. In his place, Daizell would probably be on intimate terms with everyone from the Houses of Parliament to the houses of correction, and having a marvellous time.

What might Cassian do in Daizell's place, the penniless son of a disgraced man? He hoped he wouldn't just drift around. He might become a horse trainer, he thought, or a stagecoach driver, even. Both of which would use the skills he'd acquired through owning a lot of horses, and having all the time he wanted to drive and ride. He wondered what skills George Charnage's son had beyond cutting profiles.

'I suppose you're right,' he said. 'I maintain you are

extraordinarily generous to help her a second time. Did they get away safely?'

'I trust so. I handed Miss Beaumont over and waved goodbye, and that is the limit of my responsibility.'

'Fair.' Cassian contemplated his ale. 'Were you afraid I'd be shocked by that tale?'

'You don't strike me as an unconventional gentleman,' Daizell said. 'You're clearly concerned about appearances, and correct behaviour. So ... yes?'

That was rather lowering and Cassian wasn't even sure why. He *was* conventional, mostly, and he *was* concerned about correct behaviour, and so he ought to be. And Daizell hadn't said it in a patronising way that might imply he was timid or boring, not at all. That was still how it felt.

'Well, I dare say I am,' he mumbled.

'If ready to assist an elopement at the drop of a hat,' Daizell added, a touch of amusement returning to his voice. 'So maybe not entirely conventional. Prepared to infringe convention when you dislike someone enough?'

'Or when I like someone enough,' Cassian batted back, and then felt a pulse of panic as Daizell's eyes widened. He hadn't meant to say that, or admit it, and they were once again sharing a room tonight. 'I mean, I liked Miss Beaumont. I thought she was very, uh ...'

'Yes, very,' Daizell said, a grin twitching at the corner of his mouth. 'So you can discard unwanted social strictures if you happen to like the person?'

'I ... have done that, now and again,' Cassian said, astonished at his own daring.

The smile broadened temptingly. 'That's good to know.'

Chapter Seven

Cassian was delightful when he was flustered. Daizell felt an overwhelming urge to fluster him some more.

He needed to resist it. Cassian was clearly conventional, whatever he might claim, and you never knew when a conventional gentleman might decide he didn't associate with erratic elopers of notorious family. That was a horrible prospect. Daizell needed the fifty pounds, but far more than that, he wanted the growing friendship and purpose he had with Cassian. He'd been more desperate than he realised for something to do, and someone to do it with, and, most of all, someone who wanted to do it with him.

He could forget how lonely he was for a lot of the time, because he was mostly lonely in company. He was very good at drifting with the tide, washing in and out of inns and tap-rooms and other people's homes with the rest of life's flotsam. Making himself pleasant, never showing he felt directionless and useless because that wasn't what people wanted to hear. Enjoyable temporary company was the most that anybody wanted of him, and he went along with that because crying and struggling didn't do much good. But just now and then he couldn't avoid feeling the great echoing void of his life, and it hurt unbearably.

Cassian was making it hurt. This companionship was so joyous, it reminded Daizell forcibly of how alone he'd been before and how alone he'd be again. But he had become adept at living in the moment, so he tried to focus on the pleasure of having someone to travel with, sharing meals and making plans. Cassian's quiet conversation, and the smile that lurked in his eyes far more often than it made its way to his mouth. Cassian's warmth, constantly near him. Daizell liked physical closeness and affectionate touch: waking up with his arm over Cassian had been perfect.

Nearly perfect. Perfect would have involved him moving his hands down and pulling Cassian round, and finding out what those curved lips could do, how his sun-and-rain eyes might widen, what that neat, compact body felt like and how it responded. Unfortunately, Cassian was a conventional gentleman. *Unless he liked someone enough*, he'd said, and Daizell wasn't sufficiently sure about that.

And since he wasn't willing to risk their companionship for a chance at physical gratification – really, he was becoming terribly mature – he had better leave well alone.

He took a long pull at his ale. 'What about you, then? Any luck today?'

Cassian took a second to register what he was talking about. 'Ah. Yes. No. No, I've visited every inn here, not just coaching inns, and asked questions till the words lost meaning, and got nowhere. If he came through here, he didn't stay, and nobody remembers. Of course, that doesn't mean he didn't—'

'Just that we won't know where he's gone. Although, presumably you confined your search to the town. If he changed at one of the staging-posts further out—'

'I thought that too!' Cassian said, with the oddly pleased look he often had at such moments, like a schoolboy who had the answer to a question. 'But I visited all of those within walking distance. I thought we might try the rest tomorrow.'

Daizell felt a pulse of guilt. 'We could have done it today if I hadn't been playing the fool with a vicar.'

'Miss Beaumont needed your help, and a person is more important than an object.' He said that as though he thought Daizell might argue. 'The ring matters a great deal to me, but if we'd gone looking for it, even found it, and then heard Sir James had tracked her down when we could have prevented it... No. No, you did the right thing.'

'It might not slow Sir James down at all. We don't even know he'll come this way.'

'This was the best we could do; we can't do more. We oughtn't do less, but we can't do more.'

He said *we*, and he thought Daizell was doing his best, and Daizell felt his ever-hungry heart thump. 'I still want to find your ring, though. We'll ask at the further-flung inns tomorrow, and failing that, we'll make a plan.'

'We'll do that,' Cassian said, tapped his glass to Daizell's, and smiled.

They were sharing a bed again. It was torture.

At least they'd both been exhausted the previous night. This evening Daizell was wide awake as he surreptitiously watched Cassian moving around the room, wide awake as he noted the lines of that smooth, near-hairless back and chest. (The man shaved once in two days, he'd noticed, and that seemed optimistic.) Wide awake when Cassian got in the bed next to him, his lighter weight meaning it would be so easy for him to roll towards Daizell, which he did not.

He didn't, but Daizell was so very nearly sure he wanted to.

The way he looked, the way he blushed, the glances he stole. None of which constituted an invitation to touch, or at least not a conscious one, and the problem with deciding that people were unconsciously inviting was that you could be wrong and in fact you weren't invited at all. And then there would be outrage, or dismay, or alarm, and none of those were emotions Daizell would care to evoke.

Cassian was breathing softly, shallow and even. It sounded as though he'd gone straight to sleep: Daizell had no idea how, unless of course Cassian wasn't at all troubled by the nearness of bare legs, the possibility of reaching out, hands meeting, exploring skin. He wondered if he could toss himself off without disturbing his companion's rest.

'Are you awake?' he murmured, very quietly.

There was a short silence. 'Yes.' It sounded a touch reluctant. 'Why?'

Marvellous. Now he'd started a conversation. 'So am I.'

Cassian made a noise of mild exasperation. 'Have you considered sleeping?'

'Good idea.'

Cassian shifted, turning towards him. 'Is something wrong?'

'Wrong? No. Why?'

'I don't know. You seem …' He paused there. 'I hope I didn't offend you earlier.'

'What? How?'

'Asking questions. I've no right to interrogate you and I dare say you might not wish to rehearse events which doubtless were very distressing.'

Daizell deciphered that. 'The elopement? It wasn't distressing. Somewhat wounding to my pride, and very tiresome, that's all.'

'You looked, when you spoke of it …' Cassian paused again. 'Not yourself.'

Cassian thought he was lying awake because he was upset?

That was charming in its way, even if wrong. But perhaps not entirely wrong in every aspect because Daizell found himself saying, 'Well, it's not much to be proud of.'

'What isn't?'

'Any of it. Eloping with a woman I didn't know. *Failing* to elope. Being fooled by a schoolgirl, in fact. Sir James. All the rest of it.' He paused. 'My father.'

He was sure Cassian knew, and the silence confirmed that. After a moment, his bedmate spoke cautiously. 'I did hear about your father.'

'You could hardly not.'

George Charnage had capped a career of gambling, extravagance, unpaid debts, and almost continual inebriation by losing a fortune he didn't have at whist. He'd invited the two men he'd played with for another match at his house the next night, offering as stake all he had left: the house and its contents. They came with money in their pockets, ready to reduce George Charnage and his family to beggary for their night's entertainment. Instead, he and Daizell's mother had held them at gunpoint, stripped them of everything down to their clothing, and shot one of them when he resisted.

Daizell had come home late the next morning after a night's debauchery in south London to discover an enraged man in his drawers bound and gagged in the drawing room and another lying on the floor in a pool of blood. George and Anna Charnage had left Mr Henry Haddon untended, unconscious, and bleeding all night. When Daizell had knelt to help him, the bone had been visible in his shattered shoulder. He died a few hours later.

Apart from a furious man and a dying one, the house had been bare. Daizell's mother and father had packed up everything they owned of value plus the proceeds of that candlelight robbery, and fled the country.

They hadn't told their son of their plans beforehand and they hadn't invited his company in their escape or exile. They had left him as the only one of the family there to blame, and he had been blamed. His father was cousin to the Marquess of Sellingstowe, who had given him an allowance on the basis of family obligation; at the scandal Sellingstowe had publicly repudiated the connection, cutting off Daizell too. His name was bloodstained and disgraced. George Charnage's other victim had claimed the house in lieu of the debt. Daizell found himself with nowhere to live, no income, no skills, and no connections who would give him work, if there was any work he might be fit for given his curtailed education and lack of adult occupation.

He had been left with nothing but a tenuous claim to be a gentleman, a decent wardrobe, a likeable manner, and a knack for cutting profiles. He'd survived for seven years on those things and the tolerance of hosts which, like the wardrobe, became more threadbare every year. He was unwanted, aimless and useless, and though he'd always thought he'd somehow find a way out of the mess, it had never come to pass.

He swallowed all that down. 'Well, it can't be helped. He did what he did. I would prefer it if people didn't blame me for his acts, that's all.'

'Do they?' Cassian said. 'How? That is, you were not involved, were you?'

Daizell hated the question in his voice. He'd been asked too often. 'No. I wasn't.'

Cassian didn't reply. Daizell blinked into the dark, reminding himself that he was a provincial gentleman, that he wasn't to know and had every right to ask, that it was all a long time ago and a life away.

'I was in Vauxhall Gardens all that night,' he said, slightly less harshly. 'A friend had a small party. I had no idea what my parents had planned. They didn't tell me Father had lost everything at whist the night before; they certainly didn't advise me they'd be enlivening the evening with robbery and murder. I came home to an empty house and a dying man. They didn't even leave a note. They just did it and fled.'

'But – they said nothing? Not even goodbye? Have you not heard from them since?'

'No.' He had never received a letter. Perhaps his parents had written to the house he no longer lived in, or care of friends or relatives Daizell no longer saw. Or perhaps they hadn't written at all. He'd given up wondering a while ago, because wondering meant hoping and he couldn't do that any more.

Cassian was eloquently silent. Daizell sighed. 'I told you about my name: well, my father was always like that. He was loud and he drank and I'm not sure he fully understood that other people were real too. He was convinced that anyone who behaved in a way he found inconvenient must be doing it out of personal malice towards him. We were all minor actors in the play of which he was the star.'

'Even your mother?'

'Oh, she agreed with him,' Daizell said. 'I expect it was the only way to live with him, but he was the heart of her world. She worshipped him, whatever he did. She loved me too, but only in the space he left for that, and he didn't leave much. A jealous god, my father, and didn't like to share. When he said, *Take a gun and help me commit a robbery*, she would have done it without hesitation. I expect she wept over leaving me behind, but that didn't stop her going, or leaving me to take the blame for their mess.'

'But why should you take it?' Cassian demanded. 'How could you be blamed when you weren't there?'

'Someone had to be. Vier very much wanted a scapegoat.'

'Vier? Sir James?'

'He was the other man in the house. He and his friend Haddon came ready to play deep. Apparently they intended to strip my father of everything he had left down to his home and, according to some rumours, my mother's person. Instead Vier lost two thousand pounds that night, as well as his friend, so one can quite understand he wanted vengeance. And since I was the only Charnage available, he took it out on me.'

'What did he do?'

Daizell shut his eyes, feeling the backwash of bewilderment, distress, injustice, helplessness. 'It seems my mother wore breeches and a kerchief over her face while holding the gun. Vier claimed to believe it was me. He told everyone I was my father's accomplice.'

'But you were in Vauxhall.'

'I *know*. I had witnesses. But I never had a day in court to say so, since he never tried to press charges. Instead he made a lot of remarks about how he couldn't see the face of the second robber, about the hair – my mother's was like mine – about drunken evenings and lying friends protecting me and how he can't prove it but he knows. All implications, but he's been whispering them so long – and what was I meant to do? Slam my hand on the table and say, *No, sir, I did not conspire at robbery and murder, that was my mother*? I'd lost everything – the house, the money, my parents – and Vier was spinning lies and sowing doubt, and people looked at me differently and I didn't know what to do. I just didn't know what to do.' He felt his voice fade in the darkness. 'One of the men I was with in Vauxhall went to the wars and died there, and another I barely knew and wasn't much in society himself. There was nobody speaking for me, whereas Vier was always there. And I suppose many people found it easier to believe that I had held up a man with a pistol than that my mother had. Or they didn't really believe it but enjoyed the gossip, or perhaps nobody wanted my company anyway, with my father a murderer. In any case, people turned their backs.'

'I'm so sorry, Daizell.' Cassian's voice ached. 'That is dreadful. I quite see why you loathe Vier.'

'Oh, that part only made me dislike him,' Daizell said. 'The loathing came—' He glared at the night. Cassian was so close, and a hundred miles away. 'I suppose you ought to know, if you're in my company and all that. It wasn't – shouldn't have been – dreadful, but... The thing is, I stay with people, you see, as one does when one is a gentleman lacking any means of support. A few weeks here or there. One has to be an entertaining guest, if possible, so I cut shades. My one talent. I sing for my supper with profiles, as an entertaining little trick for a gentleman which is *quite* different from being a jobbing artist. But some house parties are less reputable than others, and people have different ideas of entertainment, and to cut – as it were – a long story short, I have done some rather risqué scenes, for people who wanted them.'

'Oh.' Cassian sounded startled. Daizell would bet he was blushing, could picture how his cheeks had pinked. 'I didn't realise – that is, *can* you, with profiles?'

'Lord, yes. Full-length ones, you know, and scenes. You'd be amazed.'

'I probably would. I had no idea.'

He sounded intrigued. Daizell hadn't taken up his scissors in days – it had been a relief not to – but he had a sudden urge to snip something that would make Cassian really blush. Even more, to ask him what he'd like to see, and to watch his face as the figures emerged from the paper.

Stop it.

'It was a gentleman's entertainment,' he said. 'Something for groups of men without ladies present, or with ladies who weren't being ladylike. Entirely private. But then a couple of months later I was staying with some rather strait-laced distant cousins, who felt an obligation to me despite my father's behaviour, and they held a soirée and invited their neighbours, who included Miss Beaumont and Sir James Vier. They knew of Sir James's grudge against my father, of course, but they believed that I wasn't involved, and said they wanted amity restored. And Vier smiled at me in the most unpleasant way, and an hour or so into proceedings he took me aside and informed me he had obtained some of my more disreputable shades. He had shown them to my cousins, and told them I was secretly making obscene postures for the young people at the party. Corrupting them.'

'What? Why?'

'Why did he do it? Revenge. Why he told me: possibly because he wanted to see my face, but also so I couldn't look surprised or innocent when my cousins confronted me about it. It was a well-laid trap. I denied cutting anything unfit at their house, but they had the profiles as evidence, and there we are. That was why I agreed to elope with Miss Beaumont. Vier had cut me off from the last members of my family who'd speak to me, out of sheer spite, and I was drifting around the place wondering what on earth I'd do.'

'Great God, Daizell. I'm so sorry.' Cassian's hand groped for his, sliding under the sheets, fingers warm and close and comforting. 'This is appalling. I had no idea. Vier is a vile, hateful man and I'm disgusted, though not surprised, but your *father*. How could he do that to you? He ruined you as much as his other victims, and people blame you for it?'

Everyone had blamed him, if only by contagion. He'd been cut so often it had felt like real cuts, each turned head or blank look a blade on his skin.

Daizell was a companionable man. He'd thought he had plenty of friends, just as he'd believed in his father's careless affection and his mother's love. But when it came down to the bone, people didn't help, and they didn't stay. They looked to their own well-being and left you behind.

He hadn't helped himself, of course. He'd been tainted by his parents' crime, but he'd blackened his own reputation as thoroughly as he had ever blackened paper for a profile, in a slow steady slide out of the Polite World and into disreputability that he couldn't seem to stop.

'It's my own fault,' he said aloud. 'Well, and my parents', of course. But I haven't helped myself. I was expelled from Eton, you know.'

'I did hear. A gambling ring?'

'Quite a lively one,' Daizell admitted. There had been a few running at Eton; his syndicate had, unfortunately, taken rather too much of various young noblemen's allowances, and an example had been made. Like father, like son. 'I made plenty more mistakes too. I was a careless fool before the robbery, and after I was a drunken one for a while, and perhaps if I had stood up for myself better, people wouldn't have found it so easy to tar me with the same brush.'

'But none of that is a crime!' Cassian sounded really angry now.

'The profiles were definitely dubious. It's hardly surprising people don't think much of me.'

Cassian's hand tightened. 'Well, they're wrong. And I do.'

'Why?'

The word tore itself from a throat that was already hurting with control. Cassian took a moment to answer. With another man, Daizell would have pulled his hand away at that pause, but he was getting used to the little silences as Cassian thought about what he was going to say.

'Because you're kind,' he said at last. 'I quite believe you would make impulsive decisions, or unconventional ones, or bad ones. But you go out of your way to help people. You risked your neck in a coach crash to protect someone else's baby. I would *never* believe you were involved in a robbery or corrupting youth, or anything like that, and if anyone does, they're a fool.'

He squeezed Daizell's fingers hard, and relapsed into silence. Daizell lay, eyes stinging in the dark, not entirely knowing what he felt except that it hurt, but also that it hurt in a good way, like the picking off of a tight, ugly scab.

It didn't really matter if Cassian, a gentleman of wealth but no account, thought he was a good person. The world had decided him to be a not-quite gentleman of bad stock and poor character, and one man's opinion wouldn't change that. But all the same, here in the quiet of the room, it felt like everything.

Cassian's fingers were still entwined with his, sufficiently relaxed that he could pull away if he wanted. He didn't, and the touch was a comfort in the dark.

★ ★ ★

This time, Daizell woke up with his arm over Cassian, and his face buried in the man's shoulder.

Cassian was breathing evenly under him. Daizell allowed himself a moment to enjoy the physical contact, then peeled himself off and rolled onto his back. He tried to do it without shaking the bed or waking his bedmate, but Cassian grunted.

'Morning,' Daizell said, with determined cheer. No more soul-searching: they had a job to do. 'Are we going round the outskirts today?'

'Chasing a man in a mulberry coat. Ugh.'

Daizell rubbed his face. 'You know, if he changes his coat…'

'That has occurred to me too. Am I wasting our time, Daize?'

'I don't have anything better to do with mine.'

'And I've got a month off, so—'

He couldn't help asking. 'A month off what?'

Cassian stilled. It was a tiny quiver of tension, which Daizell wouldn't have noticed if they hadn't been so close. 'Oh, normal life and duties and whatnot. I'm not expected back for a month is what I meant, so like you, I've nothing better to do.' He paused. 'I suppose…'

'What?'

'I was wondering if it would be a dreadful dereliction to look at Stratford while we're here? There's the church, and I believe Shakespeare's birthplace is preserved.' He sounded longing.

'You should absolutely see them while you're here,' Daizell said. 'If you want, I can go around the staging posts on the outskirts while you visit the sights?'

'No,' Cassian said reluctantly. 'That would be very tedious for you, and not very fair.'

Daizell knew an impulse to suggest they both forget the whole thing since his faith in their chances, never high, was more or less exhausted. He bit it back, and thought about what a useful and efficient person might say. 'Perhaps we could try to track your quarry down today? If we get a good lead, we'll follow it, and if we don't, we take tomorrow as a holiday and decide what to do next.'

'That's a good idea,' Cassian said, perking up. 'Yes. I don't want to feel consumed by guilt at not looking, but this travelling business is rather tiring.'

'Do you spend a lot of time consumed by guilt?'

'A certain amount. I was brought up to take my responsibilities very seriously.'

'I wasn't. Perhaps we could ...' He waggled a hand. 'Strike an average.'

'That's an excellent idea,' Cassian said, a laugh in his voice. 'So we will be exceedingly responsible today and take a holiday tomorrow.'

They did precisely that. It made for a blasted long day. Cassian hired a couple of hacks, and they rode out along the cross roads from Stratford to the first stage on each, asking at inns, talking to coach-drivers, searching for the man in the mulberry coat. They had, to Daizell's entire lack of surprise, no luck at all: nobody had seen their quarry, or remembered him if they had. It was a great deal of riding for nothing, if you counted quiet, easy conversation and companionable silences as nothing.

They were everything. Daizell needed people, needed friendship and talk and laughter and touch. Solitude drained his soul, leaving him bleak and joyless; companionship had him fizzing with energy. He tried to restrain that, since Cassian was clearly the opposite, and made sure not to babble when his companion lapsed into one of his many thoughtful silences, not wanting his own presence to grate. He didn't need to be always talking anyway. He was quite happy looking around, watching the world go by, as long as he had someone to do it with.

Not just someone. Cassian, with his gentle voice, murmuring enchantments to his blasted lucky horse: Daizell could listen to that all day. He also rode superbly and made some fairly cogent criticisms of Daizell's seat, which indicated more clearly than anything yet that he was an exceptional horseman. A horseman, with things to do he didn't care to discuss, and knowledge that Daizell wasn't sure how he came by.

'How did you know about the gambling ring?' he asked as they rode back.

'The …?'

'At school. That I was sacked for that.'

'Oh. Um. Actually, I was at Eton myself, a few years below you. So, you know, I heard it mentioned.' He looked a bit pink. 'I'm sorry. I know it's not pleasant to be gossiped about.'

'I had it coming. You were at Eton? Is that how you knew me?' Daizell couldn't remember if Cassian had mentioned it on their first meeting. He hadn't paid much attention.

'I was. Didn't I say? But it hardly matters: you wouldn't have noticed me.'

Probably not. Daizell's friends at school had been as loud and boisterous as himself and he hadn't troubled to acquaint himself with younger pupils. He might have thought the name would ring a bell, though, unusual as it was. Vernon Cassian … no, he could not for the life of him remember any such boy. He did, now he thought about it, have a vague memory of some undersized shrimp with a pale face whom he was meant to have noted for some reason or other. It tugged at his mind a moment, then he lost the thread.

But, as Cassian said, it hardly mattered. If he didn't want to tell Daizell things, he probably had good reason, and Daizell didn't intend to spoil the companionship they had with pushing where he wasn't invited.

A long day on horseback, a pleasant, tired evening afterwards. The White Swan was a comfortable inn, rather better than the kind of place Daizell normally stayed. He enjoyed feeling like a man of means, even if they weren't his means, and Cassian had lost his initial air of a visitor at the zoological gardens, and seemed very comfortable.

'Should we talk about what to do next?' Daizell said as they addressed an excellent veal and ham pie. 'I know we're declaring a holiday tomorrow, if you still want to do that.'

'I do. Afterwards …' He made a face at his plate. 'Do you think we've any hope? Really?'

'Of finding John Martin? Honestly, no.'

'Oh.'

'If he was more distinctive in appearance, or if we had been sooner on his track, we might have stood a chance. Or not lost so much time to the crash and then Miss Beaumont.'

'Those couldn't be helped.'

'Not much of it can be,' Daizell said. 'Including being robbed in the first place.'

Cassian gave an unhappy little laugh. 'On the contrary. That's the only part I could have controlled.'

'In retrospect, yes, just as I could have discovered that my parents were planning to commit a violent crime and abandon me. If either of us could see the future, we'd be a deal better off. As it is, sometimes things just don't go our way. Are you going to treat everyone as a possible thief now? I'm not going to treat everyone as if they're keeping some cursed great secret from me.'

Cassian's mouth dropped open. He looked like Daizell had slapped him for a second, the colour rushing to his face, then he said, 'Well, yes – no ... That is, I see what you mean, but one can't disavow responsibility. It was my duty to keep the ring safe, and I lost it.'

'You can take responsibility for that. You *have*. What you can't do is magic the thing back onto your finger by sufficient application of guilt.'

'If I could, I'd have retrieved it days ago.'

'I believe that. Look, I don't think we'll find the man, but there's a decent chance he pawned or sold the ring straight away, as we said at the start. And it's the ring you want, yes? So we take tomorrow to recover our energies, and then we retrace our steps to where we know he was, and try the pawn shops, and find out how one gets in touch with sellers of stolen property. We'll keep looking as long as you like. No stone unturned.'

'Yes,' Cassian said. 'Yes, that's a plan. Thank you, Daize. I don't know what I'd do without you.'

Daizell did his best not to glow. He very much liked the feeling of being useful, and knew a powerful desire to earn it by finding this blasted ring. 'I'm sure you'd manage, but I'm glad I can help.'

They smiled at each other across the food, warmth lighting Cassian's sun-and-rain eyes, and another bit of Daizell's fool heart slipped out of his control. Tonight was going to be agony.

Chapter Eight

This time, he woke up with Cassian not just in his arms, but between his legs.

Daizell had to take a moment. Cassian's nightshirt had ridden up, and Daizell was wrapped around him, arm over his chest, face in his shoulder, thigh over his hip, and prick – with a serious case of morning wood – pressed against his bare arse. At least the thin cloth of Daizell's nightgown was between them. He'd fucked people less intimately than this.

They hadn't, had they? He rapidly checked his memory but no: they had not drunk to excess, they had gone to bed in a perfectly decorous manner, and apparently they'd woken up spooning like lovers. Or, at least, Daizell was spooning, and Daizell had woken. Cassian was breathing lightly. If he was still asleep, Daizell might be able to peel himself off without the man feeling like he'd been violated in the night.

Daizell didn't know what the devil he was doing in his sleep these days. He knew himself to be tiresomely mobile and very prone to outflung arms, because he'd had plenty of complaints, but he'd never woken up in this sort of tangle with a bedmate of convenience, as evidenced by the fact that he still had all his teeth. He needed to do something about this. Unfortunately, he had a very good idea why his sleeping body wanted to wrap itself around Cassian, and a lowering suspicion that he'd need the co-operation of a waking body to mend matters.

This was not the time to consider that. He needed to extricate himself without disturbing Cassian, and he needed to do it prick first because nobody wanted to wake up to someone else's unsolicited erection. If he could somehow inch his hips back and away, this wouldn't be quite so disastrous.

He took a second to listen to Cassian's breathing, so that he could judge his movements. It was soft, shallow and even. Just like the other night. When they'd talked.

Oh Christ, he was awake.

Daizell's stomach plunged. What could he do now? Simply apologise? Treat it as a joke? Behave as though he thought Cassian was asleep, and they could pretend this hadn't happened? Pretend he'd just woken up himself, with a lot of yawning?

No, wait. If Cassian was awake, why was he just lying there? Was he panicking? He didn't feel as though he was panicking, and Daizell could feel a lot of him at this moment, much of it bare skin. He couldn't possibly—

Daizell called upon every bit of nerve he had. 'Cass?'

Silence. Then, quietly, 'Yes.'

'I, uh. I seem to be—'

'I know.'

'Would you like me to move?'

Another silence. Then, almost inaudibly, 'No.'

Daizell stared at the back of his neck, the curve where it met a slim shoulder. Cassian was warm and delightfully solid, and the word 'yielding' was in his mind now. 'Um. To be clear, do you want me not to move, as in "don't move away", or not to move as in "don't make any further advances"? Not that this was an advance, as such, I just woke up like this, but for the sake of clarity and also decency, or at least good behaviour – I'm going to stop talking, but which was it?'

'I think I've forgotten the question,' Cassian said, and there was a tremor in his voice that might have been nerves or laughter or both, and which was extremely emboldening, much like the very comfortable way Daizell's prick was fitting against his neat, firm arse.

'I could stay still,' Daizell said. 'Or I could get away from you. Or I could … neither stay still nor get away.'

'Don't get away.' Cassian's voice was a whisper, a charm. 'But if you don't want to stay still, I shouldn't want to make you.' He shifted back a touch as he spoke, pressing into Daizell, who took a moment to pray he wasn't dreaming. Cassian, in his arms, rubbing against him, sleepy and perfect. 'You do move around a lot.'

'I'm restive.' Daizell slid his leg along Cassian's thigh, just to see, and almost choked at the light touch of exploring fingers meeting his skin, moving delicately up. 'Oh God. Cass. Is this—?'

'This is perfect,' Cassian murmured. 'Just like this. Or …' He reached backwards and tugged at Daizell's nightshirt.

Daizell yanked it up, bunching the fabric above his waist, then shifted forward. That put them skin to skin, his prick explosively hard now. Cassian inhaled sharply, and breathed out with unmistakable relish. Daizell let his own hand drift downwards, across smooth chest and soft stomach, down to coarse curls, and then his questing fingers found what they sought, and he wrapped his hand around Cassian's stand with a pulse of intense satisfaction.

Cassian whimpered. 'Oh, yes. Daize. Could you—' He shifted a bit, up the bed, so that Daizell's stand was at the juncture of his thighs. That seemed an excellent idea. Daizell nudged his way in, prick trapped between Cassian's legs, hand around Cassian's cock, leg over all so that he had his bedmate cradled and held, and he could feel Cassian panting soundlessly. It was a remarkably motionless way to go about things, he vaguely thought, but on the other hand he was about three thrusts from exploding, and when he rubbed his thumb over the tip of Cassian's prick he could feel the viscous wetness of arousal.

Small movements, then. Just gentle pushes between those firm thighs, and pushing back with his fist as he did it, so he was stroking Cassian in time to his own thrusts, and Cassian was simply letting him, with nothing but those stuttering, whimpering breaths to signal his desires. Tiny pleading noises, his body in Daizell's hands, just as Daizell had wanted. Perfect.

'Cassian,' he whispered. 'Cass. God, you're lovely.'

Cassian's breath caught audibly and he gave a little moan. Daizell tightened the grip of both hand and leg, by instinct, holding him closer, and Cassian moaned again, in such a hopelessly wanton way that Daizell was doomed. He moved faster, no choice at all, frigging Cassian and using him to frig himself, the pair of them a mass of harsh breath and shuddering pleasure, and then Cassian gave a little cry like pain, and he was bucking in Daizell's grasp, spilling over his fist. Daizell thrust twice more between his legs, and spent in a quivering, sticky, joyful mess.

He slumped forward, face in Cassian's lovely shoulder. They lay together for a moment, breathing, Cassian nestled in Daizell's hold.

'I'm so glad you did that,' Cassian said eventually.

'Which part?'

'All of it, really, but did *something*. I didn't have the nerve.'

'*I* didn't have the nerve: I just woke up like this. Sorry about that,' he added.

'Why? It was a very nice way to wake up.'

'Eventually, yes, but I don't suppose you wanted to find me all over you when you were fast asleep.'

Cassian made a noncommittal noise. Daizell brushed a very light kiss to his neck, since it was within reach. 'Is this – just so I know – is this something we did once, or something we might do again?'

'Oh. Um. Is *again* a possibility?'

Daizell kissed his neck again, harder this time. 'I'd call it a likelihood. Left to myself, it would be a certainty.'

'*Oh.*' Cassian squirmed around at that, wriggling round to face him, rainswept eyes warm with sleep and pleasure, and Daizell kissed him.

He couldn't have helped it if he tried. Cassian looked so lovely, aroused and dishevelled and wanton and willing, and Daizell had wanted to kiss him for days, to find out if that expressive mouth worked as well by touch. He wanted Cassian as close as he could be, because when he was close the world was a warm, soothing, easy place. He wanted to show his enchanting but oddly uncertain bard that he was entirely enchanted.

There was a tiny moment as their lips met, a tiny stillness, long enough for Daizell to wonder if that hadn't been welcome after all, and then Cassian's arms snaked around him, gripping his head, pulling him in. His lips were hungry, and his mouth was unexpectedly fierce, and everything, just for now, was perfect.

The day was bright and sunny, which was nice. Daizell would have been just as happy in torrential rain, or a blizzard. He didn't care about weather: he cared about that slow, blissful coupling, and the long, languorous kissing that followed it, and then the second fuck, which had been a great deal more energetic than the first. Exceedingly energetic in fact: frantic rutting against one another, lips locked and hands on cocks, groping at hair and skin, gasping into one another's mouths so as not to be indiscreet.

They'd washed and dressed and breakfasted in a post-coital glow, and then they'd set off to see the sights of Stratford-upon-Avon.

It was at this point that Daizell would normally have protested. He had been obliged to watch a Shakespeare play once, for reasons he could not now remember, and it had been three or four, or subjectively eighteen, of the longest hours of his life. If he wanted to see people shout incomprehensibly at one another he'd go to the Continent, and the thought of being in the company of someone who talked about 'the Bard' or, even worse, 'the Swan of Avon' chilled his blood.

Luckily, Cassian showed no signs of doing that. Nor did he declaim swathes of poetry that didn't rhyme. He did however take Daizell to Holy Trinity church, where he'd already been to have the banns declared, only this time he was supposed to look at it.

Daizell had vaguely noticed the soaring arches and stained glass on his previous visit. Cassian wanted a great deal more detail than that. Luckily it turned out that ecclesiastical architecture was a deal more interesting when someone knew what he was looking at. Cassian showed him medieval tombs and explained what the animals and symbols meant and who the dead people were; he took him to a row of almost-seats where monks or choristers or whoever could rest their arses during mass, and they spent a highly entertaining twenty minutes examining the peculiar and sometimes bawdy carvings underneath and exchanging surreptitious remarks that left them both giggling like idiots. They had to see the Shakespeare family graves in front of the altar, of course, and a bust of the old fellow himself, looking like a pompous schoolteacher. Cassian contemplated it reverently and murmured something about dead shepherds which Daizell politely ignored, but redeemed himself by pointing out some strange carved faces with leaves instead of hair, high up where Daizell would never have noticed them, and identifying them as pagan images.

It was, in fact, the most interesting time he'd ever spent in a church, although the threshold for that was not high, and he said so as they strolled out through an avenue of trees.

'I'm glad,' Cassian said. He was glowing, bright with pleasure. 'I do love a good church. Thank you for coming with me.'

Daizell's tolerance for Shakespeare's birthplace was, perhaps, a little less, since it was a once-fine half-timbered house, now looking very mean. One half of it was an inn called the Swan and Maidenhead, for reasons he didn't want to ask, and it smelled like a brewery and a piggery at once. The half that remained a house was populated by aged dodderers who offered to show them Shakespeare's own chair, his cradle, his wife's cradle, his tragically lost son's cradle, his pipe, or whatever other tatty old rubbish they had to hand, and who were all ready to recount their great-grandfather's many stories from when he was the best of friends with the Bard. This was the sort of thing a gullible man, or an excessively polite one, could be caught in for hours.

Fortunately, though Cassian was exceedingly polite, he was clearly well versed in the darkest arts of courtesy, and slid through the grasping fingers of Shakespeare hawkers like a greased pig, leaving only smiles behind. He'd had a great deal of practice in deflecting the impertinent and importunate, Daizell thought, considering he was such an unassuming young man.

They also took a look at the New Place, which would have been the house where Shakespeare spent his last years and died, except that it wasn't there.

'I read about this. The last owner cut down a mulberry tree planted by Shakespeare's own hands,' Cassian explained. 'So the residents here threw stones at his windows and broke them. Then he sought the right to extend his garden, and that was refused and his taxes put up. Whereupon he felt so tired of Stratford and the Shakespeare industry that he demolished the house as an act of spite. That was just a few years ago. What a shame.'

Daizell whistled. 'If they broke his windows over a tree, how did destroying the house go down?'

'He was chased out of the town by irate locals.'

'Oof. Still, good for him.'

'It was an act of appalling vandalism and an insult to history. That said, I know what you mean,' Cassian admitted. 'It's all rather *much* here, isn't it? I feel as if expressing a preference for the plays of Christopher Marlowe might get me strung up in the public street. And all the relics – it's like those Catholic churches, you know, where if one put together all the fragments of John the Baptist, there would probably be enough for half a dozen complete skeletons. Still, I suppose the town doesn't have a great deal else to recommend it to visitors. Have you reached your limit of seeing the sights?'

'Not if there's anything else you want to see,' Daizell said, trying to make it sound convincing.

'Well, there's Anne Hathaway's cottage, which is a mile from here, but I believe it's a farm and I don't suppose they appreciate visitors.'

'I'd expect they welcome visitors with open arms, as long as they can sell you a clod of muck that Shakespeare trod on while he was writing *Hamlet*, price a mere five shillings.'

'Also possible,' Cassian said. 'Let's have something to eat instead.'

They made a light but pleasant luncheon. They strolled down to see the new canal, which offered the town a chance at Shakespeare-free prosperity that Daizell could only applaud, and walked along the River Avon, out into the surrounding countryside to enjoy the fresh air, shoulder to shoulder. Cassian talked about interesting churches he'd seen abroad and Daizell listened with fascination, because he'd listen with fascination to anything in that soft enchanter's voice.

They roamed, and watched swans on the canal, and sat together under trees. At one point Cassian put his hand over Daizell's, just a touch, and Daizell crooked his fingers to turn the touch to a hold. They sat there like that, hand in hand, quiet and intimate, and Daizell felt peace settle over his soul. He didn't ever want this day to end.

It seemed that Cassian felt an equal desire to have the most time they could, because he didn't suggest going back either, but at length, Daizell heard a church clock chime.

'Seven. Good Lord, how is it so late? We should go back.' Back to the inn, and the shared bed. If time insisted on passing, at least it meant that bed. 'It'll be dusk soon.'

He stood. Above, a couple of birds cawed, and flapped slowly away, black shapes against the purpling sky.

'Light thickens, and the crow makes wing to the rooky wood,' Cassian remarked.

'I beg your pardon?'

'*Macbeth*. Good things of day begin to droop and drowse, while night's black agents to their preys do rouse,' he added in sinister tones.

'At least it rhymes,' Daizell said, and they set off back.

They'd walked a reasonably long way out of the town, and it was well into twilight as they crossed the river. The bridge led towards a broad street with fine new buildings, more impressive than the street on which they were lodging, and the Warwick and Birmingham roads led off from around here. The area had been busy when they crossed it earlier in the day. Now, as the townsfolk retreated to their dinners and their pipes and their minding their own business, it was quite deserted, except for the group of three men who stood by the side of the road before it forked, talking. Two were facing the bridge, and they both glanced at Daizell and Cassian. The third didn't look round.

They were just standing there. With their coach. Not doing anything but standing and waiting.

'Cass?'

'Mmm?'

'Keep an eye on those men. If they come towards us ...' What he would like to say was, *Leave them to me*, or something equally brave and useful. What he had was, 'Run for the town. Don't wait for me.'

'What?'

Two of the men started walking, towards Daizell, mere shapes in the dim light. 'Just go. Don't try to interfere.' Cassian clearly wasn't a brawler, and there would probably be sticks.

'What's wrong? Do you mean them? Oh good God, you don't think it's Sir James's men?'

'I expect so,' Daizell said grimly. 'Pull your hat down, hide your face. We don't need them getting a look at you. And stay back now ... Sir.' That was to the man approaching them. 'Stand off. If you have something to say, you can say it from there.'

'Mr Daizell Charnage?' It wasn't really a question.

'Himself. Kindly state your business.'

The man was large, and now Daizell saw him close up, he was familiar despite the dusk. One of Vier's men, and he was carrying a stick – more a club, really – which he pointed at Daizell. 'You've got in the master's way before. You won't do it again. Hand her over, and the wedding licence, and then piss off out of my sight or I'll break both your legs.'

At least he made himself clear. 'If you mean Miss Beaumont, I don't have her to hand over,' Daizell said. 'She left Stratford yesterday. I have no idea where she went.'

'You think I'm stupid?' the lout demanded. 'You going to lie to me like I'm a fool?'

'She's long gone,' Daizell repeated. 'You can ask at the inn where I'm staying: I'll happily take you there. No lady.'

The man shook his head, in sorrowful acknowledgement of human failings. Then he drove the butt of his stick into Daizell's stomach.

He didn't see it coming fast enough. The blow knocked the air out of him to sickening effect and he went over, down to the ground, knowing his head and neck and back were now horribly vulnerable to blows and kicks, but unable to do anything except gasp fruitlessly for breath. There was a flurry of violent motion above him, with a cry cut off, and then a boot landed hard in his side. Daizell curled round the pain, trying to brace himself against more.

It didn't come. There was more scuffling, but the sound was retreating. Daizell uncurled cautiously and saw the coach across the roadway, the driver standing waiting, two men dragging a third, oddly shaped figure with them. It took him a moment to realise the third had a blanket over his head.

'Cass?' he croaked.

Vier's men started bundling Cassian into the coach. He wasn't making it easy, although he was muffled in cloth: he was kicking and struggling, but there were two of them and they were big. Daizell forced himself to his feet, side and belly aching, and made himself run. It was more of a stagger, with one arm round his painful side. 'Hey!' he shouted.

The coach door slammed. The driver cracked his whip. The coach rattled off with Cassian inside, and Daizell stood staring uselessly after it.

Chapter Nine

Cassian had no idea what was going on, but it was terrifying.

Being confronted by large men in gathering darkness had been alarming, but he'd told himself Daizell would talk their way out of it. After all, they *didn't* have Miss Beaumont: they could prove it. He hadn't expected the sudden, frightening violence that doubled Daizell over, and he really hadn't expected what happened next.

As far as he could tell, someone had thrown a blanket over his head, because he'd found himself enveloped in scratchy, close, dusty darkness and hauled off with a brutal grip on his arm. He'd shouted and struggled, but someone had got a hard hand over his mouth, pushing the sacking against his lips, and then he'd been fighting an enemy he couldn't see, far stronger than himself, with no idea what they were doing or what had happened to Daizell.

And now he was sprawling on the floor of a coach, and it was moving.

A hand closed on his arm, hauling him up to the seat. 'Sit there and shut up,' growled the man who'd hit Daizell. 'Damned nuisance. Caught me on the bloody jaw.'

'What are you—' Cassian began, high-pitched with fear and indignation, and was cut off by a hand grabbing at his throat.

'I said, shut up,' the man growled. 'Little bitch. Serve you right if we treated you like your sort deserves. Keep your mouth shut now or I'll take my belt to you.'

Cassian's jaw dropped under the sacking. He had never in his life been spoken to in such a way and the urge to demand *Do you know who I am?* could only be held back by the fear that the brute might find out. He didn't speak. After a couple of seconds, the hand at his throat released its grip, dragged roughly and deliberately down over his chest, and moved off.

Little bitch. Your sort. Cassian didn't like the sound of that at all, and the fear was unfamiliar and sickening. Had he and Daizell been seen holding hands, or caught in a betraying look?

He knew very well his predilections were dangerous. They got other men in bad, sometimes fatal trouble, brought them disgrace or shame even if the cruel law wasn't involved. He'd always been excruciatingly, soul-sappingly discreet himself. And yet, if the Duke were caught with a man, the consequences would all be to his self-esteem: humiliation, widespread gossip, his family's opinions. Those were bad enough, but nobody would assault him, gaol him, pillory him. He was safe from all that because he was Severn.

Right now, he was only Cassian, and he was terrified.

He made himself breathe and think. These were Vier's henchmen, out to retrieve Miss Beaumont. If they'd taken Cassian, it was surely because they thought he could lead them to the runaway heiress. The odds were that the insults were just casual ones, aimed at his unimposing physique. He hoped to God that was the case.

Why had they kidnapped him rather than Daizell, though? It made no sense. Unless, of course, someone had recognised him.

That was a grim thought. If Sir James intended to accuse the Duke of Severn of abducting an underage heiress, things might well become difficult. And if everything had gone wrong and the vengeful Vier found out about the Duke and Daizell…

There was no point frightening himself with possibilities. Probably he'd been taken as Daizell's companion and the easier target, and all would be resolved when he explained he had no idea where Miss Beaumont was. Until he had an opportunity to do so, he ought not to make bad worse by thinking. He was a duke even if disguised, and thus untouchable, he told himself, though the blanket over his head was rasping his skin and its dust made his throat tickle, and he was unpleasantly aware of the two large men sitting at his sides.

He'd find out what was going on soon enough; in the meantime, he would not attempt to struggle against a pair of bravos in a small space. Instead, he bent his mind to considering where they might be going. He had a good innate sense of direction, and had pored over *Paterson's British Itinerary* in his plod around the staging-posts outside Stratford. Between that and the reasonable road surface, he was fairly sure they were heading up the Warwick Road.

They weren't long on it, turning off to the east on to what was clearly a wretched track. The coach jolted and jerked as it rattled along, and Cassian pressed his lips together under the cover of the blanket, and clenched his fists against the consuming fear. He wished Daizell were here, with that casually kind hand pressed to his knee, offering comfort unsought and unquestioning. He set his mind to that touch, and then to the other touches of their glorious morning, which now felt a very long time ago, and managed to keep his feelings of alarm to a manageable level until the coach stopped.

'Right. Get out. Mind those dainty feet.'

Cassian found himself half-lifted out. He stumbled along, pushed by unseen hands into a building. There were murmurs of speech, then sounds of appalled protest in a female voice, to which Cassian's captor growled, 'Shut your mouth. I want the back room key.' He let go of Cassian's arm as he spoke.

'But that's not—'

'I know what I'm doing, jade! The key, I say.'

Now he was on his feet, out of the coach, and in the presence of a witness, Cassian felt able to act. He pulled the horrible blanket off, and blinked in what briefly seemed bright light.

He was in a rather mean house; if it was an inn, it wasn't much frequented. The ceilings were low and it was lit with tallow candles. He could see his captors, and a thin-faced woman in a drab dress, and a brutish-looking man behind her. They were all gaping at him.

He'd have liked to announce, *This is an outrage!*, but they already knew that. 'What is this? Who are you people? What reason do you have for this abduction?' No answers. Everyone was still gaping. Cassian put his hands on his hips and Lord Hugo into his voice. 'Well? I demand an explanation!'

The second bravo swallowed. 'Jim. That ain't Miss Beaumont.'

'I fucking know that,' said the leader in a voice that promised retribution. 'I can see.'

'Well, why did you—'

'*Now* I can see.'

'Miss Beaumont?' Cassian repeated. It had taken him a moment to regain his breath. 'Miss— You mistook me for a *woman*?' Outrage warred with a wholly inappropriate desire to laugh. 'Great God, are you mad?'

'He's in breeches,' the woman observed, in a general, abstract sort of way. 'Not skirts.'

The leader turned on her savagely. 'They said she'd be dressed as a bloke, and with that fucker Charnage!'

Cassian took that in with some resentment. Granted he was on the shorter and slimmer side, and Miss Beaumont was a strapping young lady, and it had been dark, but even so. And, he now realised, that put the interaction in the coach in a new light. *Serve you right if we treated you like your sort deserves. Keep your mouth shut now or I'll take my belt to you.* And the hand that had dragged, he'd thought deliberately, over his chest, as padded by coat and blanket…

These were the men Sir James Vier had sent after a young woman, and righteous fury exploded through him.

'If you cannot use your eyes, the more fool you,' he said crisply. 'You have made a very bad mistake, and I will ensure Sir James hears of this. You will return me to Stratford right away, if you wish me to consider treating this as an error rather than a criminal act. At once!'

The guilty looks that shot between the Second Bravo and the woman made him think, for a second, that he'd have his way. Then the First Bravo shook his head. 'No.'

'Jim…'

'No, I say. He was with Charnage. Charnage took out a marriage licence. He knows where she is.'

'I know no such thing, and nor does Mr Charnage. Miss Beaumont left Stratford two days hence. You have lost her trail, and a good thing too, if this is how you treat a lady. Now get me back to Stratford!'

The First Bravo's jaw was grinding. 'We'll get Charnage. They're at the White Swan. We'll go in the morning and make him tell us where she is. And we'll keep this one till then. Can't have you warn him.'

'Take me back immediately!' Cassian said furiously. 'How dare you detain me like this! This is kidnapping and I will have the law on you!'

'Ah, shut up,' the First Bravo said, and dragged His Grace the Duke of Severn into a dirty, dark back room by the arm. He was shoved in, so that he stumbled and almost fell.

'Keep your gob shut,' the First Bravo advised him. 'Nobody round here to hear you, and you'll just rile me. Be a good boy and we'll bring you something to eat and a pot to piss in.' The door banged shut behind him, leaving Cassian in the dark.

He turned around, angry, astonished, and undeniably afraid. Vier's brutes were lawless to an alarming degree, and he had probably been foolish to make threats he was in no position to carry out. Once he was restored to his position he would bring the full might of his dukedom down on Sir James, he promised himself, but in the meantime …

In the meantime, he was locked in a room, and Daizell was probably back at the White Swan, where these bullies would arrive the next morning, determined to beat answers out of him that he wouldn't be able to give. Daizell's insistence that Miss Beaumont didn't say where she was going now seemed at once a wise precaution and a ghastly mistake.

Where was he? Not in a town: it was entirely quiet out here. They'd turned left off the Warwick Road, and from the distance, Cassian decided they were somewhere in the depths of Warwickshire, perhaps in the region of Hampton Lucy. The irony was biting: he knew the Lucy family of Charlecote Park, which was probably within a couple of miles of here, and had even stayed in their grand Elizabethan home. If he could get out, he could seek assistance there.

That would, of course, mean turning up with a dirty face and dusty hair, saying he'd been kidnapped, and demanding their assistance to come to Daizell Charnage's rescue. He'd deal with that when he had to. For now, he could not simply stand here feeling outraged. He needed to think of something to do.

He hadn't got anywhere on that a few minutes later, when the door opened again. The First Bravo entered. The woman followed with a chamber pot and a blanket, then went out again and returned with a plate and a mug.

'Food and drink,' the First Bravo said. 'Keep behaving and you can go tomorrow morning, no harm done.'

'Will you at least leave the candle?' Cassian said. 'There are rats in here!'

'No such thing,' the woman said with offence. 'Mice, only mice. We can spare it, Jim.'

'For a fee,' the bravo said. 'Board, lodging, and light. Let's have you.'

He held Cassian efficiently while the woman slipped her hand into his inside pocket. They both gaped at what she pulled out.

'Jim,' the woman said. 'It's banknotes. He's got *thirty pound*. Jim, I don't like it. Who is he?'

'He's the man who had thirty quid that's mine now. So shut up. See if he's got more.'

'More?' Cassian demanded. 'You have my money, damn you, do you want my fob-watch too?'

The First Bravo gave him a sardonic look, and reached for his fob-pocket, extracting the watch. The timepiece and its chain were the plainest the Duke possessed; as Jim took them out and the gold gleamed in the dim light, the woman gave a little gasp. 'We could hang for this!' she said shrilly.

'And for kidnapping,' Cassian said, and regretted it as they both looked at him. 'Let me go and I won't tell anyone. You can keep the money for your trouble, hmm? Nobody needs to know anything.'

'Jim . . .' the woman said, pleading.

The First Bravo hesitated, then shook his head. 'In the morning. After we've had our word with Charnage and found the bitch, we'll let you go, and you can have your watch back too if you're a good boy. No more talk.' He put the candlestick on a high shelf, and they both left.

Cassian reflected sourly on that interaction as he ate excessively strong cheese and tough bread, washed down with sour ale. If he'd been a heroic Corinthian sort, he could have fought his way out. That was not an option, because he was a shrimp of a man who could be mistaken for a runaway lady, if only in bad light.

He thought about his lack of broad shoulders for a moment, then stood.

There was one small window, a single square pane of dirty glass. It was high up in the wall but the walls weren't that high, and he found a broken box to balance on. The window was far too narrow for anyone to worry about people climbing through, and it was just a pane of glass, with no opening mechanism. Cassian contemplated it for a few moments. Then he took a moment to utter a prayer, and put a hand in his coat pocket.

The watch had distracted them from checking his other pockets. So they hadn't taken his knife.

One of the most striking aspects of Daizell's heroics on the day of the crash had been the casually competent way he'd pulled out a clasp knife. The Duke of Severn had never carried such a thing on his person: he had servants for that. Cassian had bought himself a clasp knife in Stratford, indulging a fantasy of being the kind of man who might produce one in an emergency. He hadn't lost it in the evening's proceedings, and now here he was.

The window was secured with thick putty, brittle with age. It took a very little effort to work the blade around the edges, and after some moments of manipulation, the pane shifted. He eased it forward, because if it fell and smashed he'd be in trouble, and put it carefully on the ground. He was left with a very uninviting opening that most people would say a grown man, even a slender one, would have no hope of getting through.

Most people hadn't grown up in a castle. Staplow was exceedingly well provided with narrow windows, and the Duke and his cousins – Leo, Matthew, and their sister Louisa – had spent a lot of time experimenting. You could get through most apertures, they had found, if your head and one arm fit.

He went to the door and listened, but heard nothing. He finished the sour ale and made use of the chamber pot. He put the knife securely in his pocket, and then he balanced on the broken box, and jumped.

He caught the window sill with his elbow first time. That was good, but getting the rest of himself up there was harder. He hadn't done this in some years, and there wasn't space to get both hands in place and heave. He had to scrabble against the wall with his feet in a frantic, undignified way, trying to make as little noise as possible. He slipped back to the ground, and glared at the wall.

He could do this. He had to.

The window aperture was not wide. He took off his coat, bundled it up, and threw it through the window, both to narrow his width and to force himself to persist. Then he jumped and scrabbled again, and got the edge of his ribs up, and then it was a matter of twisting sideways, thrashing like a landed salmon to propel himself, working his leading arm out and pulling his other arm through in angular sections, clamped against his chest. It was damned tight. If they caught him like this, arse hanging out of the window and feet fruitlessly waving, wouldn't they laugh.

That thought gave him the push he needed. He gave one more tight squirm, arm wedged against his chest, and then his second arm was through.

Now he just needed to get down to the ground without falling on his head. He pulled himself through sideways, getting his backside on the sill, folding a leg to get his foot up, and managed to hold on to a beam and work his way out to the point he could jump down.

He hit the ground with a thump that sounded very loud in the quiet of the night and stood a second holding his breath, ears straining. Nothing.

He was out. What now?

He could run, or more likely walk, but they'd come several miles. The moon was up now and three-quarters full, which helped but it would still be a nightmarish journey through dark fields and woods with no idea where he was going or what he was stepping in. Or he could stick to the road back, but then a man on a horse would catch him easily.

Of course, if he were the man on the horse …

He contemplated that a moment, then he retrieved his coat and crept silently round the outside of the house, looking for where the horses were stabled.

They were in an outbuilding. Cassian groped at shoulder height and found, as he'd hoped, a tinder box and lamp. He lit the lamp, hands shaking a little from nerves.

The building looked as though it had been used as a stables before, but not recently. It was dirty and dusty, and the straw for the two carriage horses looked sadly in need of refreshing. They both looked up at him, and one whickered.

'Shhh now. Quiet, beauty,' he murmured, approaching with slow confidence. 'Come now, my lovelies …'

They were the usual hired beasts, weary job-horses without spirit, but at least they weren't inclined to make a fuss, and Cassian invested a couple of minutes he didn't want to spare in making friends. The tack hanging up was old and stiff but it would do. He saddled the horse that seemed more amenable, keeping his movements calming and his voice soothing. He put the second on a leading rein, using a length of rope that hung on a hook. Then he poked his head out of the door.

Nothing. Nobody.

'Come on, beauties,' he told the horses softly. 'We're going to find Daize.'

He led them out, praying they wouldn't neigh, wishing he could muffle the hoofs as he'd read smugglers did. The shutters of the building were all closed. His heart was thundering. If they caught him now …

He got the horses to the road. Walked them a little way, both to avoid noise and because he had no idea how his chosen steed would react to a rider, trying not to let his tension show in his movements. Then he whispered a few endearments, and swung himself up onto the carriage horse's back.

The beast took it placidly: it seemed he'd been ridden before. Cassian clapped his heels to the horse's sides, and they jogged off into the night, leaving his prison behind.

He'd have liked to gallop, but that would be insanity on such a bad road, in the dark, on an unfamiliar beast, and with a second horse in tow to boot. He did, however, urge the horses to a trot, because his back was prickling and his ears straining for pursuit. None came, and as the slow minutes passed and he got further away, he was able to believe it wouldn't come.

He'd done it. He had actually *escaped,* from *kidnappers*, all by himself. Leo was going to choke. Cassian rode on, skin tingling with the sheer magnificence of this exploit, wanting to whoop at the moon. He had looked after himself in the teeth of some thoroughly alarming opposition, and he had not needed Lord Hugo or his valet or Daizell or anybody. He—

There was someone coming. A horse, approaching him, along the road.

Cassian's mood of infallible competence evaporated on the instant. It could be just a late traveller, but that person would be able to tell his captors he'd seen a rider with two horses, and if it was a third bravo, or even Sir James Vier himself—

It would not be Sir James. But in the unlikely event it was, Cassian was going to make him regret he'd ever been born, somehow. He would, however, feel a lot more confident doing that in a drawing room or a lawyer's office than on an empty country lane in the darkness.

It was too late for him to dive off the road behind a tree

or some such: the lane was straight and the other rider could surely see him, and he'd only attract more attention by trying to hide now. He'd just have to urge the tired horses to speed if need be, although riding *ventre à terre* in the moonlight seemed a terrible idea.

Cassian squared his shoulders, trying to look unmemorable, though he was aware he'd lost his hat at some point. The other rider seemed to be hatless as well, he noticed, and as his horse plodded closer, the moon glinted silver off curls that looked, somehow, as though they might be copper and gold.

'Daize?' he yelped.

Daizell glanced at him, looked away, swung back around, and almost fell off his horse. '*Cass?* Cass!'

'Daize.' Cassian was gaping like a fish. He rode up as Daizell pulled his horse, a big rawboned brute, to a halt. 'What the devil? How are you here?'

'I came after you. How are *you* here?'

'I escaped. They shut me in a room, the swine, and I forced the window and got out, and stole their horses—'

'I stole *this* horse!'

Daizell stared at Cassian. Cassian stared at Daizell. They both started laughing, incredulous and bubbly with relief. 'Mother of God, Cass. Are you all right? What on earth did those brutes want with you?'

'I'll tell you on the way. I haven't come very far and they might be after me.'

'Hell. Then you should go without me. This damned slug is barely moving.'

'He looks tired,' Cassian said rebukingly. 'Poor old boy. And I don't think they're on my tail precisely, since I have both their horses. These two are in better condition: do you want to change?'

'Very much,' Daizell said. 'This is about the worst horse I could have stolen, but there wasn't a choice.'

'You stole a horse,' Cassian repeated as they both dismounted, the meaning of that belatedly sinking in. 'Really stole? From the owner?'

'Well, he'd put the reins over a post while he stopped for a piss, and I didn't have time to ask for the loan, so, yes. Just at the start of the Warwick Road. It was that or run after you, and I don't think my legs are up to that.'

'We'd better bring it back then,' Cassian said a little dizzily.

'I dare say. Cass?'

Cassian had gone to take the bridle off the stolen horse, to put it on the other stolen horse, because he was a horse thief now. 'Mmm?'

Daizell slid a hand over his shoulder, up to the back of his head. He leaned in, and Cassian looked up in wonder, and then they were kissing, on the open road, under the moon. Daizell's mouth hot on his, Daizell's fingers digging into his hip.

He hadn't gone back to the inn. He'd come after him, and actually stolen an actual horse to do it, and for all that was a remarkably irresponsible act, it made Cassian's insides melt like honey in the sun. Kissing, open-mouthed and desperate and gleeful, under the night sky, while escaping kidnap. Cassian had never felt less like a duke, or more like himself.

Daizell pulled him close with a grunt, and Cassian buried his face in the sturdy shoulder. 'Lord, Cass. I was quite alarmed.'

'So was I,' Cassian said, muffled. 'They weren't pleasant.

And I need to tell you about it, but, Daize, they know where we're staying.'

'In Stratford? Hell's teeth. Right, let's get moving. We'll work something out on the way back.'

They rode back to Stratford – it was only another three miles – with the extra stolen horse plodding alongside more happily for not bearing its burden. For its sake, and because Cassian didn't trust the road, they kept to a gentle trot, and were approaching Stratford within half an hour. Cassian heard the church clock chime, and realised he'd quite lost track.

'What time is it, do you have any idea?'

'Half past nine, I think,' Daizell said. 'We should still be—'

'You!' It was an enraged bellow. 'You, sir! That's my damned horse!'

An elderly man, bewigged and of portly habit, was waving an angry stick in their direction. Daizell said, 'Uh-oh.'

'Surely we need only apologise?' Cassian murmured, hoping that was true. Was it still theft if you gave the loot back? 'And compensate him, of course. I'm happy to—'

Daizell was already leaning down to speak to the man as he approached, along with someone who looked very like a town constable. 'The grey? Is that yours? Can you prove it?'

'I *beg* your pardon, sir?'

'We found it wandering on the Warwick Road,' Daizell informed him, apparently without shame. 'We thought it would be best to bring the beast back with us. If it's yours, that saves us the effort of finding the owner.'

'That's Mr Bezant's grey all right,' the constable put in, in a heavy Warwickshire accent.

'Then all is well,' Daizell said. 'Good evening.'

'What? Wait! You're the fellow who took him!' It was hard

to say with only the light of the constable's lantern, but Mr Bezant's rubicund face seemed to be getting redder.

'I certainly am not, sir. I have ridden with my friend back from ...' Daizell waved vaguely to indicate the road.

'Hampton Lucy,' said someone in possession of Cassian's voice, albeit a somewhat strangled version. 'Just now. Visiting friends,' he added, since one might as well be hung for a sheep as a lamb. Or a horse. 'I'm delighted we can restore your property to you, sir.'

'I say that this fellow stole my horse,' Mr Bezant repeated obstinately. 'And where's his bridle?'

'I really could not say,' Daizell told him, in a witheringly superior tone. 'You have your beast; pray do not trouble to thank us for the effort involved in catching and returning him. We are quite at your service for any other small duties your convenience may require, but I really cannot be blamed for your carelessness in losing him in the first place. Good evening to you.' He set his heels to the horse as he spoke, and Cassian urged his own steed to catch up.

'Is that going to work?' he asked as they rode down the High Street.

'Doesn't matter. We'll be out of this town first thing tomorrow, and not before time. You go in and settle up – and pack, too. I'll find us somewhere to stay. If I take the horses—'

Cassian was not going to ride out of Stratford on a stolen horse, no matter how justified the theft had been at the time. 'I'll have them stabled here,' he said firmly.

He otherwise followed instructions, explaining to the landlord of the White Swan that they intended to leave very early in the morning, and paying their shot accordingly. He also paid for the horses to be stabled and fed for two days, saying that Sir James Vier's men would collect them. He'd have preferred to leave Sir James with the reckoning, but the animals' welfare was more important: they had done him good service.

That done, he packed his things and, feeling a little intrusive, Daizell's. Daizell didn't have much. A few changes of linen, another suit of clothing, the third volume of *The Antiquary*. A satchel which contained his cutting things: paper, card, paste, scissors.

Was that really everything? Did he not have a home somewhere, more possessions, more evidence of his life in the world?

Daizell came in as Cassian was checking the cupboards. 'We have a room at the Bull and Mouth, which is the coaching inn for Birmingham. I suggest we take the back way out of here so nobody knows we've left.'

'Is there a back way?'

'There's always a back way,' Daizell said, with the confidence of a man who used them frequently.

Cassian nodded. 'I think I have everything of yours?'

Daizell gave the bag a cursory glance. 'Looks about right.'

'Is that everything you have?'

Daizell shrugged and took his bag. Cassian followed, uncomfortably aware of Staplow, with its rooms full of furniture and wardrobes full of clothes, and a family who lived there, all of it waiting for when he chose to come home.

Daizell was a hanger-on, eternally a guest at someone else's table; Cassian owned the table. They usually had half a dozen people living off Staplow at any given time: impecunious artists, amusing younger sons, spinster friends of Aunt Hilda, aspiring scientific minds, foreign travellers, temporarily embarrassed politicians. They'd once had a poet stay for three months, reciting his verse every evening, and only when Lord Hugo insisted they get shot of the blasted man before he resorted to violence did the Crosses discover that none of them had actually invited the fellow: he'd simply turned up.

He wondered what might happen if Daizell turned up at Staplow.

Chapter Ten

Cassian once again woke with Daizell wrapped around him.

He lay there, quivering with the awareness, feeling Daizell's breath on his neck and the weight of his arm. The wanting was overwhelming.

He'd never woken up with anyone in his life before this trip. He'd always had his own space, in bedrooms and in carriages and hotels and everywhere else lesser mortals were expected to crowd together. A ball or rout might be a sad crush, but nobody jostled the Duke; when he travelled, crowds parted before him or, more precisely, before the people whose job it was to make the crowd part. He'd never asked anyone to get out of his way and leave him untouched; he'd never had to, since inviolability was one of the privileges of his position. The Duke of Severn was a man apart.

Cassian was a man with a handsome lover draped over him in bed, warm and intimate, and for all that they had an urgent need to leave Stratford, he gave himself a moment to luxuriate in the feeling.

Just one moment, though. 'Daize?' He shook his companion until he got a grunt. 'We have to go.'

'Oh, God,' Daizell muttered. 'I suppose we do.'

They really did, Cassian reflected as he dressed. There was the outraged Mr Bezant, for one. Cassian hoped he would count his blessings at being reunited with his horse, or, failing that, would be unable to track them down, but Daizell had unquestionably committed a serious offence. Then there were Sir James's men. He doubted they'd risk making a complaint of horse theft under the circumstances, but they now had a grudge against Cassian to go with the one against Daizell. He had a feeling the First Bravo in particular would be keen to avenge his humiliation at kidnapping the wrong person and then losing him, not to mention he'd have a long and tedious walk into Stratford, and a deal of explaining to do to his master if he failed to find Miss Beaumont. Vier's men had been both more violent and more ruthless than Cassian had anticipated, and he had to remind himself very consciously that it was good they were following Daizell. Every day Vier's men spent chasing him was a day for Miss Beaumont's track to grow colder, and Cassian knew first hand how easy it was to lose track of somebody.

'Where will we go?' he asked Daizell. 'Back to Worcester?'

'But not by the same route. There should be more coaches to Birmingham and we can shake off any pursuit there much more easily.'

That seemed an excellent plan. Cassian followed him down, and ordered breakfast while Daizell took seats on the first coach. That was scheduled to depart a half-hour hence, which gave them time for a substantial meal of eggs and bacon and a pot of adequate coffee. He was wondering about a second cup of the latter when Daizell said, 'Shit!'

Very few people had ever sworn in front of the Duke of Severn. Cassian tried not to show shock. 'What is it?'

'One of Vier's men. The big brute with the horsewhip. Outside.'

'You're joking.' Cassian fought the urge to duck under the table. 'The fellow from last night?'

'No, a different one. Appalling lout.'

'Is he coming in?'

'Don't know. He went past.' Daizell looked decidedly alarmed, as well he might. 'Hell's teeth. He'll spot me at once.'

'He's got no grounds to accost either of us,' Cassian said with more hope than certainty.

'Don't be a fool. He's Vier's man, looking for a runaway ward and I took out a marriage licence with her. And if he's talked to the men you met last night...We need to get in the coach and away without being seen, or we'll have to come up with a *lot* of explanations.'

Cassian considered the many explanations that might be required of them both, in the matters of horse theft, young ladies, and identity. 'We do, yes. How—' He cut himself off.

He had been going to say, *How will we do it?* from sheer force of habit. He didn't want to. Cassian had very much liked being the kind of man who extricated himself neatly from a tricky situation; he'd recounted the tale to Daizell before they'd gone to sleep, and basked in his admiration because he'd earned it.

Daizell had heard the question, for all he'd tried to stifle it. 'I don't know. He doesn't know you, so I suppose you could get on the coach and I can try to dodge him?'

'Don't be absurd. Here.' Cassian pushed coins across the table. 'Pay our shot while I see what's going on outside.'

He stuck his head out of the door, rebuking himself for the fluttering in his stomach. Really his nerves were nonsensical, the fears quite overblown—

No, wait. The man was terrifying.

He wasn't tall but he was thick-muscled and brutish, with a malevolent expression and piggy eyes. He couldn't help his face, of course: he might have the pure soul of a gentle saint under the menacing exterior. Cassian wouldn't have put money on it, what with the scarred knuckles and the billy club he held loosely in one hand.

Cassian slipped out, walking past him in a carefully nonchalant manner, skin prickling with the anticipation of a shout, or even an attack. It didn't come: the brute ignored him. Thankful for his insignificance, he strolled around the yard, wondering what he could do. The stage was due to leave in seven minutes by the yard clock. He wasn't sure he could distract the fellow, who was presumably standing watch for Daizell here, for that long or at all. And if Vier's other men were on their way, they'd recognise them both. He and Daizell were in real trouble, and he wasn't sure his name would protect them, or not nearly soon enough to avoid arrest, perhaps a beating. His pulse thudded unpleasantly.

A small fuss was happening at the entrance to the yard. Cassian glanced over and his heart plummeted even further. It was the man from last night, Mr Bezant, rubicund of face and ruffled of manner, expostulating with one of the ostlers. He had someone who looked like a constable by his side. Clearly, he was not taking yesternight in his stride.

This was a nightmare. If they were trapped between the man whose horse Daizell had stolen and the men whose horses Cassian had stolen, they'd never get out of here.

Mr Bezant looked around at that moment, saw Cassian, and called, 'Hey! You!'

Inspiration struck like a falling apple to the skull. Cassian didn't stop to think it through; he just strode up. 'Ah, Mr Bezant, wasn't it? Excellent. I was about to write a note for you.'

Mr Bezant looked nonplussed, but made a recovery. 'I

want you, sir. Your companion stole my horse last night, I am sure of it.'

'He did not,' Cassian said. 'We spent the day together, rode up to Hampton Lucy in the evening, and found your horse astray on our return. As you say, it was night, and you cannot be blamed for poor eyesight with your distinguished years.'

'My eyesight is *not*—'

Cassian barrelled on over him just as Lord Hugo might, wincing internally at his own rudeness. 'But I think if you look around, you will see where you made your error.'

'Look? Where?'

'That surly, disreputable fellow on the other side of the inn. He is much my friend's height, if rather more thickset. Easily mistaken in the dark. And I just heard him say, "We lost that horse last night".' He gave Mr Bezant a meaningful look. 'Of course, he might have been referring to another lost horse, but . . . Well, it is your concern, and it is up to you to decide if you want to question him further. After all, my friend and I found your horse and returned him to your possession, so you might very well think it ill-judged to confront such a fellow. Discretion is the better part of valour, after all.'

Mr Bezant swelled like a bullfrog, shouldered Cassian to the side, and marched over to Vier's henchman, visibly bristling. By the time Cassian had got to the stagecoach, Mr Bezant was poking a finger at the man, and Daizell was slithering out of the inn door behind the brute, with all their bags in hand.

Cassian grabbed them. 'Get in the coach, get *in*.'

Daizell nipped around the other side of the coach with haste. Cassian threw their bags in with the other luggage, and got in, to see Daizell had kept him the corner seat again.

Cassian made a mental note to swap with him on the next stage.

They both waited breathlessly. The stage should surely be leaving now? Daizell's fingers tapped lightly but relentlessly on his knee. Cassian heard angry voices raised outside, and a demand of 'Where is the fellow?' that clashed with the driver's bellow. Someone rattled at the door, and an ostler shouted. The stage jolted into motion, and they were off.

Cassian sagged back against the seat, weak with relief. Daizell leaned over and murmured in his ear, 'You're a genius. What did you do?'

'Tell you later.'

'You're a genius,' Daizell repeated, and Cassian glowed quietly as the coach rocked its uncomfortable way towards Birmingham.

It would be three stages to get there. The inside of the coach was full, and they couldn't talk about anything they didn't want overheard. Cassian did comment, at the first stop, 'Will they come after us?'

'Almost certainly,' Daizell said. 'But we've a head start and we can disappear into the town easily enough. We get out at the centre, and we walk some way, and I think we both need to buy new hats so as not to attract attention.'

'Your hair is memorable,' Cassian agreed, and liked the grin that won him.

They rumbled on towards Birmingham. Cassian realised with mild surprise that he was no longer particularly troubled by the jolting, the distressing proximity to his fellow men, the noise, the smell, or even the prospect of another accident, which had faded in his mind to the point he could make himself discount it. He still felt like his backside had been cudgelled and that his fellow passengers were a blight on the earth, but only in a general sort of way rather than as a matter of sharp distress. He was becoming used to the stage, and that pleased him.

Birmingham was huge. Cassian was used to London; he was not used to towns that approached London in size, or density, or grime. It had an encouraging bustle about it though, and some gracious, recently built streets indicated prosperity. He had never visited an industrial town before and he looked out of the window, intrigued, hearing the hammer and clatter of factories over the sound of their wheels. He eavesdropped shamelessly on the only intermittently comprehensible conversation of the other passengers, one an iron merchant, the other a maker of buttons and buckles, and wondered if he might find out more of this alarmingly modern world. He had an urge to see how it worked.

That was for later, when he was the Duke of Severn once more. For now, he needed to disappear into Birmingham with Daizell, and then disappear right out of it again to head back to where they started.

'What are you grinning about?' Daizell asked him.

'It occurred to me that, from some perspectives, our travels might look like an exercise in futility.'

'Well, that's my life,' Daizell remarked, but when Cassian looked around at him, he was wearing his usual smile.

They jumped off the coach in the centre of Birmingham. The air was thick with the odours of industry, metal and slag and some very sharp, unpleasant scents. It felt dirty, and caught in Cassian's throat. Daizell wrinkled his nose but didn't comment.

'Now what?' Cassian asked.

'Let's head off.'

'Do you know the town?'

'Not at all. I suggest we plunge in, and start asking directions when we're well and truly lost. If we don't know where we're going, how will anyone else be able to follow us?'

That struck Cassian as unassailable logic, and he set off happily into the elegant new streets. They passed any amount of shops selling Brummagem-ware, although Cassian rather thought he wouldn't use that disparaging term within earshot of any local, and found a very acceptable hatter who returned them both to respectability. They bought pastries on the street that were apparently called fitched pies, whatever fitching might be, and ate them sitting on a low wall watching people go by. Cassian had never done such a thing in his life: eating so informally, outside, where everyone might see. His pie appeared to contain ham, apples, onions, and cheese. It tasted like being somebody else.

They talked over the business as they sat.

'How likely are they to pursue us?' Cassian asked. 'Of course they want Miss Beaumont but it should be clear now that we aren't with her. And there is the matter of kidnap and robbery. I could swear against them.'

'Robbery?'

'They took my money and my watch.'

'You didn't say. How much? Enough to get them in trouble?'

'Very much so, yes. I had a lot with me.' He'd had vague ideas of buying Daizell some sort of gift in Stratford as they took their holiday. In the event, it had felt like it might distract from their day together and he'd decided he could do it later.

Daizell blinked. 'You didn't think to mention that at the inn?'

'Well, not with Mr Bezant shouting about you stealing his horse, and also, I didn't think they'd run away if I threatened to call a magistrate and accuse them of theft and kidnapping. Do you think they would have?' he added, suddenly feeling rather foolish. 'Should I have confronted them?'

'Probably not,' Daizell said. 'We'd doubtless have all ended up thrown in gaol accusing one another of things, what with the missing heiress and the stolen horses. No, you handled things perfectly. You always do; I don't know what you thought you needed me for.'

That entirely took Cassian's breath. He sat, heart thudding and lips parted, for a few seconds before he could answer. 'I did need you. I *do*. I couldn't have done anything if you hadn't showed me how.'

Colour surged in Daizell's cheeks. 'I think you'd have managed, you know, but – glad to be of service.'

They smiled at one another. Daizell cleared his throat. 'On the subject of money, though, how much did they take? That is, do you have enough to keep going?'

'Oh.' He hadn't even considered it. 'Uh. No. I have— Oh.' He had no idea what to do now. If he wanted money, and he rarely did, he just told his people to give it to him. A sense of panic swept over him, as though he found himself hopelessly adrift on an open sea. 'Oh God almighty. I've only got about twenty pounds left.' It was a tiny sum, a nothing. When it ran out, he wouldn't have anything else. He stared speechlessly at Daizell.

'Twenty? Lord, that's all right,' Daizell said with staggering airiness. 'I thought we had our pockets to let. You, I mean; I already do. Er, you can get more, yes?'

'I have plenty of money. I can send to home.' But that would doubtless mean he'd lost the wager, and he'd have to admit he'd been robbed *again*. Leo would laugh, the aunts would flap, and Lord Hugo would say he'd known all along that the Duke would come to this. No. He would – how did people get money?

'We're in Birmingham,' he said, thinking it through. 'I can surely find a bank. Of course I can.' He looked a disgrace but he had his card case, which had, thankfully, been hidden at the bottom of his luggage. 'We might need to stay here a night or two if they have to send to verify that I have the funds, but – yes. Bank.' It was a plan. He wasn't going to be destitute. He could breathe again.

'That seems very sensible,' Daizell said. 'Shall we find a place to stay and then you can do that?'

It took Cassian a while. He banked with Coutt's in London, but they had no office here; he eventually discovered that Birmingham offered a branch of Taylors and Lloyds. There he had a stroke of luck: the manager was an ambitious man who had used to work in Gloucester, and knew the Duke of Severn when he saw him even in an ill-fitting coat. He insisted on serving tea with great ceremony, promised absolute discretion, made no comment at all about his dishevelled appearance or unattended presence in Birmingham, hinted that Taylors and Lloyd's would provide His Grace with exceptional service at all times if they should be so fortunate as to have his business in the future, and furnished him with a hundred pounds.

Cassian emerged after a couple of hours with money in his pocket, a little soothed by the comforting exercise of privilege. He didn't want servility but it was undeniably pleasant to be recognised. He also felt slightly guilty, as he wasn't entirely sure if this fell within the terms of the wager, but decided it was fair: he'd never agreed to be a pauper.

That said, he was irritated at himself for having lost so much money to thievery. He added it to his list of reasons to resent Sir James Vier, who would under no circumstances be getting his greys.

He returned to the Spread Eagle inn where they had decided to stay, and found Daizell cutting a profile. A little crowd stood around him, chanting. 'Fifty-seven, fifty-eight, fifty-nine ...'

'Said he'll do it before a count of a hundred,' a fellow watcher informed him in a very strong accent. 'Start to finish. Mr Bignall said he couldn't, but look at them scissors twinkle!'

Daizell was moving the paper rapidly in that smooth manner, gleaming eyes flicking from subject to scissors. His face was intent but a smile curved his lips as the count carried on. 'Ninety-one, ninety-two—'

'Done!' Daizell said, triumphantly holding up the profile. The crowd gathered round to judge it against the subject, and made loud noises of admiration.

A man, presumably Mr Bignall, handed over what looked like a banknote and shook Daizell's hand. 'Well, sir, you made good on your word. That's a fast hand and a good eye you have. I wouldn't have thought it possible.'

'Thank you kindly,' Daizell said. 'Would you care to be cut yourself, as a memento? Not quite so fast this time, my fingers wouldn't take the strain.'

Within a moment, Bignall was sitting for a profile. Cassian watched from the outskirts, fascinated. Daizell had slipped into what was clearly a practised persona, charming and friendly when he wasn't locked in concentration on his work, and several more people asked for their profiles, at three shillings a time. By the last, Daizell looked in his satchel and clicked his tongue. 'I've no more blackened sheets, I'm afraid. How about a hollow cut?'

'What's that, then?' asked his hopeful customer.

'Watch.' Daizell pushed a scissor blade into the middle of a sheet of white paper, piercing a hole rather than starting at the edge, and began to cut. Several people leaned forward, obscuring Cassian's view, and by the time he'd moved round to see, the cut was almost done: an oddly shaped hole in the middle of the paper. Daizell found a dark blue card in his bag and pasted the paper to it, and there it was: a profile made of empty space, surrounded by white.

Daizell accepted the acclaim with becoming modesty, let Mr Bignall buy him a drink, and put away his things, giving Cassian a slightly embarrassed look as the watchers dispersed. 'Hello, there. Success?'

'Yes, it was easier than I had feared. You seem to have been busy?'

'Well, you seemed a little worried about funding, so ...' He shrugged. 'A few shillings here and there, it adds up. Street-corner flummery, I know.'

'But impressive. Did you really cut that man's profile in a count of a hundred? Do you not have to draw the outline?'

'I taught myself to do without. I had a lot of time on my hands.' He shrugged again. 'It's a party trick, nothing more.'

It seemed to Cassian to be a remarkable skill, if not a profession. 'Are there not studios for profilers?'

'There are, yes. John Miers in London has a positive factory now, with people tracing shadows and drawing from them, and there's another fellow, Charles, doing the same. Both of them undercutting the other's prices and making life harder for everyone else. You can charge five shillings for a painted shade in the provinces where you'd only get a shilling in London now.'

'Weren't you charging three?'

Daizell looked distinctly embarrassed. 'Well, these are just cuts, no paint. And I'd already won a pound off that fellow.'

Cassian wasn't generally a wagering man, but he had witnessed many a bet, and was quite used to stakes in two, three or even four figures. There was something so small, so vulnerable about betting a pound and having the outcome matter. It ought not matter, and Daizell ought not to be so close to disaster that a pound seemed worth betting. The hundred pounds in his own pocket felt uncomfortable and obtrusive.

'What if you hadn't been able to do it, though?' he asked. 'If you'd lost?'

'Please,' Daizell said. 'I can cut a profile in a count of sixty if I have to. The hard part is timing it to ninety-something.'

'Oh.' It seemed rather unethical to bet if he knew perfectly well he could do it. 'Is that quite fair?'

'I'm sure you disapprove,' Daizell said, flushing. 'I dare say you should. But I make my living, such as it is, cutting profiles in inns for shillings, betting on my skills, and performing at parties to earn my place. I don't have the option of going to a bank to refresh my pockets. I'm well aware it isn't the occupation of a gentleman, but I don't have a great deal of choice.'

Cassian recoiled at his tone. 'I didn't say anything.'

'You were thinking it.' There was tension in Daizell's face. 'Cutting profiles for my supper allows me to maintain a little more self-respect than out-and-out begging, that's all. I dare say a man of actual self-respect finding himself in my position would have fled to the Continent, or won a fortune at the gaming tables, or taken up honest labour, but I don't speak French, play, or have any other talents, which rather limits my options.'

He was sounding disturbingly brittle. Cassian put a hand on his arm and felt tension twanging along it. 'I see you must feel your position painfully, but you're doing what you can in the circumstances. And if you want to know what I think, it's that this whole business is horribly unfair – what your parents did and how you were blamed, and Sir James, all of it. It's miserably unjust that you should be reduced to this—'

'Reduced. That's the word,' Daizell said. 'That's the point. I'm less than other people – than Vier, or you – because of my father, and Vier's lies, and all of it, but really because of this.' He gestured at the scissors and bits of cut paper. '*Gentlemen* don't exploit their skills for profit in alehouses. A *gentleman* exhibits his talent purely for the amusement of his friends. Well, forgive me if I'm no longer a gentleman, but I should rather bring in a few shillings than be left high and dry. That isn't a comfortable position.'

'You didn't have to do it now,' Cassian said blankly. 'I was fetching money... You didn't think I'd come back? Daize, were you worried I wouldn't come back?'

Red bloomed over Daizell's cheekbones, though he made a fine stab at airiness. 'It's not unknown for a gentleman to cut his losses, or abandon his obligations, when he feels the pinch.'

'I would not do that. I swear.' He slid his hand down, grabbing Daizell's fingers. 'I just went to get money! I don't abandon people I care for. I would not abandon you.'

The words came without thought, without the consideration a duke should give his every utterance. Daizell gave him one desperately open, hopeful look and then shut his eyes tight.

Cassian's heart was thumping, with panic and with a sense of teetering on the edge of something huge and frightening and wonderful. He squeezed Daizell's fingers and released them, too aware they were in public, wanting to say—

He couldn't say it. He only had the remains of his month as Cassian. Then he would be Severn again, and everything would go back to how it had been.

He didn't want that.

He had no idea what he wanted instead.

He shoved the thoughts aside for now. The important thing for the moment was that Daizell should not have that hurt, lost look in his eyes. 'I wouldn't do that. And I think you're marvellous.'

'Oh, come.'

'Truly. I don't know how you talk to strangers so well but I should like to learn, and as for the cutting, it seems to me to be pure sorcery. I admire it immensely, and I admire that you have developed a skill and use it.' He would have liked to mention some of the many unrewarding hangers-on who had lived off Staplow – they'd had an exceptionally dull ex-military friend of Lord Hugo's for a full twelvemonth – but any story would have raised questions he didn't want to answer. 'I wouldn't know what to do in your place, or how to go about making a life I didn't expect to lead, alone.'

Cassian had never feared for his own finances, or his social position, which he would probably have to commit public murder to lose, and no matter how exasperating and domineering his family were, he'd never doubted their love or loyalty. To lose all that in a night was unthinkable. 'It was terrible, what your parents did to you,' he said intently. 'And you have done your best with what was left. It is hardly your fault you cannot behave like a wealthy gentleman when you aren't wealthy.'

'The problem is, one quickly ceases to be a gentleman of any sort,' Daizell said. 'Which is all very well until one has aspirations to mix with gentlemen again. Maybe I should have picked one or the other. Fought harder to retrieve my name and preserve my standing, or given up and settled to profile-cutting: it's made Miers rich. I should have done that, but I thought, I kept thinking, I could retrieve my position one day. Well, I couldn't and I haven't, and now I wish I had done everything differently.'

He sounded so bleak. It looked so wrong on his face. 'Oh, Daize,' Cassian said. 'Surely we can do something.'

'Don't. It's not— Ugh, I'm sorry. I didn't mean to spill all that out on you. It's just been hitting home in the last days that most people wouldn't count me fit company for a gentleman. For you.'

'Daize, you are,' Cassian said, knowing it wasn't true, or not for the Duke, at least. 'I hope I haven't made you feel otherwise. Have I done something?'

'Reminded me I'd rather not be notorious, that's all. Forget it. I'm being foolish. Let's talk about something else. Please?' he added, as Cassian began an objection.

He sounded like he meant it, and Cassian didn't know what he could say anyway, except for things that he couldn't say at all. He bit back the urge to say them anyway, as he had long learned to do because the Duke of Severn weighed his words and considered his commitments. The silence still felt like a betrayal.

* * *

Cassian was exhausted by nine that night. The last couple of days had been so absurdly up and down that he felt quite adrift: from the exquisite pleasure of his day with Daizell to its terrifying ending; the sense of need for urgent action coupled with the staggering monotony of his hours on the stage or the lengthy time waiting in the bank, and then Daizell's distress. His eyelids were heavy when Daizell said, 'Let's go to bed.'

It was another large bed to share, which they had because Daizell had indicated to the innkeeper that they were unconcerned about sharing if that was more convenient for the inn. As simple as that. Cassian washed his face, noting that he definitely needed to shave tomorrow. He would have put on his nightgown too, out of habit, except that Daizell was even then swinging himself into bed stark naked.

He was lovely in the candlelight. The flickering light caught bronze and gilt and copper hairs, making him glimmer, and Cassian stared at his chest, and the glittering hairs that trailed downwards, and then looked back up to a face that was grinning at him.

'I wasn't going to trouble with a nightshirt. Unless you object?'

'I don't object.' Cassian caught himself from dropping his own nightshirt on the floor, and draped it over a chair instead. He stripped off his breeches and walked, very aware of his own nakedness and his slim build compared to Daizell's far more satisfyingly solid form.

Daizell didn't seem to be complaining. He reached for Cassian's hand, his laughing eyes alight. 'You are lovely. Come here.'

Cassian would have given one of his minor estates not to be so tired. Daizell was so warm, so beautiful, and Cassian shifted willingly under him, feeling Daizell's thigh settle between his own, and reached up to pull Daizell's head down. Daizell kissed him gently but thoroughly, and Cassian wrapped himself around whatever of Daizell he could, straining up into him with relief and joy and a sense of wonderful rightness, and very aware his eyelids were sagging.

Daizell broke off to kiss his ear, then snort in it. 'You look half asleep.'

'Don't mind me.'

Daizell nuzzled his way down Cassian's neck. 'Go to sleep. We've all the time in the world tomorrow.'

'I'd rather . . .' Cassian tightened his grip indicatively.

'Don't be silly. Look at you. You'll fall asleep half way through.'

'I don't mind. I'd like it.' The words were out before he realised, his sleepy brain betraying him.

'Well, I wouldn't,' Daizell said. 'There I'd be, having my wicked way with you and you'd be snoring. Aside from the questionable morals, it would be quite offensive to my self-esteem.'

'Uh,' Cassian said, stifled. 'Yes. Sorry. I—'

'Cass.' Daizell pushed himself up on an elbow. 'Is something wrong?'

'No.'

'It is. Did I just say something stupid?'

'No.'

'*Cass.*' He spoke with a touch of exasperation. 'I felt you tense there. What did I say?'

'It wasn't you. Nothing. I'm just sleepy.' He could have kicked himself. If he'd just kept his mouth shut they could have been kissing and stroking still. He tried to tug Daizell back down to him.

Daizell resisted, contemplating him with a little frown. 'Did you – were you just trying to tell me something?'

Cassian felt the tide of blood flood his face, thickening his throat so he wasn't sure he could answer. Daizell was looking down at him with an expression that was mostly baffled, and a little worried, which made everything worse. 'It doesn't matter,' he mumbled, turning on his shoulder, away.

There was a second's silence, and then Daizell settled behind him, arm coming over Cassian's waist and curling up to hold him close. 'It matters to me,' he said softly. His breath tickled Cassian's neck 'It matters that I don't say stupid things to you, and it matters that something I said made you unhappy. And it matters very much if there's something you want from me that you haven't said, because there's nothing I'd like more than to do whatever it is you want. So could we go back to the part where you said you'd like it and I didn't listen?'

Cassian squeezed his eyes shut. 'It's stupid.'

'You've come to the right place then: I've done more stupid things than you've had hot dinners. If you want to tell me, I promise I'll hear you out. You don't have to but I wish you will.'

Cassian glared at the sheets. Somehow, wretchedly, from being on the verge of passing out, he wasn't tired at all any more. He sent a curse in the general direction of whatever controlled sleep. 'It's just… a thing I thought about. Think about. Sometimes.'

'This is the kind of thinking one does with a hand on one's cock, yes? I would *love* to know what you think about.'

He'd never told anyone this. He hadn't had anyone to tell, and he simply couldn't with paid company, and he was the Duke of Severn. Except here, where he was Cassian, with

Daizell. 'I ... being with someone who'd ... you know. While I was asleep.'

There was a short pause. 'Really?'

'Mmm.'

'Actually asleep? That is, and I'm not being difficult, but wouldn't one wake up?'

'Well, one might, but ... I don't know. It's just a thing I think about.' If he blushed any harder, he might set fire to the sheets.

'No, I see that,' Daizell said. 'Is it something you've tried, at all?'

Cassian shook his head. Daizell leaned in, resting his own head on Cassian's shoulder. 'Well. So one would want to wake up and find oneself being, uh, manhandled?'

'It's all right. You said you wouldn't want to.'

'I wouldn't want to do it to someone who didn't want it done to them. Although, if you think about it, that covers everything from kissing to two-at-a-time buggery. I asked because – well, actually, I have woken up with someone manhandling me, very much *not* someone I'd invited to do so, and in what you might call the ensuing discussion, I broke his nose. Which was very much a matter of instinct, and I'd rather not have my nose instinctually rearranged by someone else. But I suppose if one was expecting it or familiar with one's bed partner, that would be different.'

'I've never broken anyone's nose,' Cassian managed. 'You seem to make a habit of it.'

'Once. I've done it *once*,' Daizell said indignantly. 'Or twice, I suppose, if you count that prick in the crash.'

'How could you not count him? You broke his nose!' He knew very well what Daizell was doing, easing the mood with absurdity. It still worked. 'I – can't promise I wouldn't strike out, I suppose. It's probably—'

'Don't say a stupid idea. It isn't stupid to want things.'

'It can be,' Cassian said, with feeling.

'No, it isn't. Sometimes it's stupid to try to get them, or we go about getting them in stupid ways, but you can desire whatever you want. And if this is something you've thought about a lot, and you want me to—'

'But if you had a bad experience—'

'That wasn't a bad experience. I've had lots of those, but this was just a prick in a shared bed who got a five-second feel before I put my elbow into his face. No, I'm happy to try. Two things, though, Cass?'

'What?'

Daizell's hand moved, gently stroking his hip. 'First, if you wake up and you don't like it, don't hold it against me? The fact of doing it, I mean.'

'Of course I wouldn't. Why would I do that?'

'Plenty of people prefer not to take responsibility for their mistakes. Just remember I'm not trying to take anything you didn't want to give? And actually, another thing: if you don't like it, promise me you'll say so. Don't pretend anything's all right if it's not, or feel you have to go through with it.'

It was slightly embarrassing to feel quite this known. Cassian said, 'I promise but – Daize, are you sure you want to do this?'

'Not at all,' Daizell said cheerfully. 'Suppose we find out tomorrow morning?'

Cassian's chest tightened a little with alarm and anticipation. 'Really?'

'If I wake up first, I'm happy to give it a go. If that suits you?'

'Yes,' Cassian said. 'Please.'

'Then it's a bargain. Right: that's one thing. The other…'

'What?'

Daizell's hand slipped downward, to his groin, not provocative, just covering him. 'You might tell me what's so exciting about the idea. So I understand.' His hand tightened a fraction. 'So I can make it good.'

Cassian attempted to clear his throat. 'Uh. I… it's the idea of…' He wasn't sure how to voice it. He'd been tossing himself off with this in mind for years, one way or another, and the idea of exposing the details of those private dreams was excruciating. The only worse prospect was that of holding back now and wondering for the rest of his life what might have happened if he were braver. 'Just, that someone could just *do* that. Not in an unkind way, not unwanted, but to wake up to your body being used by someone – that sounds dreadful.'

'Not to me.' Daizell's voice was gravelly in his ear. 'Not if you want it. And since the only people hearing it are you and me, tell me more.'

'I want you to touch me while I sleep.' He said it in a breath. 'I want you to – to take whatever liberties you care to, because you can, and to be trying not to wake me so you can carry on doing as you please.'

'Sweet Jesus.' Daizell swallowed audibly, and, Cassian realised, he could feel the hard line of a cockstand against his back. 'And that's what you think about when you stroke your prick at night?'

'Sometimes. Yes.'

'And you look so innocent. I am going to do my very best to live up to this.' He crawled over Cassian, tugged him round, and kissed him, hard. Cassian kissed him back, snaking his arms over those sturdy shoulders, feeling himself relax into Daizell as the kisses became slower, more gentle, decidedly sleepier.

Daizell shifted off, snuggling against him. 'Thank you for trusting me, Cass. I will do my best. For which we both need some sleep.'

Cassian couldn't argue. He blew out his candle as Daizell did the same, and felt a solid arm settle over his waist again as his eyelids fluttered closed.

Chapter Eleven

Daizell woke first.

He was, as ever, spooned against Cassian, his arm over Cassian's hard hip bone, chest to back. It was very warm and comfortable, and he enjoyed the sensation for a moment before he remembered last night.

Well.

He wouldn't have imagined that Cassian harboured such peculiar desires, but then again, if peculiar desires were obvious, he supposed they wouldn't be peculiar. This one did no harm, or at least he hoped it wouldn't. Daizell had not in the slightest enjoyed waking up to find a strange hand rummaging between his legs, and he had not forgotten the sense of violation, the fear, the fury. He couldn't help wondering what would happen if Cassian woke up with a similar set of sensations.

But he'd been asked, and it had cost Cassian something to do the asking, and if it worked, well, that would be something he'd have given Cassian that nobody else ever had. Something he'd wanted and not been able to have, something he'd remember and be happy for. Daizell, leaving a mark on Cassian's life for the better.

He wanted to get this right.

He dwelled for a moment on those whispered words from last night. *Take whatever liberties you care to, because you can. As you please.* Cassian had sounded so lost, so longing, and the tone as much as the words had gone straight to Daizell's groin. He'd woken with a reasonable case of morning wood: now he pressed gently against Cassian's bare arse, wondering how to go about this.

He shifted his hips, pressing a little closer, rubbing against the soft skin of Cassian's back and buttocks. It felt undeniably wrong to be doing this to a sleeping man, and he reminded himself he'd been asked. Cassian had trusted him with this strange wanting; Cassian trusted him enough to hand over his unconscious body. The thought quivered through him.

He could do this. He'd just take his time. And be wary of flying elbows, because he liked his nose the way it was.

So he moved a little more, just a little, thinking of that soft pleading voice, imagining Cassian's murmured endearments whenever he got near a horse. *Such a good, willing boy.* Gently frotting himself, moving lightly, finding the groove of Cassian's arse and rubbing against it.

He felt it when Cassian woke. A slight shift in the body he pressed against, a slight change to the breathing that Daizell had come to know so intimately. He froze for a second with a feeling of dreadful guilt at being caught, and indeed an instinctive desire to shield his face, but Cassian didn't react, just stayed unmoving. Pretending to be asleep.

That brought a couple of other mornings to mind. Daizell found himself wondering if this was what he'd wanted the first time they'd woken tangled together. The cheeky little beggar. The thought was a spur, and he started moving again, perhaps a touch harder, rubbing himself against Cassian's unmoving flesh, ears twitching like a bat's for the tiny shifts in breath.

He'd bet money Cassian was loving this. Something in the quality of the silence, the shallowness of his breathing:

Daizell couldn't have put his finger on it, but now he was sure, and it spangled through his veins. And since he was in fact awake ... He slipped a very light hand down, between Cassian's legs, gently parting the meat of his thighs with as much care as if he had believed him asleep, and so slowly, so carefully, eased his stand between Cassian's thighs, quite as if he intended to pleasure himself at Cassian's expense.

No reaction. Cassian must have been very good at statue games as a child, or had been taught a deal of self control. Daizell frigged himself gently against the warm pressure, wondering when he might force his lover into reaction, and suddenly realised he was enjoying himself enormously in this odd game of pretence.

He wasn't going to touch Cassian's prick. That was not in the spirit of his instructions. Therefore ...

Daizell applied a little pressure, just a little, easing Cassian onto his front with immense care, and now he had Cassian under him, now he could thrust just a little harder, just as he might do if he didn't care about waking him up any more. As if all he wanted was his own climax, and he was going to take it. He ground his hips against Cassian's firm arse, and heard an audible moan of pleasure, no more pretence, and, driven by an impulse he didn't understand or question, he put a hand to the back of Cassian's skull, pushing his head down into the mattress. He held him there as he thrust harder, quite as if he only cared about finishing himself off, and as Cassian bucked under him, he spent as if his balls were on fire.

Once his head cleared, that seemed a slightly less good idea.

'Hell,' he said, snatching his hand away. 'Cass?'

Cassian groped behind him, and grabbed his hand, holding

it hard. He didn't speak for a moment, then he made an incoherent noise into the pillow.

'Cass?' Daizell said again. 'I got carried away.'

'So did I.' Cassian twisted his head round. The one eye Daizell could see looked wet. 'Oh God, Daizell. That was the best – my whole life – *God.*'

'Oh. Well, then.'

Cassian exhaled, apparently breathing out his bones as he did so, because he flattened into the bed like an unset jelly. 'Perfect. Perfect. If you want to be unbearably smug, feel free.'

'That went as you hoped, then?' Daizell was milking this shamelessly. He felt he deserved to.

'Yes. God, yes. I woke up, and I felt you – Lord above.' He twisted round, and Daizell did too, so they were lying in one another's arms, legs tangling stickily. 'Perfect. Was it – did you like it?'

'More than I'd thought I would,' Daizell said honestly. 'Though I felt like quite a bad person for a while. I, uh, thought you wouldn't want me to bring you off with my hand?'

'You didn't need to,' Cassian said, with deep sincerity and a touch of awe. 'All over the sheets, good Lord. That was magical, Daize. Thank you.'

'It wasn't a hardship,' Daizell assured him.

Cassian put a hand to his cheek. 'I mean it. You asked me what I wanted, and you cared to give it to me. And I realise you weren't quite comfortable with the idea, and I feel rather selfish for pressing.'

'Nonsense. I offered, and I'll very happily do it again if that's what it does to you. Not without discussion beforehand,' he added hastily. He wasn't going to make a habit of grabbing sleeping partners without a by-your-leave. 'But if you insist on saying that I'm the best fuck of your life, I suppose I'll just have to live up to it.'

'You absolutely were. Are. How are you so marvellous?'

Daizell was not used to being marvellous. He rather felt he could be led around like a dog on a string by Cassian telling him he was marvellous. 'Well, you asked me to be, so it's probably your fault. Uh, at the end, when I held you down, it seemed a good idea at the time, but—'

'Perfect,' Cassian said again. 'Which – that's not really something I'd want normally. I know some people do, but it doesn't appeal at all as a rule. But just then, it was exactly right.'

'Thank God.'

Cassian nuzzled into him. 'Goodness. Is there – while we're here – is there anything I can do for you?'

'I did very well already, thank you.'

'Not now: I need a moment. I meant – well, is there anything you want? You did that for me, and I don't want to be selfish.'

He was such an odd fish, with that tiny line of worry between his eyes. Daizell kissed it. 'That wasn't selfish. It was a marvellous idea. If you're asking if I'm harbouring any secret desires: no, not really. I'm a fairly straightforward sort of man, I'm afraid.'

'You needn't apologise.' Cassian paused. 'Um, we haven't discussed whether you might want to … you know.'

'Know what?'

'Buggery?'

Daizell choked. 'There's a question. I don't much care for it on the receiving end. Or do you mean you'd like me to fuck you?'

'Um. I don't much like receiving either, but if that's

something you want, I could try? I imagine it would be better with you.'

And that was another chunk of Daizell's foolish heart broken off and floating away, like a melting icicle. 'I hope it might, but I've no great urge to find out. It's not something I greatly care about in either part.'

'But you must want something. Really, Daizell, you just gave me something I've thought about since I thought about these things. Isn't there anything I can do for you?'

'It's not a quid pro quo,' Daizell pointed out. Had Cassian not had a lover before? Well, no, clearly he had, but he seemed oddly uncertain of the etiquette all the same. 'I'm honoured you trusted me with that, and it was magnificent for me because you loved it. And I would absolutely share my secret desires with you if I had any.' He wished he did now, just to give Cassian something back for his gift of trust. 'Uh, maybe—'

Cassian cocked his head. 'What was that?'

'Oh, nothing very meaningful. It's just ...' This would sound dreadfully stupid, but then so did *Please molest me in my sleep*, and Cassian had found the courage to voice that. 'Well, it's only that I like the way you talk when you want, well, to give instructions. Encouragement.' Cassian was looking blank. Daizell said, muffled by embarrassment, 'I like the way you talk to your horses.'

Cassian's eyes opened wide, the sun-and-rain mix glowing with something that might have been laughter. 'Are you asking me to ride you, at all?'

Daizell winced. 'Apparently.'

'Oh, but I could do that.' Cassian's voice dropped into that spine-tingling gentle croon. 'I could ride you just as you want, my Daizell, my very wonderful Daizell, and tell you how wonderful you are as I do it.'

A small whimper escaped Daizell's throat. Cassian tightened his arms, and then they were tangled up in kisses again, blissfully lost to the clock, or pointless missions, or anything except one another.

Eventually, Cassian squirmed down a bit to lie on Daizell's chest, toying idly with a nipple, to interesting effect. 'I feel I should thank you.'

'For what?'

'Not assuming that I must like to, uh, receive, just because I'm not a great hulk of a man. That's at least one thing John Martin got right.'

'It makes no sense,' Daizell said. 'Why should that— Hold on. What?'

'Oh.' Cassian's ready blush flooded his face. 'Yes. I wasn't entirely honest with you about how I came to be robbed, was I? Well, I couldn't be, at the time. But it's how I came to be in an inn with him overnight, that's all.'

That did make rather more sense, now Daizell thought about it. He hadn't troubled to consider the story deeply. 'The thief was your lover?'

'Hardly that. We met in a park. He paid me some very flattering attention, and persuaded me to meet for a night together. He was exceedingly charming and it was – well, I'm not used to being courted and it felt like he was doing that. I was quite taken in. And we met, and had a very nice meal, and he plied me with drink and had me ride him. It was good, I think – it's not quite clear in my memory, but I'm reasonably sure I enjoyed myself up until I fell asleep. And then I woke up with my clothes and possessions and ring stolen. I did not enjoy that part.' He was trying to sound light, but Daizell could hear the hurt. 'Granted he wanted to rob me, did he have to make me feel quite such a fool? He even left me a note saying it was my fault.'

'Your fault that he robbed you?'

'He said I shouldn't put temptation in people's way, I suppose by having a few costly items with me, or perhaps by falling asleep too soon. I felt it was rather an unkind jab.'

'Temptation in people's way,' Daizell said. His voice sounded hollow in his own ears. 'About your height, dark hair, hazel eyes … he didn't, by any chance, have a purple birthmark on his arse?'

'He did, actually,' Cassian responded, and then his face changed as his brain caught up with the words. 'How the devil do you know that?'

'Because I've seen it. The same way as you did.'

Cassian sat up in a jerk. 'He robbed you too?'

'Of course not: I've nothing to steal. His name's Martin Nichols. He's a … friend, I suppose.'

Cassian was staring at him. 'You knew who he was all along?'

Daizell rolled his eyes. 'If I had, I'd have spared myself a lot of time in stagecoaches. I *would* have known all along if you'd told me you'd tupped him and what happened. That's a lot more distinctive than a mulberry coat.'

'You're friends with a thief?'

'He's a valet,' Daizell said. 'Or he was, until an unfortunate incident left him with the sort of reference that does you no good.'

'You mean he robbed his master?'

'Yes and no.' Daizell had no great urge to defend Martin, but he also had strong feelings about false accusations. 'His master, uh, wouldn't take no for an answer. He had his way by force, and told Martin afterwards it was his fault for putting temptation in his way. So, working on that principle, Martin helped himself to all the valuables he could carry, and left. I grant that's theft, if you want to apportion blame, but in the circumstances—'

'No.' Cassian looked rather sick. 'I see.'

'He's got a bit of a temper, and little fondness for gentlemen, and if you heard some of his stories, nor would you have.'

'I see. And you are, or you were, lovers?'

'We used to fuck,' Daizell said, which wasn't quite the whole truth. 'He can be charming – you know that. We got on very well for a while, only … ugh. He was determined to be independent. *I care for nobody, and nobody cares for me*, that was his song. But, like a fool, I did start to care for him, and he didn't like it. We had quite the pretty row, in which he made it very clear I wasn't necessary to his happiness, and he walked out.'

'Oh, the swine,' Cassian said, with startling venom. 'The miserable swine.'

'That's Martin. Anyway, now we know who stole your ring, which means we can find him, pick him up by his heels, and shake him till the ring falls out.'

Cassian's face changed, as if he hadn't realised what this meant. 'You can *find* him?'

'I should think so. I bump into him now and again.'

Cassian scrubbed his face with the heels of his hands. 'I am going to need a moment to grasp this. I'd given up, in truth. I was going to drag myself round a string of pawnshops to prove to myself I'd tried everything, but I didn't really believe we had a chance. And now – Daizell, you are astonishing.'

'I'm nothing of the kind. It's pure good fortune we both happened to fuck the same man.'

'I wouldn't call it good, myself. Why is he your friend still?'

Daizell opened his mouth to reply, and realised there wasn't much to say. 'When you've nothing to do and you drift, and you meet the same person drifting the same sort of way… well, an awkward friendship is still better than nothing. He's not a bad fellow, truly, underneath. But he was badly treated, and he passes it on to people he shouldn't.'

'Is it that bad, Daize? The way you live?'

He felt himself redden. 'Oh, well. I feel lonely, sometimes, but it suits some people. I expect you'd do perfectly well in my shoes, because you're not needy.' *Needy and tiresome*, Martin had said, when Daizell had attempted to suggest they try something more than drifting in and out of one another's orbits. It still hurt.

'You aren't needy,' Cassian said, which just went to show he wasn't that acute, or that Daizell had finally learned to conceal his desperate craving for affection. It was about time he did: his parents had taught him how pointless it was, and Martin how unappealing. 'And I don't know about that. I have plenty of aunts and uncles and cousins. This journey is the first time I've done things on my own in my life.'

That explained a lot. Daizell nodded. 'What about your parents?'

'My mother died when I was a baby, and my father when I was six.'

'Oh, that's hard. I'm sorry.'

'I wasn't deprived of care by that,' Cassian said. 'The opposite, really. My father was… preoccupied, and quite vague, and didn't know what to do with a small child. I don't remember him very well, to be honest. He used to come into the nursery sometimes, and I thought he was terribly tall and grand, but mostly I remember him after. When he was dead, I mean. I remember that very clearly, because they brought me in to see him and gave me the ring from his hand and I didn't want to put it on. It was still warm, you see, although he was dead, and it felt – well, children have fancies, don't they?'

Daizell gaped at him. 'Literally off his hand? Why on *earth* . . . ?'

Cassian, who had been looking rather lost in memory, blinked and went very red. 'Oh, it's a tradition. My great-grandfather's ring, heirloom, you know. Lots of families do it.'

'It's demented,' Daizell said frankly. 'What a thing to do to a child, good Lord. And that's the one Martin stole? Er . . . you do *want* it back, do you?'

'Yes!'

No accounting for taste. 'Then we'll get it back, by hook or crook.'

Cassian swallowed. 'Thank you. But what I had intended to say was that you needn't feel sorry for me for lacking parents. Nurse was always wonderful, and my uncle went to the greatest possible lengths to act in loco parentis, far more than my actual father would have, while the aunts – I had five – gave a non-stop commentary on how well or poorly he was doing. I have been surrounded by people who look after me all my life. If anything, I could do with a great deal less coddling. I love them all, and I am truly grateful, but sometimes it makes me want to scratch my skin off.'

Daizell blinked at the sudden snap in his voice. Cassian raised a hand, the brief expression of frustration dissolving. 'I have no reason to complain, none in the world. But I have come to find it a little stifling, so I leapt at the chance to take this month away, as generously granted by Mr Martin, or whatever his name is. I was desperate to be myself alone, whereas you have a great deal more solitude than you want. Things are very poorly distributed.'

Daizell had snagged on 'alone'. 'Are you saying that you want more time on your own now? Because if—'

'No!' Cassian said quickly. 'No, not at all. Your company isn't, oh, overbearing, not in the slightest. It never is. You're wonderfully easy. The best companion I could have asked for.'

'Oh.'

Cassian gave him a glinting smile. 'And full of ideas, and going to find my ring with a bit of luck, and – I think we mentioned this earlier – the best, um, you know.'

'What was that?'

Cassian pinked. He wasn't prone to bad language, and Daizell could see him gather his nerve. 'The best, er, fuck of my life?'

'You can say that whenever you like.'

Cassian looked wonderfully flustered. 'The point is, I don't at all want time on my own. Actually, if we could – well, keep on being with one another, I'd like that very much.'

Daizell couldn't quite find a reply. Or, he could, but it would entirely explode Cassian's bizarre idea that he wasn't needy or overbearing, because what he wanted was to demand exactly what 'being together' meant, and precisely how long 'keep on' might mean. He failed to answer for long enough that Cassian's smile wavered. 'If you want to, I mean, once we have the ring. It's up to you. I do realise I'm not terribly exciting—'

'What? No. Yes. Yes, of course I'd like to carry on, but what the devil do you mean by exciting? My *father* was exciting. I've been exciting, and it's got me expelled and disgraced and nearly horsewhipped. And you …' He groped for words. 'It's not even that you aren't exciting yourself, it's just that you do it so quietly. You quietly calm a set of panicking horses, and quietly let yourself out when you're kidnapped, and quietly scheme to bamboozle parsons. Good God, Cass, you're like a cool drink on a hot day. Anyone who tells you otherwise isn't paying attention.'

'That …' Cassian looked far more struck than the remark deserved. 'That is very lovely, and – goodness. I intend to think about that. Um, I have two questions.'

'Mmm?'

'What do we do next? And' – his hand slid meaningfully down Daizell's flank – 'do we have to do it yet?'

'I'll work on it, and no,' Daizell said. 'We most definitely do not.'

Once they got up, which was shamefully late, Daizell turned his mind to the matter of finding Martin Nichols. It wasn't a problem he'd considered before. It was a long time since he'd wanted to find him.

Martin had had the stuffing knocked out of him rather worse than Daizell had. He'd been a valet to a baronet and had high ambitions of improving himself, snatched away by a selfish swine who took what he wanted and left wreckage in his wake. Daizell had only sympathy with that, and he quite understood Martin's reaction both to escape, and to do something vengeful on his way out.

Unfortunately, that reaction had ruined him. He'd robbed his abusive master and made himself a criminal by it, and he was still stewing in anger at himself and the world when he and Daizell had had their affair. Daizell had been desperate to care and be cared for; Martin had wanted to care for nothing and nobody; the affair had ended up hurting them both for no good reason. It didn't do to want more than people were willing to give.

Daizell had never set out to find the man in his peregrinations, and had absolutely no idea how to go about it. But Cassian was regarding him with a calm, confident expectation that he'd perform some piece of wizardry and Daizell felt a strong urge to live up to it.

'I've several times met him at the Green Lion in Coventry,' he mused as they pored over a map Cassian had acquired. He put his finger on the town. 'He's the landlord's cousin or some such. And I've met him in Kidderminster, and Leamington Spa. And you met him in Gloucester.'

They contemplated the map, obscured by his splayed hand. Cassian said, 'We need a pen,' and then, conscientiously, 'I'll get it.'

He returned with a poorly cut pen and a pot of execrable lumpy ink, which was about what Daizell expected from an inn, especially one in a provincial town. Cassian clicked his tongue but circled the places they'd met Martin between them.

Daizell contemplated it. 'I don't know if that tells us anything at all, honestly.'

Cassian frowned at the map. 'Is it him sticking to the Midlands, or you?'

'It's not me. I've never met him outside the Midlands, though.'

'I suppose, given he recently robbed me in Gloucester, he would want to stay away from there. And we know he headed to Stratford.'

'Going east. And I've met him in Coventry several times. For want of any better ideas, shall we start there?'

'So we have to get there from here. Ugh.'

'Ugh, indeed.'

'Might this be the time to hire a coach?' Daizell suggested.

Cassian's head came up with a startled, almost wary look. 'Sorry?'

'It wouldn't cost so much more to take a private coach and pair than to go on the public way, and we'd get there a deal faster and more comfortably. I'm not telling you how to spend your money,' he added, since Cassian didn't look as if this was a welcome suggestion. 'Do as you please. But it would seem to make sense.'

'Yes, it would,' Cassian said. 'I, uh, can't.'

'Can't what? Drive?' He didn't believe that for a second.

'No, of course I can drive. I can't hire a private chaise. Ugh. The thing is, I made a wager.'

'A wager? To do what?'

'Take the public coach for a month, or at least, not hire my own carriage. My cousin told me that I, uh, lacked experience of life and wouldn't be able to manage on my own. We had something of a dispute and we made a bet.'

Daizell sat back with a sigh. 'Seems harsh. Granted you were something of a greenhorn initially, you've learned fast enough, and there's nothing praiseworthy in using the stage for its own sake. It's just a damned uncomfortable means of transport. Still, if it's a wager . . .' He shrugged acquiescence.

Cassian tipped his head. 'You don't mind? It's inconvenient and uncomfortable for you, and for a rather foolish reason.'

'But it's a wager. I take it you want to win?'

'Yes.'

'Well, then,' Daizell said, trying not to let his weariness show, and reached for *Paterson's British Itinerary* again.

Chapter Twelve

It was a long way to Coventry. That would help throw any possible pursuer off, which was good. On the other hand, it gave Daizell too much time to think about things.

He was beginning to fear Cassian was richer than he'd thought – the pack of concerned relatives, the fact that he'd barely taken the public stage before, the absurd wager, the heirloom ring. That was disheartening. A quiet country gentleman possessed of a competence might live very happily with a companion out of the public eye. Rich men had responsibilities, and people around them who guarded their wealth, and perhaps pressures to marry.

Not that Daizell had any right or reason to dream of that imagined quiet existence. He knew perfectly well it was too much to ask of life. Unfortunately, that knowledge didn't stop him hoping. He always hoped. He wished he could stop.

Cassian had called him the best companion he could have asked for, and Daizell felt so much the same that it hurt a little. Cassian was delightful in his unobtrusive way – a good friend, a fascinating lover, a competent ally, an entertaining partner in absurdity – and Daizell didn't want to think about parting. About Cassian going back to his established life where people poked at him to be louder and thought he was a nonentity, and nobody listened to what he wanted. About Daizell being alone again, but far more alone now because he'd feel Cassian's absence. About the fact that if Cassian was wealthy they'd unquestionably have to part, because nobody would be pleased to see a well-off young man turn up with George Charnage's son in tow. Cassian would know that as well as anyone.

And yet he had said he wanted to keep on being together.

Daizell couldn't let himself draw too much significance from that, or he'd destroy himself with hoping. Almost certainly Cassian had just meant until his month was up. But still he had said 'keep on', not 'keep on for the rest of the month', and Daizell's idiot heart couldn't be persuaded to let that go.

He ought to do something sensible, such as talk to Cassian about what he really meant. He didn't dare. For one, they'd only known each other a handful of days, for all it felt like a lifetime. For another, he didn't want to press Cassian to anything. He was the one with a life and a family and things to lose. Daizell had lost those things, and he couldn't bear to think of Cassian going through that, especially not with himself as the cause. For a third, the reason he was trying to hide behind the rest, he remembered very clearly the disgust in Martin's voice. *Christ, stop* wanting *things of me, it's revolting.*

Martin had not been at his best then, and he'd apologised since, but the words still hurt. Daizell liked people, and liked to be liked, and 'revolting' had sat under his skin for a long time now. So no, he was not going to make demands of Cassian, who was a grown man perfectly capable of saying what he wanted when, or if, he wanted it.

God, Daizell wished he would.

Brooding at least distracted him through the tedious journey to Coventry. It was well past four when they arrived.

'It's this way for the Green Lion,' Daizell said. 'I vote we head there first, see if Martin's there, or if anyone knows where to find him. And, indeed, take lodgings while we're at it.'

Cassian nodded. 'It seems ridiculous to say I'm tired when I've done nothing but sit all day, but I'm exhausted. I am sorry for inflicting this on you.'

'Can't be helped. Nevertheless, unless we have a very firm lead, may I suggest we don't spend tomorrow in a coach? Coventry has a wonderful cathedral. It would be a shame for you to miss it.'

That was shameless manipulation, and Cassian duly perked up. 'Yes, of course. Would you care to come? I suppose you've been a dozen times already.'

'Never set foot there in my life. You can tell me all about it.'

The Green Lion was much as ever. Forster, the landlord, gave Daizell a warm welcome and Cassian an interested once-over. 'Room, is it?'

'For a couple of nights,' Daizell agreed.

'One bed or two?'

'One will do very well. How have you been, old fellow?'

They caught up with news, talking of this and that for a few moments, before Daizell went for the question. 'By the way, has Martin, Martin Nichols, passed through recently?'

'No, not for a couple of months.'

Cassian didn't curse, or sag, or anything dramatic, but Daizell heard just the faintest resigned sigh. 'Blast.'

Forster cocked his head. 'You want to see him? Thought you weren't on terms.'

'I've a bone to pick with him.'

'You'll have your chance if you can hang about for a few days. Which you usually can,' Forster added unkindly.

'Martin's always here for my Gracie's birthday. She turns ten on Friday, so I dessay he'll pitch up.'

'Will he,' Daizell said. 'Excellent. Then we'll be staying till Friday.'

Forster showed them up to the room, where Cassian dropped his bag on the floor and put his hands on his hips. 'I have at least fifteen things to say at once. Have we truly found him?'

'With a bit of luck.'

An incredulous grin spread across Cassian's face. 'Good God, Daizell. I could never, *ever* have done this without you.'

'Thank me when we get the ring back off Martin,' Daizell reminded him, but he was smiling too, caught by Cassian's joy. 'I hope to blazes he's still got it.'

'Even if he doesn't – because I am not going to pin my hopes on that at all – I will know that I tried my best and did what I could. Um. If he does have it, do you think he'll give it back?'

'If he knows what's good for him. What else was it you wanted to say?'

'Well, the bed – the landlord—'

'He's trustworthy,' Daizell reassured him. 'This is a safe sort of place. No maids barging into rooms, or awkward questions about linen or who sleeps where.'

'It's a molly house?'

'It's an inn. Just a friendly one, where one doesn't have to bribe the maids or leave by the windows.'

'Oh.' Cassian frowned. 'But what about everywhere else we've stayed?'

'We've left most of them after a night. And you've tipped lavishly, which ...' Which he'd assumed was buying complaisance, but Cassian's blank look suggested otherwise. He just tipped to excess as a matter of principle. *Rich*, Daizell thought again. 'I'm not advising indiscretion in the public rooms. Just saying, the landlord's a decent fellow.'

'But...' Cassian winced. 'If people found out I lodged here, would that be suggestive?'

'What people? You live over the far side of Gloucester: who would notice or care where you stay in Coventry? And in any case it's not a brothel. It's an inn, albeit one where you might find like-minded company if you were looking for that. There's usually somewhere in a good-sized town if you know where to go.'

'But I don't know.' Cassian looked a little lost, somehow, almost bleak. 'I've only ever really gone to one place and it's quite... quite exclusive, you know, and awfully careful. I've never been to a normal sort of molly house.'

'I could take you, if you like,' Daizell offered, and saw on his face that was wrong. 'Or not. Do you not want to stay here? I assumed you'd want a safe place.'

Cassian rubbed his face. 'Because this is a safe sort of place for you.'

'Well, yes? Is there something wrong?'

'No. No, I dare say not. It's a new experience and I'm supposed to have those. I'm sorry, I'm being very silly, when you've found our quarry and a good place to stay while we wait.' He shook himself. 'Forgive me. Could we perhaps take a stroll and stretch our legs? I don't know Coventry at all and if we'll be here a while, I should acquaint myself.'

'You're just itching for the cathedral, aren't you?' Daizell said, and led him out.

It was a pleasant afternoon, and Coventry was a lovely town. It wore its medieval history on its sleeve, with some surviving town gates though the walls between them had long gone, and two churches whose exteriors had Cassian rapt with admiration. Daizell had never considered them beyond 'tall and pointy'; he expected to learn a great deal more in the near future, and found himself rather looking forward to it. They strolled in a leisurely way, and returned to the Green Lion for an excellent dinner and a pleasant evening in the taproom.

It was pleasant indeed. Daizell's wanderings around the country and friendly habits meant he had a wide acquaintance. The Green Lion was where he always came when he passed through the area, and he greeted familiar faces with pleasure. Cassian said little, but he was an excellent listener, a trait which would win him popularity in any drinking establishment. Daizell told a couple of amusing stories, got belly laughs, laughed immoderately at other people's stories, and made half a dozen new passing friends. He was thrumming with energy when they retired upstairs.

'Goodness,' Cassian said, sitting on the bed. 'What a lively evening. You enjoyed yourself.'

'I did. Did you?'

'Yes.' He sounded as though he was slightly surprised. 'It was very entertaining. I usually find big, noisy gatherings rather exhausting. I think the trick is not having people particularly want one to talk. It's much more enjoyable when I can just listen without feeling obliged to say something.'

'If you want to be surrounded by people who talk so much you couldn't get a word in if you tried, you've come to the right place. With the right man,' he was forced to add, since he was well aware he'd been chattering all night.

'Yes, that was perfect,' Cassian agreed quite seriously. 'Everyone allowed you to talk for both of us. I wish you could do that normally.'

Daizell frowned. 'You've plenty to say for yourself.'

'When I want to. The problem is when I've nothing at all I want to say, and yet people still press me to converse. I find that dreadfully tiring.' He cocked his head. 'Whereas you look quite invigorated. Have I been keeping you from the social whirl?'

'Yes, all those invitations to soirées I've turned down,' Daizell said, a touch more sarcastically than he'd meant. 'No, not at all. I like company, but if it's too much for you—'

'If I find it too much, I shall retreat and read a book, and be as happy in my solitude as you are in company. Unless that would be offensive?' he added quickly. 'I don't want to be standoffish.'

'Nobody will mind in the slightest. We can find a bookseller tomorrow.'

'Oh, perfect. Buy books, explore the town. And I thought, perhaps you could cut me one of your special profiles? I have wondered about that a great deal, you know. How you'd do it.'

'I'll need you to inspire me,' Daizell said, and reached for him.

The next few days were quiet bliss.

They bought books – several, since they both liked the Waverley author. They saw the sights of Coventry, with Daizell discovering once again that a man who was interested in everything made everything interesting. They took long walks that alternated talking and comfortable silence, and spent entertaining evenings with the regulars of the Green Lion. It all made for remarkably full days. And then there were the nights.

Oh Lord, the nights. He didn't think he'd ever forget this

time. Cassian had taken Daizell's request to heart, whispering those glorious endearments, telling Daizell he was so marvellous, so giving, such a very good boy, and Daizell was almost embarrassingly weak-kneed under the onslaught of lips and fingers and most of all those soft words in that bard's voice. It was ridiculous how the praise went straight to his prick, and he didn't care. Partly it felt too good; partly, Cassian had thrown himself wholeheartedly into the role, and was revelling in the effect of his words, and if it made him happy to bring Daizell to whimpering bliss, Daizell wasn't going to complain.

He'd returned the favour with another planned 'good morning' fuck, every bit as successfully as before, leaving Cassian as sated and boneless as a cat in sunlight. He might possibly be dead and in heaven, except he didn't think he'd done anything to merit this.

He had their mutual pleasure, and Cassian's company and friendship, and their growing intimacy. He had no stagecoaches rattling his bones, no worries about money. He might have worried about time because Cassian's month was running down with every day that passed, but that would spoil things, so he cut off the thought when it came and set himself to enjoy each moment as he lived it.

Something in Cassian seemed to melt away over those days too: some reserve, or worry. He stayed up with the raucous crowd a couple of times, and was once persuaded to tell a mildly warm story that was greeted by great applause and hoots of laughter. He'd glowed as if he'd never got a laugh in a public bar before, and Daizell didn't know how his heart could keep expanding like this.

He cut Cassian's shade, showing him the whole process, starting with smearing thick paper with lamp-black. He didn't trouble with a pencil outline: by now he could have cut that quietly elegant profile in the dark. He did two, a standard shade of Cassian ruffled and smiling, which he pasted opposite a hollow cut in more serious pose. He also did an extremely questionable full-length version, which involved a great deal of giggling, and which he insisted, with regret on both sides, they burn afterwards. He'd learned his lesson there.

Everything was perfect until Friday.

Forster hailed them as they came in after a morning's walk and leisurely luncheon. 'Daize? You might want to know, Martin's here. He's giving Gracie her birthday present.'

'Good,' Daizell said. 'We'd like to have a word when he's done. Can we have the parlour? And don't tell him it's me, will you? I'd like to surprise him.'

'I bet you would. You sit down, I'll send him along.'

Daizell gestured Cassian towards the parlour. 'Shall we?'

'Yes. Or – I was wondering, is it a good idea for me to be there? That is, if he feels he has a hold over me, might that not make for a more difficult bargaining position?'

'He doesn't have a hold over you. Does he?'

'Well, the indiscretion—'

'If he threatens to use that against you in this place, Forster will rip him limb from limb,' Daizell pointed out. 'That said, I dare say he's more likely to ask you for money than he would be me, since I haven't got any. It might be best if you stayed out of the way, unless you want to tell him what you think of him.'

Cassian sighed. 'I just want my ring back. I am reluctant to pay him for it, since he's already had my pocketbook and possessions, but if I have to—'

He would not be doing any such thing, and if he was

considering it, Daizell wanted him well out of the way, where Martin wouldn't be able to read his face. 'Look, you go and read *Kenilworth*, so I can have it off you sooner. I'll get your ring back, or find what he did with it. All right?'

Cassian gave him a smile that twisted Daizell's heart in his chest, wistful and happy and trusting all at once. 'Thank you, Daize,' he said softly. 'Can I kiss you in here?'

'Very much so.'

Cassian caught his face with both hands, bringing their mouths together, kissing him with a breath-sapping intensity and then resting his head against Daizell's. 'I … you mean so much to me, Daizell. I'm so glad I met you.'

'So am I,' Daizell managed. Cassian's hands were on his shoulders now, hanging on tight, almost desperate, and he needed to say something. To ask for what he wanted, and find out if it even remotely resembled anything he could have. 'I – look, I want to talk about this. About us. Being together.'

Cassian looked up at him with huge, rainswept eyes, and Daizell's heart contracted like a clenched fist. He took a deep breath. 'The thing is, I love you.'

Cassian's eyes widened, lips parting in what looked like shock. Daizell hurried on, because it was too late to stop. 'I know it's not been long but I've been falling in love with you since we met, and I had to say so, and I can't let this end without trying to keep it because this has been the best few weeks of my life. I'm well aware I've no money and a tainted name, and I quite see the difficulty, and if – if it can't work, if you don't want to or have other obligations, I shan't make a fuss. Don't fear that. Only, if you want to be with me at all, then you should know I want that more than anything. Because I love you.'

'Oh God.' There were tears in Cassian's eyes and his fingers were tight on Daizell's shoulders. 'You really mean that? Me? Just me?'

'Who else is there?'

Cassian made a hoarse noise, and pulled him in hard, making Daizell realise how much he'd feared him pulling away. 'Yes. Absolutely yes. I want to be with you so much, Daize. You've changed everything, and the way you make me feel – I *need* you.'

Daizell kissed him, with all the urgency he felt. Cassian's lips met his fiercely for a moment, then he pulled away. 'Wait, listen. We have to talk. There's things I need to tell you, important things.'

'Not with Martin about to walk in on us.' Good God, this had been a stupid time to make a declaration. But he'd done it and Cassian had said yes, and Daizell couldn't stop grinning. Cassian wanted this, wanted *him*. Perfect. 'You should go, and I'll be up soon.'

Cassian nodded. 'If you have to offer him anything to get it back—'

'Do *not* say that where he might hear you. Go on, clear off. Leave it to me.'

'You're wonderful, and – I love you. I do.'

'Oh God, Cass.' Daizell kissed him again, grabbing his hair. 'Go, or he'll walk in on entirely the wrong thing.'

'Good luck.' Cassian added a last swift kiss, and left him alone, quivering with joy.

Cassian felt the same. He hadn't called him needy, or cut him off without a thought. He wanted Daizell.

Wanting wasn't everything, he reminded himself. He had a disgraced name and dubious reputation; Cassian had an overbearing family and responsibilities – presumably the things he needed to talk about – and that might be hard or impossible to overcome. Love didn't conquer all; in Daizell's experience it had yet to conquer anything at all.

But he'd still asked, because he loved Cassian, and the last few weeks had been perfect, and the only thing worse than the prospect of rejection had been the idea of losing that happiness because he was too afraid to ask for it. He'd asked, and Cassian loved him, and just for now he'd let himself hope for the best, because the best was more joyous than he'd dared to dream of in so long.

He was thinking of new ways to say *I love you*, feet up on a stool to aid cogitation, when Martin came in.

'All right, Daizell,' he said with a nod.

It was hardly a greeting for once-lovers who'd not seen each other in a year or more. But Daizell also saw warmth in the other man's eyes, and what looked like rueful embarrassment. He rolled his own eyes demonstratively. 'Good to see you too.'

Martin took a chair, apparently feeling that the civilities had been dealt with. 'So, what news? Forster tells me you're big with it.' He gave Daizell an assessing look. 'You seem well-fed.'

That was the result of more than a fortnight eating at Cassian's expense: Daizell had noticed his clothes were better-fitting. 'I hope that's a compliment.'

Martin shrugged. 'I hear you've got a … now, what would it be? Patron?'

That took Daizell's breath for a moment. '*What* did you say?'

'Wealthy, mousy, sharing your bed?'

'Go to the devil.' Daizell found his fists were clenched. 'Really, Martin, go to hell, and if that's what Forster said—'

'I drew conclusions.'

'I'll draw your arse into the street if you don't mind your tongue.'

Martin's brows were up now. 'I heard you were here with some pliant, plump-in-the-pocket sort. Am I mistaken?'

'You're a prick. He's a damned fine man, and he's *quiet*, not pliant, and I'm not sponging off him—'

'What, you've paid for your own food?' He raised a hand as Daizell took a deep breath. 'All right, all right, I'll take your word. You've a wealthy – not patron – *companion*. Good for you. What are you doing with him, then?'

'Helping him with something. Enjoying his company. One can do that, you know: be pleasant to one another and not treat people one cares for like punching-bags. One can talk about things, and care what each other thinks, and be ...' He waved a hand. '*Together*.'

'Good Christ,' Martin said. 'Are you in love or something? Oh my God, you are.'

'It's none of your business.'

'You *are*. Well, that puts a different complexion on it. A fellow with funds, though? I'd watch that if I were you.' Daizell took a deep breath; Martin held up both hands. 'Just saying. Rich men buy things and throw them away.'

'I am not bought, and Cassian is not buying. He has money, yes, but there are more important things. He trusts me. He *trusts* me, Martin. He thinks my father wronged me, he's trusted me with personal matters; he believes I can do well by him. It's ...' He gestured, since he had no way of voicing what that was or what it meant, and if he did find those words, they would be for Cassian. 'He trusts me.'

'Do you trust him?' Martin said. 'Can you? Really?'

That was a brutal question from him. Daizell met his

eyes. 'I love him. He loves me. I don't know if we can make something of this but I trust him to try. That's all anyone can ask.'

Martin pressed his lips together. Daizell couldn't quite make out his expression. 'Well,' he said after a moment. 'You deserve to be happy, Daize, and I'm glad for you. I'll buy you a drink, you and your beau. We can toast your future. Don't make more of a mess of it than you can help.'

'I don't intend to, and I'll hold you to that drink. But, talking of messes, I have a bone to pick with you.'

'About what?'

'Cassian, that's what. My lover. Under the name—' Damnation; he'd forgotten. 'Another name. You met him in Gloucester, bedded him, and robbed him, calling yourself John Martin ... Don't make faces,' he added, because Martin was staring at him with a look of stunned horror. 'If you're ashamed at being caught for it, you shouldn't have done it.'

'How—' Martin swallowed. 'How did you find me?'

'He told me about it and I realised it was you. He wants his ring back, the one you stole off his finger. God rot it, what did you have to be such an arsehole for? What terrible thing did he do that you felt obliged to take everything down to his clothes and the ring – his dead father's ring, for God's sake – off his finger? Did he dare to enjoy your company and say so? How long are you going to punish everyone you meet for one man's acts?'

He regretted that last immediately, since Martin's face had gone an unattractively grey shade. 'I'm sorry, I shouldn't have said that. But you—'

'Shut up. No, stop talking, Daize, let me think. That man – him – *he's* your lover?'

'We met, he asked me to help him retrieve his ring, we took a shine to one another. If you even think to use that—'

Martin licked his lips. 'Do you know who he is?'

'Cassian. His name's Vernon Cassian.'

'Oh Christ.' Martin pressed his fingers to his temples, making white dints in the flesh. 'Hell and damnation. I'm so sorry, Daizell. Truly, I am.'

'As you should be, and you can tell him so yourself. He's just upstairs.'

'Sorry for *you*, not him. I'm extremely sorry for you.' Martin exhaled hard. 'Just to be sure, we're talking about a short, inconsequential sort of fellow, yes? Brown hair, soft voice?'

'How many men did you fuck and rob in Gloucester?'

'One. I hoped he might have sent someone to retrieve his ring for him.'

'What? Why would he?'

Martin squeezed his eyes shut for a second, visibly bracing himself. 'Because the man I robbed – the wonderful lover who trusts you so – is the Duke of Severn. And it doesn't sound like you know that.'

Daizell turned the words over in his mind, gave it some thought, and said, 'Are you drunk?'

'I wish to God I was. What did you say he called himself?'

'Vernon Cassian.'

'He told me Wotton. In fact – this is burned on my memory – he's Vernon Fortescue Cassian George de Vere Crosse. Duke of Severn, Earl of Harmsford, Baron Crosse of Wotton, and Baron Vere.'

'No,' Daizell said. 'No, that's not— No.'

'Yes. And I know this for a fact, because when I attempted to pawn the ring, the pawnbroker asked me if it was a replica of the Severn ring. He showed me a picture of the bloody thing, so I went and found a likeness of the duke. It's a damned cheek to look that insignificant when you bear quite so many titles. Sailing under false colours.'

Daizell was barely listening. He couldn't seem to think. 'Severn,' he repeated. The child-duke of Severn had been to Eton at the same time as him, a few years below. Daizell remembered again that small, pale boy, and thought of Cassian with his dead father's ring put warm on his finger, and his responsibilities, and his Grand Tour, and how he had dropped shirts on the floor as if someone would pick them up. 'Oh Jesus.'

'I'm sorry,' Martin said again. 'I quite believe you trusted him and thought he trusted you, but you shouldn't have, and he didn't. He's a *duke.* And as for how I treated him, I know. I only meant to take the money, but he had so much – money, things, silver and gold – and it made me angry, and I just got ... carried away. Since when I've spent the last fortnight looking over my shoulder in a state of sheer terror, which I dare say I deserve. You're welcome to his damned ring. Good riddance. I was tempted to throw it in a ditch but I decided I'd rather be able to give it back.'

He fished the ring out of his pocket as he spoke. Daizell held out his hand, which was shaking a little, and took it: an odd, lumpy, rather misshapen thing in red gold.

'Doesn't look like much,' he said, because he couldn't think of anything else to say.

'A very unremarkable object at first glance, but if you examine it closely, it's a dragon,' Martin said. 'Much like its owner. I'm getting out of here. You're sure he doesn't have men with him?'

'Yes. Go.' Daizell should probably get more answers out of

him but he didn't think he cared any more. He didn't think he cared about anything at all.

He'd known Cassian was keeping his background private, but thought it was because he had not wanted to rub in his own prosperity to a man who had only the clothes he stood up in. That he was holding back out of natural reluctance to boast, that he didn't want to be seen to buy. He'd thought Cassian had trusted him. He'd said as much to Martin because he'd wanted to proclaim the joy of what he'd found.

What a fool. What a lie. What an embarrassment.

'Daize?' Martin was standing, looking down at him with pity that stung like a handful of nettles. 'I've seen that look on your face before, and may God punish every man who's ever put it there. You didn't deserve it from me and you truly don't from him, and if you want company, I'll wait for you. I swear not to be a prick about this.'

Daizell didn't reach up for his hand. Martin's sympathy wasn't comforting and he didn't want it. He wanted Cassian's hand on his shoulder, Cassian's comfort.

Cassian didn't exist.

He swallowed. 'I'd rather be on my own, I think.'

'Christ,' Martin said. 'I'm glad I took that titled nonentity's clothes; I wish I'd given him clap. I'm heading to Leamington Spa, then probably down to Oxford. I'll leave a note at the Rose and Crown in Leamington, if you should want to catch me up. For God's sake be careful, Daizell. Dukes are hazardous creatures.'

Chapter Thirteen

Cassian had retreated to their bedroom. It was a pleasant room for an inn, with a reasonably sized window, a reasonably comfortable bed, enough space for two men to share without being irritatingly on top of one another. Admittedly that was in part because neither he nor Daizell was particularly big, and in part because they enjoyed being on top of one another, but still, he was pleased at his own contentment in this small, bare room, decorated only with Daizell's shades.

Cassian's bedroom at home was three times the size. It had a luxurious bed that could fit five of him, a Canaletto and a lovely painting of his mother by Sir Joshua Reynolds on the walls, fine porcelain and beautiful furnishings and velvet curtains. It was a palatial room, and he was undeniably looking forward to sleeping in it again, but at this moment the thought of it had a very empty feel.

What was he going to do?

Daizell loved him. Daizell wanted to be with him, not just now but in the future, for as long as they could have. Daizell didn't know who he was, because Cassian had lied to him every single day.

Cassian wanted time too. Not just the remainder of his dwindling month, but proper time, long time, all the time. He'd stopped himself from making Daizell promises he didn't yet know how to keep, but he would make them, soon. He wanted to give Daizell everything, starting with himself.

They'd had day after day with nothing to do but enjoy one another, in bed and out, and with the inevitability of gravity, Cassian had tumbled headlong from liking to love. He craved Daizell painfully; he had wild thoughts of simply not going home that he knew were impossible but in which he allowed himself to indulge for shameful moments here and there. He needed cheerful, absurd, erratic Daizell with him, because when Daizell was present, he felt like himself.

And it was him that Daizell loved. *Him*, Cassian. Not the Duke, with his money and grandeur acting as compensation for his personal insignificance.

So all Cassian had to do was work out a way to tell him the truth, and also a means by which Daizell Charnage could be in his overly examined, ever-correct, scandal-free ducal life, and everything would be perfect.

There would be a way, he told himself. Daizell was ingenious, and Cassian was a duke, with all that entailed: wealth, power, authority. Between them, they'd come up with something, just as soon as Cassian admitted that he'd been lying to him from the moment they'd met.

He thought about how to do that, sitting by the window with *Kenilworth* unread in his hand, feeling rather sick. Daizell would surely understand that there had never been a good time; that saying it too early would have killed everything that had grown between them. He was still thinking about it when Daizell came in.

Cassian looked around, starting a greeting, and leapt to his feet as he saw Daizell's face. 'What's wrong? What happened? Are you all right?'

'All right? Well. That's a question. Here.' He walked over, grabbed Cassian's unresisting hand, and dropped something into it. Something small, cold, and gold.

'My ring!' Cassian hadn't let himself believe this was possible. He couldn't have borne imagining getting it back, only to learn it had been pawned or sold or lost. 'You got it. You found it. Oh God.' He pushed it on his finger with a shaking hand, feeling it slide into its rightful place, filling a gap whose yawning depths he only now let himself realise. The Severn ring, back where it belonged, and he would never, ever be so foolish as to lose it or risk it again. He gripped his right hand in his left, clutching the ring to himself. 'I can't believe it. Daizell, I owe you everything. I . . .' He looked up and his throat dried.

He'd seen Daizell's face as he walked in, wearing an expression he didn't recognise or like. That had been quite driven out by the joy of having his ring back, and as he'd looked up, he'd expected Daizell would be smiling. That he'd put on that grim look as a jest, a pretence something had gone wrong, in order to enjoy Cassian's happiness all the more.

He wasn't smiling now. He wasn't smiling at all.

'Daize?'

Daizell met his eyes in a long, hard, stare. 'Your Grace?'

'What's wrong?' Cassian asked, and then, too late, the words sank in. He felt colour draining from his face. 'Daize—'

'You have the ring you hired me to retrieve,' Daizell said. His voice was stiff and thick. 'The Severn ring. So that completes my period of service to Your Grace. You owe me fifty pounds.'

'No. Yes, but— Daize, listen!'

'To what?' Daizell demanded, the stiffness cracking like a thrown glass. 'To you explaining why you've made a fucking fool out of me for weeks and lied to my face? How could you do that to me? Why? Jesus Christ, did you think I needed to feel stupider than I am? Or did you just not think about me at all while you got what you wanted?'

'That's not true!' Cassian's face was burning, his throat closing. He hated being shouted at. 'You must see, I couldn't just say.'

'You couldn't just say who you are?'

'No! I couldn't! I was incognito!'

'So? What, if there's Latin involved, it's not a lie?'

'I couldn't say at first, and then, later, I didn't want to be the Duke,' Cassian said, the words spilling out urgently. 'I wanted to be myself with you. Not to have that standing in the way, because it would have done, you know it would—'

'It would. It *does*. And if I'd known it stood in the way before, I wouldn't have said and done a lot of things. I wouldn't have cared for you, and believed you cared—' Daizell was crying, Cassian realised with horror, angry tears in his brown eyes. 'I said things – felt things – This isn't fair. You had no right to make me love you when you always knew I couldn't.'

'No. Daizell, please.' Panic was creeping through him in a cold sweat. 'I should have told you before, and I'm sorry, but things were so perfect. I didn't want to spoil them before I had to. How could we have had that time, this week, if I'd said? It's been the best week of my life—'

'And as long as you're happy, that's what matters?' Daizell snarled. 'Listen to yourself. We couldn't have had this week if I knew you were a duke, because I wouldn't have done it! You've been fucking me in my sleep, and I never gave you permission for that!'

Cassian's stomach was roiling now with a sour brew of guilt and fear. 'I'm sorry! I really am, but when should I have said it? And for God's sake, is this really the worst thing in the world? Yes, I'm a duke. That gives me—'

'Money?'

'I wasn't going to say that, but since you ask, yes. I have money, and I have power. That means I can make things work for us!'

'How?'

'Uh – well, I don't know yet, but we can—'

'You don't know. If you could just fit me into your life with a wave of your hand, you'd say so. For God's sake, I don't know anything about your life – about *you* – and even I can tell how much scrutiny you're under. You had to go through this absurd wager of yours to get even a month—' Daizell stopped short. 'This wager. What was it? What were the terms?'

'Um—' Cassian could hardly remember at this point. 'That I could live as – as a normal person for a month. Not using my title or privilege, taking the stage and so on—'

'Living as a commoner.'

'Yes, exactly.'

'So telling me you were a duke would have meant you lost your bet.'

'Well, yes,' Cassian said, and then, 'No! That is not the reason, I swear. I didn't keep it from you for the bet!'

'You dragged me around half the Midlands in a set of miserable stages for your bet. You've got me mixed up with Sir James Vier again and Christ knows what other trouble coming my way, when you could have made everything we've encountered go away with your calling card and your purse any time you liked, for your bet. And you lied to me about who you were and let me love you, all for your damned bet!'

'It wasn't about the bet!' Cassian protested, but he knew deep down it was, a little, and he feared the guilt showed on his face. 'I wanted to manage for myself, not to just rely on my wealth—'

'And you've landed me in a pit of troubles while you got your experience. Why has all this been about what you want? What about what *I* might have wanted? Not having a half-mad brute on my tail, for one, and not to be made a fool of *again* by someone who never cared for me, who'll just leave—' He angrily dashed a tear away. 'But what you wanted was all that mattered, because you're a duke and other people aren't as important as you.'

'That – but— Daize, no, I didn't—' He had, though. He knew he had. 'I didn't mean to do that. I was trying to be like other people!'

'You succeeded triumphantly,' Daizell said. 'You're exactly like everyone else. I'm going.'

'No. Stop. I know you're angry, but don't leave now, not like this. *Please*.'

'What am I supposed to stay for?' Daizell shouted. 'To hear you explain why you didn't trust me? Why you led me this damn fool dance over a damn fool wager? Why you let me tell you everything I said when you knew bloody well you'd be going back to whatever ducal palace in a week or so, with your whole month's experience of being "like people", and I was nothing but a diversion?'

'You weren't that,' Cassian said. 'That's not true. I've been sitting here for the last hour thinking of a way for us to be together!'

'But there isn't one, is there? You've known that all along, and you made sure I didn't. I thought you were someone I could be with, and you let me think that, you let me hope. That was cruel. I didn't think you were cruel.'

'I didn't mean to be,' the Duke said, his voice dry and scratchy.

'But you were. Stop talking to me. I don't want to hear any more.'

He was throwing his things into a bag, haphazardly. So few things. The Duke swallowed down the lump in his throat. 'I have that fifty pounds—'

'Keep it,' Daizell said, not looking round. He fastened the bag.

'I owe you—'

'Yes. You do. And I'm not having you tell yourself it's all right because you gave me money.' He hoisted the bag and walked out. The Duke stared after him, hand over his mouth, and as Daizell slammed the door behind him, he crumpled to the floor.

He left the Green Lion an hour later, when he was sure Daizell had gone, sped on his way by an extremely unfriendly look from Forster. He'd stay in a different place tonight, and leave Coventry in the morning, he decided, although he had no idea where he'd go.

He ought not stay in a place with a reputation for mollying, even if that reputation was confined to people who wouldn't object. He was, after all, a duke. He went instead to one of the better hostelries Coventry had to offer, and commanded a room of his own, a bath, and the cleaning of his linen and boots, and sat in one of the public rooms afterwards with a book he didn't want to read, alone.

If he'd been in the Green Lion, he could have talked to the casual friends he'd made. Except they all liked Daizell, and he'd hurt him, so none of them would have talked to him any more. If he'd been in the Green Lion *with* Daizell—

If he were there he would be happy. As it was, he was as lonely and miserable as he'd been in his life.

He had some ten days left of his holiday, which felt more like an exile. He ought to make use of it somehow, though all he wanted to do was curl up on his empty bed. Leamington Spa was south of here, but his married cousin Louisa lived there with her husband, a solicitor, and there was too great a risk he might bump into her. He adored Louisa, who came between Leo and Matthew and had grown up racing around Staplow with the boys, and he would have liked nothing more than to stay with her now, the bet be damned.

But if he did that he'd have to talk about how he was. That meant lying, if only by omission, and he couldn't stomach any more lies to people he loved.

Not Leamington Spa, then. He flicked through *Paterson's British Itinerary*, and saw Kenilworth. It was only a single stage away. He'd go to Kenilworth because it was somewhere to go, and because moving was better than staying still, and because he had absolutely nothing better to do with his stupid ducal self.

He went the next morning, after a mostly sleepless night in an excessively large bed. He found where the stage went from and took a ticket and claimed his place, wondering as he did it how this had all seemed so daunting just a few weeks back. Because he'd been inexperienced, of course, and because he'd been alone. Everything was worse when you were alone.

Kenilworth proved to be a pleasant market town. It wasn't hard to find the ruins of the castle: a great mass of red stone, still standing tall, its bones bare and magnificent. The Duke strolled around, trying to make himself be awed by the history. Here Simon de Montfort had besieged Prince Edward, unless it was the other way around; here the Lancastrian kings had plotted in the Wars of the Roses. Here Queen Elizabeth had stayed, entertained and courted by Robert Dudley while he concealed his illicit marriage. That had ended badly, for everyone: Dudley's tragic wife, and Dudley who was suspected of her murder, and the Queen herself, who had died a virgin, or at least unwed.

He didn't care. He'd have cared if he was telling Daizell all about it, and Daizell would have cared while he listened, but they weren't doing that, and the misery of that fact left him too exhausted to walk further. He plodded to a grassy bank that seemed reasonably dry, and sat on it. It was another thing dukes didn't do, and he didn't care about that either.

He'd wanted to be a nobody, and now he was and he hated it. He'd liked being Mr Cassian very well indeed, thanks to Daizell, but having nowhere to go and nothing to do and nobody to do it with – one couldn't enjoy that. That wasn't leisure, or holiday: that was just filling time to get the day over with.

Was this how Daizell felt, drifting around in constant purposeless movement? He'd said he was lonely, but he'd never really elaborated on it, and Daizell elaborated on most things, except the ones that hurt. That urgency to talk, the readiness to fall in with any plan as long as it was a plan – the Duke could understand those things, given the sense of yawning purposelessness he felt after a single day without Daizell.

Daizell needed company, and he thought he'd found it in Cassian. And the Duke had seen that, and let him believe it and go on believing, never admitting that Cassian didn't exist, because he'd put his own selfish wants first. Because dukes always came first.

He hadn't meant to abandon Daizell. He clung onto that fact as if it was some sort of argument in his own favour. He had truly intended to find a way forward and – what, present it as a fait accompli? *I've lied to you, but to make it better, I've decided your future for you as well.*

Daizell might not even have minded that so much: heaven knew he was easy-going. If the Duke had told him the truth and offered him some sort of future, or even if he'd said, *Help me think of something*, Daizell would have come to terms with it, he was sure. If the Duke had just told him.

But he hadn't. He'd let Daizell hope and care under false pretences because he'd been enjoying the pretence. That was what it came down to, and the shame made him writhe.

'You shit, Severn,' he said aloud. It seemed the only possible word in the circumstances. 'You utter shit.'

He could have explained it. If Daizell had given him a chance to talk it out, he could have persuaded him, made him understand. Except that he'd had that chance every second they'd spent together, and hadn't taken it until his hand was forced.

No wonder Daizell had walked out. No wonder he hadn't wanted to hear any more. Lord Hugo had told the Duke a hundred times he needed to be more determined, more forthright. If he'd spoken up when he should have, he wouldn't be moping round a ruin, and Daizell wouldn't be—

He tried to think of what Daizell was doing, and could only see his face, red with anger, glistening with tears. Was he alone? There had been no sign of the man Martin Nichols and they'd been lovers once: would Daizell have gone with him, for lack of other comfort? The Duke almost hoped so. He couldn't bear the thought of Daizell alone again. Betrayed again.

He couldn't do this. He couldn't just sit here and let the man he loved drift away; he would not. He'd find some sort of answer to how they could be together that didn't founder on the rocks of his dukedom and Daizell's shoddy, shabby reputation, and he would find Daizell and present it to him. Just as soon as he thought of what it would be.

Restlessness propelled him to his feet. He marched around the picturesque scene, cudgelling his brains. He cursed Daizell's father, the wretched villain, and the damn fool position it had left Daizell in: notorious, barely educated, at once too much a gentleman and not quite enough of one. Could he be a permanent guest at ducal Staplow, when his own family didn't count him worthy? Would he even *want* to live at Staplow, with Lord Hugo and Aunt Hilda and probably their strong opinions on George Charnage? The Duke very much doubted it. Sometimes a hundred rooms didn't feel enough.

He had to find an answer of some kind. He couldn't let this go. Even if they couldn't be together, he couldn't let Daizell be lonely. It wasn't fair.

He strode forward, brow ferociously knit, and almost collided with a tall lady.

'I beg your pardon,' he said briskly.

'Not at— Oh! Mr, uh …'

The voice was terribly familiar. The Duke actually looked at her, and saw, with a sinking feeling, Miss Beaumont.

'Good heavens,' he said. 'Miss Beaumont. I thought you were in Scotland. Or – have you come back?' he added with a sudden hope. 'Should I be offering my congratulations, Mrs Marston?'

'No.'

'Oh.'

'I did not get married,' she said, in a tight sort of voice. Her big grey eyes looked rather red. 'Mr Marston chose – we had an argument—'

'Oh.' The Duke glanced around. 'Where is he?'

'I couldn't say. I left him in Manchester.'

'Oh.' He wished he had something else to say to this litany of disaster. 'Then who is your attendance?'

She shot him a vicious look. 'I don't *have* any attendance. I ran away from my guardian to elope and now I haven't even eloped and I've nowhere to go, so how I could have *attendance*—'

'You came down from Manchester alone?' Dear God. But, regrettably, his duty was clear and the Duke always did his duty. 'There is a bench over there. Would you like to sit down and talk about it?'

Miss Beaumont would. She poured out a tearful but reasonably coherent account of the journey from Stratford to Manchester, in which she freely admitted becoming exasperated by her intended. 'He was so *slow*. He was so dreadfully bad at all of the deceiving people we had to do, and Mr Charnage said we should get to the coast and take a boat, but Tony, Mr Marston, wouldn't because he gets seasick, of all the stupidnesses, and I dare say I was terribly impatient with him, but *really*. He exasperated me dreadfully. And – and then by the time we got to Manchester and we'd argued for a day or so, he asked me, did I truly love him or did I merely want to marry him to escape Sir James? And I just couldn't say it. I suppose that's even wickeder than eloping, isn't it? Eloping with someone I didn't even love – only I did, I'm sure, when I was seventeen, but I'm twenty now and we haven't spent much time together in years and I'm *sure* he wasn't so tiresome before – but he said I wasn't even marrying him for his money, I was marrying him for *my* money, which was worse, and he didn't want to be a cipher in his own life, and I'd just used him as a means to my freedom. That was awfully unkind, you know, because it was true. I wished it wasn't, but it was.'

'Yes,' the Duke said. 'That does hurt.'

She sniffed. 'He said if I didn't care for him, he certainly didn't want my money.'

'That was good of him.'

'I dare say it was very noble, but I was furious. We'd come all the way up to Manchester and gone through all this inconvenience so I could marry him and there he was refusing, which left me in the most dreadful scrape. And really, what was I to *do*? I suppose he wanted me to tell him I was sorry and he was wonderful, but honestly, I thought he was being a self-centred oaf. I *was* marrying him to be free of Sir James, and if he wanted something more it was quite right he shouldn't marry me, but for heaven's sake, could he not have raised the subject before *Manchester*? So I left.'

'And he let you come back all this way on your own?'

'He said, if I didn't love him, then I should do as I pleased. I think he was expecting me to cajole him into a good humour.'

The Duke thought about that – a young lady, unchaperoned and miles from home, being told by the man with power over her future to prove her love – and took a breath. 'I would like a word with Mr Marston.'

'I did hurt his feelings awfully,' Miss Beaumont said fairmindedly. 'I know I shouldn't have done it but I truly thought we'd rub along so much better than we did. After all, once we were married we'd have lots of money and that solves most problems, doesn't it? And I didn't lie to him. One might have thought he'd prefer an honest arrangement to a flattering deception. But then, if he'd truly thought I was heels over head for him in the first place, I can see why he was disappointed. I've made an awful mull of this.'

'Something of one,' the Duke was forced to admit. 'And what now? Why are you here?'

'I have to be somewhere,' Miss Beaumont said bleakly. 'I took the stage south, on my own, which has been really quite unpleasant. I bought a ring, on Mr Charnage's advice – is he not here?'

'No. No, we're not travelling together any more.'

'Oh,' she said, with clear disappointment. 'Well, the ring helped, but all the same— Anyway, I got to Birmingham and I realised I didn't know what I was coming back *for*. I've no family and my trustee has made it very clear he doesn't want to be troubled and I cannot go back to Sir James.'

'No, you can't. Not after this escapade. If he finds out—'

'But I don't know what else to do.' She sounded very young as she said that. 'I've made such a dreadful, dreadful mistake. I should have lied, shouldn't I? I should have told Tony he was wonderful and flattered him into a better mood—'

'No, you should not,' the Duke said. 'What you should have done from the start is found a lawyer who would act on your behalf if your trustee won't.'

She shot him a look. 'I wrote to five lawyers. Only one of them wrote back, and he did so directly to Sir James, as my guardian. I am under age and a woman. They won't listen to me.'

And the rush to a hasty marriage would not make her

seem any more worth listening to. The Duke didn't point that out. 'Have you met anyone you know on your travels? Can anyone – except Mr Marston, I suppose – say for certain you eloped?'

'Well, I did leave that note for Sir James, saying I was running away with Mr Charnage.'

'But you can argue that was to throw him off the track. What we need is— Oh.'

She straightened at his tone. 'Have you had an idea? What is it, Mr, uh—'

'Cassian,' the Duke said, yet again. 'What we need is a respectable married woman who will take you in and be ready to swear you have been staying with her these past days. You left that note and ran to her house – we'll say she's an old friend. And you can stay with her while we instruct a lawyer who will look into your case, or at worst fend off Sir James until you come of age.'

'I do see that would be marvellous,' Miss Beaumont said politely. 'Do you happen to know any such lady?'

'My cousin Louisa. She lives perhaps six miles from here.'

'Oh! Really? But are you sure she'll agree to that, if she is a respectable woman?'

'She is a very respectable woman indeed, married to a successful solicitor, and she has the soul of a pirate. Shall we pay a call?'

Miss Beaumont clasped her hands, face alight, then something changed in her features. 'Wait. You are very kind, to offer that, but why would you?'

'Because you are in a deal of trouble, and it appears to be my role to help you out of it. You can't expect me to say *I'm sorry to hear it* and leave you in trouble.'

'You could,' Miss Beaumont pointed out. 'Lots of people

would. Almost everyone, actually. And, Mr Cassian, I don't at all wish to offend you, or to make unfair implications, but I also don't wish you to have the wrong idea just because I have happened to elope with two gentlemen already. I think I have learned my lesson.'

'Good. And, if I may reciprocate your frankness, I have no designs on your person, your hand, or your money,' the Duke said firmly. 'I am very well breeched on my own account, I doubt you and I would suit, and my affections are already and entirely given elsewhere. In fact, I must beg you to take the greatest pains to avoid any possible imputation of impropriety. We will travel by the public stage.'

She gave him a glowing look, apparently believing the precaution was for her benefit rather than his. Call it both, the Duke thought. 'Thank you. That is exceedingly gentlemanly.'

Chapter Fourteen

Miss Beaumont's courage lasted until they arrived at Louisa's house. The Duke's was faltering a little too. It was evening, and Louisa might well look askance at his arrival. It couldn't be helped.

A maid answered the door. Mrs Kentridge, wife to a country solicitor, lived in significantly less magnificence than had Miss Louisa Crosse, grand-daughter to Severn, but from all the Duke had seen, she was blissfully happy in her provincial surrounds.

'Please tell Mrs Kentridge it is her cousin Sev,' the Duke said, hoping the maid wouldn't make the connection. She apparently did not, escorting him and Miss Beaumont in without much ceremony, and they waited in the drawing room until Louisa entered, wearing a very wary look.

'Good eve—' she began, and then, 'Sev! It is you! What on earth?'

'Hello, Louisa.' The Duke jumped up and kissed her soundly on the cheek. 'I told your maid your cousin Sev: did she not say so?'

'She said exactly that, and I assumed she'd run mad. Is this to do with your absurd wager? Yes, I have heard all about it. But good heavens, I beg your pardon,' she added, casting an assessing eye over Miss Beaumont. 'Sev, you will surely introduce your companion?'

'Miss Eliza Beaumont, Mrs Louisa Kentridge.' The ladies

exchanged bows. Miss Beaumont was now bright red. 'Miss Beaumont is a friend of mine who has suffered a misfortune.'

'Misfortune,' Louisa repeated.

'Yes. In fact I have come to ask if she can stay.'

'Stay … with us?'

'With you.'

Louisa looked at her, then at him, and inhaled deeply. It was very like the way Uncle Hugo inhaled before explosion, and the Duke cut her off in some haste. 'Pray listen. Miss Beaumont has been through a shocking time, and she is in grave need of help. I require a respectable matron of unimpeachable virtue to stand for her, and an excellent lawyer to fight for her. So I came here. She has been shockingly treated.'

'I dare say. It is quite amazing how many pretty young ladies are shockingly treated and require the help of susceptible young men,' Louisa said, with a decided chill in her voice.

Miss Beaumont made a stifled noise. The Duke said, 'Louisa, that is grossly unfair. You know very well that I am not susceptible, and you know nothing of Miss Beaumont at all. I quite agree this situation is unconventional but I am trying to make it conventional as quickly as possible, for the sake of a lady. I hope that you will help me.'

She did not look to be in helpful mood. 'This seems scarcely appropriate.'

'Indeed, it is not,' the Duke said. 'But I am not bringing immorality into your house and I am sorry you should think that of me.'

'I should not make any such accusation,' Louisa informed him loftily. 'So what precisely are you bringing into my house?'

'It's a long story which I shall tell you presently, but—' He needed the big guns. 'Harum-scarum, Lou.'

It was the term they had used as children, the one that commanded utter loyalty in the teeth of authority. A call of *Harum-scarum!* obliged the hearer to tell barefaced lies ('No, I have not seen Louisa anywhere. Is it really time for her piano lesson?'), or take any measure necessary to support the caller. Leo had invoked harum-scarum on the never-to-be-sufficiently-bemoaned-by-Uncle-Hugo occasion they'd decided it was necessary to walk round the complete span of the castle atop the battlements, and the Duke had even claimed it was his idea when retribution descended.

He had scarcely ever invoked it himself. Maybe it was time.

Louisa's lips had parted. She said, with concentrated force, 'Brothers. *You*. Goodness me.'

'Please,' Miss Beaumont said, with difficulty. 'If Mrs Kentridge does not – does not wish to accommodate me—'

'Not at all,' Louisa said swiftly. 'No. I made a foolish assumption, and I beg your pardon. And it is certainly too late for you to go anywhere this evening.' She moved to ring the bell. 'So I shall have a room made up, and you shall go upstairs and wash, Miss Beaumont, while my cousin explains to me *exactly what is going on*. Will you stay with us tonight, Sev?'

'No, I shall take a room somewhere.' He had no intention of spending a night under the same roof as Miss Beaumont, for both their sakes.

'You must at least remain for dinner. I shall send to the Star for a room for you.' A maid arrived: Louisa gave a series of orders that ended with Miss Beaumont being swept upstairs with a programme of tea, washing, and settling in.

Louisa waited for the door to shut, turned to the Duke, and said, 'Is this an elopement? Oh, Sev, is it a wedding?'

'It is neither and I intend to keep it that way. Miss Beaumont has no interest in me—'

'Fiddle.'

'She's an heiress in her own right. Listen. You know about my wager with Leo?'

'Of course. He is staying here too. He and Father have been arguing up hill and down dale, over the bet and his losses to that ghastly Sir James.'

'Ah.' The Duke grimaced. 'I hope he doesn't consider my calling on you to infringe the terms. I needed to do something with Miss Beaumont.'

'Leo will do as he's told. I want to know everything, immediately.'

He explained the situation. Louisa had the quality, rare in the Crosse family, of being able to hear a story without undue interruption. She listened as the Duke outlined his travels, touching as lightly as possible on his travelling companion because he did not trust himself to talk about Daizell. He explained Miss Beaumont's predicament and actions very frankly, since Louisa should know what she might be getting into, and at the end she drew a long breath.

'Good heavens, Sev. You *have* been going it.'

'I know.'

'No wonder you look exhausted. And you have taken Miss Beaumont under your wing because—?'

'Someone had to. Could you have walked away, seeing her alone?'

'Yes,' Louisa said crisply. 'The little fool seems to have brought much of her trouble on herself, and encountered a great deal less than she might have, running around the country with men. I suppose she's an innocent: one would have to be, to be so very stupid.'

'She isn't stupid. She's inexperienced, and she was facing the prospect of Sir James pressing his suit.'

'True,' Louisa admitted. 'Is he as vile as all that? Leo holds strong views on him, but then he owes the fellow a lot of money.'

'Dreadful. He is a vicious swine who employs violent brutes and beats his horses unmercifully. I have no doubt he would beat his wife. But if he was the most virtuous man alive, she doesn't like him, and that should suffice.'

She nodded slowly. 'You are a good man, Sev, and Miss Beaumont is fortunate. What do you intend?'

'I'd like you to keep her. Perhaps give her some useful advice,' he added in the certain knowledge that Louisa wouldn't be able to stop herself. 'If you felt able to say that she came directly to you from Vier's house—'

'Are you asking me to lie, Your Grace?'

'We could call it a benevolent deception if you prefer.'

'I'll have to talk to Kentridge about that,' Louisa said. 'What else?'

'Kentridge's help. Miss Beaumont needs a lawyer who will prod her trustee into action, and take steps against Vier. Break the guardianship if possible, or at least keep her out of his clutches. I don't know what can be done, but he doubtless will, and he is welcome to use my name.'

'That is liable to attract comment. Are you quite sure—'

'Positive. She has no interest at all in marrying me, nor I her. Indeed, she would not have accepted my help if I had not assured her that it came without any expectation on my part or obligation on hers.'

'Fiddle,' Louisa said again. 'I don't wish to offend you,

Sev, but one might see this as a well-woven trap, and you are a catch.'

'I think you will find she's rather too straightforward for that,' the Duke said. 'And she doesn't know who I am.'

'I beg your pardon?'

'Hence the 'cousin Sev'. She knows me as Mr Cassian, because of the bet, and I have not disabused her. I—'

He'd put yesterday's confrontation to the back of his mind for a little while, relieved to be concentrating on Miss Beaumont's woes and enjoying Louisa's company instead. Now his betrayal and Daizell's hurt came rushing back, with all the more force for having been briefly pent up. He swallowed. 'I hid my name all the time. Lied to people.'

'Sev?'

'It's nothing. Nothing. I – It's been a peculiar time for me.'

She gave him a long examining look, and shook her head. 'Bother Leo and his foolish wagers.'

'Don't blame Leo. I wanted this and it has been ... I would not have missed it for the world. With everything, I would not have missed it.' She was watching him, looking puzzled and a little concerned, and he forced a smile. 'I have learned a great deal. Partly, I have learned that anonymity is a curse as well as a blessing, and now I shall have to tell Miss Beaumont I am a duke, which will be embarrassing.'

'More so for her, I expect.'

'Yes.' The Duke winced internally on Miss Beaumont's behalf. He was deeply glad she had spoken so frankly about her sentiments, or lack of them, towards him, but he suspected she might not feel the same. 'Could we perhaps tell her *after* dinner? I should prefer her to be comfortable.'

'She would not be more comfortable with me if I started by colluding to deceive her,' Louisa said. 'For goodness' sake.

Now, that sounds like Leo coming in. You may greet him, and at least wash before we dine because you may be anonymous but there is no need to look like the scaff and raff. I shall have Miss Beaumont down here for you to speak to after that.'

Dinner was a great deal more enjoyable than the Duke could have predicted. Leo greeted him with great good humour, and was easily persuaded, under his sister's quelling eye, to agree that this family dinner lay outside the terms of the wager. Miss Beaumont had been incredulous and horrified to learn of Mr Cassian's true identity, but she carried on bravely despite her natural mortification, aided by Leo's clear admiration. He was a tall, well-built man with a deal of charm, most unlike his titled cousin, and he chaffed the Duke about his deception in a way that soon had Miss Beaumont daring to giggle.

'It does seem a quite extraordinary thing to be doing, Mr—Your Grace,' she said.

'Severn,' the Duke said. That was a perfectly respectable mode of address for a family friend. 'And perhaps it is a little odd—'

'Absolutely absurd,' Louisa said. 'You and Leo are nothing but a pair of schoolboys.'

'I don't quite agree, my dear,' James Kentridge remarked. He was rather older than his wife, an intelligent man with a deceptively sleepy look. 'As I understand it, Severn set out on his adventure with a purpose.'

'I did.' The Duke caressed the ring with the pad of his thumb, checking it was there as he had done no more than fifty or sixty times that day. 'I wanted experience of life which one cannot get from a castle window, or the Bow

Window either. I wanted to encounter people and see how they saw me – *as* me, not as my position. I wanted to prove to myself that I could manage. I don't know if I have achieved that entirely. I have failed badly at some things. But I have certainly learned.'

'To use the stage?' Leo asked.

'To use the stage, to order my own meals and tend to my own belongings and to decide the course of my own days. That may not sound much to you, but then, you have not always been wrapped in lamb's wool.' He paused. 'Also, I escaped from kidnappers.'

That created a suitable effect: in fact, Leo choked on a mouthful of wine. The Duke told the story, eliciting gasps and laughs in a very satisfactory manner. Possibly he had learned a little from the evenings in the Green Lion. Miss Beaumont seemed entirely unsurprised by his account of the men Sir James had sent after her, but Leo grew red with fury on both her and the Duke's behalf.

'The man is a dashed villain,' he said. 'A villain, I say. To send the sort of beasts who would manhandle Miss Beaumont—'

'And who did manhandle Severn,' Louisa said. 'I trust you intend to repay that, Sev?'

'I do, yes,' the Duke said. 'Mostly by removing Miss Beaumont and her wealth from his grasp. Kentridge, I hope you will be able to act for me there?'

'I can certainly speak to your lawyers in London. And I know George Boyson, Miss Beaumont's trustee, slightly,' Kentridge said. 'He is disinclined to take trouble on himself, but I expect he might be persuaded that your displeasure is potentially more troublesome than Vier's.'

'Do tell him that. I shall be happy to make it good.'

'Absolutely right. Vier must not be allowed to get hold of Miss Beaumont again,' Leo said. 'I won't have it.'

'You are so very kind, Mr Crosse,' Miss Beaumont said, cheeks pinking, apparently unaware that the Duke and Mr Kentridge would be doing all the work.

'It sounds as though Sir James is as malevolent as Leo has said,' Louisa remarked. 'Why did your father put you in his hands, Miss Beaumont?'

'My father wasn't terribly pleasant either. They were business partners. And Sir James can be charming, and plausible.'

Leo snorted disbelief. Louisa, ever sisterly, remarked, 'Well, he persuaded you to play with him. Repeatedly.'

'Oh, I hope you did not,' Miss Beaumont said. 'He cheats.'

Every head turned to her. 'I beg your pardon?' the Duke said.

'Sir James cheats at cards. At whist, at least. He has a system with his friend Sir Francis Plath. I hope you weren't playing with them, Mr Crosse?'

'They played as partners,' Leo said grimly. 'When you say *cheat*—'

'They have a way of signalling what cards they have, and want the other to play. If he says "gentlemen" before they start, he's saying he is strong in hearts – that is, has good cards or a lot of them,' she glossed helpfully, 'and "trifle" indicates strong in diamonds. So he might say "excuse me, gentlemen, a trifling cough" or "let me not trifle further, gentlemen" and both of them mean that he has hearts and diamonds. "Come", as in "come, your card" or "will you come to dinner tomorrow?" means he wants Plath to lead a spade, but if he says "Plath" with it, it means to play a low spade. That sort of thing. It has to be very subtle, so as not to be obvious when they do it. I have heard them rehearse it.'

Leo was going purple. Mr Kentridge said, 'Really? That is exceedingly interesting.'

'*Interesting?*' Leo exploded. 'It's bl— blasted disgraceful!'

'Yes,' said Kentridge. 'Do you think you could write down everything you recall of his system, Miss Beaumont? And, Leo, not a word of this. No posting back to London to confront him. Don't tell anyone at all.'

Leo blinked at his formidable brother-in-law. 'What? Of course we must.'

'I think Kentridge means, keep quiet until the right time,' the Duke said.

Kentridge gave him an approving nod. 'This may be an opportunity. A weapon, even. But he must not be alerted too soon. Does he know you know about this, Miss Beaumont?'

'I don't think so. I was eavesdropping,' she said frankly. 'One had to in that horrid house.'

'We will consider the matter well before we act,' Kentridge said. 'The first concern must be to extricate Miss Beaumont from Vier's guardianship. She should, I think, stay here, as Severn has suggested. I shall go down to London to put matters in motion. If Vier is capable of sending bravos after her, it might be best if Leo also stays in my absence.'

'It would be my privilege,' Leo told Miss Beaumont.

'We shall cut our cloth depending on what I can find out. As to the matter of cheating, we shall keep it in hand, and consider when best to strike.'

'Goodness me, Kentridge,' Louisa said, with a curl in her voice. 'How ruthless.'

'What about you, Sev?' Leo asked, evidently reluctant to observe his sister making eyes at her husband.

'I'm not going to act until Kentridge has had a chance

to get the lie of the legal land,' the Duke said. 'Meanwhile I have some ten days to go on our wager—'

'Oh, nonsense,' Leo said, in chorus with Louisa. 'You must see this is more important. I absolve you.'

'You will do no such thing. It is a wager, and I want to complete it. And, really, this is best not in my hands. I don't greatly want Vier to find out that I was directly responsible for aiding his ward's flight, or abetting the deception of a vicar—'

'Of a what?' Louisa demanded.

'Oh, but that wasn't you. It was Mr Charnage,' Miss Beaumont said.

'Charnage?' Leo repeated.

He couldn't avoid it any longer. 'That's right. A gentleman I travelled with for a while.'

'Which Charnage? Because as far as I know, of the men of that name—'

'Daizell.'

'You cannot mean that.' Leo sounded distressingly like his father. 'Are you serious?'

'No relation of George Charnage, I hope?' Louisa put in.

'His son.'

'*What?!*'

'Sev, you've gone mad,' Leo said bluntly. 'Daizell Charnage? Travelling with *you*? For the Lord's sake, man! It's one thing not to be high in the instep, but—'

'He is not responsible for his father's crime. It is a great shame he has been punished for it.'

'He was very kind and pleasant,' Miss Beaumont offered, looking from face to face.

'Oh, pleasant, absolutely,' Leo said. 'Very likeable fellow. Nevertheless—'

'No, not *nevertheless*.' The Duke could feel his cheeks heating. 'Daizell cannot be blamed for what his father did.'

'Oh, yes he can. The sins of the fathers are visited on the children, like it or not,' Louisa said. 'And as I understand it, he's done plenty of his own accord. Was there not an elopement?'

'That was me,' Miss Beaumont said meekly, looking at her plate. 'But it was not his fault, precisely.'

'It was a complicated situation,' the Duke said. 'And half of what is said about him is Vier's spite, which comes back to what George Charnage did.'

'He was unquestionably running a gaming ring at Eton,' Leo said. 'I should know; he cleaned me out twice. Honestly, Sev, there is adventure and there is mere recklessness. What are the chances he recognised you? What will you do if he goes around claiming a close friendship with you? If he uses your name or turns up at Staplow, presuming on your acquaintance?'

'I should be very glad to welcome him to Staplow.' Under the cover of the table, the Duke was twisting his napkin, tighter and tighter. 'He is my *friend*.'

'For pity's sake. I can see you have been living it up on your holiday and I always liked Charnage, and I dare say it isn't fair, but life is not fair. Severn cannot be friends with his sort and that is all there is to it.'

'Perhaps Severn can't,' the Duke agreed with a dry mouth. 'As with all the many things that Severn must and must not do. I understand they matter. But do I not matter? I cannot be Severn all the time, only doing what Severn does and behaving as Severn must, with no life of my own that is not Severn. I will *die* in there.'

Louisa frowned. 'Are you all right, Sev?'

'I've no idea what you mean,' Leo said briskly. 'The fact is, you have your position and you have its obligations, and can you imagine what Father would say, knowing you were associating with George Charnage's son, giving him countenance? Still, he won't let the fellow set foot in Staplow so I dare say there's no great harm done.'

The Duke stared at his plate. Then he looked up.

'Remind me,' he said. 'Who is the Duke of Severn?'

Louisa and Leo exchanged glances. Louisa said, 'Sev—'

'Who?'

'You,' Leo said. 'Of course. But—'

'Who is master at Staplow?'

Leo tried for a joke. 'Well, that's a tricky—'

'Who?' the Duke shouted, and saw his cousin recoil. 'By God, I will not have this! Constant dictation of what the Duke may do, and how, and who with – *I* will decide what I do, and make my friends as I please! Who the devil are you to tell me otherwise? If people don't like my choice of friends, they may set themselves outside my acquaintance, and if the family don't like *my* guests in *my* house, they are not obliged to live there! I will have no more of this accursed trammelling. I am a grown man, and the obligations and duties of my station do not extend to having my friends selected for me! How *dare* you tell me who I may care for?'

He was standing, fists planted on the tablecloth. He wasn't sure when he'd got up. Leo and Louisa were both bright red. Kentridge watched with interest. Miss Beaumont's eyes were wide.

'And I will tell you this,' the Duke added furiously. 'Daizell Charnage has been unfairly maligned, and I will not have it. If he has my countenance – and he does, because he is my friend – then any man who chooses to abuse or to cut him on his father's account offends Severn. I shall make that known, and we will see how the sheep of the Polite World behave when the dog barks!'

He stopped there, for lack of anything else to say, heart pounding. He'd never in his life lost his temper so comprehensively or shouted so much.

Leo's mouth was set tight. 'I must beg Your Grace's pardon for any offence I have given.'

'Shut up, you fool,' his sister hissed.

The Duke looked between them, and quite suddenly could not bear any more. 'I apologise for raising my voice, but – you must understand – it is not tolerable. I will not tolerate it. I think I should go; I have some way to travel tomorrow. I hope I can safely leave Miss Beaumont with you?'

'Of course,' Louisa said. 'Take whatever time you need, Sev. I hope we will see you soon.'

The Duke nodded to them all, and walked out. As he left, Leo started to speak. Louisa told him to shut up again.

The Duke set off for Coventry the next morning, in a curricle hired at the best livery stable Leamington Spa had to offer, drawn by the fastest pair they could provide. Be damned to the bet; he'd learned the hard way how difficult it was to track a man down once you no longer had his trail.

He was going to find Daizell. He was going to apologise – fully, humbly, as he should have done at the time. And he was going to offer all the power at his disposal to end the ostracism that Daizell had suffered for his miserable parents and Sir James Vier's spite, along with the odd indiscretion that was really no worse than anyone else's. He'd do that whether Daizell wanted any more of him or not, because it was right.

That vow, and the pleasure of driving himself in a well-sprung conveyance at a satisfactory speed, carried him all the way to the Green Lion in Coventry, where Forster the landlord seemed unexcited to see him, and suggested he might want to leave. Cassian felt warmly towards him for his defence of Daizell, but had no intention of taking the dismissal.

'I need to know where Daizell went,' he repeated politely. 'It is important I find him.'

'Look, mate, your quarrels aren't my business—'

'No, they are not. Answer me, please.'

Possibly the landlord saw something in his face, because he said, 'He headed south. Went to meet Martin at the Rose and Crown in Leamington.'

Where Cassian had just come from. Marvellous. He changed horses and headed back, cursing Martin Nichols – why was Daizell travelling with that blasted man? – and fate, and mostly himself.

At the Rose and Crown, he learned that he had missed Daizell by some thirty-six hours. He and Nichols had taken the coach towards Worcester. Cassian took this news with as much grace as he could, considering he seemed to be fated to drive in circles. He was going to find Daizell, and he was going to apologise if it was the last thing he did.

Two days later, he broke the journey at the March Hare in Broughton Hackett. He hoped only to get some sort of lead there before arriving in Worcester. Instead, he walked into the inn, and straight into John Martin.

'You!' Cassian said.

'Oh God.' Martin sounded exhausted, and looked it too, his eyes dark-ringed. 'Look, sir, Your Grace, if you're planning to have me arrested—'

'I don't care about you. Where is Daizell?'

Martin opened his mouth, hesitated, and considered him for a moment. 'What for?'

'Because I want to talk to him.'

'What do you intend by him?'

'That's none of your affair.'

'Hurt or help?' Martin demanded. They were having this conversation in a passageway, in low voices. It was probably indiscreet. Cassian didn't care. 'Because you've given him quite enough hurt, and if you mean more – well, which is it?'

'I want to speak to him, and I mean him no harm, and—' He had no desire to reveal anything to Martin, considering, but the man was defending Daizell. The Duke had a momentary mental image of Daizell taking comfort in his old lover's arms, and quashed it. If he'd driven Daizell to that, it was his own fault. 'I need to apologise. I hope he will hear me. Maybe he won't but that is his choice, not yours.' He held Martin's gaze. 'If he doesn't want to speak to me, I'll leave.'

Martin examined his face a moment longer. 'And what if he needs help? Would you act for him, Your Grace, or is it more important to stay incognito?'

His tone was aggressive, but there was something raw in it and Cassian's spine prickled. 'What do you mean, help? What's happened? Is something wrong?'

'You might say so. He's in gaol.'

Chapter Fifteen

Daizell sat in the cell, arms on his knees and head in his hands, wondering if he could identify the point at which his life had gone quite so badly wrong.

It depended where you wanted to start. Being fathered by George Charnage had been a tactical error from which he'd never recovered. Expulsion from Eton had primed the world to take a dim view of him. He could have handled himself better around his father's crime, instead of his bewildered efforts to defend his parents, not to mention the drinking. The obscene profiles had been enormous fun to do at the time, but he should have ensured they were gathered up and burned. He probably shouldn't have tried to elope with Miss Beaumont. And he should never, ever have talked to Cassian, or agreed to travel with Cassian, or fallen in love with Cassian.

Perhaps that wasn't the stupidest thing he'd done in his life, but it felt like it. His wretched idiocy, his self-delusion, his pathetic need for once not to be disposed of as a trivial obstacle to someone else's life: they stewed miserably in his stomach, unless that was the gaol food.

If he wasn't a bloody fool, he would have realised that Cassian was far more than he said. Perhaps they might have set up a sensible sort of arrangement, one where they could be friends who fucked, and Daizell lived at the Duke's expense. A kept man, as Martin had suggested. That would have been the sensible thing to do, if he could have borne it, if he'd kept his head and negotiated a satisfactory bargain, if he hadn't wanted Cassian to love him.

He didn't want to be Cassian's shameful secret or paid bedmate. He wanted Cassian as he'd had him over the last glorious weeks, friend and lover and companion, there all the time with his sun-and-rain eyes, that wondering hopeful smile.

But he wasn't going to have that, because Cassian was the Duke of Severn. If he wasn't a damned needy fool, he could at least have taken the news with grace and had another week. He could have taken the fifty quid, come to that. It would have helped.

And, while he was on the subject, he could have refrained from punching Mr Thomas Acaster in the face.

He'd quite forgotten about that business on their travels, relegating the coach spill to his collection of unwanted memories, and entirely disregarding the little turd who'd caused it. He certainly hadn't considered the matter as he and Martin had made their desultory, unenthusiastic way towards Worcester: he'd had other things on his mind. It had been a miserable journey. Martin might have intended sympathy, but nothing he said had actually supplied it, and in any case he wasn't Cassian. Daizell wanted Cassian so badly he felt sick with it, and couldn't seem to come to terms with the fact that he didn't exist.

They'd got off the stage at wherever it was, some place so trivial Daizell couldn't even recall its name, because they were both fed to the back teeth of the journey and each other's company, and who had they encountered but Mr Tom Acaster. Daizell hadn't even noticed him. He'd spotted Daizell all right, and brought a constable.

Daizell had been promptly hauled before the local magistrate, one Sir Benjamin Acaster. That had gone as well as might be expected. Sir Benjamin had listened to his son's complaint, 'examined' Daizell by bellowing abuse at him without letting him get a word in, and committed him to prison to await trial. And here he was in a cell, glaring alternately at the dirt-streaked lime-washed walls and the earthen floor, cold and damp and hungry, in expectation of a trial that was to be conducted by, wait for it, Sir Benjamin Acaster.

Which meant he was doomed. In a fair hearing he might point out the context of his assault on the young man, but he wasn't going to have one of those, nor would there be anyone to appeal to. Magistrates were meant to sit in pairs, but the turnkey had informed him that Sir Benjamin sat alone, and liked it that way.

Sir Benjamin wouldn't want to send Daizell to the Assizes, where he risked a more severe punishment but would at least get a hearing. Instead, he would use his powers of summary justice. That, as he had said with relish at the preliminary examination, meant a whipping. There would probably be a fine too, and since Daizell had no way to pay such a thing, he was inevitably looking at a spell in gaol as well.

Daizell wasn't sure which prospect was the worst. He did not want to be whipped: the idea made him feel sick. He'd been caned at school and that had hurt, but whipping – he'd seen the mess that made of men's backs, he was not stoic about bodily harm, and his gorge rose at the thought of the pain, the shame, the scarring.

He didn't want to be a gaolbird either. He hadn't conducted himself with any great righteousness throughout his adult life and was used to being a gentleman of uncertain fortune and degraded reputation. But whipping and imprisonment meant a fall he'd probably never recover from.

This was it. This was the moment he stopped being a not-quite-gentleman and became a marked, degraded scoundrel. He'd broken the magistrate's son's nose because he was a stupid, thoughtless fool, and he was going to pay in blood and skin and pain, and nobody was going to help him. Martin probably would if he could, but he couldn't, and Daizell had seen nothing of him since the arrest. Doubtless he had vanished away, like a sensible man. And nobody else in the wide world cared an iota for Daizell.

He wasn't going to wonder if Cassian cared. He'd felt a panicked impulse to call on the Duke of Severn's name in front of the magistrate, and choked it down. It wouldn't work anyway: who'd believe him? How could he prove it, with Cassian miles away and Lord knew where? And he'd consigned Cassian to the devil so it wouldn't be fair to drag him into this.

It wouldn't be fair anyway. This was Daizell's mess, self-created, self-inflicted. It was time he faced up to that, and to the fact that nobody else was going to bring order or certainty or purpose to his life. He wouldn't find value, in himself or anything else, by drifting along, seeing where the currents took him, for the rest of his life. He knew very well where they would take him: inexorably downward till he drowned.

So he'd endure the whipping and whatever other spite Sir Benjamin chose to mete out, and wait for it to be over, and then he'd… do something. Go and seek a place in one of the profile studios in London or, better, set up one of his own in a provincial town. Give up trying to be more than he was, use the skill he had, cut shades for shillings all day every day, and if that felt desperately bleak, it was at least better than the pointless existence to which he'd let himself be habituated until Cassian had made him dream that he mattered.

Daizell set his mind to that, trying to imagine himself enjoying life as an independent artisan rather than starving in a gutter, until the turnkey came to get him.

He was marched into a mean and dingy room for trial, hands chained. It was hardly a courtroom, but justice round here was rudimentary at best. Sir Benjamin sat at a table that represented the Bench. Daizell was shoved into a pew, with the smirking Tom Acaster on the other side. His nose had set very badly, Daizell was pleased to note. A scattering of people sat to watch. Daizell didn't look at them: he didn't want to be gawped at.

Sir Benjamin cleared his throat. 'In the matter of common assault, brought against Daizell Charnage by Thomas Acaster—'

'These proceedings are unlawful.'

That was Martin's voice. Daizell looked around sharply, and saw him standing in the small crowd.

The magistrate swelled. 'I beg your pardon? Who are you, sir?'

'My name is John Martin, and I object. It is not right for the prosecutor's father to sit in judgement of this case. It should be heard by another magistrate.'

'How dare you?' Sir Benjamin retorted. 'I am the magistrate here! I rule without favour! Is my son to be denied justice on the basis of his father's name? I think not, sir. He is the victim of a vicious assault, and I will judge the case with impartiality and discretion.'

Martin scoffed. Daizell tried without success to catch his eye in order to indicate *Stop it!* 'Sir, you are bent on vengeance rather than justice. This is not right. You should release the prisoner until a fair judge is found, since you are clearly no such thing.'

If Martin was trying to get him hanged, he was going the right way about it. Daizell would have liked to have his hands free, just so he could put his face into them. He contemplated the reddening magistrate with a sinking heart.

'How dare you insult my impartiality?' Sir Benjamin bellowed. 'Be silent or I will commit you for contempt of court!'

Martin shrugged. He didn't back down easily in the face of threats, though that trait was less admirable when Daizell would be the one paying for his insolence. 'Very well, your honour. If that's how you want it, I submit a witness for the court.'

Sir Benjamin's eyes bulged. 'What witness? None has been bound over for the prosecution except my son. No other will be heard.'

Martin smiled. It was not a pleasant smile. 'I think your honour will find you're wrong about that.'

He sat down. Cassian stood up.

Daizell's mouth dropped open. He'd been so busy gaping at Martin that he hadn't even noticed Cassian behind him, slim and unobtrusive. Now he walked up to the bench, and Daizell had no idea how he could have missed him. How anybody ever could.

'What is this?' the magistrate demanded. 'Who are you, fellow?'

'I am the Duke of Severn,' Cassian said. 'You will address me as Your Grace.'

'Nonsense,' Sir Benjamin said with an incredulous laugh.

He was seated. Cassian stood in front of him, but he didn't have the posture of most men in front of a magistrate. He was very definitely looking down, with an expression of remote displeasure. He wore his old coat, but the golden card-case he took from his pocket was engraved, and when he placed a card on the bench with a click, the wrought gold ring gleamed on his finger.

The magistrate picked up the card and his face changed. Probably a duke's cards felt expensive.

'I am Severn,' Cassian repeated, and his voice was different, somehow. Remote, and very, very superior. 'I was travelling with the prisoner when the reckless stupidity of this man, your son, illegally tooling the coach in contravention of numerous by-laws, caused an accident. At least three people were extremely badly hurt, perhaps killed. I note none of them are here, in this room where you propose to try Mr Charnage.' A touch of anger in his voice now. 'Mr Charnage saved the life of a child in the wreck, acted heroically afterwards in preventing further accident, and aided wounded passengers to escape the coach. While he did so, your son reeled around drunkenly, making oafish jokes, uncaring of the damage he had done. And now you propose to abuse your position and carry out judicial vengeance on Mr Charnage for his very natural anger, while *your son* goes unpunished for his reckless, drunken destruction. You disgrace your office, Sir Benjamin. This is contemptible.'

The magistrate was the red-purple colour of a raw steak, or an oncoming apoplexy. Cassian went on, voice low and steady, slim form upright, staring down at him as he sat. 'You are committing an egregious abuse of power and I will not tolerate it. You are unfit for your post, sir, and your son is unfit for the company of gentlemen. I will make both of those things known across England.'

The magistrate opened his mouth. Cassian held up a finger. 'Weigh your words. I will brook no insolence.'

'I – but— How do I know you are who you say you are?'

'I beg your pardon?'

His words fell like stones, clear and separate, and the magistrate swallowed. 'That is, how do I know, Your Grace?'

Cassian gave him a few seconds' silent scrutiny. 'You may send to my seat, Staplow, or to London to my solicitors, should you choose to doubt my word. If I am delayed on my travels by this, I will hold you responsible for any consequences. You will in any case release Mr Charnage on my cognizance, now, while we wait for the proof you require. It is regrettable you have not applied such high standards of evidence in your judicial duties.'

'Your Grace, please.' Sir Benjamin was sweating visibly. 'I'm sure we can discuss this. As men of goodwill.'

'Goodwill?' Cassian repeated. 'I think not. You take up my time. Will this prosecution go forward?'

The magistrate swallowed again, and made a surreptitious gesture to his son, who croaked, 'No.' His father positively snarled at him, and he amended it to, 'No, Your Grace.'

'So Mr Charnage is free to go.'

Sir Benjamin nodded eagerly. 'Yes, Your Grace.'

'Then why is he still in irons?' Cassian enquired, and the edge to his voice did more than any bellow could have achieved.

'At once, Your Grace. Get on you fool!' the magistrate snapped at the turnkey. 'Your Grace, please believe that this unfortunate misunderstanding – a very natural inclination on a father's behalf – I beg your tolerance—'

'You seem not to grasp the issue, Sir Benjamin,' Cassian said. 'I was in that coach. Your son could have killed Severn. There *will* be consequences.'

Sir Benjamin's mouth opened and shut. Cassian stood in silence, back stiff with hauteur. His coat might have been ermine.

He waited for Daizell to be freed, then turned and swept forward without a word to the magistrate, Daizell and Martin scrambling along in his wake.

Daizell stepped out into his first fresh air and sunlight for two days, blinking. Cassian stopped in front of him, and gave a tiny shudder, like a horse shaking off flies. Daizell shot a glance at Martin, who pulled an appalling face.

When Cassian turned he looked like himself again, without the cold, superior expression and upright bearing. 'Daizell. Are you all right?'

'Uh. Yes.'

He couldn't think of anything to say. Probably 'thank you' would be appropriate, except he didn't want to, unless he did. He was suddenly very aware of his gaol-stink, of the fact he hadn't slept, washed or shaved in two days, still less changed his linen. His coat was torn, his only coat, and he looked like what he was, a shabby ruffian. Cassian was a duke.

Daizell wanted to demand, *What are you doing here? Why did you come?* but he wasn't sure he could bear the answer.

Cassian seemed equally tongue-tied, for all his earlier poise. They stared helplessly at each other. Martin looked between them, and gave a sigh. 'Daize, he wants to talk to you. If you want to hear him out, he's taken a parlour in the inn. If you don't, we can go.'

'Please,' Cassian said scratchily. 'Would you hear me out? Or even just let me apologise?'

Daizell nodded. Martin touched him on the arm. 'I'll get your things from the gaol, and be in the public if you need me.'

There was indeed a private parlour in the inn. They walked in, and Cassian shut the door. Daizell wandered over to the other side of the room. He was slightly concerned this might be a dream: that of course the Duke of Severn had not appeared to save him, that he would wake again and still be alone and facing a whipping.

'Daize,' Cassian said. He sounded real, for what that was worth. 'Oh, Daize. I have so many things to say to you, but before I start, I really didn't mean what I said then. About the crash, and the important part being what might have happened to me. I truly don't believe that, and please don't think it. I just wanted to give him the worst time I could.'

Daizell couldn't argue with that. The magistrate's face had collapsed in on itself with horror, and young Master Acaster was probably getting pepper at this moment. 'How were you there? How are you here? Why is Martin here?'

'I came to find you, and met him on the road,' Cassian said. 'He said you were going to be prosecuted for hitting that fool, so we, uh, came up with a plan.'

'For Martin to object, and you to come in if that didn't work. Why?' The answer was all too obvious, but it still hurt enormously, churning miserably in his gut. 'Were you – were you trying not to lose your wager?'

'Oh God. No,' Cassian said urgently. 'Not at all. I wanted him to intervene because I didn't want to do that. I didn't want to sweep in as the Duke of Severn come to rescue you. I hoped that he could make the magistrate realise that his corruption wasn't going unobserved, and get you out of trouble. I didn't want you to owe your deliverance to me when it was all my fault you were in that position in the first place.'

'No, it wasn't. I hit that idiot.'

'You were on that coach in the first place because of me. Because of my wager, and my foolishness, and my lies, and I'm so sorry, Daizell. I hurt you horribly, and I will regret it for the rest of my life. You have every right to be furious, and I know an apology means very little when I chose to act as I did, and you don't have to listen if you don't want to. But I'd like to explain myself if you'd hear me out.'

They were standing in the parlour, watching one another. Daizell's pulse was thumping in an unpleasant thready way. He moved to lean on the mantelpiece. 'You did hurt me. A lot. For a *bet*.'

'It wasn't,' Cassian said urgently. 'That was how I got into the situation, but it isn't the reason I lied. Please, could I – are you all right?'

'Fine.'

'No, you're not. You're awfully pale. Have you eaten?'

'Not for a while,' Daizell said. 'The accommodations in gaol weren't very generous.'

'Sit,' Cassian said urgently. 'And, oh Lord, you want a wash, don't you? Not to listen to me chatter. And your coat— Oh, Daize, this is all my fault. Will you let me put this right, for now? And if you want to hear me once you've had a chance to recover yourself, we'll talk later and if you don't, we won't. But let me do something because you look shocking. *Please*.'

Daizell was painfully hungry, quite thirsty, unpleasantly aware of his dirt, and entirely exhausted after the battering of the last days. A prouder man might have refused anything from Cassian, even so. Daizell was fresh out of pride, and he had empty pockets and nothing to his name.

So he nodded, and Cassian strode out into the hall, calling for attention. He'd learned. Or he was using his title; Daizell wasn't sure and didn't have the energy to care.

He was conducted to a comfortable room, and brought lavish quantities of food and ale, which he ate in a borrowed gown because his clothes, retrieved by Martin, had been taken for washing and his spare linen had been stolen in gaol. He ate alone while a hot bath was prepared, of which he made good use, scrubbing away the visible evidence of humiliation and misery, and then he slept because he couldn't keep his eyes open any longer. He woke for long enough to devour another good meal, and slept again, and woke the next morning feeling at least physically back to something like normal.

That meant he was restive. In fact, he was on tenterhooks, because he was going to have to speak to Cassian and he didn't want to.

He didn't want to hear apologies, or explanations. He absolutely didn't want declarations. He didn't want any of it unless it came with something he was determined not to hope for, because hope was no longer something he could afford to indulge. The cost was too high.

He would have liked to take up his bag and leave, slip away quietly, but he couldn't because he had nothing to wear. This was absurd.

He ate the large breakfast provided in a dressing gown and a bad mood, and then sat by the window, cutting very unkind profiles of Sir Benjamin Acaster for want of anything else to do, when there was a knock and Cassian came in.

He offered Daizell a small, uncertain smile. 'Good morning. You look a little better?'

'I feel better, for the sleep and the food. Thank you for those – I assume you're paying; I can't. I'd apologise for my undress, but my clothes have been removed.'

'Your things will be ready by the afternoon,' Cassian said. 'Please command whatever you want in the way of food or drink or anything else. And I owe you fifty pounds. I know you didn't take it before but I owe it to you and I'd like you to have it now, before anything else.'

'What anything else?'

Cassian's shoulders sagged a fraction. 'I was hoping you'd talk to me, and let me talk to you. It's up to you, but I wish you would. But please take the money first because I owe it to you and you earned it. You found my ring, and nobody else could have done that.'

Daizell took the note he held out, because he'd be a fool not to. This would at least replenish his wardrobe, and if he was sensible it would see him through the year. He intended to be sensible. It was about time.

'Thank you,' he said again, trying to sound a bit less grudging. 'I don't want to go over everything. I can't see the point. But you didn't have to come back, or rescue me, and certainly not identify yourself to do it.' The Duke of Severn intervening to rescue a gaolbird Charnage: he wouldn't want that story to spread. 'So if you want to call it quits here, we could part friends?' It sounded more hopeful than he'd meant. He hadn't quite realised until he spoke that he did want to be friends, or at least to believe in Cassian's friendship.

Cassian stood still, his eyes fixed on Daizell's face. He swallowed before he spoke. 'Is that what you want? To part?'

'We *have* parted. But it wasn't how I'd have wanted to end things, and if you want to put matters on a more amicable footing—'

'That's not what I want at all.' Cassian had gone rather pale. 'I don't want to end things. I didn't come back to say goodbye. If – if that's really what you want, though, if you don't care to hear me out because you're not interested, then—'

'How can you not have come back to say goodbye?' Daizell demanded over him. 'What else is there to say? You're Severn! I appreciate what you've just done for me, I truly do. But if what you're going to say boils down to, "I'm a duke and I have to go back to my palace", I'd rather we just agreed you have to, and didn't go over it all. What's the point?'

'I am a duke, and I do have to. The point is, I don't want to.'

Daizell didn't think Cassian was a man for scenes, but his rainswept eyes were wild. This was going to be awful. 'What is it you want to say that will change anything?' he demanded. 'You're talking about apologising, but what you need to apologise for is that you were always out of my reach, and you knew that, and I didn't. And however much you apologise for that, you'll *still* be out of my reach, and I don't need to have that hammered home.' His throat ached. 'You lied to me and now I'm left loving a man who was never real, and there's no point in you explaining why you did that to me. It won't make things better.'

'Oh God. Daize, did you mean that?' Cassian took two steps forward and dropped to a knee, grabbing Daizell's hand. 'You still love me?'

'We are not going to do this!' Daizell almost shouted. 'Do

you have any idea what it feels like—' He'd had perfection for a handful of days, and briefly believed he could keep it, and he didn't need to be told this mess was bad for Cassian too. 'You were always on a lark. I understand that. You don't need to rub it in.'

'No. Listen.' Cassian's eyes were fixed on his. 'Actually *listen*, Daizell, because you have entirely the wrong idea. I am begging you to hear me. Please.'

He didn't want to listen. He wanted to run away, to find a blanket and shove his head under it and not have to plough through a conversation that, at best, would only make him feel worse about what he'd lost.

But he couldn't leave the room in a borrowed gown, and the Duke of Severn was kneeling by him with what looked like real pain in his eyes.

'All right,' he said, with less grace than he'd have liked. 'Go on.'

Chapter Sixteen

For someone who had begged for a hearing, Cassian didn't start talking at once. Daizell didn't hurry him; he didn't want to listen. He felt miserable and harried and haunted, and Cassian had put all those feelings there.

Maybe he had something to say that would take them away. Maybe not.

Daizell pulled his hand free, because he didn't need to be touching. Cassian took that hint, rising and pulling over the other chair so they faced each other across the table with its cut paper and scissors.

Cassian took a deep breath, visibly steeling himself. 'All right. First, the bet. I made it with my cousin Leo as an excuse to get away without attendance and find my ring. I told you all that. What I didn't say is that I wanted, *needed* to stop being Severn for a while. That's why I made the assignation with Martin in the first place. I needed, just for a little while, not to be a duke.'

'What's wrong with being a duke?'

'I wouldn't know,' Cassian said. 'I don't know about being anything else. My father died when I was six. Before that I was Harmsford, the courtesy title, and when he died, I became Severn. I haven't been called by my first name in my life. Not that I like my name, but I have been Severn and only Severn almost since I can remember. The only people who ever played with me as a normal child were my cousins. The whole world puts me at a distance because of my position. I have friends, of course, but as Severn. My uncle has spent two decades grooming me to be Severn, him and my valet and everyone around me, always saying Severn must do this and that, Severn is obliged, Severn may not lower himself. Severn, Severn, Severn. That's my whole purpose in life: to fill a Severn-shaped hole. I don't suppose I do it well, but nobody asked me if I wanted to do it at all. And it is a very luxurious, privileged hole, far better than the holes most people find themselves in. Nobody asked you if you wanted to be George Charnage's son any more than they asked me to be Severn's, and clearly I had the preferable lot in life. But it's stifling all the same.'

He looked up then, as if expecting an interruption. Daizell didn't have anything to offer. Dukedom wasn't a problem he'd ever considered, and he was fairly sure he'd prefer it to his own troubles, but Cassian was speaking with unusual urgency, venting something he'd been holding on to for a while.

'So, you wanted to get away?' Daizell tried.

'Cabined, cribb'd, confined. I needed to be not-Severn, just for a little while. That was when Martin approached me – and he didn't know who I was, he wasn't carefully respecting me. I had, or thought I had, one evening where I was being judged on my own merits and found satisfactory. Well, that went poorly. I felt useless, worse than useless. Held up by the scaffolding of my privilege, Leo said, and he was right, and I thought, if I don't find a way to – to carve a space for myself, Severn is going to close in around me until all that's left is the scaffolding. All outside and no inside. I don't know if I'm explaining this very well, but… I wanted to be someone who wasn't Severn so very much, just for a little while, to see. And then I met you, and I *was*. Oh, goodness, Daize.' He rubbed a hand over his face. 'You didn't treat me as the Duke, or carefully *not* treat me as the Duke, which is worse. I was Cassian with you for the first time in my life. Nobody's ever called me that before. I never dared ask anyone to.'

'What? Why not?'

'Because—' Cassian's mouth moved, then he picked up the paper on the table. Daizell had cut the caricature in one piece without any further snipping, so the surrounding excess paper might have formed a hollow cut except for the one long snip for access. Cassian put that sheet down so the wood of the table formed the magistrate's profile. 'Look. This is Severn, or at least, something that makes a Severn-shape. And this is Cassian.' He put down the inside cut, the solid image, next to the other piece. 'One is the opposite of the other, and I don't know how to be both at once. I've always tried to be Severn as well as I could but that didn't allow any space for Cassian, because – well, I've seen you make a hollow cut. When you do it properly, you start by destroying the inside part of the paper, don't you? You pierce a hole in the inside and cut it all away bit by bit, to make the perfect unsullied outside shape.'

'Cass—'

'Only, you don't have to.' Cassian sounded urgent, almost feverish. 'You showed me that. I want to be ...' He gestured at the hollow cut on the table, with its surrounding paper cut just once, otherwise intact. 'It isn't quite perfect, it's a little bit damaged, but it's almost right. There's an outside and an inside and they both work, and that's what you gave me. When you saw me, and listened to me, and expected me to do a good job of things. You didn't have any Severn-shape at all, you just saw Cassian, and I didn't want to change that. I couldn't bear to lose it, and if I'd told you, I would have. And, as you pointed out, all I was thinking about there was myself. It was selfish and deceptive and unfair to you. I know that. But I liked who I was with you. Who you were, and who I was, and what we had together. I liked it so much, and – and every day we had together helped make Cassian into a real person.'

'You are a real person.'

'Cassian wasn't. He didn't even have a name.' Cassian swallowed. 'And then I was, and I could be, because of you, and if I'd told you the truth that would have ruined it.' He tried a smile. 'My uncle likes to say, if the truth shames you, the fault lies with you, not with the truth.'

Daizell wasn't so sure of that. There were lots of things one could be ashamed of that weren't one's fault. 'You can't help being a duke.'

'But my silence was for my benefit, at your expense. And that was dreadful of me for all sorts of reasons – cowardly and dishonest, but also ungrateful. Because you're wonderful, Daize.' His rainswept eyes were wide and intent. 'I don't think you know how wonderful you are. How much you care, how kind you are, how ridiculously tolerant and loving and practical and ingenious, and accepting. That most of all. I've never in my life been myself as I have been with you. And you didn't do all that because I'm Severn; you did it because you're Daizell. So wonderfully, perfectly Daizell. And I wished I could just travel with you forever and keep you company and see if I could make you as happy as you make me.'

'But you couldn't,' Daizell said, voice thick. 'Because you are Severn, and you always had to go home.'

'Yes,' Cassian said. 'And also no. Because you found out, and I went to see my cousins, and they were saying – oh, things about what Severn could do and who he could associate with, as usual, and I realised that I can't have two separate lives.'

Daizell set his jaw. 'Is that not what I said at the beginning?'

'No. Because the point is, I need to be ...' He moved the inside cut, dropping it into the empty outline, filling the gap. 'Not Severn with Cassian as a guilty secret, and not Cassian playing a game of pretend that he isn't Severn. Cassian must be Severn, but Severn has to be Cassian *as well*, for purpose and humanity and living. I realise I'm talking about myself in the third person as though I'm Julius Caesar, but do you see? I want a whole life. I want you in it, as my friend, my lover, my Daizell. As *yourself.* Because I could be myself with you and I think – I thought – you could be happy with me and I want you to be happy more than I can say. I know I didn't behave that way—'

'You did,' Daizell said. 'Except at the end, you did.'

'I want to be happy with you,' Cassian whispered. 'Or sad with you, or angry with you, but *with* you.' He swallowed. 'If that's what you want, of course. If you don't, or not any more, I do understand. My position is going to make everything very tiresome, and I conducted myself appallingly, and I'm not terribly special other than being a duke. I know all of that. But I've spent the last three weeks falling quite desperately in love with you, and even if I have already ruined everything, I need you to know that I love you, I wish I hadn't hurt you, and when I did, it was never, never for something as foolish as a bet. I was hollow, and you let me be there. I want to be with you. So the only question is if you'd like to be with me.'

'It's not the only question. I wish it was that easy.'

'Do you? Really? Oh God, Daize. Please tell me I haven't spoiled everything and I swear I will make this easy, or at least possible. It has to be possible.' Cassian slid to his knees again, by the chair, urgently grasping Daizell's hands. 'You're so generous and ridiculous and wonderful and – my good, my very good Daize.' He bowed his head over their joined hands. 'I hurt you, and I missed you, and I love you.'

'Cass.' Daizell whispered it. Cassian's hands tightened on his. 'I missed you too. I wanted there to be something for us.'

'There can be. There has to be.'

'But what? I have to know. I need to. It's been so lonely and so pointless and I thought I had something with you—'

'*Daize—*'

'I can't be thrown away again. I don't know why people find it so easy to throw me away.' He blurted that out, feeling the horrible childishness of it: the bewildered realisation that his mother cared only for his father, and his father for nobody at all. 'My parents, and everyone I thought was my friend, and Martin, and then you – no, let me finish. I can't keep only mattering when other people care, because they always stop caring. I can't be disposable all my life.'

'I don't want you to be!'

'But if I can't see you or be seen with you, or visit you – what do you have in mind? That I should sit somewhere rural and wait for you to call when you're not busy with your dukedom?'

'I'm not asking that at all. I want you *with* me, and I want you to have your life back. Surely we can manage that between us. I'm a duke, and you're brilliant.'

'No, I'm not. I lurch from crisis to crisis and I ended up in gaol! What sort of companion is that for a duke?'

'One that changed me,' Cassian said. 'And you're entirely wrong. You tracked Martin down and got my ring back. You saved a child's life. You taught me how to negotiate the world and kept me safe when I was a hopeless greenhorn and came to save me when I was kidnapped—'

'I *got* you kidnapped. You rescued yourself.'

'You stole a horse to come to my rescue!' Cassian said indignantly, and then his mouth twitched. 'Which perhaps was not entirely sensible. But I wouldn't have even thought to do something about being kidnapped before I met you. I only had a knife with me because I was copying you, and the way you deal with the situation in front of you. Not in that awful efficient way of bear-leaders – I had the most tiresome man on my Grand Tour, always sweeping in to make everything easy for me, and demonstrating how wonderfully competent he was all the time, which meant I never did a thing. You're not like that—'

'No. I'm really not.'

'Good!' Cassian said vehemently. 'I don't want another person to run my life for me. I'm fighting off dozens of them as it is. I want to do things for myself, and I want to be myself, all of me, and I want you with me because if I tried to do it alone the castle walls would come pushing in again, and the duty and the ceremony, and my space to be Cassian would get smaller and smaller until I was squeezed to death. I need you to be the person who keeps the space clear and who doesn't let me hide away from the world, or disappear under a pile of ermine. When I was with you, I told stories in an inn and people *laughed*.'

'I knew you loved that,' Daizell said, his heart aching like a bruise.

'You showed me how. You looked so pleased with me, for me. I need you, Daize. I dare say I could manage on my own. Perhaps I could still be Cassian without you. But I don't want to.'

Daizell made a noise in his throat. Cassian let go his hands, grabbed his shoulders, and kissed him, and Daizell sank into the kiss, feeling tears running down his face, not caring.

He'd come back. He wanted more. They surely couldn't have more but he still wanted it, wanted Daizell, and that knowledge was everything. That knowledge plus Cassian in his arms again, the grip of his fingers, the urgency of his kiss.

They didn't speak as they stripped one another, Cassian pulling the gown off Daizell's shoulders, Daizell wrenching off Cassian's sadly battered cravat. There wasn't much to say, unless there was far too much, and the silence was soothing. Lips and fingers and skin could do the speaking for now.

Daizell pulled Cassian to the bed, laid him down, and lay with him, relishing the closeness as much as anything. He could simply have stayed there and held him, but Cassian's hands were roaming frantically, urgently, as though he needed to persuade himself Daizell was really there, and his need was contagious. Daizell hauled him round, so he lay on his back with Cassian over him, and Cassian crawled down his body, kissing his way as he went, and got his mouth to Daizell's prick.

'Oh God,' Daizell said aloud, on a breath. 'Cass. Please.'

Cassian had a clever mouth, he knew. They'd done this a couple of times, but he was giving it everything he had now, using lips and tongue and teeth and the roof of his mouth, sucking hard and soft, changing the pace as though he was trying to drive Daizell out of what passed for his mind, and by God it was working. The Duke of Severn, giving him the gamahuching of a lifetime. He'd got his fingers in Cassian's hair at some point, grabbing a handful, and Cassian's hands were hard on his hips, because he was only using his mouth, keeping this going for an agonisingly long time that passed far too fast. Daizell moaned and bucked under him, and spent in his mouth with sobs of pleasure that could all too easily have been the other kind.

Cassian stayed where he was crouching over him for a moment, then made his way back up the bed to pillow his head on Daizell's chest.

'Really, you ought not be a duke,' Daizell said at last. 'You should do that professionally.'

'I try to please.' Cassian's head was heavy on him. 'I'm not assuming I've been forgiven, by the way.'

'You don't have to make anything up to me. I don't know if I understand what it's like to be you, but I heard what you said. I don't suppose there was ever a good moment to say *By the way, I'm a duke.* And I don't blame you if you weren't able to trust me, in your position.'

'I did! I *do*. It wasn't that.'

'Well, it should have been! You need to be more careful. What were you thinking, making assignations with someone like Martin? If he'd known who you were—'

'You think he'd have blackmailed me?'

'Not him, but someone like him might have tried it, and then where would you be?'

'I know.' Cassian's head felt a little heavier on his chest as he said it. 'That's why— Ugh.'

'What?'

'I never, before— I've only ever had, uh, paid companions.

You know. An extremely discreet, very expensive brothel. It was better than nothing, of course. Probably. Actually it was awful. Not the people, they were very pleasant, but I went four times and every time I felt wretched afterwards. But it was all that was available because at least that way one could guarantee discretion.'

Daizell squinted down at the top of his head. 'You couldn't just fuck an – well, not an equal, but at least an earl or some such?'

Cassian gave a laugh without mirth. 'The opportunity has never arisen. For one thing, I'm Severn, and for another, I'm me.'

'Rubbish. Don't say that.'

'It's not false modesty. I know I'm not much to look at. I can't complain, given everything else I was born with.'

'You're everything to look at. The problem is that people *don't* look,' Daizell said. 'They don't see. Anyone who actually looked at you would see you're beautiful, and if they let your dukedom get in the way of that, they're a fool.'

Cassian raised his head at that, and the look in his yellow-grey eyes, the shape of his lovely, wistful mouth … Daizell pulled him up, and kissed him hard, and Cassian wrapped himself around him, clinging on. Daizell kissed his hair, his ear, anything that he could reach, and Cassian kissed his neck open-mouthed, hungry and urgent. 'Daize. Lord. My good, my lovely Daize.'

Daizell knew that tone by now. 'Talk to me,' he whispered. 'Please.'

And Cassian did, so gentle, so loving, whispering endearments, taking it long and slow so that Daizell spent again, soothed and shivering and cherished, in his tight embrace.

Chapter Seventeen

They lay in silence for a little while after that. Cassian was exhausted by all the talking, and Daizell looked much the same, but the desperate, sick misery had gone from his eyes. Even if they couldn't make this work – and they would, he was determined they would – Cassian would always be thankful he'd been able to repair some of the damage he'd done.

'Thank you for giving me a chance,' he said aloud.

'Mph. I'm glad you came back.'

'So am I. And that I found you. And was there in time.'

'That part was particularly good,' Daizell said. 'Not to say spectacular.'

'Oh, don't.' Cassian buried his face in Daizell's glinting chest hair. 'Dramatic entries are not my forte.'

'They truly are. It was a marvellous sight. Stalking up and giving that magistrate the fish-eye.'

'I think you mean to say, asserting the natural authority of my position.'

'Swinging your duke around.'

Cassian gave a yelp of startled laughter. Daizell grinned down at him, and Cassian smiled back, feeling a ridiculous bubble of joy expanding in his chest. 'I may say, it is a great deal easier chasing people across the country in my own vehicle. I am proud that I have acquired experience of the stage, but I'm never taking it again as long as I live.'

Daizell blinked. 'Wait. Your own? Does that mean you lost your bet?'

'It doesn't matter. I had to find you, and I didn't want to lose time.'

'What was the stake? Or – no.'

'No?'

Daizell made a face. 'If it was a guinea, or some such, I don't think I want to know.'

Cassian grabbed his hand. 'It was truly never about the bet. But since you ask, it was my greys. That is, I have a matched pair of—'

Daizell sat up, jolting Cassian's head off his chest. 'Your greys? You don't mean the Duke of Severn's greys?'

'*My* greys. Yes. Leo wanted it to be a stake that counted. Which it did,' he added with a grimace. 'I trained them myself, and they are a wonderful pair.'

'But you've lost them!'

'Rather them than you,' Cassian said. 'If I had delayed, and you had been convicted and gaoled or whipped while I dallied— No. If letting Leo have my greys is the price of finding you then I count it cheap. But I don't want him to give them to Vier.'

'Sir James? Why would he do that?'

'He lost a great deal of money to Vier at cards. He thinks, no doubt correctly, that the horrible man will take my greys in settlement: he covets them. I will not let him have them while there is breath in my body, so I shall have to – ugh. I don't know what I can do. Leo won't take my money.'

'Really?'

'My uncle always bent over backwards to avoid exploiting his position as my guardian.' He sighed. 'It was a difficult path to tread, and hard for my cousins too – growing up in luxury that wasn't theirs, with their shrimp of a cousin as the special one. Other people might have been resentful about it, or greedy. Leo is, oh, punctilious. He absolutely will not take my money, and if that ends up being painful for me, as now – well, I can understand why he might feel justified in a little jab here and there. But if my greys suffer for it, that would be my fault, and I can't have that.'

'Could you not explain that to him?'

'Leo isn't sentimental about horses. He thinks they're just animals. And he does owe Vier a great deal of money, so he's in rather a bad position. Although given Vier probably cheated to win it—'

'What?!' Daizell yelped.

'Oh goodness, I haven't told you. I had a time of it in your absence.' He outlined the meeting with Miss Beaumont, and the revelation of Vier's system of cheating, through which Daizell choked and spluttered with outrage. 'I left them at Louisa's house,' Cassian concluded. 'Lord knows what's happened since. But never mind Leo or Miss Beaumont either: what are we to do about us?'

Daizell flopped back on the bed. 'That – I want to say, it's up to you. You're the one with responsibilities, and power, and money.'

'No. That won't work. You can't feel as though it's my life and you're an addendum to it, still less that I have all the power. I don't *want* all the power. If I wanted someone who would do exactly and only what I choose in a way that suited me, I could have paid for that.'

'You could,' Daizell said. 'You could have paid someone to give you a rude awakening at any time, come to that. Why didn't you?'

'Because—' Cassian had to stop and think through it.

'Because that wasn't an act I wanted performed for the sake of it, not really. It mattered because of how you did it. Because I could trust you with it – telling you a secret truth, believing you would not abuse it. Because you wanted to do it for me. Because it was *you*.'

Daizell stared up at the ceiling, silent, for a long moment. 'And what about marriage?'

Cassian had heard that men conducted their own ceremonies, sometimes in a spirit of misrule and sometimes in one of seriousness. He wasn't sure about that. 'Um, it's not legal? But if you want that—'

'What? I meant you, you fool. You're a duke, you need heirs. Haven't you an arrangement lined up?'

'I *have* heirs.' This at least was solid ground for Cassian. 'My Uncle Hugo and his two sons would all do as well as I. And there will be no arrangement. I have never in my life inclined to women, and I may be obliged to distort my own life to fit round the edges of Severn, but I'm cursed if I inflict that on someone who has a right to expect better. I will not make vows of love and fidelity to another person and before God, when I have neither the ability nor the intention to keep them.'

'People will expect it.'

'Then I will disappoint them,' Cassian said rather crisply. 'The men of my family tend not to marry early anyway, and my father inherited from his own uncle, it's hardly unusual. I will happily put off all enquiries as too early till I'm forty, and then move seamlessly into being a confirmed bachelor. I would rather be disappointing to matchmakers than an unfaithful husband to a wife and an unfaithful lover to you.'

Daizell's lips parted. Cassian rethought what he'd said. 'Uh, that made a number of assumptions.'

'It did a little.'

'I really am not asking you to sit in a cottage, or a London house, waiting for me to call. You already said you wouldn't want that; I don't want it either.'

'Which brings us back to what you do want. How this might work.'

'It works when we can be together,' Cassian said. 'I don't know exactly what that looks like, but I know it requires you to have your reputation back.'

Daizell lay there unblinking, then rolled over and propped himself on an elbow. His bronze and copper chest hair was unbearably delicious; Cassian stopped himself from burying his face in it, or at least postponed that thought. 'Say that again?'

'You need to return to society. You should not be cast out because of what your father did. And everything else is Vier's spite, and I don't see why his opinion of you should count for more than mine.'

'Not quite everything,' Daizell said. 'I don't have any money.'

'No, but I do. I have money and I have power and place, and I have sat on my own for years with my money and power and place between me and everybody else. Is there any way we could not let it stand between us? Because if the obstacle to us being together is that you don't have money, and the solution is right here in my hands—'

'It's not the sole obstacle.'

'But it's a big one. Forget where the money comes from. If you had a decent wardrobe say, and no need to cut profiles except for entertainment, and the Duke of Severn as your friend, do you not think you might be able to return to society?'

Another long silence. 'Maybe,' Daizell said at last. 'Possibly. Although, with Vier continually spitting venom – I don't want to be feeble, but it hurts when people make digs, or turn away, or sneer. I decided I wouldn't play again because – well, the obvious, but also because I don't think I could sit at a gaming table and wait for someone to make a joke.'

'No. I see.'

'I don't mean to be difficult. If you think we can do this – I mean to say, I've the Duke of Severn begging me to be with him. An actual duke. Good Lord, you're a duke,' he added with something like his usual energy. 'You should do something ducal.'

'I have robes somewhere? And a coronet, a ridiculous crimson velvet arrangement with fur trim if that helps.'

'Try it on for me sometime. Let me sort this out in my head. I would love not to ever think about money again in my life, and I quite see you could solve that problem for me. But I don't want to be an appendage, or an addendum, or whatever the word is. I want to be useful. Needful. Tell me the truth, Cass. Can I make your life better?'

Cassian grabbed his hand. 'You already have. If you left me today, you would have still made my life better, and I will always remember that. But please don't leave, because I want you to keep on doing it. You make my life so much better, and I say that as one of the most privileged men in England. I want you with me because you are necessary to me.'

'I don't want to be an addendum,' Daizell said again. 'But if I can play a useful role in Severn's household, even if that role is keeping Cassian happy—'

'It's a great deal more than that,' Cassian said, the joy sparkling through his veins. 'You got my ring back. You have *ideas*. I need you as a … a confidential facilitator of all sorts of things, including but not limited to my happiness.'

Daizell gripped his hand, tangling their fingers together. 'I mean it. I want to be valuable, Cass.'

'I will lean on you so heavily, you will stagger under the weight,' Cassian promised. His heart was thudding with the possibilities: seeing Daizell happy, content, *there*. 'Do you suppose you could think of a way to keep my greys, or at least prevent them going to Vier? Because I have lost the bet, and I have also upset Leo quite badly, and I must say I feel apprehensive. And then there are Miss Beaumont's affairs, which I have rather made my responsibility, and your rehabilitation in the eyes of Society, and talking of Vier, I have several scores to settle there. So if you have any ideas on all that—?'

Daizell grinned at him. 'I'll give it my best shot.'

Daizell's clothes were delivered an hour or so later. Cassian had paid quite a lot of money to expedite what he wanted, in case Daizell had been determined to leave. He might, also, have gone a little overboard in his guilt and remorse.

Daizell stared blankly at the delivery. 'What the—?'

'Your coat was ruined, and your linen was stolen at the gaol. I had to replace it. And, um. Your shoes were in an awful way too, and it was my fault, so …' He gave an embarrassed smile. 'I got carried away.'

'Two coats, three pairs of breeches, two waistcoats, five shirts – Cassian, this is a wardrobe!'

It was the bare bones of one in Cassian's view, though admittedly rather more than Daizell had originally possessed. Cassian had sent the remaining sorry garments to the best tailor in the vicinity and demanded clothing made to the same size, overnight, for suitable recompense. He'd need to visit a bank again. 'Try them on,' he said. 'If anything doesn't fit or is missing, Martin can get it dealt with.'

'Martin?'

'He's staying here. I, uh, felt I should pay for his stay, and reassure him of your well being, and I thought you might want to speak to him. And you said he was a valet so I asked him to help me.' He was usually attended by tailors when he needed a new coat; linen and other necessaries simply appeared. He would, he thought, have been very capable of tackling the tailor himself, and rather regretted not doing so, but with Daizell in urgent need, it seemed more sensible to call on an expert.

Daizell was gaping at him. Cassian shrugged awkwardly. 'He was determined to help you, and you said he wasn't that bad, and honestly, if it hadn't been for him I shouldn't have met you. I thought I might forgive and forget?'

'You are a remarkable duke,' Daizell said, and kissed him.

The tailor had done a good job. Daizell's two new coats – one in a similar green to his old one, one in a rich blue – fit very well. It all did, in fact, down to the shoes. Daizell stood, in new, clean, unworn finery, staring at himself in the spotty mirror. He looked like a gentleman of very certain fortune.

'That makes a difference,' he said at last. 'Thank you.'

'You look marvellous. Better than me, in fact.'

'I didn't like to say.'

Cassian stuck out his tongue. 'I've sent for my own clothes to be delivered to Louisa's house. I ought to go there, and I wondered if you'd come. I think we need to put our heads together about Vier and Miss Beaumont, and to be honest I ought to apologise for shouting at Leo, but also – well, perhaps this is a place to start bringing you back to the world. You know Leo, don't you, and he's popular.'

'I know him,' Daizell said. 'He ceased to know me after my father's incident.'

'Oh.' Cassian hadn't quite put that together. 'Oh, I'm sorry. Would you rather not meet him?'

'No, I might as well. See how it goes, I suppose, and I'll have to get used to it. And he wasn't unkind. I can't blame anyone for being revolted. Do you want to go tonight?'

'No,' Cassian said. 'Not tonight. I'd rather – could we go for a walk? A walk, and eat together, and have the rest of the day just for us before we move onto everything else?'

Daizell walked over and rested his head against Cassian's, forehead to forehead. 'Let's do that.'

Cassian had to admit he was nervous as they drove back to Leamington Spa. He had hired a good pair of horses, and drove at a clipping pace. Daizell sat beside him on the box. It was infinitely better than the stage; it was also far superior to plodding along in the ducal coach with outriders, a valet, all the trappings of attendance.

He did want his valet, since he was tired of being a scruffy mess and of packing clothes and organising laundry – so tired, in fact, that Daizell had got Martin to deal with it all in return for a lift to Leamington Spa. Still, the freedom of movement of the last month was something he wanted to experience again.

They arrived at Leamington in the early evening, tired and windswept. Cassian took a room – two beds – at the Star, and sent a note to warn Louisa while they made themselves presentable, and they made their way over to the Kentridges' home.

They were shown into the drawing room, where Kentridge, Louisa, Leo, and Miss Beaumont were waiting.

'Sev.' Louisa rose. 'And Mr Charnage.'

Cassian made introductions between Daizell and the Kentridges. Miss Beaumont greeted him enthusiastically. 'Oh, Mr Charnage, I am so pleased to see you again. I have told Mr Crosse and Louisa all about how kind and clever you were. I hope you're well?'

'Excellently, thank you,' Daizell said, saluting her hand. He straightened to look at Leo, who was glowering. 'Crosse.'

'Charnage,' Leo returned. 'It's been some time. I understand you've been getting my cousin in trouble.'

'Actually, it was the other way around.'

Daizell said it easily enough, but Cassian could feel his tension, and Leo's bristle as he returned, 'The Duke of Severn isn't known for making trouble.'

'You suggested yourself that it would do me good to do so,' Cassian put in.

'I didn't know how much trouble you had in mind! Or that you intended to take your responsibilities so carelessly.'

'Leo, for heaven's sake—'

'You made the point that you are Severn, Your Grace. You are obliged to live up to your title.'

'You overstate matters, Leo,' Kentridge said, in his mild way. 'People tolerate a great deal more and worse from all corners of the House of Lords than anything Severn has done. I might even suggest that Lord Hugo's very natural desire to fulfil his obligations in loco parentis, and Severn's exceedingly tolerant nature, have led to rather an oppressive set of expectations around his conduct which, so far, has been faultless to a fault.'

'*Kentridge*,' Louisa said. 'If you're going to talk like that, stand for Parliament.'

He smiled at his wife. 'That is, I don't think it's good for anyone to be obliged to be perfect. It's not in human nature. I cannot see that Severn has done anything mean or unkind, so perhaps we could end this argument, which smacks of moralising.'

'I am not moralising!' Leo protested furiously. 'If I do not approve of Severn's associations, it is because Charnage's disgraceful behaviour has caused the greatest harm to the reputation of a lady whom I admire and respect above all others!'

'Now, wait a moment!' Cassian snapped. Louisa said, 'Leo, for goodness' sake,' and Miss Beaumont put in, louder than anyone, 'Mr Crosse, that is unfair!'

'It is, on Miss Beaumont's own telling, most unfair,' Kentridge said. He was a remarkably self-possessed man, and rather more authoritative than any of those present. He also had a knack of saying things in a manner that made the Crosse family listen, which Cassian intended to learn. 'And it is also discourteous to a guest in my house.'

Leo reddened. 'That is all very well, but look at the situation Miss Beaumont is in! You have achieved very little with her trustees, and all Vier needs to do is spread this story of a second elopement to ruin her entirely!'

'Well, that is my fault,' Miss Beaumont said, with colours flying in her cheeks. 'And I said so, and I don't see why you must blame other people for what I asked them to do!'

'He should have known better!'

'I was there,' Cassian said. 'At least, on the recent occasion. So if you want to blame someone—'

'—you should blame Eliza,' Louisa said briskly. 'She has made it quite clear she was the motivating spirit in both these escapades, with Sev and Mr Charnage merely her catspaws. Although honestly, Sev, how *you* should not have known better is beyond me. Nevertheless, she has not made excuses for herself so Leo needs to stop trying to make this anyone else's fault – no, we all see that's what you're doing so shut up.'

'Yes, please stop, Mr Crosse,' Miss Beaumont said. 'I don't want to blame my mistakes on other people and I don't want you to do that for me. It isn't fair. I am not a child who needs to be absolved of responsibility for a broken toy. What I did was my fault, all of it, and if it makes you think badly of me I am very sorry for it, but it will not help anyone to pretend otherwise.'

Leo opened his mouth, closed it, and finally said, 'Miss Beaumont, I should rather have your faults than other people's perfection.'

'Oh good God,' Louisa muttered.

He ignored her. 'I beg your pardon. And yours, Charnage. I, er. Possibly got a little carried away.'

Daizell nodded acknowledgement in a very serious manner. He didn't catch Cassian's eye.

Louisa rolled her eyes. 'Marvellous. If you are harbouring a desire to play the knight for Eliza, what we actually need is a way to get her out of this tangle.'

'Both of them,' Cassian said. 'Daizell has a reputation to salvage too. If Sir James Vier chooses to speak of the recent incident, it will do a great deal of damage to them both.'

'Possibly more than you're aware,' Louisa said. 'Kentridge has rather run up against the rocks of Eliza's trustee, who seems to be quite appallingly sluggish. If or when Vier chooses to make this story public, suitably embroidered, it will be most unpleasant for Eliza, for any gentleman who might wish to marry her without being ridiculed as a fortune hunter with low standards, and for Mr Charnage if he does not care to be known as a dangerous abductor and abandoner.'

'I would rather not be.' Daizell was red in the face too now. 'You should be aware that Vier has had a great deal to say about me in the past, and I dare say he will bring it all out again, which will not help matters. I'm sorry about that.'

'It is not your fault,' Cassian said through his teeth. 'He has slandered you continually because of your father's wrongdoing and it has to stop!'

'It seems to me we have a number of people in this room for whom Vier is a problem,' Kentridge said. 'Might I suggest everyone put their cards on the table?'

'Over dinner,' Louisa added. 'Leo is both more pleasant and more intelligent when fed, and I dare say Cook is in a fury by now since we should have been eating twenty minutes ago and everything will be quite spoiled. Let us go in.'

The dinner was not spoiled, but it might as well have been for all the attention anyone paid to the excellent meal. Kentridge presided, drawing out the problem with forensic care.

'Miss Beaumont's situation,' he said. 'Vier is legally her guardian. He could insist on her return to his home, at least attempt to compel her marriage, and certainly raise objections to any marriage attempted without his consent. We can resist that at law, and hope to draw out a case until she attains her majority, but that is several months off. Moreover, any case will involve her attacking his character, which is not known to be bad, and him attacking hers, which has this matter of two elopements attached to it. Further, Miss Beaumont remains a very rich woman and a rich woman with a damaged reputation is liable to attract men of questionable motives. Which would be distressing for her, and cast an unflattering light on any decent man with aspirations to her hand.'

'A decent man would not care a button for her fortune, or people's opinion,' Leo said, chin up.

Miss Beaumont pressed her lips together to avoid wobble. 'But if the world believes a man is marrying a ruined woman for her money – people are so cruel. I would not want to do that to a man I – cared for. Oh, I wish I hadn't eloped!'

'You aren't ruined yet,' Louisa said firmly. 'If this Mr Marston keeps quiet, and I say you came directly to me, and only used Mr Charnage's name to muddy your trail—'

'You could indeed say that, my dear, but not in court,' Kentridge informed her. 'Your lightest wish is my command in general, but I must require you not to commit perjury, even in a good cause. Let us turn to Mr Charnage's problem. Vier seems to dislike you rather, Mr Charnage.'

'My father robbed him at gunpoint and killed his whist partner,' Daizell said. 'I don't blame him for taking that poorly. He also manufactured a scandal about me at my cousins' home. He had hold of some profiles I had cut – it's a hobby – which were, uh, for a gentleman's party, and claimed I was distributing them to the young people there.'

'*That* was a lie,' Miss Beaumont said. 'I heard it said, but I was there and I never saw any such thing. And Mrs Swain did not ask me or anyone if it was true.'

'Anna Swain? Sellingstowe's cousin? No, she would not. What a dreadful prig of a woman she is and her husband is worse,' Louisa said. 'They are unquestionably the most righteous people I have ever met. Appalling bores.'

'Mr Charnage's cousins, my dear.'

'Pshaw. Nobody could be related to the Swains and be happy about it.'

Daizell made a face that suggested Louisa had the right of it. 'All the same, Vier did have some rather unfortunate profiles, even if I had not meant them for that audience, and then I did attempt to elope with Miss Beaumont.'

Kentridge tapped his fingers on the table. 'It seems to me that Vier has a number of unfortunately accurate things to say. He can demand Miss Beaumont's return, accuse her of various misbehaviours, bring up Mr Charnage's offences – justified or not – to stoke the flames of scandal, invoke Leo's debts, and quite probably drag Severn into it all. This entire business could become quite unpleasant for all of you. And it would make it very difficult indeed to argue that Miss Beaumont's wardship should be struck down, by marriage or otherwise.'

Miss Beaumont had gone pale. Leo reached out to her, and she gripped his hand. 'You must have some ideas, Kentridge,' he insisted. 'The man is a villain.'

'One with the law on his side, and who will have public opinion on his side too.'

'He had me kidnapped,' Cassian said. 'Admittedly while trying to have Miss Beaumont kidnapped, but I don't see that's better.'

'You'd be the one ridiculed for that,' Louisa pointed out. 'And his reason was your involvement in this second elopement, which is not information we want to set about.'

'He is a cheat!' Leo said. 'We can surely use that.'

'It will be hard to prove,' Kentridge said. 'Consider, Leo. The only way to demonstrate that he is a cheat would be for him and his partner to play a game under the eyes of neutral parties who had been made aware of his methods in advance, because otherwise they will not remember or notice what he says and plays. That means people who can be trusted not to give anything away, because all he need do not to be caught is not use it. Could you really tell people, enough people, about his system in all its subtleties, and have them memorise it, and watch him play, and be sure they would not let anything slip, *and* that they would be prepared to assert what they heard and saw – and, after all that, have other people believe their account? Perhaps it is achievable, but—' He made a face.

'We are talking a great deal about public opinion,' Cassian said.

'Because that is what we need,' Louisa returned. 'Eliza's future will be determined by public opinion: if she will be admitted to good society even as a married woman, for example.'

'Many ladies are who have done worse,' Leo muttered.

'Better-born ladies who already have friends in high places. I never said it was fair,' Louisa added.

'Yes, but am I not a friend in a high place?' Cassian asked. 'Can I not direct opinion? Quite seriously, I am Severn. If I give Daizell and Miss Beaumont my countenance—'

Louisa rolled her eyes. 'Dear Sev, you are not, with the best will in the world, an arbiter of Society: you've never tried to be. You would have to make a deal more of a splash than you currently do.'

'And it is not the be-all and end-all in any case,' Kentridge said. 'We need to free Miss Beaumont legally and Vier has the upper hand given what he can say about her, and indeed about Mr Charnage.' He held up a hand as both Cassian and Leo spoke. 'I realise you think that unjust, but it is not I who needs persuading of it.'

'No,' Daizell said. 'As Cassian – Severn – said, it's public opinion. If public opinion could be turned against Vier, if he *could* be exposed as a cheat, that would surely make it easier to fix him in the public mind as a liar, and in the courts as an unfit guardian?'

'Absolutely,' Kentridge said. 'It would be ideal. Unfortunately, as I just explained in some detail, I don't see a way to do it, which makes this tangent fruitless.' He paused, his eyes narrowing. 'Unless you have something in mind, Mr Charnage?'

Daizell glanced at Cassian. 'I might.'

Chapter Eighteen

The next period was as busy as Daizell had been in a while.

Cassian's valet turned up. Waters, a very correct and elderly man about three times his master's age, was appalled to see the Duke looking so scruffy, more appalled to be informed that he would not be staying in the Star in Leamington with his master.

'I told him to take my things down to Wotton House, open it up, and make all ready for the six of us,' Cassian said. 'He came in the ducal coach, of course, so I told him to take it down and I would drive myself.' He sighed. 'I feel rather unkind, and distinctly ungrateful.'

'You should at least be grateful.' Cassian had been very thoroughly valeted before Waters' departure, and was admiring himself in the mirror. He deserved to. Fine clothes made the man, Daizell supposed, but Cassian's were extraordinarily fine: superb quality, superb cut, perfectly fitted. He might look like nobody in an old coat, but properly groomed and clad, to Daizell's eyes, he was every inch the duke.

Maybe that wasn't entirely Daizell's eyes. Cassian seemed a deal more natural in his ducal identity than Daizell might have expected, and a deal less unassuming while occupying it. Judging by the frequent raised eyebrows, looks of surprise, and occasional heated exchange with his cousins, this was new. Cassian had said he needed to be Cassian in order to be the Duke: maybe this was what he'd meant.

He moved behind his quiet nobleman, stroking the flanks of his coat. 'This is marvellous. Why are you being unkind to your valet?'

'Because Waters wants nothing more than to go home to Staplow. He's too old to be jaunting about the country, but I would break his heart if I simply told him so. He will do better if he reaches that conclusion himself. I will move him into some sort of sinecure position where he can retire in all but name, and keep his dignity. I owe him that. I owe him a great deal. But I also need a new valet.'

'Is that urgent?'

'Yes,' Cassian said, turning and slipping his arms around Daizell's waist. 'Crucial. We'll have enough people to hide from; we need an ally in the house, someone whose duties involve letting me wake up with you, and ensuring nobody else sees.'

'That sounds good if it's possible,' Daizell said slowly. 'Do you have such a paragon in mind?'

'I had an idea. I wondered what you'd think – though I don't know if paragon is the word I'd choose—'

'Martin? Are you serious?'

'I'm seriously asking,' Cassian said. 'After all, he knows about us, which is a start. And you said he was ambitious. I am not a leader of fashion, of course, but then, he's unlikely to get another post at all.'

'So he might settle for a duke. I see what you're saying, but, Cass, he *robbed* you.'

'Yes, but I understand why. We had a frank conversation while you were sleeping. He was treated shockingly. I grant he has behaved very badly himself, but – well, if I wanted you to forgive me, and I want people to overlook anything you may have done, surely I should extend grace to others in my turn?' He gave a slanted smile. 'I'm even called His Grace. That seems to suggest an obligation.'

'I doubt it's one felt by many dukes. You realise he is a wanted man?'

'For a theft that took place in Northumberland as Martin Nichols. I see no reason he shouldn't be John Martin in London and Staplow, in my service, and have a new start. I can offer him that, if he wants it.' His lovely lips curved. 'I do owe him something, for bringing me to you.'

Daizell looked at him, so earnest, so determined to get it right, and wondered how happiness could make your heart hurt. 'If you're willing to harbour a felon—'

'I'd rather you didn't put it *quite* like that.'

'It's wonderful. And I do think it could work. You, uh, don't mind – prior relations and all that?'

'Not if you don't. He may, of course, in which case he can decline. But a valet on our side would make life a deal easier, and once I don't have to consider Waters, I can move around a great deal more.'

Daizell raised a brow. 'Going somewhere?'

'I'd like to travel. *Not* on the stage,' he added firmly as though Daizell was likely to argue. 'Birmingham was fascinating, and I want to spend more time on my own lands without stewards all over me. I think I need to see things directly, without people mediating my view for me. I do realise you've been wandering a long time, and I don't want to drag you around—'

'You can drag me around.'

'Not to Staplow,' Cassian said with deep feeling. 'Not yet. My *aunts*, Daize, you have no idea. I don't want to dislodge them, but I have one or two other properties that might become more of a home—'

'One or two?'

'Or so,' Cassian said with a look of ridiculous embarrassment. 'And if things go well in London and you like Wotton House, I thought we could spend quite a lot of time there.'

Daizell pulled him closer, hanging on, and rubbed his face in Cassian's hair. 'You are marvellous,' he said, a little muffled. 'And I want this to go well, more than I can say, but what if it doesn't? All Vier has to do is not cheat, and then we're stuck.'

Cassian caught his hand. 'Then I will pack Leo and Eliza off to Gretna in my own coach – I think things are going that way, don't you? – and face down anyone who bothers them or you.'

'You'd hate that. Leo said his father would have a stroke.'

Leo had entirely forgotten his objections to Daizell once he'd come up with a scheme to help Eliza and scotch Vier. They were all on first-name terms now, except for Kentridge, who Daizell suspected didn't have a first name. Cassian had offered his new name to his cousins, who both said it sounded very well but they were used to 'Sev'. He didn't seem to mind. To be Cassian for Daizell was all he needed, he said, and Daizell had no objection to having Cassian all to himself.

'Uncle Hugo wouldn't be pleased,' Cassian agreed. 'He fought at least one duel in his youth, and sowed plenty of wild oats, so why he is quite so insistent I ought to be respectable, I can't say.'

'It sounds exactly right for your family,' Daizell pointed out. 'The terribly respectable veneer cracks at the slightest opportunity. Look at Louisa suggesting we kidnap Vier. Thank the Lord Kentridge stepped in.'

'That may be true, actually,' Cassian admitted. 'But Uncle

Hugo would hate more than anything to see Leo accused of mercenary motives if he and Eliza make a match of it: he worked so hard not to be accused of that himself with my fortune. And if he gets into his head that Leo is taking another man's leavings for money, it will go horribly. Whereas if we can present Eliza to him as a wronged woman who took her fate in her own hands, he will defend her to his last breath.'

'The story of the woman who escaped from a villainous guardian and the gentleman who assisted her without thought of reward or reputation,' Daizell agreed. 'For which we need to pull this off. And, in turn, that means you need to sharpen your skills.'

Cassian groaned. 'I have already played three hours of whist today.'

'And we have another two hours to go,' Daizell said implacably, or as implacably as he could, which wasn't very, since he didn't want to force the issue. Cassian loathed card games, with their competition and shouting, and his mind visibly drifted. 'If it's any consolation, I don't like it either.'

Cassian stepped back to look at him. 'I had wanted to ask. Is it difficult, doing this?'

Daizell had not played for years because the sight of cards made him see again the empty room, cards scattered over table and floor, the ten of spades sodden to pulp with a dying man's blood. Cassian wouldn't touch a card again if he blurted all that out. 'It's … tainted, yes. But the truth is, I can't see the pleasure in gaming any more. It's nothing but patterns on pasteboard and a night's meaningless, manufactured excitement, and for that I lost my schooling, and my father lost everything else. We'd have been ruined even if he hadn't killed Haddon. Frankly, it all seems a very bad idea to me now.'

'Yes, I suppose it would,' Cassian said slowly. 'Although lots of people play deep and lose, and most of them don't kill the winners.'

Daizell blinked, unsure why he would rub that in. 'Yes, I realise that. My father was peculiarly unwilling to accept his own failures.'

'So he held the winners up with a loaded gun which he was prepared to fire. He planned it in advance, knowing what it would do to his wife and son, and he left Haddon to die. Doesn't that strike you as more than not accepting failure?'

Daizell had no desire to defend his father, and yet the words rose to his lips anyway, driven by hurt. 'They'd ruined him!'

'Yes. Haddon ruined him, *playing with Vier*.' He was looking at Daizell, his luminous eyes wide. 'And Vier cheats. Did he cheat with Haddon, as he does with Plath? Did they cheat your father together? Daize, do you think your father guessed?'

Daizell stared at him. It hadn't even crossed his mind to link the two before; now he couldn't see how he'd failed to do so. 'Oh sweet Jesus. You don't think—'

'I don't know.' Cassian had gone pale. 'I don't know, but for anyone to resort to such violence—'

'He thought he was owed the world on a platter as it was. If he felt sure he'd been cheated, and could do nothing about it, he'd have been – oh, beyond enraged. And my mother always took his side. Oh God, you're right. They didn't just commit a robbery at gunpoint, did they? It was vengeance. And Vier—'

'Lost his partner in crime at your father's hands,' Cassian said. 'Would have had to find another man, and train him, with the risks and the loss of winnings that entailed. No wonder he wanted to punish you. No, wait – good Lord, Daize, he wanted to *discredit* you. That's what this was about, all of it, those endless spiteful attacks on your name. He wanted to make sure, if your father told you he and Haddon were cheats and you told the world, that you wouldn't be believed. Hey. Sit down.'

He had grabbed Daizell's arm, and now walked him stumbling backwards to the bed. Daizell sat heavily. His head felt peculiar, as though he'd drunk too much gin too fast.

His father was a murderer, that was beyond question. He'd left Daizell twisting in the wind, and nothing could change his feelings about that. But if his father had been provoked into that act by being cheated in a way it was so very hard to expose or prove …

It hadn't had to happen. None of the last miserable seven years had had to happen. His father might have spent his worthless life without doing significant harm to anyone. Daizell might have encountered Cassian – not on equal terms of course, but at least not kneeling in the wreckage of his name. He could have been spared seven years of cuts and insults, whispers and sneers and shame and the slow sucking away of hope.

But Vier had robbed his father, and put Daizell's destruction in motion, and then set out to ruin what was left of his name as a precaution, just in case he knew too much.

'The shit,' he said dizzily. 'The shit.'

'If we're right,' Cassian said. He was kneeling by the bed, his hands hot on Daizell's unless Daizell's were cold.

'We are. It fits.'

'It does. Though how we might prove it, I don't know. Are you all right?'

'No, I am not. Why would he do that – no, I know why, but Christ! I never threatened him. I never knew. I was *sorry* for the man, curse it. I apologised to him!'

'But your father could have written to you at any time. Said, *this is why I did it.*'

'I doubt I have crossed my father's mind from that day to this,' Daizell said. 'The idea that he might write at all, let alone stoop to explain himself as though he'd done something wrong... ha. I suppose my mother might have written, but if she did, it never reached me. Vier wasted a great deal of unnecessary effort in ruining me.'

'I'm so sorry,' Cassian whispered. 'Or – no. I'm not sorry.' His hands tightened. 'I'm *furious*. I am so angry. How dare they? How dare any of them? Your father, Vier, Haddon and Plath, Acaster, that swine who outraged Martin – they're all the same in their different ways, and none of it is right, and I am going to do something about it. About all of them and more. And we will start with Vier, but by God I will not be finishing there.'

His eyes were bright with wrath. Daizell looked at him, stiff and fierce in defence. 'Swinging your duke around?'

'*Hitting* them with it.'

'I'm looking forward to this.' Daizell took a brief moment to wonder what he might have let loose on the world in the person of an enraged duke, and decided the world deserved it. He pulled Cassian's hands up, kissed the knuckles. 'Cass. I'm so glad I have you with me.'

'Always,' Cassian said. 'Always. Now teach me to play whist properly, because I'm going to *do* this.'

★ ★ ★

They played for another couple of hours, until Daizell's head was swimming. Cassian looked positively dizzy, and when he forgot what card he'd just played for the third time in a row, Daizell called a halt.

'You look befogged.'

'I am befogged. Where is the fun in this?' Cassian wailed. 'It's more luck than skill, unless one can remember every card played in every hand and then forget it again when one starts the new hand, yet people bet money they can't afford on it. Ridiculous. Wagering is foolish enough – as I should know, but at least I had some chance of controlling the outcome.'

'Gambling isn't about controlling the outcome, though, unless you're a professional, or Vier. It's about…' Daizell thought back on his own days of play. 'Excitement. Recklessness. Staking more than you can afford on a matter of pure chance even if everyone says they've a system, or a lucky way to roll a die, or a good tip on a horse. The truth is, gambling is pitting yourself against the world, and winning confirms what everyone secretly believes: that they're Fortune's favourite.'

'Unless they lose, and it turns out they're her fool.'

'Yes, well, that's the other outcome. Don't you feel any appeal in it at all?'

'No, honestly. I would feel dreadful if I lost the sums Leo did. I could afford it a dozen times over but how wasteful, how unappreciative of my own good luck it would be to throw that away.'

'Yes, I suppose a duke doesn't need to prove he's Fortune's favourite, does he? You already know. On which subject…'

'Mmm?'

Daizell sighed. 'I know we've spoken about this. I know you're determined. But the truth is, it's going to be a challenge to have Vier play and cheat and be caught. It may not be manageable, and we both may end up looking ridiculous, and you may find yourself in the position of having people think you're a fool on a number of levels, including your association with me.'

'I realise that,' Cassian said. 'People might well think I'm a ridiculous gull. But, you know, if they think that, they will be wrong.'

'That isn't much consolation.'

Cassian took his hand. 'I expect it has not been, for you on your own with the world against you. But you aren't on your own now, and nor am I. And I'm *right*. If the world thinks badly of you, the world is mistaken. And perhaps the world will think badly of me for thinking well of you, and if so, that's something I will live with, because I know what matters, and it is not the opinion of people who aren't in possession of the facts.'

Daizell's experience had been that the opinions of those people mattered a great deal. Then again, he wasn't a duke. And Cassian wasn't without his own experience of being disregarded or mocked, in its way: he knew what it felt like, he was always in the public view, and he had a great deal of reputation to lose.

And yet here he was, putting himself at hazard for Daizell.

'What is it?' Cassian asked. 'You look struck.'

'I'll tell you what it is,' Daizell said. '*You* need to lie down and have a nap. *I* am going to have a word with Martin about valeting, and then I am going to come back up here and find you as close to asleep as may be.'

Cassian's lips parted and curved. 'I am rather tired, now you mention it. All those cards.'

'Good,' Daizell said. 'I will see you in an hour or so. Sleep well.'

Martin heard the proposition out with a very wary look indeed. It took him a little time to understand that this was an offer of a position without strings or dangers; that he might have safety and prosperity and a secure occupation – not just secure but stellar – within his grasp. He then accepted the post in a very proper manner, expressed his fervent hope that he would give satisfaction, and spent ten minutes weeping uncontrollably on Daizell's shoulder.

Daizell didn't begrudge his damp coat. He knew exactly how it felt for a drifting man to be granted safe harbour, all the more when it came unexpectedly, and he loved Cassian for the thought and kindness. Not to mention that he was quite right: Martin would keep their privacy, guard the ducal bedroom like a mastiff, and revel in obstructing anyone who attempted to overrule him. Daizell suspected he'd have the time of his life fending off butlers or uncles.

This was a stroke of genius on Cassian's part. Daizell sent Martin off for a celebratory drink with his cronies in Leamington, and headed upstairs to show his appreciation.

He pushed open the bedroom door very gently, and locked it with the greatest of care. Cassian had pulled the curtains across and the only sound in the room was his quiet, steady breath. If he wasn't asleep he was doing a fine job of seeming so. He was also lying on the covers naked, which Daizell took as the hint it was.

He stripped himself with excruciating caution, to be sure, easing his boots off and barely allowing a rustle of cloth. Needing to be quiet, because he very much wanted Cassian to be asleep under his intruding hands. The sense of transgression tingled through his veins, and hardened his prick in a frankly disgraceful way. He ought to be ashamed, he thought with absolutely no sincerity, easing himself by inches onto the bed.

Cassian was sprawled half on his front, half his side, one leg bent. The curve of his neck was the most perfect thing Daizell had ever seen, except perhaps for his elegantly limp hand, adorned with its gnarled lump of gold.

He shifted closer, agonisingly slow, because if Cassian was asleep he needed to stay that way for now, and if he was awake he could enjoy the anticipation. Daizell intended to behave as if the former was the case, so he gave a moment's consideration to what a villain might do to a helplessly sleeping naked man. Then he knelt up, moving so he was straddling his duke's shoulders without touching, gripped the headboard, and gently rubbed the tip of his erection across Cassian's lips.

No reaction. Nothing but warm, deep breath. Daizell did it again with a touch more pressure and felt Cassian's lips part a fraction. Kneeling over him, gently pleasuring himself with Cassian's slack mouth: he could thrust it in if he cared to, and Cassian would know it, and Daizell chose not to glance at his prick. They had discovered that if he knew for sure Cassian was awake, that knowledge showed itself in his demeanour, in a way Cassian could identify if not define. It was better if he believed his lover to be deep in unconsciousness, which was not a thought he'd ever imagined himself having.

He pushed a little harder. Cassian's loose lips parted a little, perhaps by reflex or perhaps not, and Daizell worked the head of his prick between them, and only just stifled a moan. All those years telling himself he was truly not the rogue the world thought, and it turned out he was a colossal degenerate after all.

Cassian's lips were so soft, so yielding. Daizell indulged himself for a few moments that way, then got a hand to his prick, stroking himself in time with the gentle thrusts, feeling the momentum build, with Cassian quite untouched except for his mouth, but his breath unquestionably just a fraction faster.

God love him, Daizell's ordinary, extraordinary duke. Daizell made his cautious way back down the bed and the limp body, considered his approach, and decided subtlety was overrated. He nestled against Cassian's back, cupped the lightest hand over his groin, not quite touching but so close he could feel the heat and knew Cassian was painfully hard, and rubbed against his arse. Featherlight touches, and then a little firmer, a little faster, and then Cassian let out a strangled noise, and his prick was fully in Daizell's hand, and Daizell pushed and pulled to plaster them together, skin to skin, rubbing and gasping and frotting and finally, too soon, both bucking with pleasure, biting back the cries.

Cassian subsided, chest heaving. Daizell flopped over him, but didn't loosen his hand. He liked the fistful he had.

'Lord,' Cassian said. 'Lord.'

'I love you,' Daizell remarked into his neck. 'I love your kindness, and I love that you love me, and I particularly love that you want me to do that to you.'

Cassian considered before replying, in a way that might have seemed offputting if you didn't know him. 'I love how you sparkle. Sparkle and shine. And I love that you make it so easy for me to be me. And I particularly love that you're happy to do those things to me.'

'It's highly convenient we found each other, really.'

'Sometimes one can believe in a well-ordered universe,' Cassian agreed, and snuggled back against him, sweaty, sticky, and entirely perfect.

Chapter Nineteen

They arrived in London a week later, the whole Severn party down to Eliza Beaumont, who had refused to be left in Leamington Spa even if she couldn't show her face in London for reasons of her safety. They also had the officially renamed John Martin, temporarily as Daizell's valet until Waters could be eased into the lavish retirement his age and devotion deserved. Martin had adopted the impossibly correct demeanour of a man determined to be the perfect valet. Cassian could only hope he calmed down a little before he turned into Waters the Second.

In any case, he could now be ticked off Cassian's list of Things Needing To Be Dealt With. It was a long list, which he suspected would only get longer. He had put enquiries in motion as to the stagecoach crash, with an eye to offering assistance to the injured or bereaved and mounting a prosecution against Tom Acaster, and had also composed a letter about Sir Benjamin's fitness to be a magistrate, for his lawyers to take up in the proper quarters.

Apparently the dutiful duke had always wanted to be a troublemaker. But he was still Severn, despite it all, so he was going to make trouble as only Severn could, for Daizell, and Martin, and Eliza Beaumont, and whoever else required it. It was what his position was for. The thought gave him a sense of steadiness, as if he'd settled into place.

He did not like the other thoughts that came with it,

about Daizell's seven purposeless, wasted years and how they had scraped his self-esteem to the bone. Sir James Vier was accordingly at the very top of Things Needing To Be Dealt With, and Cassian steeled himself to the task.

So, that evening, he went to speak to Sir James.

There were a number of things he would have liked to say to the man, about slander and cheating and abuse of young women and kidnapping, but all those subjects had to be avoided. He was there only as Severn, and only to talk about his greys.

Sir James was not a member of White's; they found the fellow in the Cocoa-Tree instead. It was a hell frequented by the best people, Leo had assured him, which was to say it was a pit lit by wax candles instead of tallow, and where the dead-drunk men reeked of French brandy rather than London gin.

The Duke came to the door with Leo in tow, and was stopped by a smooth-faced maitre d' with a sly look. 'Ah, Mr Crosse. Is your friend a member?'

'This is my cousin,' Leo said. 'Severn.'

The man's face changed. He bowed the Duke in with grovelling servility, and took his hat and stick, while movement and whispers up ahead indicated that the news of his arrival was spreading.

He considered the place as he walked in with Leo, ignoring the fuss. He had every intention of broadening his horizons and his circles – he had enjoyed those nights of companionship and stories at the Green Lion in Coventry more than he would have thought possible – but he wouldn't have cared to include this place even if Daizell had wanted to frequent a gambling den. It had a sordid, aggressive feel to it, the faces around him greedy and needy, and he was fairly certain that was informed judgement on his part rather than fear born of inexperience.

He walked through the groups of men, stopping to acknowledge some few acquaintances most of whom he disliked, and turning off remarks about his unexpected appearance and offers of play with a polite, faint smile, until they found Sir James Vier.

Sir James was a man aged about fifty, very well dressed in the plain style, with a lean, distinguished sort of look and thin lips set in a polite, faint smile of his own. Cassian made a mental note that polite, faint smiles were actually quite dislikeable, and therefore kept his own firmly in place.

'Sir James,' he said.

'Ah, Your Grace.' Sir James gave a little bow. 'Good evening. I trust you are keeping well? I had the honour of meeting your cousin earlier today.'

'That is why I am here,' the Duke said, his voice pitched a little louder than was his wont. He was normally soft-spoken to a fault, but people were listening and he wanted them to hear. 'I understand he offered you my greys in lieu of vowels you hold, to the tune of a thousand pounds.'

Sir James raised a brow. '*Your* greys? Mr Crosse assured me he had title to them.'

'You're selling your greys, Severn?' asked a man named Mowbray who had been at Eton with him. 'I wish you had mentioned it to me.'

'I am not,' the Duke said, keeping his eyes on Vier. 'Leo had my greys off me by a wager, Sir James. I do not care to lose them. You will oblige me by taking my note of hand for the sum.'

'You propose to buy your greys back from me?' Sir James

Vier's thin lips stretched. 'But suppose I do not feel inclined to sell, Your Grace?'

'My cousin acted precipitately.' The Duke allowed his dislike to creep into his expression and voice. 'There was no need for him to use my horses to settle his debts. I do not wish them to go into – another man's ownership.' He didn't say *yours*; he didn't have to. Everyone would remember the incident when he had rebuked Sir James in Hyde Park for his savage hand with the whip, and been sent packing under the lash of the older man's withering tongue.

Sir James certainly remembered, because his smile widened further. 'Let me be sure I understand. Crosse informed me he had taken possession of the greys, and had every right to exchange them for his vowels. Was that the case?'

'You will oblige me by not calling my cousin's word into doubt,' the Duke said tightly.

Sir James bowed. 'In that case, my ownership is a matter of fact, Your Grace, whereas your wishes are – merely wishes.' He puffed airily at his fingertips, as if blowing thistledown away. 'The horses are mine now. You may offer to buy them from me, and I may refuse to sell. I look forward to having them delivered to my house at your, or your cousin's, convenience.'

The Duke clenched his fists. They were at the centre of a group of listeners now; he could feel the interest and the amusement. 'Sir James, the horses should not be in your ownership. You exchanged them merely for a debt—'

'For your cousin's note of hand. Surely that is as good as gold. Or do you mean to imply his vowels are worthless?'

'I do not care to play games with you. I will pay you fifteen hundred pounds for my greys.'

Sir James locked eyes with him. 'No,' he said softly, tauntingly.

'I do not haggle,' the Duke snapped. 'Name your price and have done.'

'Sev,' Leo said, sounding worried.

'I said, name your price!'

'I will not take a price,' Sir James said. 'I have a fancy to keep the greys. *My* greys.'

'Mine, and I want them back!' the Duke said, voice rising. 'They should not have been offered to you, and a *gentleman* would acknowledge that and act accordingly!'

Several people inhaled. Sir James's face stiffened. 'Your Grace is unjust,' he said, a bite in the words. 'I accepted the greys from Crosse as payment for a debt I am owed. You do not dispute the debt, nor Crosse's ownership of the horses at the point he chose to exchange them with me. Therefore, they are mine. You cannot force me to sell them, any more than you can order me to sell you my house or my coat, or otherwise dictate what I, an Englishman with an Englishman's rights and liberties, do with my property. You exceed your authority, sir.'

The Duke could feel he'd gone red, between anger, profound embarrassment, and the heat of the room. He was making himself a spectacle, brawling in this sordid gentleman's hell, all but shouting demands he knew very well were utterly unreasonable. People would talk.

Which was exactly what they were supposed to do. They just needed to talk about the right thing.

'What is this prating of rights?' he demanded in a conversational dog-leg modelled on his uncle. 'I am speaking of *horses*. I am offering to pay you twice the worth of a pair you haven't even driven and I doubt are up to handling, and your refusal smacks of nothing but spite. Or do you hope to push up the price like a costermonger?'

That landed with the audience, he could tell. So could Sir James, because he retorted, 'On the contrary. I will not sell them at any price: I have a great fancy to drive them, and in this matter my fancy trumps yours. If you did not wish to lose your horses, Your Grace, you should not have wagered them.'

'Play for them,' Leo said suddenly.

'Quiet,' the Duke snapped at his cousin.

'No, listen, Sev. You must see Vier doesn't have to sell them to you – though I must say, fifteen hundred – but he's a sporting man. Let's make it a game. A return match, even. What do you say, Vier? A few rounds of whist, you and Plath against Severn and me, with the greys on the table, and there will be no question of who owns what.'

'There is no question as to my ownership now,' Vier said, but his eyes were calculating. 'A game, you say? I was not aware you play, Your Grace. And I play deep. Are you sure you can meet your cousin's expectations?'

'I can certainly meet my obligations, whatever they may be,' the Duke said icily. 'But as to gaming—'

'Of course you shall play, Sev,' Leo said. 'Come, now, if you want your greys back, what choice have you?'

The Duke looked round sharply at his cousin. Sir James Vier laughed, an unpleasant sound. 'Quite, yes. In this particular circumstance, I fear His Grace has no choice at all. Shall we say two days hence?'

They were to meet for the game in Lady Wintour's hell: a public match after the public argument. Lady Wintour – a hostess from a faro den who had married well above her station – had run her establishment for some years. Its veneer of respectability was thinner than the sheerest of muslins, but at least it wasn't the Cocoa-Tree, and more importantly, Daizell was an old friend of the proprietress. He had gone for a chat with her a few days previously.

It was crowded when Cassian and Leo arrived. Apparently the word had got round that the Duke of Severn had lost his temper, forgotten his breeding, had a vulgar public argument, and would probably be losing a great deal of money to Sir James Vier.

Cassian knew several of those present, and didn't greatly care for any of them except Daizell, who was deep in conversation with Lady Wintour. He took a glass of brandy, watching the room, and realised his face had slipped once more into his usual public expression of that polite, faint, offputting smile. No wonder people didn't talk to him.

To blazes with that. He turned to the closest man who looked friendly, and said, 'Good evening. I'm Severn. How's the play here?'

'Deep but honest,' the man replied. 'Lady Wintour takes a firm line, and Ned – the big one there whose hand looks incomplete without a cudgel – applies the line firmly, if you follow me. The brandy is drinkable but I wouldn't call for champagne, she watches the pennies too closely there. Loxleigh, by the way.' He gave Cassian a nod, paused, then said, 'It has just occurred to me – when you said Severn, you didn't mean—'

'Yes, but "Severn" will do very well, please.'

Loxleigh took a second to digest that, then opened his hands with a smile. 'A pleasure to meet you, Severn. First time here?'

He proved to be as friendly as he looked, and the next

few moments passed in enjoyably inconsequential chatter. The Duke had never been good at that before Daizell: he'd been taught that a duke's speech was always heavy with consequence. Now he managed a very satisfactory idle conversation with remarkable ease, since his companion was a fluent chatterer, and was almost distracted when Sir James Vier walked in.

Sir Francis Plath was behind him, a smooth sort of fellow. There were grunts of greeting from around the room, but Vier ignored them, approaching Cassian as Leo came to his side.

'Your Grace. Crosse.' Vier nodded at Leo. 'I thought you might have reconsidered, considering the sums you already owe me. I trust I may expect those in due course.'

Cassian felt Leo inhale, trod hard on his foot, and gave Vier a chilly look. 'We have an appointment to play. Let us do that.'

'Certainly. My dear Lady Wintour—' He turned, and saw Daizell. 'What is *he* doing here?'

It was loud enough to attract attention. Daizell was still speaking to Lady Wintour; he entirely ignored Vier, who said, louder, 'You, Charnage!'

Daizell looked around, keeping his poise though his cheeks were rather red. 'Vier.'

'What the devil are *you* doing among gentlemen? Lady Wintour, I am surprised at whom you let through your doors.'

Lady Wintour's nostrils flared. 'If His Grace don't object to my friends, I dare say you can deign to tolerate 'em, Sir James.'

'I am very happy with the company,' Cassian said. 'Good evening, Charnage, I didn't see you there.'

'Ah, Severn, good evening,' Daizell said with a cheery nod. 'Hello, Crosse.'

Sir James looked between them, pantomiming surprise and disapproval. 'You are acquainted? Really, Your Grace, I must venture to give you a little advice.'

'Must you?' Cassian said. He said it very gently, in the manner of his more dangerous aunts, and noted that Loxleigh's eyes widened. Possibly he had aunts too.

'Your Grace, that individual assisted his father in a notorious robbery that left my dear friend Haddon dead. His father is a murderer and he an accessory to murder. Deny it all you please,' Vier went on loudly over Daizell's response. 'I have made it my business to warn Society of him, even if the law will take no action. Your Grace must consider your acquaintance better.'

'I – beg – your – pardon,' the Duke said, and he put all the duke he had into each stony word.

Sir James's faint smile slipped a fraction. 'Excuse me, Your Grace. I should have said "might".'

'But you said *must*. To me.' He let that hang for a moment. 'I would not venture to tell a gentleman what he "must" do, Sir James, so I will merely observe that there are laws pertaining to slander, and if Mr Charnage chooses to use them, he will have a number of witnesses, including myself. No, I will not hear any more of this,' he added sharply. 'You know very well it is nonsense and I will not be an audience to untruth or spite.'

The room was absolutely silent now. Sir James's expression was vicious. 'I beg Your Grace's pardon if I have offended you. However, the man Charnage—'

'Has witnesses placing him in Vauxhall at the time of the robbery,' Leo said. 'Which you know very well, Vier. If you really thought he was involved you'd have brought a prosecution.'

'With his carefully picked "witnesses" prepared to swear an alibi?' Sir James flashed back, the quotation marks audible. 'One can hardly trust to justice in such circumstances.'

'Hoi!' A loud, gruff voice. Cassian turned to see a burly man with a remarkably Roman nose, and the look of a building thunderhead. He took a step towards Vier. 'You, fellow. Did you just say the witnesses to Charnage's whereabouts swore false?'

'I merely suggest—'

'Be damned to your suggestions, and to your implications, and to you,' the man said, with force. 'I *am* one of those witnesses. I was one of the party in Vauxhall that night, with Charnage, and said so at the time. What the devil do you mean prating about "carefully picked witnesses" in that tone?' He jabbed an aggressive finger at Sir James. 'Are you calling me a liar?'

'Hart,' Lady Wintour said, warning. 'I won't have brawling in my house, thank you.'

'I have no intention of brawling,' Sir James said, smoothing his cuffs.

'Well, I do,' the man retorted. 'Daizell Charnage was in Vauxhall Pleasure Gardens that night, and I was there with him till the small hours. I've said so whenever I've been asked, and I'll say so again, under oath, whenever you like. Understand?'

'Who's he?' Cassian murmured to Leo.

'Sir John Hartlebury. In trade, not the best ton, but a good fellow.'

Vier's mouth had tightened. Clearly this was the first time

his implications had been overheard by one of the witnesses. 'I hear your words, Sir John.'

Hartlebury took another step toward him. He wasn't tall but he was distinctly intimidating. 'Is that a mealy-mouthed way of saying you don't accept them? I am telling you that I was with Charnage in Vauxhall while his father killed that fellow in Town. Do you refuse to accept that? Because if so, you will do it here and now, to my face, or you will shut your mouth on the subject for good. *Well?*'

Sir James's expression was poisonous but he didn't reply. Hartlebury waited a few seconds, then snorted. 'Didn't think so. Keep it that way. Spiteful prick,' he added, not really under his breath at all. 'Evening, Charnage. Not seen you in a while.'

'Hart.' Daizell gave his usual cheery smile, but his eyes were gleaming bright.

'I think that matter is now clear,' Cassian said. 'Sir John Hartlebury, I believe? I'm Severn.'

'*Duke*,' Loxleigh said, low and urgent.

Hartlebury visibly recoiled, then bowed with some self-consciousness, as was only fitting for a man who'd just picked a fight in the ducal presence. 'Your Grace.'

Cassian inclined his head. 'I'm pleased to make your acquaintance, Sir John. I am engaged to play with Sir James now, but I hope we can speak later.'

'Honoured, sir,' Hartlebury said, looking understandably baffled by this turn of events.

'If that's all clear, shall we get on?' Leo said. 'We did come to play.'

Lady Wintour indicated a table for four in the middle of the room, with decks of cards laid out and waiting, a decanter of brandy, four glasses. The Duke felt rather sick.

For all the last week's practice, he would never be a good player.

They went over the stakes, playing for a pound a point, which was deep. Vier had a nasty look in his eyes. 'I hope we have all brought funds, gentlemen. As I mentioned, I am reluctant to accept any more of Mr Crosse's vowels.'

Leo stiffened with wrath. Cassian said, icily, 'What an extraordinary remark to make of my cousin.'

They began to play. As the first hand progressed, Daizell put a chair behind Leo, pulled out a sheaf of paper and his scissors, and began snipping.

Sir James didn't stop play. He did, however, stare incredulously over his cards, and at the end of the hand, he said, 'What are you doing?'

'Profiles,' Daizell said cheerfully. 'I cut them. Well, you know that.'

'I do know that. I wonder if everyone else in this room does.' His tone was heavy with meaning.

Daizell glanced around. 'I should imagine they can all see.'

'I refer to the type of profile you cut.'

'What's that?' asked Loxleigh, drifting over with Hartlebury in tow.

'Profiles,' Daizell said, glancing up. 'Let me show you; I should think you'll find it interesting.'

Sir James looked around the room full of men, plus Lady Wintour, who looked like she'd enjoy a ripe profile as much as anyone, and changed tack. 'If you are mumming for pennies, among gentlemen—'

'Sir James, I came here to play,' the Duke said. 'If you cannot give me your attention, you are at liberty to resign the game.'

'For heaven's sake, Vier, let us get on,' Sir Francis added, which was the first time he'd spoken. He looked rather uncomfortable at being the centre of attention as they were.

Well, they would be. The open hostility, aided by Hartlebury's intervention; the fact that Severn was playing, and likely to be mulcted – everyone was fascinated when a very rich man lost a lot of money – and of course Daizell. He was doing hollow-cut profiles as they played with his usual speed, and handing out the sheets with a few murmurs. Soon quite a lot of people had pieces of paper in their hands, or were showing them to their friends with muffled exclamations.

Cassian couldn't afford to pay attention to that; he needed to give all his thought to the game. He and Leo needed to do their limited best to make this enough of a match that their opponents would be obliged to cheat.

They did have the advantage that Sir James's signals were known to them. If he said, 'Let us commence, gentlemen,' he was strong in hearts and spades. Cassian did not find that as helpful as one might have hoped: certainly not as helpful as Plath.

He and Leo were soon badly down. The points were mounting against them; the candlelight was very bright; the smell of molten wax and sweaty male bodies and brandy overwhelming. He could afford the losses, he knew he could, but he did not want to lose and the tension thudded under his breastbone in a sick drumbeat.

Leo looked sick too. Cassian wondered how it had felt when he had lost three thousand that he could not in the slightest afford. He wondered how George Charnage had felt, and how many people Sir James and Sir Francis and Henry Haddon had rooked and ruined.

He wasn't paying attention, he realised. He played a high

heart in a spirit of hope rather than confidence, and Vier gave a hiss of satisfaction. Damnation.

He bent his mind to the game. He had to do this: if he didn't make it a contest, Vier would take his money and keep his horses, and Daizell would go unavenged. The thought spurred him; he forced himself to attend, as he had to the many tedious lessons in his past. He and Leo won the next hand, then another. Vier glowered at Sir Francis. 'Wake up, man.'

'Eh? I'm very well.' Sir Francis shook himself as though tired. 'Fact, it's time to raise the stakes. What about those horses?'

'Ah, yes, the famous greys.' Vier's lips curved. 'You do seem to have plunged a great deal recently, Your Grace. Let us add that stake to the outcome of the next rubber. Shall we say, the greys against… oh, five thousand pounds.'

The room had been mostly silent, with people clustered around them, but that stake caused a deal of exclamation. Cassian let it subside. 'The greys and Leo's remaining vowels.'

'Certainly,' Vier said, fished out a paper, and tossed it casually onto the table. 'The addition makes little difference.'

Leo's face darkened at the implication. Cassian kicked him under the table: they needed to concentrate now, because Vier would not want to lose this rubber.

The entire room was watching now. Most of the spectators were gathered behind either Vier or Sir Francis's chairs, naturally enough since Cassian had the wall at his back, and Leo had Daizell at his, now standing to watch. There had to be twenty of them holding Daizell's sheets of paper with hollow-cut profiles, including Sir John Hartlebury. Cassian dreaded to think what Daizell had made of that impressively Roman nose.

The rubber began with hearts as trumps. Sir Francis murmured, 'Very warm in here.' *Strong in clubs.*

'A trifle so,' Sir James agreed. *Diamonds.*

Cassian concentrated furiously on his lessons. Return your partner's lead. Count trumps. Second player plays low. The maxims didn't feel like much protection, especially since Leo frequently ignored them. Possibly this was one reason he'd lost three thousand pounds.

Sir James was to lead next. 'Come, your play,' Sir Francis murmured. Sir James played the queen of spades, Leo played the king, and Sir Francis the ace. He took the next round with the jack. There was a murmur from the watchers.

'Quiet, please,' the Duke said. His hands were trembling with tension.

Sir James and Sir Francis took the game. The next hand was dealt; hearts were trumps again. The Duke looked at his cards and nearly dropped them: six hearts to the ace and king, and the aces of spades and diamonds.

With a hand like that he could not lose, and he did not. Sir James's face darkened as Cassian and Leo took all but one trick. One game each. Everything now rested on the third game that would make up the rubber.

Cassian and Leo were close to two thousand pounds down so far; if he lost now, Sir James would keep the greys and Cassian would owe him and Plath seven thousand pounds, since he had promised Leo he'd cover all the losses. He didn't want to pay the swine a penny.

Sir Francis dealt. Cassian took his cards and glanced up, meeting Daizell's eyes. Daizell gave him a smile, small, quick, but there, like a fleeting touch, a brushed kiss.

Trumps were cut as clubs. Sir Francis mopped his brow. 'Really, it is most uncomfortably warm,' he remarked peevishly to the spectators. 'Do move away a little.' *Strong in clubs.*

'Yes, kindly let us concentrate,' Sir James agreed. *Spades.*

The Duke's hand was not so good this time: very few clubs but ace and queen of hearts and ace of spades, and a long string of diamonds. He and Leo collected the first three tricks; Sir James took the fourth with the king of spades. He considered his hand, then reached for his brandy, and frowned. 'Is this cracked?'

'Is it?' Lady Wintour came forward. 'Where?'

'My mistake. I thought I saw a crack.' He held it to the light, then gave a smiling shrug. 'Merely a mark. My eyes fail me.'

Whatever part of that was their code didn't appear in Eliza's list. Cassian thought he could make a guess, though: Vier was asking for instruction in what to lead. And, indeed, Sir Francis said, 'Allow me to refresh your glass, Severn.' *Allow*: the code for *Play a diamond.*

Sir James looked at his hand a moment longer, then led the six of diamonds. Leo played the ace. Sir Francis dropped the three of clubs on the table, trumping it.

'Ha!' he said with the mild satisfaction of a fortunate man, and put out his hand to collect the trick.

Sir John Hartlebury leaned in and slapped his hand on Plath's arm, holding it to the table.

'What—!'

'That will do, I think,' Hartlebury said in a low, savage rumble. 'Evangeline?'

'It will undoubtedly do.' Lady Wintour's voice was edged like a razor. 'Turn up your hands, gentlemen, Your Grace. I said, hands *up*.'

She turned over the trick on the table, showing the four

cards. The Duke spread his remaining hand on the table, heart thudding. Leo did the same, as did Sir James, revealing a disappointing set of cards. His face was bland and unmoved but Cassian thought his skin looked rather waxy.

'Sir James,' Lady Wintour said. 'You had king, six, three in diamonds. Do you care to tell us why you led the six?'

'Why should I not?'

'Try again,' she said. 'Now.'

His eyes narrowed. 'Hearts and spades have both been played; clubs are trumps; I thought my poverty in diamonds might mean my partner's strength. A matter of probability. I took a chance.'

'Probability, my arse. Posterior,' she amended with a glance at Cassian. 'You underled a king!'

'Should I have led the king instead, with the ace as yet unplayed?'

'You shouldn't have led a diamond at all, with those cards,' she said. 'But you did. And we all know why.'

She slapped a piece of paper on the table. It had a hollow-cut at the centre: Sir John Hartlebury's highly distinctive profile leapt to life, revealed by the white paper against dark wood. There were a couple of chuckles, but only a couple, because the paper was not otherwise blank. It also held quite a lot of neat writing, headed, in large letters: VIER AND PLATH CHEAT. READ THIS. KEEP SILENCE. DON'T SHOW THEM YOU KNOW.

Miss Beaumont had an excellent, very legible hand. She had written out the code some thirty laborious times, leaving a space at the centre of each sheet for Daizell to cut a profile. He'd been passing the sheets out to the spectators under Vier's nose all evening.

'Allow': play a diamond. 'Come': play a spade...

Sir James picked up the paper, frowning. 'What does this mean?'

'Don't waste my time,' Lady Wintour snapped. 'We have all heard each of you use these words a dozen times this evening. We've all seen what you played in response.'

'How long have you been doing this?' demanded a man named Tallant, a well-known gamester. 'I lost two thousand to you not two months back!'

'I lost three,' Leo said, and there were other comments to similar effect.

'Their luck certainly has been in for a long time,' Lord Myers said. 'How did you spot this, sir? Mr Charnage, is it? You have done gentlemen a great service with this.' He brandished another sheet of paper with its neat writing and hollow cut. 'Most ingenious, I must say. Wouldn't have believed it otherwise.'

'These are lies!' Vier snapped. 'Charnage's lies! His father murdered my dear friend Haddon and robbed me—'

'What has that to do with you cheating at cards?' the Duke asked.

'He is a liar and a pornographer, a rogue and fortune hunter—'

'You cheated my father!' Daizell shouted. 'You and Henry Haddon took him for everything he had! The reason he robbed you and shot Haddon is that the pair of you had ruined him! And you didn't let Haddon's death stop you, did you? You merely acquired Plath as partner, and kept on cheating, and lying, and stealing, you wretched sharper!'

'Haddon?' Hartlebury demanded. 'Because I recall Vier and Haddon taking a great deal of money off Lord Arvon – Miles Carteret as was – some years ago, and if that is the case—'

'You did that to Miles?' Loxleigh said, and his friendly face wasn't friendly any more. 'You *bastards*.'

Sir James started a response to which neither Loxleigh nor Hartlebury listened. They were shouting in angry chorus, and they weren't the only ones. The outrage and expostulation rose deafeningly; one of Lady Wintour's house bullies shoved his way through the crowd in an ominous manner. Cassian wanted to call for control, but knew his own voice would be lost in the mayhem.

He took the clasp knife from his pocket, and started to tap it against the brandy decanter. The steady chinking cut through the noise, which dwindled as people turned and saw its source. He kept tapping as mouths closed until the room was completely quiet.

'Thank you,' he said, folding the knife with a deliberate click and returning it to his pocket. 'Gentlemen, Lady Wintour. Mr Charnage brought this matter to me when he learned that Sir James had rooked my cousin Leo for a very large sum at whist. Sir James has been attempting to destroy Mr Charnage's character for some years now, out of fear of this very exposure. I trust his slanders will receive no further credence.'

He paused there, looking around. Everyone stayed silent, but there were several nods. Daizell was scarlet-faced but bright-eyed.

'Mr Charnage explained that Sir James and Sir Francis were cheating in this way,' the Duke went on. 'We agreed that Leo and I would play, and he would expose them in this ingenious manner—'

'Entrapment!' Sir Francis spluttered.

'All you had to do was not cheat,' the Duke said, icing his voice. 'As Lord Myers observed, Mr Charnage has done a great service to gentlemen tonight. I add my thanks to yours, my lord.' He inclined his head; Myers and Daizell bowed. 'Vier, Plath: I will not be paying you your so-called winnings from this game, nor will you have my greys. Moreover, my cousin's debt of honour to you was not won honourably and is thus no debt. I will take his vowels.'

He reached out. Sir James snatched up the paper first; Hartlebury slapped his wrist down on the table with unnecessary force.

'Thank you, Sir John,' the Duke said, part of him observing his own aplomb with astonishment. He plucked the IOU from Vier's pinned hand, held it up ceremonially, and tore it across. 'I will fully support anyone who has lost money to you in declining to pay, or retrieving their losses. You are both unfit for the company of gentlemen, and I must decline your further acquaintance.'

'*Whereas*, me and my boys will be having a very long talk with this pair of tosspots,' Lady Wintour said, fizzing with wrath. 'Cheating in my house! Get 'em, Ned.'

The oversized bully moved purposefully, grabbing Sir James's collar with a huge hand. The Duke held up his hand commandingly. 'Stop. I cannot countenance violent retribution, Lady Wintour.'

'Oh, come off it!' Loxleigh said furiously. 'Uh, that is—'

'No. I must decline to witness any such thing.' Cassian gave it a couple of seconds, as Sir Francis and Sir James shot him looks of desperate hope, and concluded, 'So let me leave the room before you start.'

Chapter Twenty

'So we went to the back room and had a drink with Hart – Sir John Hartlebury – and Tallant, and Lord Myers, and, uh. Everyone.'

It was the next afternoon. Cassian's head hurt and his stomach was still uneasy: Lady Wintour's brandy might be drinkable, but not in the quantities he'd imbibed. At least he'd been more abstemious than either Daizell or Leo, who both looked very much the worse for wear. As well they might: there had been a great deal of excitement and the evening had become correspondingly raucous. It was the kind of night he had heard a great deal about, and never attended in his life.

'Did they believe you?' Eliza demanded.

'About the cheating? Entirely. Well, it was clear, and Sir John had already made Vier look bad.'

'How did he come to be there?' Louisa asked.

'Evangeline, Lady Wintour, whistled him up when I told her what we were about,' Daizell said, grinning. 'Bless her. I don't really know the man, but we were both in her party that night at Vauxhall, although she left early. He let it be known he was with me at the time, but he was in rather bad odour himself then, some family affair, and he doesn't spend much time in London anyway. Otherwise I've no doubt he'd have fought my corner before now. Excellent fellow.'

'Yes, I liked him very much,' Cassian agreed. 'He had all

sorts of interesting things to say about brewing, which I should like to learn more of.'

'Nobody else would be in the middle of the greatest scandal of the Season and talk about brewing,' Louisa said. 'Good heavens, Sev.'

It was the kind of remark that had all too often made the Duke cringe with awareness of his social ineptitude. He considered that now, and found it wanting. 'On the contrary. I had a very pleasant conversation with an interesting man, while Daizell and Leo did all the gossiping that anyone could require. I had spoken my piece.'

'And wonderfully,' Daizell said. 'I don't know if it will entirely revive my reputation, but you could not have done more.'

'Oh, blast your reputation,' Leo said. 'Nobody cares. If you ask me you could have brazened it out at the time.'

'Do shut up, Leo. But it is possible fewer people believed it than you feared,' Louisa remarked. 'People will happily repeat stories they know to be lies as long as they are entertaining. Now, however, the entertaining story is all on our side. I do wish I'd been there.'

'So do I,' said Eliza, with feeling. '*Did* Sir James cheat your father? Was that why he robbed him?'

'I think so. I can't prove it, but then, Sir James can't prove he didn't.'

'Only give his word, and that is no longer worth much. On which note, I must go and see your trustee, Eliza.' Kentridge rose. 'I dare say he may be more amenable to a conversation once I have advised him of the news. I will have you free soon, my dear.'

Eliza clasped her hands together, eyes sparkling. She was very pretty indeed in a state of enthusiasm, and Leo regarded her with an expression that the Duke might have called imbecilic admiration if he hadn't suspected he might himself sometimes look at Daizell like that. Louisa glanced between her brother and her very rich friend, and beamed.

Daizell cleared his throat. 'While we're here, on the topic of bets, Leo?'

'Eh? Oh yes. Sev, you should know I made a wager with Daizell.'

Louisa's benevolent expression fled on the instant. 'Oh good God, what now?'

'Nothing to concern you. Just, Daizell bet me that we'd pull it off, and the stakes were your greys returning to their rightful owner. Thank you, Sev.' Leo held out a hand, with no less sincerity because he didn't actually leave his chair and the Duke had to get up to take it. 'I would say I'm sorry for the wager in the first place, but it seems to have done you a power of good, so really you should be thanking me for making it.'

'I stand in your debt,' Cassian assured him. 'Daizell, could I have a word with you?'

They retired to his room, which, Cassian had earlier noted with annoyance, had no bolt to the door. Martin was in there with Waters, so deep in conversation about the intricacies of caring for buckskin that they didn't notice their master's arrival. He coughed.

'I beg your pardon, Your Grace,' the older valet said. 'You were not expected.'

'Sorry to intrude,' Cassian said, earning a look of dignified rebuke for that bit of cheek. 'What are you up to?'

'I am acquainting Mr Martin with your wardrobe, Your

Grace. As your London valet, he requires a great deal of education.'

That was the agreement: Waters would hold on to valeting rights at Staplow for now, and pass on his wealth of experience to his new junior, in order to mould him in his own image. That was a terrifying prospect, but Daizell had a great deal of faith in Martin's stubbornness.

'Excellent,' Cassian said. 'Nevertheless, I want you to leave for Staplow tomorrow, to keep an eye on things there. Martin will manage, I'm sure.'

'Your Grace.' Waters bowed and withdrew. As Martin followed, Cassian added, 'Make sure I'm not disturbed, will you? I have business to attend to.'

'Your Grace,' Martin said, with a bow so respectful that Cassian wasn't sure if he imagined the wink accompanying it.

He shut the door behind him. Cassian said, 'Do you know, I think this will work. Waters seems quite—'

'Oh, damn the valets,' Daizell said, and Cassian found himself hauled bodily into a ferocious embrace. 'You utter wonder. You glory, Cass. You did it.'

'*We* did it. You organised everything with Evangeline, and thought of how to hand out the papers without Vier suspecting a thing—'

'And you picked a fight, and played cards to the manner born. Despite Leo's help. I can't believe I was sacked from Eton for cleaning him out at cards: a child could do it.'

'He didn't return half of my leads,' Cassian said, with some resentment. 'Honestly. Thank goodness Vier cheated, or I'd have owed him a fortune.'

'But he did. You set him up, and he took the bait, hook

and all. I hope this soothes the sting that you didn't get to bamboozle the vicar in Stratford.'

'Somewhat. Not entirely. But there are always other vicars.'

'I will take you on a vicar-bothering tour of the English countryside,' Daizell promised. 'And if my head didn't feel like someone used it as a jakes last night, I'd carry you to the bed and ravish you into blancmange.'

Cassian was quietly grateful for Daizell's head: his stomach roiled at the very mention of food, or indeed ravishment. 'Yes please, but definitely later,' he said. 'Good God, how do people have the constitution to drink like that regularly?'

'I don't remember: I'm too old. Still, what a night. You enjoyed it?'

'I did, actually, more than I would have thought.' He had spoken to a dozen people, all of them too flown on excitement or brandy or both to care excessively for his title. He'd retold a couple of the best stories that he'd heard at the Green Lion in Coventry, and got proper laughs, and seen his own pride reflected in Daizell's eyes as he did it. Mr Tallant had even slapped him on the arm and called him a dog, a bit of manly informality about which he was probably writhing with belated mortification. Cassian made a mental note to be affable when they next met. 'Myers is much more pleasant than I recalled, and Loxleigh is charming, and if I were to play regularly, I should do it at Evangeline's hell.' Lord Hugo would probably call it far too vulgar a place for the Duke. 'In fact, I should like to visit again even if we don't play. Can we?'

'Of course.' Daizell kissed his ear.

'And Hart invited me to see around his brewery, although he may not remember doing so, but I should like to arrange it. But first we need to bring you back into Society, don't we?'

Daizell was officially one of his party at Wotton House now. He would stay while they were in London, and they would travel together afterwards – including an anonymous trip to the Green Lion, he thought. And whenever they were in a Severn property, he'd fill it around them with guests and visitors and people who needed a place. Daizell would be one of a crowd until everyone was so used to his presence they wouldn't think to question it. Cassian had absolute faith in the Crosse family gift for not paying attention; it would be satisfying to have it work in his favour.

'The invitation cards are already arriving,' he went on. 'Many of them will want to meet you and hear the story. And I dare say Louisa and Eliza will like to go out as much as they can, so we will all surround one another. She would like Eliza to have the entertainment of which she has been deprived all these years.'

'It seems to me Eliza made her own entertainment,' Daizell remarked drily. 'Yes, it will be a social whirl. Do you mind?'

'No,' Cassian said, a touch surprised that it was true. 'No, I don't mind at all. As long as you come back here with me, and I have time *not* to be in Society too, I shall do very well indeed.'

Daizell smiled at him. 'Perfect.'

'Yes.' Daizell was warm and comfortable, the two of them in each other's grasp and leaning on one another, and there was nowhere else in the world that Cassian Crosse, Duke of Severn should be, and nobody else he should be with. 'Yes,' he repeated. 'It truly is.'

Acknowledgements

I tapped my father for help working out the specifics of cards and cheating for the gambling scene. He promptly sat down with a notepad, laid out a full hand for each of the four players in the last round, identified how the decisive play would go, and spoke with feeling on the topic of Underleading A King And Why You Shouldn't. Love you, Dad.

The word 'silhouette' was not used in English until around 1825, hence the use of 'shade' or 'profile' in this book. You can't find this more annoying than I did. *Mastering Silhouettes* by Charles Burns is an excellent guide to the history and practice of cutting silhouettes; any mistakes on the subject are mine.

Huge thanks to Rhea Kurien for a really insightful edit, to Sally Partington for a very acute copy-edit, to the whole Orion team for their help and support, and to Chloe Friedlein for the lovely cover.

As ever, thanks to my utterly fabulous agent Courtney Miller-Callihan, to May Peterson and Elisabeth Paice for invaluable early reads, to the KJ Charles Chat group for keeping it (sur)real, and to Charlie and the kids, of course.

Credits

KJ Charles and Orion Fiction would like to thank everyone at Orion who worked on the publication of *The Duke at Hazard* in the UK.

Editorial
Rhea Kurien
Sahil Javed

Copyeditor
Sally Partington

Proofreader
Linda Joyce

Audio
Paul Stark
Jake Alderson

Marketing
Hennah Sandhu

Design
Tomás Almeida
Joanna Ridley

Editorial Management
Charlie Panayiotou
Jane Hughes
Bartley Shaw

Contracts
Dan Herron
Ellie Bowker
Alyx Hurst

Finance
Jasdip Nandra
Nick Gibson
Sue Baker

Production
Ruth Sharvell

Publicity
Frankie Banks

Sales
Jen Wilson
Esther Waters
Victoria Laws
Toluwalope Ayo-Ajala
Rachael Hum
Ellie Kyrke-Smith
Sinead White
Georgina Cutler

Operations
Jo Jacobs
Dan Stevens